THE LOST

Mari Hannah is a multi-award-winning author whose authentic voice is no happy accident. A former probation officer, she lives in rural Northumberland with her partner, an ex-murder detective. Mari turned to script-writing when her career was cut short following an assault on duty. Her debut, *The Murder Wall* (adapted from a script she developed with the BBC) won her the Polari First Book Prize. Its follow-up, *Settled Blood*, picked up a Northern Writers' Award. Her Kate Daniels series is in development with Stephen Fry's production company, Sprout Pictures. She is currently Reader in Residence for Harrogate International Crime Writing Festival. Mari's body of work won her the CWA Dagger in the Library 2017, an incredible honour to receive so early on in her career.

Find out more by following Mari on Twitter @mariwriter or visiting her website www.marihannah.com

Also by Mari Hannah

KATE DANIELS SERIES
The Murder Wall
Settled Blood
Deadly Deceit
Monument to Murder (aka Fatal Games)
Killing for Keeps
Gallows Drop

RYAN & O'NEIL SERIES
The Silent Room
The Death Messenger

THE
LOST

Mari Hannah

ORION

First published in Great Britain in 2018 by Orion Books,
an imprint of The Orion Publishing Group Ltd
Carmelite House, 50 Victoria Embankment,
London EC4Y 0DZ

An Hachette UK company

3 5 7 9 10 8 6 4 2

A CIP catalogue record for this book is
available from the British Library.

ISBN 978 1 4091 7405 9

Typeset by Input Data Services Ltd, Somerset

Printed and bound in Great Britain by Clays Ltd, St Ives plc

www.orionbooks.co.uk

For Mo

THE LOST

THE LOST

Prologue

Without Tim, Alex would be dead. Every time that thought entered her head she loved him a little bit more. Right now, the urge to see him was greater than it had ever been. Apart from business trips, this was the first time they had been separated since they married. Seven days felt like a year. She should never have agreed to the holiday without him. Seeing Kat had been worth the sacrifice, but now Alex wanted her life back.

She looked up, a tinkling sound grabbing her attention. Long faces with straggly beards stared at her. There was nothing sinister about them and yet she felt tense. Fortunately, goats slept at night. Their cowbells hadn't kept her awake. Shame the same couldn't be said for her sister. Kat had whined continually, complaining that the villa's owner should have warned them that they would get no peace. She cared less than Alex that farming was important to the economy and culture of Majorca and its people.

She cared less than Alex, full stop.

Looking left along the driveway to the dusty road, Alex focused on their redundant hire car, eyes straying beyond the garden gate to the southern face of the Serra de Tramuntana dominating the near distance. In the foothills beneath, white villas baked in the searing heat. Alex longed to look inside. Not that she had the means to purchase one just now. Her money was tied up in Tim's business and her own expanding public relations company.

More than once this week Kat had pointed out that being married to an ambitious entrepreneur had its downside. She viewed Tim as a reckless risk-taker. As far as Alex was concerned, her opinions were immaterial, although it pained her to think that two of the three people she loved most in the world had never really hit it off. Last night, as she floated the possibility of owning a holiday home within striking distance of the UK, Kat reminded her that there was no cash for second homes when the first was re-mortgaged to the hilt. Alex got that. She did. All the same, she bridled at the dig. Apart from Daniel, her ten-year-old, Tim was her world. He had plans her sister was unaware of – ones that Alex was OK with if it made him happy.

She owed him.

Lifting her wine glass, she savoured an aged Rioja, a blend of grapes local to the area, rich, earthy and well rounded. Alex eyed the vines all around her, long branches and thick leaves flourishing in the warm climate. Tim would appreciate the simple lifestyle here, the relaxed pace, the opportunity to read and swim and feel hot earth beneath bare feet. But, as it had for Alex, the novelty of living the island dream would soon wear off.

They'd be bored in a few days.

'Welcome to Casa Pegueña.' Kat was reading the visitors' book over Alex's shoulder. 'You're not going to write *War and Peace*, are you, Ali? Check-in closes in four hours. There's time for one last dip and a shower before we head off. C'mon, get your kit off.'

'No, you go ahead. I'm done.'

Sulking, Kat sat down, stripping the shirt from a deeply tanned body. Alex felt pale by comparison. While she'd enjoyed her break, much of the week the heat had been oppressive. Most days she'd taken refuge in the shade of the terrace. She'd not ventured up the Puig de Maria to the monastery to take in its amazing views, walked the kilometre to the Roman town of Polença or driven to the port. Other than trips to the supermarket, she'd not gone out – not even to the beach. And whilst the idea of a place here held a certain appeal, she'd be glad to get home to Northumberland where it was green and cool, she thought, but didn't say.

A breeze picked up. It swept across the parched land, rustling surrounding vegetation, kissing her face. Though the rippling pool water was enticing, she didn't move, except to remove her sunglasses, the better to see her sister.

There was mischief in Kat's eyes.

'What?' Alex said.

'I was just wondering what state your place will be in when you get home.' Kat's point was that, unlike Alex, she had a tidy bijou flat to return to in upmarket Marylebone. No kids. Never wanted any. No clutter. Probably no soul. Alex hadn't yet seen the property. She would, as soon as she got the opportunity. Her life had been crazy of late.

'It'll be spotless,' she said.

'Yes, I forgot you had a maid.'

'Justine's not a maid.'

'You sacked the last one, as I recall.'

'That's not strictly true.'

'That's right,' Kat teased. 'You let her go. Either way, Maria ended up on the dole.'

Alex went quiet. When Daniel was born, she'd returned to work within weeks of giving birth. With a husband and two businesses to support there was no other choice. Maria was her saviour. During Alex's second pregnancy things were different, financially and in every other way. She was happy, hopelessly in love with the new man in her life – in a totally different place. After ten years of loyal service, she'd dispensed with Maria with no inkling that she'd live to regret it. The plan was to take a year off to spend time with her newborn – a decision her husband supported wholeheartedly. Little did they know that there would be no baby to stay home for . . .

Tim had been heartbroken when told that it was too dangerous to try again. Her biological clock had beaten them, a diagnosis he accepted without apportioning blame or making a fuss. Unable to live with the guilt of losing their child, his first, Alex had returned to work at the earliest opportunity. By then Maria had found another family to care for and Alex accepted Justine in her place.

As dark memories faded, Alex ached to be home. Although she'd hidden it from Kat, she had been planning her return journey from the moment she left the UK. Not a second had gone by without thinking of her family. She'd been parted from Tim for too long. They had undoubtedly lost their way as a couple but things were set to improve when she got home. This break had given them time to get their shit together. Thinking of him stirred her physically.

Soon . . . she'd be home within hours.

Poised to write in the visitors' book, she picked up her pen and put it down again, unable to describe her top tips of exciting places to visit, favourite restaurants or points of interest – and there were many on this beautiful Balearic island. She was losing the will to make any comment on their stay.

'Coming in?' Kat was poolside now.

Alex made a lame excuse that she didn't want wet washing in her suitcase. Begging her to change her mind, Kat stepped in at the shallow end one final time, bare legs shimmering as she splashed them with water. When Alex wouldn't be persuaded to join her, she disappeared beneath the surface, emerging at the other end a few seconds later, hauling her body out in one athletic motion.

Alex turned more pages, looking for inspiration, not wanting to sound dull for having done so little during her stay. People from far afield had paid homage to the villa, naming nearby towns and coastal locations worth a look, amazing drives and lunch venues:

Perfect for two; ticked all our boxes; you can't leave without exploring the beach at Formentor – divine! Reading last week's message about ants makes me smile. They returned!

Alex's heart almost stopped beating as words crawled across the page like an army on the move. She tried to still them but they kept coming, growing larger by the second. A feeling of dread crept over her, soaking through her skin until it filled her. Kat was lying on a sunbed, eyes closed, unaware of the unfolding drama. Tim was over a thousand miles away. Alex palmed her brow, unable to think, utterly helpless. As panic attacks go, this one was sizeable and sudden. She would never recover from it.

1

Tim Parker waited for action. It didn't come. For the ump-teenth time since he'd arrived at the police station he checked his watch: 11.30 p.m. It had been hours and still there was no news. The door to the interview room stood ajar. Two detect-ives loitered outside talking in dull tones: a confident male, mid-thirties, short-cropped hair; a female about the same age: a little on the petite side for a copper, brunette, sharp eyes, a grave expression on her face. They appeared to be having words.

The station was noisy – on the outside as well as in – the scream of sirens a constant reminder of the danger out there. There was no let-up of foot traffic toing and froing past the open door, a succession of uniforms and civilian personnel. The squawk of radios was getting on his nerves. There was laughter but also agitation. Tim didn't need to see it. He could feel it through the walls. The stress was unbearable. How could people work in a place that never slept?

A scrawny lad with earphones hanging around his neck was being escorted along the corridor by the arm, moaning about the length of time it had taken for police to deal with his complaint. Tim knew the feeling. He'd been there since nine thirty, just after dark. He was beginning to think that he should have driven to meet Alex at the airport before reporting Dan's disappearance to the police. With a mind full of possi-bilities too painful to contemplate, he'd bottled it, unable to face her.

Where the hell was Dan?

Guilt tormented Tim. The fact that he couldn't get out of a meeting to pick his stepson up himself was not an excuse his wife would accept. Dan was her precious boy. No matter how successful she was in business, her son always came first. He was the thing she was most proud of. Tim could hear her now: It's a question of priority. You promised to keep him safe.

And she was right . . .

A lump formed in his throat. Alex never wanted to go to Majorca. He'd encouraged her to. After the sad loss of their child she needed a break and so did he. He couldn't get away from work. If he were brutally honest, he'd not tried that hard. And when her sister had twisted her arm to accompany her to the Balearics, it solved a problem, even if potentially it might cause another.

The trip was an impulse buy. Paid for with a hefty divorce settlement. If Tim knew anything about Kat, anything about money – and he did on both counts – that pot of gold would be gone within the year. Still, he couldn't fault his sister-in-law on a point of generosity. She and Alex hadn't taken a vacation together since they were students at universities three hundred miles apart, Alex in Edinburgh, Kat at Cambridge. And they had gone through some rough times since.

Tim's hopes rose as the female detective in the corridor grabbed the door handle. Instead of pushing the door open, she pulled it to. Whispers diminished and footsteps moved away. Tim's head went down. Traumatised by nightmare thoughts, he shut his eyes, trying to calm himself. This was no bad dream.

It was all too real.

More chatter outside involving the red-faced sergeant he'd seen at the front desk. He was ambling past with a colleague, his casual attitude spurring Tim into action. Impatient for information, he shot out of his seat, hell-bent on speaking to police, whether they were ready to listen or not. As he raced into the corridor, the man with three stripes on his epaulettes turned to face him.

'Can I help you, sir?' His colleague walked on without him.

8

'I wish you would,' Tim said. 'You know why I'm here and it's been hours. Please, what's happening?'

'Take a seat in the interview room and try not to worry. I realise this is difficult for you but, as I suggested earlier, Daniel probably took a detour on his way home. He'll turn up soon enough, suitably repentant with his tail between his legs.'

'You don't know that—'

'It happens every week, sir. Believe me, it's common with lads his age.'

'And we just wait? Is that the best you can do?'

The sergeant bristled.

Tim tried not to sound pissed off. 'With respect, officer, I'd love that to be true, but as I explained when I reported Dan missing, he's not the type. His mother and I drilled it into him: never talk to strangers, never accept a lift. He's a sensible, sensitive kid. There's no way he'd have gone off without telling anyone. Besides, "probably" isn't good enough.'

'You need to be patient—'

'No! You need to start listening.'

'I am and I have. I've—'

'Please, Sergeant, I'm not challenging you or trying to put your back up, but you have to listen to me. Daniel is genuinely missing. I need to speak to someone in authority now. Unless you'd like me to ring the Chief Constable. I have his mobile number.' It was a veiled threat but Tim was getting desperate.

A face off in the corridor.

'Is there a problem here?' A female voice.

Tim swung round to find a woman in plain clothes. She was checking him out, taking in his gold cufflinks and the silk handkerchief flopping out of his breast pocket. She was also the one bending the ear of the detective outside a moment ago and had obviously overheard the escalating row.

'I'm DS Oliver, sir. Is everything OK?'

'Tim . . . Parker. Please, I need your help.'

9

As soon as he gave his name, she seemed to know who he was.

She eyeballed her colleague. 'I'll take it from here, John.'

The man in uniform moved away.

DS Oliver had been attentive and much more sympathetic than her colleague. After a brief conversation, in which she'd pointed out that she'd read the missing persons report, she'd asked Tim to wait while she spoke to her boss. She hadn't been gone long and had promised to update him. Tim sat down, relieved that someone was finally taking positive action. The interview room was muggy. Wiping a film of sweat from his brow, the reality of his situation hit him hard. The newspapers were full of appalling crimes against children, including murder. Child abuse was rife, a large proportion of it carried out by adults they knew: carers, parents, priests and counsellors were in the firing line, if not high on the list of suspects.

Right now, Tim could see their point.

Looking up at CCTV in the corner of the room, he wondered if he were under surveillance, if DS Oliver was watching him . . . judging him. Those you looked to for protection could turn on you in an instant. He was feeling the heat and it had nothing to do with temperature.

How much longer?

Another check on the time: eleven forty-five.

Tim imagined a plane touching down at Newcastle airport. So vivid was the image, he could almost hear the screech of brakes, the scream of the engines as the aircraft raced along the tarmac before leaving the runway and pulling up on its stand. It would signal instant and profound relief for one passenger. He should've been collecting Alex about now. Worse than that: he should've been doing it with Dan. It wasn't a school night and his mother had decided he could stay up late and meet her at the terminal.

A text alert pierced the silence of the interview room.

Fumbling his mobile from his pocket, expecting, praying for his au pair to put a contrite Dan on the phone, his hopes died as Alex's name appeared on screen:

I'm down . . . See you when I clear baggage control.
A x

Tim lost it. Alex was home and he wasn't there to pick her up. She travelled all over with her job but hated flying. He pictured the stress leaving her face as she walked toward passport control, phone in hand, dying to get through security, grab her luggage and head out to be reunited with her son. His absence would trigger a panic attack.

Christ!

Tim was hyperventilating, unable to get his ragged breathing under control. His wife was a formidable woman but, after all she'd gone through recently, could she, would she, cope with this? How could he look her in the eye and tell her he'd lost Dan and didn't have a clue where to start looking?

Pressing the home button on his iPhone got rid of the text. The background image on the screen made him weep. The cute, embarrassed smile of a shy ten-year-old who hated having his picture taken. It was one of very few photographs in existence, taken by his mother before Dan could turn away. Tim thought about phoning Alex but he couldn't do that. She'd know instantly that something was up. He imagined her reaction when she finally heard the news, worst-case scenarios worming their way into her head.

His eyes found the door.

Was that the reason for the delay? Were detectives waiting until his wife arrived so they could tell her what an irresponsible arsehole he was, that he should never have been allowed to fly solo and wasn't up to the job? Or maybe that she ought not to have abandoned her child to someone who clearly had no parenting skills.

Self-hatred consumed him.

He took out his mobile, his forefinger hovering over the speed-dial options. He had to be the one to tell Alex. No, he couldn't do it. He just couldn't. He didn't want to be the one to break the news. He slipped the phone back in his breast pocket. For the first time in his life, he cowered in the face of adversity. He was good at communication, even when there were unpalatable truths to convey. This was different . . .

This was personal.

Rigid with fear, he sat down and waited, the last few hours rewinding again and again like a nightmare loop inside his head. Panic was a strange thing. The realisation that there was something terribly wrong, something sinister, began like a punch to the gut, making him retch. His ability to think straight seemed to stutter and slow, like a toy running out of battery. Alex had left Dan in his care. He was her child. The only one she'd ever have. It would kill her to learn that he was missing.

2

Detective Inspector David Stone had been in the job less than a month, having transferred from the Metropolitan Police and returned to his roots in Northumberland. The last thing he needed right now was a bolshie detective sergeant on his case. In London kids went missing every second of every day. Unless they were very young or there were extenuating circumstances, finding them was a uniform task, not one for the CID. And yet his new Northumbria sidekick, Detective Sergeant Frances (call me Frankie) Oliver, was like a coiled spring, itching to involve them in a misper case.

For ten minutes, they had been quietly arguing the toss; even so, she had yet to explain herself properly. David liked her a lot. She'd shown no resentment when he blew in from the south as a replacement DI. His predecessor – an old soldier who'd retired with a bad back and good pension – was a hard act to follow. Everyone said so and David was on orders from HQ to prove his worth. That he could confidently do to his superiors. Not so to the live wire he was presently facing across the corridor.

'It's a feeling I have,' she said.

'I need more than that, Frankie.'

'I have no more, beyond the fact that he's a child and it's getting on for midnight.' Her eyes were pleading with him to change his mind. 'Boss, I'm asking you to forget protocol and take the lead.' She'd not called him boss for days. David had asked her to drop the formality of rank. And she wasn't finished yet. 'Look, I know what's in the manual,' she said. 'I'm asking you to show some common sense.'

'Then give me the rationale.'

'I can't.' Frankie spread her hands in a gesture of frustration.

'Write it up as gut feeling. Intuition. Sixth sense. Anybloody-thing you like. Just *do* something.' She thumbed towards the occupancy indicators above the doors of the interview suite. Only one was lit. 'Exactly what is your problem, David? We're hardly run off our feet, are we?'

'That's beside the point. We're not talking about a four-year-old. If we were, you could have air support and every other kind of resource. The lad is ten. He's probably pushing the boundaries, dicking his parents around, in a strop because his mother didn't take him on holiday. You know what kids are like—'

'Yes. Do you?'

It was a direct challenge to his authority. She knew fine well he had no children. Puzzled by her tenacity, David frowned. Frankie held his gaze defiantly. A flicker of distress in her eyes made him hesitate before knocking back her request a second time. He wondered what was driving her point of view.

Time to clear the air.

'Is there something you're not telling me?' he asked.

'No.' Clearly there was.

'You'd never win at poker.'

His comment didn't raise a smile. It had angered her more than it should and she didn't give a damn that he knew it. David hadn't yet sussed her out. Her file said she was single, no children, a third-generation copper with a great track record and personality to match. Having been deployed in many departments, she'd found her niche as a DS in the CID where she'd worked for the past two years. She was diligent, confident in her abilities, but underneath the surface he detected a hidden vulnerability.

This woman had a story to tell.

'Suck it up or persuade me, Frankie. My office. You have five minutes.'

*

Frankie flung herself down in the chair, trying not to show her frustration. Stone had a valid point, but she had the bit between her teeth and wasn't letting go. New into the department, she could understand his position; on the other hand, Daniel Scott was out there in the dark. She wouldn't rest until he was found. She couldn't explain herself. Why should she?

For a moment there was a deadlock.

Frankie allowed the silence to stretch out between them. Stone was nothing like her former boss and mentor, DI Drake. If only he was. She could twist him around her little finger. They had known each other since she was a little girl. He'd joined the force in the same intake as her father and was under instruction not to argue with DCI Frank Oliver's pride and joy. Drake had been ready for retirement for a couple of years. The man facing her now was different. He was ambitious and couldn't afford to put a foot wrong in the first few weeks of his tenure.

So here they sat, staring each other down.

From the second they had been introduced they had hit it off. There was an instant spark, something intangible that drew her to him. And she wasn't the only one intrigued. The station grapevine was on fire. There was some suggestion that he'd left London in a hurry. With no details available, speculation was rife. Whatever it was, it must have been catastrophic if he'd taken a demotion to run from it.

It can't have been a kid, or he'd be eating out of her hand.

Stone relaxed into his swivel chair, deep penetrating eyes glued to hers. He didn't need telling that it was their duty to safeguard the child, but things were not that simple. Frankie had to make a case for treating Daniel's disappearance as a serious crime and she couldn't. Not yet, anyway. There were very clear guidelines in situations like these. On a hiding to nothing, she climbed down, prepared to beg if necessary.

'David, trust me on this.'

'Believe me, I'm trying.'

'I've spoken to the stepfather, Timothy Parker. He claims Daniel isn't a kid who'd run away. He's not a street kid. He's cared for 24/7, mollycoddled in a way that makes him inherently vulnerable. He even has a nanny. What he doesn't have is the means to communicate. Parker doesn't approve of kids having mobile phones. The guy is past himself. I think we should treat this as high profile, log it on HOLMES and run it as a major incident.'

'On what grounds?'

'I've given you grounds.'

'With respect, you've given me sod-all.'

Much as she might like to, Frankie couldn't argue with his logic. Stone was right, but she wasn't listening. 'I've done some checking on Parker. The man is minted, something he failed to mention when questioned. For all we know, Daniel could've been abducted—'

'There's been no demand—'

'Yet.' She held up a hand by way of apology. 'David, this isn't the Met! We care about our bairns up here. They're not all little bastards who need a good hiding. Wherever he is, and for whatever reason he went AWOL, Daniel is exposed to harm. If that's not good enough reason to look for him, I don't know what is. Please reconsider. He needs our help.'

Stone's eyes were warm. 'Run it by me one more time.'

Frankie bit the inside of her cheek, considering the angles, working out what to say, feeling under tremendous pressure to perform. This was far from a done deal. The fact that Daniel's future came down to her ability to convince her boss that he was in imminent danger scared her.

She took a deep breath. 'Parker claims the boy's nanny, Justine Segal, should've picked him up from footy training because he was tied up – an important business meeting.'

'And was he?'

Frankie nodded. 'When the meeting was over he allegedly checked his phone. There was a voice message from Justine berating him for having picked Daniel up without letting her know. He hadn't, or so he says. Confused, he drove straight home. By the time he got there, Justine had calmed down. She apologised, said she'd missed his message that he'd collect the child himself, then freaked out when she realised the boy wasn't with him.'

Stone was beginning to give a little.

Not enough.

A pause in the conversation didn't last. Frankie had to keep up the momentum. 'Parker claims he sent no message. At first, he thought it was a wind-up, that Daniel was hiding somewhere in the house, that he and Justine were playing a practical joke. That wasn't the case. So, if neither of them collected Daniel, who did?'

The question hung in the air unanswered.

Stone stroked the stubble on his chin, eyes fixed on Frankie. 'What kind of message was it? Email, text . . . ?'

'DM.'

'Who communicates through Twitter?'

'Dunno. Personally, I'd rather eat worms.'

'Did you check his mobile?'

Frankie gave a nod. 'The DM wasn't there. The discrepancy bothered me, so I got Justine to send a screenshot of her phone. Twitter streams don't lie. It's there all right, in black and white. David, trust me, there's something suspicious going on here.'

'We'll revisit this. When is the mother due in?'

Frankie checked her watch. 'Now.'

'Did you speak to the call-taker?'

'There wasn't one. The informant is Parker. We didn't go to him. He came to us.'

'Who was the last person to see Daniel?'

'His football coach, Roger McCall. He witnessed the boy wave at a car and walk towards it after training, a vehicle he wasn't sure he'd seen before.'

'Any form?'

'No. But how could he not question that? Dan was under his supervision. It was *his* responsibility to hand him back in one piece, not let him wander off alone. Listen, if I'm wrong about this you can slap my hands later. I'll take full responsibility. You can transfer me. Send me blue forms. Do what the hell you like, but we need to act now. The longer we leave it, the more difficult it will be to pick up the scent.' Frankie waited, Stone's hesitation irritating her all over again. The formality was back. 'Boss, clearly one of them is lying—'

'Who did you say Daniel's mother went on holiday with?'

'I didn't.'

'You don't know?'

'Yes, I know! I just didn't say. She went with her sister, Kathryn something or other. Posh double-barrelled name. She lives down south somewhere. What does it matter? The important thing is, the boy needs our protection and he needs it now.'

'Back off, I'm thinking.'

Frankie eyeballed him across the room. 'Are you going to do something, or sit there until we have a corpse on our hands?' It was the sucker punch she felt guilty using, but one she hoped would force a reaction from her new boss. No copper wanted the death of a child on their conscience.

Stone picked up the internal phone, hit a couple of keys and waited for an answer. 'Brian, we have an interest in the missing boy. Run everything you have past Frankie until I say otherwise. And while you're at it, raise an action to search the kid's home. Yes . . . now!'

Stone hung up and got to his feet, gesturing for Frankie

to do likewise. She couldn't speak as he opened the door to let her out of his office. Her smile was the nearest he'd get to a thank you. She'd never be able to tell him why it meant so much.

3

Alex Parker eyed the female passport controller expectantly, urging her to get a move on. It seemed she'd picked the wrong security queue yet again. Despite having been out of her seat the moment the aircraft's forward door was open, one of the first to set foot on UK soil, she was going nowhere fast. The parallel line of weary travellers was moving much quicker, a young male controller letting people through with hardly a glance. Hers wasn't dawdling exactly but the woman checking ID was under supervision – new to the job, Alex assumed – examining every traveller, the man standing behind her watching her every move.

Alex shuffled closer to the happy family in front of her. Their wide-eyed kids were in a state of high excitement, desperate to get into the baggage hall where their parents would collect luggage, lift them on to a trolley and wheel them through customs into the arms of doting grandparents waiting in the international arrivals hall.

Alex was almost as impatient and, it had to be said, a little annoyed that Tim had ignored the text she'd sent as she ascended the steps and crossed the tarmac into the warmth of the terminal building. He was probably running late, panicking as time ticked towards her ETA. Alex smiled, pictured him screeching to a halt in the short-term car park, jogging into the concourse with a plausible excuse for being late – as always.

From his position behind the controller, Stone looked on as passengers from the Palma flight passed through passport control. Leaving the line of passengers, one woman moved to the point of entry desk, holding her passport up for perusal.

Instead of a nod and friendly welcome home, the controller took the document, carefully scrutinised it before passing it over her scanner, showing no emotion as she did so. Stone seized on the monitor, checking identity: this was Alex Parker. Of all the women in the queue, he was hoping that *she* wasn't the one he'd come to see.

Taking the passport from the controller, he studied it, then stepped from the booth, clearing his throat as he spoke to her. 'Ms Parker?'

'Yes.'

'Could you come with me please?'

'May I ask why?' The woman flushed, conscious of heads turned in her direction.

Stone witnessed the sniggers, finger-pointing and hushed whispers from fellow travellers, everyone wondering why she'd been stopped, making up a reason to suit the retelling later: *You'll never guess what happened as we arrived at the airport . . .*

'Am I under arrest?' Alex asked. 'Because, if I am—'

'You're not.' Stone's voice was measured, his attitude polite.

'Well, that's a relief.'

The silence seemed to last for ever. Her brain would be processing a list of scenarios, none of them palatable. Like most people, she'd probably been frisked on outward journeys but never prevented from re-entering the country of her birth. It was embarrassing for anyone to assume the position, though sadly, it was commonplace nowadays in the counter-terrorism fight.

Alex Parker didn't move.

It was clear that she had no intention of going anywhere without an explanation for the gross embarrassment his intervention was causing. This close to her, Stone was finding it hard to concentrate. He needed to calm down.

'Has something happened?' Her words came out like a terrified whisper.

'We need to go somewhere more private, ma'am.' He swept a hand out, inviting her to follow him along the corridor.

She was rooted to the spot. 'Look, I'm sorry, I'm not trying to be awkward. I have a right to know why I'm being waylaid. My husband and son are waiting for me landside. I'm tired. I've been in transit for hours. At least identify yourself.'

'I'm Detective Inspector David Stone.'

'Now you're really worrying me.'

So, she now knew he was a copper, not airport security. He was there for a specific reason and she was it. He'd checked in with the station before he left the car. There had been no sign of her son.

'What are you?' she asked. 'Special Branch?'

It was a stupid question. Stone would hardly tell her if he was. He didn't answer, merely repeated his request politely, suggesting that she step aside to allow others through.

She did as he asked. 'Inspector, you're making a big mistake—'

'They all say that,' some smart arse said.

The lad standing beside him laughed.

Alex shot the two morons a look.

'Keep moving,' Stone told them.

Onlookers were being marched through security even quicker now, rubbernecking as they reached the front of the queue. Alex Parker was desperate to follow.

Frankie had given Stone a head start. The Traffic car had followed fifteen minutes later, taking no more than ten minutes to get her and Daniel's stepfather to the airport. She was out of the vehicle before its wheels had properly come to a stop. She walked round the car, holding the rear door open for Tim Parker, ushering him into the terminal with a sense of urgency and up the escalator to the first floor. By now, Stone would have broken the news, informed Alex Parker of her son's disappearance. They had agreed to rendezvous in an area where they wouldn't be disturbed.

A member of airport security was guarding a door marked *Border Force*. Frankie asked Parker to hang back a moment, greeting the guard with a handshake. She glanced over her shoulder to ensure that her charge hadn't crept forward. Daniel's stepfather was straining to hear what was being said.

Let him.

There were questions that remained unanswered. If he was involved in the boy's disappearance, in any way, Frankie would cut him no slack. She turned to face the guard. 'How was the boy's mother when Stone met her?'

'Unhappy about being intercepted,' he said. 'Demanding an explanation—'

'And who can blame her? The last thing you want when you fly in at this time of night is a hairy-arsed polis preventing you from going home to your bed.' It had been several hours since Alex Parker had returned her hire car to Palma airport. Frankie had established that before they left the station. 'Hold your position. We don't want any interruptions. When we leave, stand down.'

The guard nodded his understanding.

When Frankie entered the room, Stone was on his feet, Alex Parker sitting down, head in hands, elbows on knees. She looked up, seizing on her husband's arrival in the room, oblivious to anyone accompanying him. She sprang to her feet, practically flung herself into his arms and then stepped away.

'Tim! What the hell's going on?'

Oh fuck, Frankie thought. Stone hadn't told her.

And then before she could speak, Alex's attention flew past everyone to the door. She staggered backwards as if she'd been struck, her voice reduced to a whisper. 'Where's Daniel?'

4

Aided by a blue flashing light, designed to get them home as quickly as possible, the unmarked police car left the airport northbound. As the countryside flashed by, Tim Parker couldn't help but notice that he was under surveillance. From time to time, DS Oliver's eyes met his through the rear-view mirror. While he didn't know her well enough to make a judgement, he could swear there had been a shift in her attitude towards him. Initially sympathetic to his plight, she now appeared to be viewing him with suspicion.

Tim understood that – Dan had been in his care.

Alex was rigid on the seat next to him, eyes front, refusing to hold his hand. They hadn't spoken since they left the interview room. As always, she was keeping up appearances, trying to give the impression that she was coping when she was barely hanging on. It's what she did when she was sad, angry or troubled. Tim suspected she was all three.

He exhaled, heart pounding in his chest. He'd seen Alex like this twice before. She'd kept her emotions in check, fury building like steam in a pressure-cooker seeking release, finally exploding with devastating consequences. It wasn't pretty either time.

Tim put a hand on hers. She pulled away. He was desperate to embrace her, tell her how sorry he was and beg forgiveness, to comfort her while they waited for an update, but there was no news to share, nor any clue as to what might have prompted Dan's disappearance. It would be cruel to give her false hope of a satisfactory resolution. If the worst came to the worst . . . Tim couldn't think about that now. Neither could he ignore it. Their precarious relationship would surely collapse. It would be the end of everything.

Close the door on your way out, pal.

His wife hadn't meant what she'd said at the airport. She was only sounding off, venting her anger. She couldn't bear to think of Daniel out there in the cold, let alone consider how he got there or what may have befallen him. Her negative reaction was nothing less than Tim deserved. She was projecting her rage on to the one closest to her, a common reaction when faced with such a horrendous state of affairs. Professionally or privately, attack had always been her best form of defence – she'd hardly blame herself, would she?

Tim threw a glance in her direction. On the surface, she was more composed than when DS Oliver broke the news. The pretence was killing him. Beneath that hard exterior, his wife was in bits, as he was. So why didn't she let it out like any normal woman? Why did she make him feel so fucking inferior? Tim needed a fix – and so did she by the look of her. When they got home, he'd call Jeremy Owen, a GP he played golf with, and ask him to come over. It was against the rules to administer drugs randomly but Tim didn't give a shit. After losing their baby, Alex had fallen ill and needed medication to calm her down. Benzodiazepines had helped her then. Maybe they would now.

DS Oliver's eyes were on him again.

Thankfully she couldn't read his mind. It was bad enough that Daniel had gone missing on his watch. Any negativity toward his wife would heap even more suspicion on him, something he didn't need right now. Stone and Oliver were smart, which meant Tim had to be careful or they'd notice he was a user and the cuffs would be out. He'd been around coppers long enough to know how their minds worked.

The tone of an incoming text message filled the car.

Alex went for her bag, checked her mobile's display. Whatever it was, it didn't move her. Her gaze returned to a front windscreen streaked with rain, the road slick and shiny in the vehicle's headlights. Tim eyed the phone held loosely in her hand, wondering who would text at this late hour. He didn't bother to enquire. It was probably Kat. The woman never slept.

If the message wasn't from or about Dan, it was of no consequence.

Tim looked out the side window, the weight of the world on his shoulders. If anything had happened to Dan, his marriage would be over. His life would be over. Alex had practically bankrolled his business and he was in no position to pay her off. He stood to lose everything. They passed through Scots Gap from where they would turn off for the home his wife had inherited from her parents. When the car pulled up at the electronic gated entrance, there were several police vehicles on the driveway, one with a blue light flashing. She lost it then, shrugging off his attempt to comfort her as she emerged from the car.

Frankie Oliver was in awe of the eighteenth-century, three-storey Grade II listed Georgian country house. Surrounded by extensive grounds, it boasted a swimming pool, three-car garage and stable block. She pulled up sharply as she walked through the front door. The interior of the house was equally magnificent, designed to impress visitors, imaginatively renovated and incredibly special. The wow factor didn't come close to describing it. The spacious entrance hallway was festooned with balloons of all shapes and sizes. Strung across the width of the room, a homemade *Welcome Home Mummy* sign seemed to poke fun at everyone. Frankie wanted to rip it down but the damage was done.

Alex was tormented; the au pair, Justine Segal, even worse.

Stone cut her off at the pass. She'd be questioned in due course, though not in the hearing of her employers. Parker gave Justine a nod, an unspoken message that they would chat later.

What was that about?

Frankie watched them carefully. Justine was a vital witness, as distressed as Daniel's mother by the presence of the search team. The use of a cadaver dog seemed to rile Tim Parker. He froze as the animal was brought in and went to work, voicing his objections firmly.

'You're wasting your time,' he said. 'Dan's not here.'

'It's basic procedure,' Stone said. 'There's no need to be alarmed.'

'How can I not be alarmed? For fuck's sake, I've searched the house already. I was frantic. It's the first thing I did.'

The DI didn't answer.

Frankie did it for him. 'Then it shouldn't take long to confirm your findings. We did ask your permission—'

'Yeah, for a fucking search team!'

'Which includes the use of the Dog Section. Yours is a big house, sir. The sooner they get started the better.' She nodded that the handler should continue. He headed for the open well staircase, his dog's paws tapping across the polished oak flooring as they moved towards it. Frankie turned back to face Tim Parker. 'We appreciate how distressing this is for both of you, but we're going to need your help and cooperation.'

'Leave Alex out of this,' Tim Parker said. 'Can't you people see that my wife is exhausted? I won't allow it—'

'I'm sure Alex can answer for herself, sir.' The contempt on Frankie's face matched that of Parker's wife.

Stone intervened, inviting everyone to move into the drawing room and sit down.

Frankie had overstepped the mark and knew it. She glanced at her boss. His attention was elsewhere. She held her bottle, eyes drifting to Tim Parker. 'As Daniel's mother, Alex may have information to give that you're not aware of, sir. DI Stone is right, it's basic procedure. We're going to need a comprehensive list of Daniel's friends and teammates before we leave.'

'Yes, of course.' Parker climbed down.

Frankie could tell he wasn't feeling the love and didn't want to put her back up. Since that first encounter at the station, whatever he said made him sound inept.

What's more, he knew it.

Alex was welling up, trying hard not show it. Every mention of Dan's name produced the same reaction. She may not be hysterical but she was fragile. Angry too; she looked as though, if her husband so much as laid a hand on her, she'd break. Frankie couldn't imagine what she was going through. Whatever her husband's feelings for his stepson, Alex had given birth to Daniel – it stood to reason that mother and son shared a bond that Parker could never hope to achieve.

Asking Alex to provide a contact list was pointless. Tim went to his study to do it himself. While there, he called Jeremy, expecting a knockback. Instead, he got sympathy. One less battle to fight, or so he thought. When he returned to the living room, Alex had other ideas. Oliver was keeping a close eye on her. His wife was exactly where he'd left her with her coat on. She was clutching a stiff drink.

'You don't need that.' He pointed at the tumbler in her hand.

Alex looked like she might throw it at him.

'You're right,' she said softly. 'What I need is my son.'

'They'll find him, Alex.'

'You don't know that.'

'I called Jeremy.'

'What for?'

'He's a GP—'

'I know what he is! That's not what I asked.'

'He'll give you something to calm you down.'

She raised her glass. 'I don't need his drugs.'

'Too late, I've made arrangements—'

'Well, you'd better unmake them.'

'I'm trying to help.'

'I won't take them. They make me feel like a zombie.'

'It's a temporary measure, like last time—'

'Don't you dare bring that up!' Alex gave him hard eyes. 'Maybe it's you who needs help.' Her expression was clear: *How you can live with yourself?*

'I don't know what to say—'

'There's nothing you can say. You promised to keep Daniel safe . . . you failed . . .' She let the sentence trail off.

Under Frankie's watchful gaze Tim wandered away, pulling his mobile from his pocket. 'Jeremy, it's me. Sorry for the inconvenience. There's no need for you to call. Yes, yes, she's fine . . . well, no she's not, but she won't take any medication. No, please don't. Yes, I'll call her GP in the morning if she changes her mind. Thank you . . . yes, I'm sure he'll turn up.'

'Are the police with you?'

Tim closed his study door. '"With you" might be stretching it. They're making the right noises. I wonder if they're actively looking for Dan outside of our home. They kept me hanging around for hours at the station. Before we left to pick up Alex, they asked my permission to search the house.'

'What? That's insane.'

'They made it clear that they would drag a magistrate out of bed to obtain a warrant if I didn't give it.'

'No way!' He paused. 'It's probably routine. Surely they can't . . .' He rephrased: 'Can't they leave it till morning?'

'Apparently not,' Tim said. 'The search team were here

when we arrived home. I overheard the officer in charge give an order to search every inch of the house, including cellar and loft. This is serious shit, Jeremy. I appear to be under suspicion.'

5

'What the hell happened back there?' Frankie whispered under her breath, one eye on the grief-stricken parents, the other on Stone – *dependable, honest . . . floundering.* The DI wiped his face with his hand, acting as if she hadn't spoken. She wasn't having that. 'Talk to me, David. You froze – you know you did – and I want to know why.'

Stone looked away, eyes on Alex Parker: classy, composed, difficult to read. Frankie's father would call her posh. He'd probably question her relatively calm reaction to the news of her son's disappearance. Frankie didn't see it that way. She was a strong female personality. Every individual's response to crisis or tragedy was different, much of it reflected in their upbringing. Besides, the full impact of Daniel's disappearance hadn't yet hit home.

It would . . . in time.

Stone couldn't take his eyes off the woman.

Frankie's stomach took a dive as a thought forced its way into her head, such a terrible idea, she didn't want to give it houseroom. The more she studied her boss, the stronger the notion became. She wanted, needed, to understand why he hadn't told Daniel's mother that her son was missing, why he'd left that task to her.

'Fuck! Tell me you don't know her.'

'What do you take me for?' It was neither admission nor denial.

Stone had shown no hesitation. That was good . . . wasn't it? Frankie took a deep breath, trying to ignore the unfathomable sadness in his eyes. She had no clue what had brought it on – only that it was there.

'What then?' she said. 'David, be straight with me. You owe me an explanation—'

'I owe you nothing.' He loosened his tie. 'Don't you have work to do?'

His attention strayed again.

Frankie followed his gaze across the impressive drawing room, so stylish it took her breath away. The dream space contained alcove shelving, media units, contemporary art and exquisite wallpaper designs, expertly put together with relaxation in mind. Sumptuous furniture was complemented by rugs and cushions, subtle lighting. The flat-screen TV was the biggest she'd ever come across outside of a public cinema.

Stone was seeing none of it.

His focus was Alex Parker, uncommunicative despite her husband's efforts to engage her in conversation. It occurred to Frankie that the woman had very little tan considering she'd spent the last week in Majorca. Her hair was chestnut brown, tied in double French braids; eyes like pools of icy water. She looked dreadful – justifiable, given Daniel's disappearance – though not enough to hide her beauty. She was a little older than Stone but not so you'd notice. They both looked like they could do with a stiff drink.

Frankie began to panic. Did Stone and Alex Parker have history that her husband wasn't aware of? Was that why the DI had been reluctant to investigate Daniel's disappearance? As far as Frankie was aware, he'd not seen the job when it came in. Conceivably he might have checked the force-wide incident log without her knowledge and recognised the name and address. No, what was she thinking? That scenario didn't make any sense. If that had been the case, he'd have said so when she was trying to persuade him to run with the enquiry. He'd hardly rock up there as if nothing had happened and hope to get away with it. Unless he was so besotted with Alex that he saw himself as a hero, riding to the rescue. Except that didn't work either. Instead of leaving it to Frankie, he'd have delivered the bad news himself – and tried to comfort the woman, surely? – then removed himself from the investigation.

Not knowing what to believe, she turned away.

The search team coordinator gave an almost imperceptible shake of his head as he approached. He'd lucked out. Nothing had been found. Frankie looked at Stone. After the debacle inside the airport terminal, he'd thrown her the keys and walked Alex to the police car without a word, leaving Frankie to act as escort to the husband. Somehow, her boss had managed to compose himself on the journey, enough to offer words of reassurance to the couple. The scenarios Frankie had imagined were so bizarre that she began to doubt herself. Maybe she'd seen something that wasn't there. Or perhaps Stone was testing her, giving her a chance to prove herself? They'd yet to move beyond that first stage, getting to know one another, falling in step. She'd once been paired with a detective who, whenever there was bad news to deliver, insisted she take the lead. At no other time was she handed the privilege. Was that what this was about? She could do the shit jobs and Stone could take the credit . . .

Think again, mister.

Frankie had never seen herself as the harbinger of doom and was disillusioned to think that he might expect that of her. She'd do her bit, of course – on equal terms. From the outset, he'd insisted that they would be partners despite the variance in rank. That's the way it had always been with her. The way it would continue to be, else she'd ship out.

Seeing her suspicion, Stone dropped his gaze.

He looked at his mobile, an avoidance tactic, leaving her to wrestle with his lack of action at the airport and since. All coppers had their own way of operating – Frankie had been in the job long enough to have spotted idiosyncrasies in colleagues – still, this was off the scale. Stone hadn't merely taken his foot off the pedal, he'd slammed their relationship into reverse, allowing her to take over their first case of any note since he'd arrived in the north. A professional partnership was all well and good but, as the senior rank, it was his responsibility to show the way.

Frankie sighed.

Challenging him while they were on duty hadn't been very diplomatic. Stone would hardly open up – let alone confess all under someone else's roof – but there *was* something wrong, Frankie was sure of it. Over the years, she'd learned to trust her instincts. She'd get it out of him eventually. Until then she'd take up the slack.

She let it go . . .

For now.

6

Alex was supposed to go for a lie-down. She was exhausted after all the travelling. The claustrophobia of being thirty thousand feet in the air in a tin tube, followed by her detention at the airport, had been replaced by a new fear. Tim had offered to call Kat. Alex wouldn't let him. Her sister would be on the next train north and wouldn't take no for an answer. Her inability to organise her life had triggered the current situation.

Alex couldn't bear to see her . . .

Not now . . .

Maybe never.

She'd had a belly full of her selfishness. She couldn't listen to her whining a moment longer: *Please, I need you . . . I've already booked it. I know I should've asked first. I thought you'd be thrilled. Come with me, Ali . . . It'll be good for you, good for both of us. What can possibly happen in a week?*

Alex slipped into Daniel's room, her eyes straying to the blackened wall of glass on the gable end, floor-to-ceiling windows designed to bring the countryside into her son's room. Having grown up in a city suburb, getting him close to nature was something she was keen on. Her reflection in the glass shocked her to the core. A wizened creature twice her age stared back at her, shoulders hunched, face a ghostly white. She threw a switch, turning the intelligent glass wall opaque, wiping out the wretched image. Muffled whispers reached her through the open door.

She wanted everyone to leave now.

Daniel's room was cold without him in it. Alex imagined him sitting at his desk doing homework or lying on his bed playing some game she didn't and never would understand.

Her eyes travelled from surface to surface, evoking memories of shopping trips to buy the items on display: a complete first edition set of Harry Potter; an acoustic guitar, his new Premier League football; her father's county cricket bat; a set of Beats headphones – an extravagant tenth-birthday present from Tim. The gift had caused a rift between them. Since Tim had come into her life, he'd tried too hard to impress her son. He should know better. No item, however trendy, could buy a way into Daniel's heart. The lad was wary of men for good reason. His biological father was no role model and Daniel's affections weren't for sale.

A thought arrived, unbidden. Communication was a two-way street. Hers with Daniel had been deficient of late. After losing her second child, she'd paid him less attention than he deserved, far less than she would under normal circumstances and she intended to put that right. Her gaze landed on his Storm Trooper clock on the bedside table: 01:32. As the seconds ate their way into the night, DS Oliver wandered in.

'Can I get you anything, Alex?'

'That's kind, but no.'

Frankie made no move to leave. 'Can I ask if you've noticed any unusual behaviour from Daniel recently?'

'He'd been spending a lot of time in his room.'

'Why do you think that was?'

'I put it down to studiousness. At private school, he gets a lot of homework. He's always head down at his desk. If he was really engrossed, I assumed he was studying, closed the door and left him to it.' Alex was searching Frankie's face. 'I can see you're not so sure.'

'It's important to know if Daniel has been talking to anyone new.'

'If he has, it must've been on the Internet. There's no phone in his room and he doesn't own a mobile.'

'Yes, I know. Does he have an iPad?'

Nodding, Alex sat down. She opened the deep bottom

drawer of her son's bedside cabinet where he kept the device, shoving a neat stack of papers out of the way, removing his calculator and the book he was currently reading: *Boy X* by Dan Smith. Daniel had enjoyed the author's recent visit to his school and thought it was cool that they shared a name as well as a love of reading and writing.

She looked up. 'It's not here.'

Impatience took over. Like a woman possessed, she hauled the drawer from its runners and tipped it upside down. Large items and small spilled out on to his duvet cover, but not the device she was looking for. She got down on the floor to look under the bed.

Nothing.

A suggestion. 'Maybe Tim has it.'

Through the bedroom door, Alex could see him pacing.

He walked towards her, a sad look on his face.

'How could you allow this to happen?' she said, thoughts of the iPad overtaken by the more serious issue of her son's disappearance. 'How? You begged me to go! You said you'd look after him. Don't look at me like that. One minute I'm leaving the aircraft, dying to hold him in my arms, the next . . .' An animal-like wail escaped from deep inside her body. 'The next, DS Oliver is telling me he's missing.'

'They're doing all they can to find him—'

Alex rounded on her. 'Not enough!'

'His description has been circulated,' Frankie said. 'Officers force-wide are on alert.'

Alex glared at her. 'With the greatest of respect, those are just words! I want action: a nationwide campaign if necessary, a TV appeal – whatever it takes to get my son back. What good are you doing here?'

Tim was visibly distressed by her outburst. 'This is no time to fall out with anyone, Alex. We need to be strong for Daniel's sake. The police are doing all they can.'

Her husband was right.

Alex took a deep breath, trying to calm down and be reasonable. She held out a hand to her husband. 'I'm sorry, Tim. It was cruel to blame you. You weren't the one who swanned off for a week's R & R in Majorca. This is my fault, not yours. No one forced me to go.' She turned to face DS Oliver, apologising for any embarrassment her comments might have caused.

Frankie left them then.

7

Stone knew he'd have to face Alex Parker – sooner rather than later – although the thought of it filled him with dread. She'd broken down at the airport and then composed herself, only letting her emotions go in the privacy of Daniel's room, according to Frankie. He could see Alex through the bedroom door, weeping gently, hugging her son's stripy pyjama top. The material looked soft and warm. It would carry a bodily scent she'd recognise blindfolded. She appeared to be looking straight at him but her husband was in the foreground talking on the phone. He was the focus of her attention.

Those eyes.

Stone simply couldn't cope with those eyes. They were the exact same as—

'No joy.' Frankie's voice pulled him from his reverie. Her appearance at his side was a welcome distraction. He'd asked her to wake Daniel's football coach and quiz him about the vehicle the boy was seen getting into. Roger McCall was the last known person to have seen him as he left the football pitch. 'McCall is no petrol head. He can't remember the make or model, only that the car was old and not very well cared for. He only saw it from a distance. He gave me a list of other kids he thinks were there.'

'Thinks?'

'Kids turn up or they don't, apparently. He said they arrive in dribs and drabs. He hasn't got time to write their names down. I'm betting the parents don't know that. If I have my way, he'll not be a coach for long. I called the office. Brian Tilley's on nights. He'll follow up with other mums and dads to see if anyone else saw the vehicle. It was dark grey, McCall reckons, which is not a lot of use to us—'

'He didn't get a registration number?'

'Not even a partial. He has to be the worst eyewitness I've ever come across.'

'How many in the vehicle?'

'He said two initially, then qualified that with "maybe".' Frankie rolled her eyes. 'Training takes place on Ponteland High School pitch, so there may be CCTV. McCall claims the car drove off in a southwesterly direction towards the fell road. Not that it helps – it could've been going anywhere. I told him to stay put. We'll need a statement from him in the morning. Ditto Justine Segal, the au pair, unless you want her now. She's not gone to bed yet.'

'No, we should get off. I need to speak to the mother first.'

'You want me to?' Frankie obviously had misgivings.

Stone cleared his throat. 'No, I can do it.'

He glanced at Alex through the gap in the door. She was curled up in the foetal position on the edge of Daniel's bed, the boy's nightclothes clutched tightly to her chest. She wasn't sleeping. Her eyes were open, staring into space. A casual observer might think she was dead.

'David?' Frankie's stare was intense. 'Are you sure you want to do this?'

He nodded, appreciating her concern. In the short time he'd known her, she'd shown herself to be compassionate. An officer who cared for colleagues and the community she served, victims her top priority. Policing was in her blood, passed down through the generations. Frankie Oliver was the real deal. She was also done waiting for a response.

'David, let me help.'

'You can't.' He walked away.

At the bedroom door, Stone lifted his right hand, tapping gently so as not to startle Alex. Her eyes moved but not her head. It was as if the strength had been sapped out of her. He knew the feeling. Seeing her lying there made his heart bleed, a pain so acute he was ready to turn around and take Frankie up on her generous offer.

Daniel's mother sat up as he moved across the threshold.

He approached her slowly, hoping she might not notice that he was wavering. It wouldn't do to show his emotions when hers were so raw. A child's disappearance crushed the life out of anyone. He couldn't imagine what she was thinking right now. The effect it was having on both parents was so profound they could hardly bear to look at one another, let alone talk.

Cases of child abduction – if that's what this turned out to be – were paramount. Many officers had kids of their own. Stone drew comfort from the fact that his small team would be utilising every method at their disposal to find Daniel. The flip side of that thought was depressing. The DI was pain-fully aware of the discrepancy that existed between family expectations and what he could realistically deliver in terms of manpower. Government cuts had left uniformed personnel stretched to the limit force-wide, every shift depleted, par-ticularly in rural areas. There were fewer detectives now than there used to be. Had it not been for Frankie's insistence that they should act, coupled with a remarkably quiet night for the CID, they would not be involved.

Selfishly, he wished the missing boy were someone else's problem.

Alex was staring at him, a look of terror on her face.

'I'm sorry,' he said. 'I didn't mean to intrude.'

'You have news?' Her words were almost inaudible.

Stone shook his head. He'd frightened her and felt guilty for it. 'It's early yet.' His legs felt like lead. He gestured at the only chair in the room. 'May I? I need to talk to you.'

Alex gave a nod.

It was a mistake to sit so close. Stone hadn't figured the effect it would have on him. His heart almost stopped as their eyes met. Memories were dragging him back in time, towards a deep, dark pit. The more he resisted, the more he dug his heels in, the greater the pull towards the edge. His eyes found the floor, the blue carpet morphing into pools of icy water, a metaphor for the eyes he was trying so hard to ignore. He was in trouble and hadn't the courage to face her.

He must . . .

He couldn't fail a second time.

Somehow, he managed to free himself from his fit of terror and concentrate on what he had to do. A smile of encouragement didn't quite make his lips. 'I thought I'd check to see if you'd like some company – someone other than your husband and housekeeper, I mean. I can arrange for a Family Liaison Officer if it would be of benefit.'

Alex appeared relieved that he didn't have bad news to share but couldn't keep the disdain from her face. He didn't blame her. His offer of an FLO sounded hollow and unimpressive.

'That's very kind,' Alex said. 'If it's all the same to you, I'd prefer to be on my own.'

'In that case, DS Oliver and I will head off. We'll be in touch the minute we have something to report. I'll brief you in the morning.' He trotted out the party line, hating himself for doing it. 'My officers will be working round the clock to find Daniel.'

Another meaningless statement was lost on her. What Alex Parker required was action, someone to take charge and save her boy, an investigator with the nous to hunt down the person or persons who'd taken him away. Stone wanted to tell her that he was that detective. That with Frankie's help he'd find those responsible and make them pay, but he couldn't make that promise on such a doubtful outcome. He'd made life and death decisions before, pledged to make the pain go away, given assurances he hadn't delivered.

I won't let that happen, I swear.

A wave of nausea slammed into him like a wrecking ball, demolishing what little confidence he had left. He turned his head away, making out he was interested in the artwork on Daniel's wall, telling the boy's mother how talented he was. Stone couldn't allow her to see his distress. She might misconstrue it. Eventually, the feeling subsided, enough for him to face her.

'You should try and get some rest,' he said.

'How can I? I have a million questions and not one answer.'

'I have many too. They can wait.'

As he made a move to stand, Alex grabbed his wrist, preventing him from leaving. Her icy hand sent a shiver right through him. The dark pit was back. One minute Stone was standing on the edge, staring into the abyss, the next he was hurtling, down and down, on his way to certain death. His desperate cries went unanswered. There was no help, for him or her.

8

'Boss, we should get going.' Frankie had gone to Stone's rescue in the nick of time. She'd seen Alex's attempt to keep him in the room. That touch, however momentary, was inappropriate between the parent of a missing child and an SIO. Fortunately, Tim Parker's back was turned or he might have been the one charging into the room to find out what was going on.

Whatever it was, Frankie wanted no part in it.

Alex spoke before Stone could. 'I don't want to delay you, but I have many questions.' She was looking directly at Frankie. 'DI Stone seems to think they'll wait till tomorrow. I'm not so sure.'

'It is very late,' Frankie said. 'We really should get going.'

'May I trade you one question before you do?'

'Of course. You can ask us anything.'

Two pairs of eyes were fixed on Frankie. She was finding it hard to concentrate with no inkling of what Alex had a mind to ask. The detective sergeant was suddenly on her guard: what the hell had she interrupted?

'You first,' Alex said.

Frankie chanced her arm, asking a question she wouldn't dare ask her boss. His fault. If he wouldn't share, perhaps Daniel's mother would . . .

Lie detector primed and ready.

'Mr Parker told me that you've been married before and that he's not Daniel's real dad.' Frankie felt the heat of Stone's glare and ploughed on regardless. 'I was wondering, has there been much contact between your son and his biological father since you split up?'

'As little as I can get away with.'

'You don't approve?'

'That's two questions and I'm rather tired.'

Frankie detected a change in attitude. To be fair, Alex Parker did look exhausted, though she was more together now than she had been when Frankie entered the room. Her tears had dried up. The transformation was amazing. No longer was she the wretched parent who couldn't cope. She wanted answers and wasn't about to air her dirty linen in public to get them. She'd have to explain that relationship eventually, though.

Nevertheless, her response had put Frankie on the back foot. 'I'm only trying to establish if Daniel might have run away and if his father is a local man.'

'My ex is from the area but no longer has a house here. Last I heard, he was living in the London borough of Camden. He moves around with alarming regularity.' Frankie glanced at Stone. No concern visible, though his face was set in a scowl. If Alex noticed the exchange she didn't show it. She was still talking . . . 'I hardly think it likely that my son had the motivation or means to get to London all by himself.'

'Children can be very resourceful,' Frankie said. 'You said yourself that he was an able young man. Such a trip would require a certain amount of planning. I assume he had access to pocket money. Perhaps he'd been saving up without your knowledge and bought a ticket online—'

'He has money but his relationship with his father is, at best, distant.'

'You wouldn't happen to have an address?' Frankie took in her nod as well as her irritation. Clearly there was no love lost between the divorcees. So where did that leave Daniel? Frankie felt sorry for kids like him. Playing piggy-in-the-middle was never easy. They almost always wanted what they didn't have, even if it wasn't good for them. However bad the relationship between Alex and her ex, the guy was Daniel's father. Frankie nudged her again: 'In case he's moved, your ex-husband's full name and date of birth would help us locate him.'

Another glance at Stone.

No reaction.

'His name is Robb Scott. Date of birth: 10 November 1977.'

Frankie had never been so relieved. Daniel wasn't Stone's kid. Even so, she suspected that he knew Alex Parker. Why else react to her in the way he had? She refocused on the boy's mother.

'Can I ask what Mr Scott does for a living?'

'You presume too much, DS Oliver.' Alex added: 'My ex is a pig, a drunk who finds and feeds off women of means, bleeds them dry, then mistreats them horribly. They eventually get wise to him and, in my case, buy him off. Divorce hands him the opportunity to move on to the next meal ticket.'

An email pinged into Frankie's inbox, the sound catching them all by surprise. Alex looked at her expectantly. The email was from Parker's business partner in response to one Frankie had sent him before they left the station. He'd just come from a charity dinner and was apologising for the delayed reply. The content was illuminating, to say the least.

Alex stared at Frankie, a question in her eyes.

'Nothing,' Frankie lied and faked contrition. 'I apologise. It was personal.'

Alex dropped her head, searching through her son's paraphernalia for pen and paper on which to write a note. With her back turned, it gave Frankie the opportunity to convey a message to her boss that she was bluffing about the email. It *was* case-related.

Stone gave a nod in return: message received and understood.

Having found what she was after, Alex scribbled down Rob Scott's name, date of birth and last-known address, handing it to Frankie. 'My son's training ended at seven o'clock,' she said. 'I'd like to know how long my husband waited to raise the alarm.'

Frankie stalled. 'Wouldn't you rather ask him?'

'I'm asking you.'

Sidestepping questions never worked with the upper class. The exact time was etched on the inside of Frankie's brain. Such details were pivotal to any enquiry. Facts and good detective work solved cases, not approximations and guesswork. Rough calculations simply wouldn't do. Following evidence was always key but therein lay the rub; police and witnesses were fallible; when human error crept in – as it invariably did – lives were lost, offenders went free.

Stone had noticed Frankie's hesitation.

She dropped her head, avoiding his eyes.

So, they were both hiding stuff, running from a dark past. In her case, an event that had shaped her future, an incident that happened long before she threw on a uniform. She'd tried hard to keep her secret locked away, representing as it did an ever-present threat that returned to haunt her time and again. If she was reading him right, it was the same for Stone. When he blew in from the south he'd led her to believe that they would work well together, suggesting that a tight and loyal unit was on the cards. It was quite a speech.

Some partnership they turned out to be.

Alex was staring at Frankie. 'How long, DS Oliver?'

'Two hours.' It was probably wise not to be too specific until there was more information on the table. Now Stone had spoken to the family, he'd want a full debrief at the station. If pushed, Frankie would give an exact time. Daniel's mother had a right to know.

'That's a bloody long time,' she said.

'I expect he waited a while. That's what most parents do, faced with a missing child.'

Frankie had her doubts about Tim Parker. Maybe he was a different kind of predatory male to Alex's first husband. It was a well-documented fact: paedophiles often sought out unattached mothers for the sole purpose of getting close to children. With no proof of that, Frankie found herself defending him. Innocent until proven guilty had always been her watchword. 'It was light until about twenty past nine,' she said.

'DS Oliver. No offence, but I'm not "most parents" and my son isn't "most children".'

'I didn't mean—'

'I know.' Alex cut her off. 'But he's a little boy! I beg you to view him as an individual. Trust me, I know him better than anyone. Look, I admit, I'm over-protective when it comes to Daniel but I assure you it's for all the right reasons and, paradoxically, that makes him more, not less, exposed to harm. On his own, he'll be utterly lost. More than anyone, my husband knows this. He should've reported him missing immediately, not waited until it was almost dark. I was stupid enough to believe that he'd look after him. I will never forgive him if anything has happened to my child.'

'I know how difficult this is for you—'

'How could you possibly?'

'I'm only saying that in his position you might have done the same—'

'If I'd been here, you mean?' Alex snapped.

Frankie felt wounded by the comment. She'd never upset anyone in Alex's position or apportion blame. On the contrary, she'd do anything, *anything*, to make them feel that it wasn't their fault, giving assurances that she'd try her utmost to find the son or daughter and bring them home. Before she had the chance to convey that sentiment, Stone jumped to her defence.

About time . . .

'That's not what DS Oliver meant. No one blames you, Alex. Please don't think that. Of course you look out for your son – you're his mother. My colleague is merely suggesting that, faced with the same situation, there's probably nothing you'd have done differently. You'd have waited a while, called his friends – all of which Tim did before he arrived at the station.'

Alex looked unconvinced.

Lifting a Lego figure from among the odds and ends on the bed, she turned it over and over in her fingers before wrapping it in the palm of her hand. She glanced at Frankie, tormented by her son's absence. 'Wolverine is Daniel's favourite super-hero. He takes this to bed with him every night.' Unable to hold on to her emotions any longer, she finally let go.

Her sobs were hard to take.

When Stone glanced up, Frankie looked away, wearing the woman's grief as if it were her own. Tim Parker was standing outside the door, an eyewitness to the distressing scene, in no rush to comfort his wife.

Realising he was being watched, he turned away.

Frankie laid a hand gently on Alex's shoulder. 'We'll do everything in our power to find him,' she said.

Alex wiped her nose with the back of her hand. 'I know you will. I'm just so worried.' Her focus was Daniel's bed.

Frankie followed her gaze. 'Have you mislaid something?'

'I don't understand why his iPad's not here.'

'The search team have it,' Stone said. 'Sorry, I should've mentioned it. Technical Support will examine the device. They'll check your son's browser history and other data to get a handle on his interests and to locate who, if anyone, he's been talking to, in and outside of your immediate family. He may have friends you're not aware of. Kids meet all sorts online.'

'You mean offenders, don't you?'

'We're not going to lie to you,' the DI said. 'Much as we like to think we have safeguards in place, the criminal fraternity find their way around them. These devices are never one hundred per cent secure. Please, try not to worry. Our technicians are the very best there is. I assure you, if there's a clue to Daniel's whereabouts on the iPad, they'll find it.'

The woman fell silent.

Frankie received the message Stone wasn't sharing with the boy's mother. Statistically, when a child – boy or girl – was abducted or abused, the perpetrator was someone close to home: father, grandfather, uncle, brother – stepfather. Occasionally, that person turned out to be female, though it was far less likely. Outside of that family dynamic and the police were in trouble. A random abduction was enough to scare the most hard-nosed cop.

Frankie had studied cyber-crime. She'd made it her life's work warning friends not to upload photographs of their children on to the Internet. Technology was a wonderful tool but it was also dangerous, providing sex offenders and murderers with the means to access the bedrooms of children, an opportunity to groom them without even leaving home.

The thought made her flesh crawl.

'Daniel may not have a phone but he doesn't need one . . .' Frankie thought it best to be upfront from the outset, but sensitively, so as not to spook the child's mother. She explained: 'An Apple ID and/or email address will allow him to use iMessage, Facetime or join a social media platform.'

'At his age?'

'As hard as it is to swallow, children lie,' Frankie said. 'Even the good ones. Do you happen to know if Daniel has an account anywhere?'

'I shouldn't think so.'

'Were parental controls set on the device?'

Alex gave a shrug. 'I have no idea. You'll have to talk to Tim. He bought the damned thing. I'm sure he has that covered. As ridiculous as it sounds, given Daniel's absence, his stepfather is very protective—' She didn't finish. Her head went down, then she looked up, a horrified expression on her face. Slowly she opened her left hand to reveal a scrunched up note she'd been hanging on to for almost half an hour. 'I found this in his drawer.'

Frankie took the slip of paper from her. It was damp from sweat and tears. The ink had bled but she could make out the words, a name: Charlie Dawson. A shiver ran down her spine, anxiety levels rising. 'Who is Charlie Dawson?'

'I've no idea. That's what's so worrying.'

'This is Daniel's handwriting?'

'Yes, I'd know it anywhere.'

'You're one hundred per cent certain?'

A nod. 'For years, I've watched the way he forms his letters, carefully and neatly. Words matter to him almost as much as they do to me.' She pointed at a framed certificate on his wall attesting to the neatness of the boy's handwriting as a six-year-old, the first of many he'd picked up.

Frankie wanted to believe that Charlie was a school chum – even though Daniel had never mentioned the name to his mother, but it was odd. She took a deep breath, telling herself that there was nothing sinister in the note.

'Try not to panic,' Frankie said. 'Maybe Charlie is a boy at Daniel's school.'

'He isn't – at least, not one I've heard of.'

'Unless Charlie isn't a boy . . . your son is growing up.'

Alex almost smiled, but Frankie could see that the alternative scenario was in her head and hated herself for planting it there. She ran both hands through her hair. Maybe Alex didn't know her son as well as she thought she did. Or was Frankie so paranoid, so hard-bitten by years of investigating crime, she couldn't see an innocent explanation for the scribbled note? Alex, Tim and Justine all said that Daniel was a trustworthy kid who was bright enough to know that online identities were unsafe and not something to be relied upon.

Then again, all mothers liked to think they knew their sons. That they were innocent and good. That they took notice of their parents. Frankie knew different. Like any kid of his age, Daniel would have secrets. She'd been led to believe that he was also patient, endowed with good sense beyond his years. She prayed he had the nous to get himself home.

Alex was welling up, as if the worst-case scenario had suddenly occurred to her. Paralysed by fear, her eyes locked on to Stone and then Oliver. What passed between the two women was a moment of menacing clarity Frankie would never forget.

9

It was a clear night, the stars bright against an inky black sky. Frankie was awed by the lack of light pollution as they left the Parkers' house. No matter how many times she saw the Milky Way in all its glory, she never tired of it. It was an amazing sight, four hundred billion stars, a show like no other. At home in the fishing village of Amble, she would stare at it through her grandfather's telescope for hours.

She followed Stone to the car.

He didn't say a word as he blipped the doors open and got in. Pulling his seat belt across his chest, he started the engine and took off at speed. The search team had left the gate open for ease of exit. Just as well. It looked like he wanted a clean getaway. Frankie was itching to ask him what was wrong but it was late; the small hours wasn't the most appropriate time for a deep and meaningful.

Whatever it was would have to wait.

As they hurtled south towards Newcastle, he kept his eyes on the road and his mouth shut. Frankie followed suit, wishing he'd lighten up. He'd been in the south way too long and had lost a lot of the humour Geordies were famous for. Not that there was much to laugh about at present. Her previous professional partner was a joker, an open book. Her new DI was different. He was deep, a charismatic loner, a detective whose name didn't fit his character. Stone was no hard man. He was thoughtful, intelligent, doing his best in a job that chipped away at his spirit every day.

'I can hear you thinking,' he said.

Frankie wondered if it was an invitation to start a conversation she'd already decided to put off till morning. Discounting that thought, she kept her mind on the job rather than pry into his personal life, believing that she'd be on a hiding to nothing if she brought the subject up.

'That's some house,' she said. 'Might have to revise my description of Parker as minted. It's probably an understatement. The art alone must be worth a fortune. Alex is no fool, is she?'

'She had a point to make and she made it.' It was a curt reply.

'Any ideas on why it took Parker so long to report Daniel missing?'

'None. Didn't you ask him?'

'Not yet – I will.'

'While you're at it, raise an action on the DM he claims he didn't send. He's got some explaining to do.'

'At home or at the station?'

Stone took a moment.

'Home,' he said. 'We might get a complaint if we drag him in. As soon as the media realise who the boy's parents are, they'll be camping outside the gates taking pictures, trying to get the low-down on the investigation. The first thing they'll want to know is why neither stepfather nor au pair thought to dial 999 within the hour.'

'Too right. If he'd been my kid . . .' Frankie let the sentence trail off.

'Two hours isn't that long.'

'It's long enough for a scumbag to bundle a child into a car and do off with him. You'd have thought a man of Parker's intellect would have the sense to know that.'

'He's not a copper, Frankie. We know stuff he's not aware of. Stuff we'd rather not know, if we're being honest—'

'C'mon! He must read the papers, switch on the news. There are photos of missing kids posted online every day by the public and the police. In the last fortnight, there have been three attempted child abductions in the south, prompting warnings to be vigilant. You think they haven't made Twitter?'

'You're very clued up—'

'That's what I'm paid for,' Frankie said. 'If Parker is a fan of social media, and he clearly is, it beggars belief that he missed these warnings, or that they didn't make him stop and think when Daniel went missing. Any sensible person over the age of eighteen would have called the law.'

'He doesn't strike me as the type to panic,' Stone said.

'He doesn't strike me as the type to tell the truth either,' Frankie bit back. 'And tomorrow we'll find him out. I've not warmed to him, have you? The guy's a creep. No wonder Alex shrugged off his attempts to help her. Did you hear him? "I won't allow it!" What century does he think this is?'

'Your opinion of him doesn't make him guilty.'

'Yeah, yeah. What was it he said right before we left?' She quoted Parker: '"My wife is subject to panic attacks. I know what's best for her." I nearly stuck my fingers down my throat. I don't like him, David.'

'You don't say.' He smiled.

'Just telling it like it is.'

'I'm not saying he's not a suspect.'

'Good.' Frankie huffed. 'Have you seen my detection rate?'

He glanced sideways, a half-smile this time. 'Like father like daughter, eh?'

'Aye, and don't you forget it.' She was pulling his leg. There had been a Detective Frank Oliver in Northumbria force for over half a century, starting with her granddad who signed up in 1966. He and her father were formidable detectives, the latter regarded as the most successful of his generation. No one could touch him when it came to investigating murder.

Frankie tipped her head at Stone. 'You'd really get on with my old man.'

'If I'm lucky, I might even get a word in edgeways.'

She laughed. 'Whatever you do, don't go inviting him to the station. Any excuse and he'll be there in a shot, taking over, poking his nose in where it doesn't belong, quizzing you about our caseload, about me. I love him dearly but we'll

55

never get rid of him. Gateshead CID practically had to prise him out the door on his last day. I'm sure I heard him scream.'

Stone chuckled. 'Must be hard, living in his shadow.'

'Think again. Frank Oliver the third intends to outrank him one day, him and my granddad. They like to think they taught me all I know about policing. To be fair, they did . . . including Rule 1.'

'Rule 1?'

Frankie narrowed her eyes. 'Learn how to handle your supervision. I did, so you'd better be on your guard.'

Stone changed down as they rounded a bend, then floored the accelerator, throwing her back in her seat. Having spent years in a Met firearms team he was supremely confident behind the wheel, better than anyone she'd come across in fifteen years of service. They might not be in an armed response vehicle but she could get used to such an exhilarating ride.

He dipped his headlights. The oncoming car did likewise.

As it shot past, she said: 'You actually remind me of him.'

'Thanks a lot! What is he, sixty?'

'Fifty-five.' Frankie saw an inroad and took it. 'You're cast from the same mould. There's a dark side to *his* character too.' When he didn't respond, she kept digging. 'He has the tendency to shut down when troubled. Ring any bells?' She didn't wait for an answer. 'You never quite know what he's thinking. That's how he got so many offenders to cough during his career. His facial expression alone scared the shit out of them.'

'Tell me about your email.'

'Is that a euphemism for lay off?'

'The email, Frankie, or keep it buttoned.'

Stone was a totally different guy to the one she'd encountered at the Parkers' house: relaxed, unruffled, in charge. The transformation was astonishing. Gone was the sad look on his face, the lack of communication. Hell, he was practically ready to take a joke. Except Frankie wasn't laughing. Whatever had happened to him in London sat on his shoulder like a heavy weight, a closely guarded secret he was unwilling to share. She hoped to God it didn't involve Alex Parker and couldn't help thinking that Daniel's mother might be the reason he'd returned to his old stamping ground. Frankie could think of no other explanation for his weird behaviour earlier. She'd made her play and decided not to push it.

'Not talking to me now?' he asked.

She glanced at him. 'Sorry, I drifted off.'

'You were about to tell me about the mystery email. Who was it from?'

'James Curtis: Parker's business partner. Remember Parker's excuse for not picking Daniel up?'

'Important meeting, you said.'

'Well, there's a discrepancy between their accounts of what happened afterwards that needs further investigation. Curtis claims the meeting ended shortly before six thirty. Parker told me he checked his phone the minute business was concluded and found Justine's voicemail. He couldn't have done. She didn't leave the message until ten past seven.'

'No wonder you were so cagey with Alex.'

'Yeah, well either Parker is lying or Curtis is. For the record, Ponteland High School is less than a twenty-minute drive from their workplace.'

'Which means Parker could've picked the boy up himself—'

'Maybe he did.'

'Maybe he didn't.' Stone was playing devil's advocate. 'If Parker had time to pick Daniel up, then logically so did Curtis. It would be interesting to know how long the two have been in business together. How close Curtis is to the family. Presumably he knows the boy personally. You work with a lad's father long enough, you get wind of their routine. Stands to reason he might have knowledge of Daniel's move-ments, collection times, that kind of thing.'

'Clever. For a moment, I thought you meant Charlie Dawson.'

'He's another possibility. Then there's Daniel's biological father and his football coach.' Stone had a point: suspects were piling up.

Frankie went quiet, sifting the possibilities. Timothy Parker could have been mistaken when they spoke at the station – not unusual for someone under so much duress. Equally, he could have deliberately misled her and made a false statement. The jury was out on that one. Or maybe Curtis had. They both had the means and opportunity to collect Daniel. With Dawson, Rob Scott and Roger McCall also in the mix, the detectives were spoilt for choice. Her priority was finding Daniel before it was too late.

10

Stone slept badly, every missing kid he'd ever come across, dead or alive, invading his dreams, a procession of lost souls and unfulfilled potential filing slowly past, girls and boys, the unlucky ones cut down in the prime of their lives. The image faded, only to be replaced by the names of bereaved parents scrolling through his head like movie credits. His eyelids flickered, distorting the image. He tried to open them, to climb out of the distressing nightmare, but *she* was in his head again, standing right in front of him, icy pools for eyes, pleading with him not to let her go. She looked SO much like Alex Parker.

Stone gasped, a sharp intake of breath waking him suddenly.

For a moment, he was disorientated. Gone were his possessions, his music and artwork, the street view he was so familiar with. In its place, a dilapidated, seventeenth-century cottage in need of a full refit, his late grandmother's home he couldn't bear to sell. Drenched in sweat, he swung his legs over the edge of the sofa and headed to what he'd named the torture chamber, an ancient shower that hung over a rusting bath. Pipes banged as he turned on the tap. He could piss quicker and the water was cold. He was in and out in minutes, clean but shivering uncontrollably and covered in goosebumps. The north-facing property was never warm even in the height of summer. The sooner he could get to the car, the sooner he'd defrost.

A shaft of light crossed the room as Stone opened the door to the incident room allocated to their case. Frankie had beaten him in. She was standing in silhouette, the sun streaming in through the open window behind her, a million dust mites dancing around her head. As she walked towards him, ready for a tough day ahead, the names that had invaded David's sleep rolled in front of his eyes. Not one had he been able to forget. Nor did he want to. Their identities acted as a reminder never to stop looking – never to give up without a fight.

He must find Daniel.

'Blimey!' Frankie grimaced. 'You look rough.'

'I'm not the only one.' It was out of his mouth before he had time to stop it.

'I was asleep for less than four hours – who were you expecting, Madonna? What's up with you anyway? You been listening to Jimmy Nail on the way in?'

Stone laughed.

Since he'd arrived on Tyneside, she'd been ribbing him relentlessly about his nostalgic ramblings of growing up in Northumberland as a kid, mocking him about his homesickness, the reason he'd given for his sudden departure from the Met. He was beginning to wish he'd used a different excuse. He could never, would never share the real one.

'Don't suppose—'

'No.' She'd anticipated the question. 'There's no news. Day shift are all out knocking on doors. Civvies are manning the phones, working through that list Parker gave us. I just got off the blower. The caretaker at the Royal Grammar School gave me a number for the head teacher, Teresa Bowlby. Charlie Dawson is not a name she's familiar with, but that means nowt. She's recently home from a sabbatical, not yet up to speed.'

'She'll check it out?'

'And so will we . . . I need a coffee hit.' Through a gaping yawn, Frankie held up an imaginary cup and waggled it in the air in lieu of speech to see if he also wanted a brew. 'I can't manage a short macchiato or any fancy shite you've been used to in the south. It's cheap instant coffee or builders' tea, if you'd prefer.' She lifted her hand, fending off a response.

'I know, we really should up our game, but this is Middle Engine Lane, not Drury Lane.'

Stone grinned.

Middle Engine Lane was the home of Northern Command Headquarters. It was close to Wallsend – a former shipbuilding and mining town on the River Tyne – so named for its location on the eastern end of Hadrian's Wall, once occupied by a different kind of force: a garrison of soldiers housed at Segedunum Roman fort.

'Builders' tea is fine,' he said.

Frankie walked away singing 'Big River', a cheeky glance over her shoulder to make sure he was smiling. He was. His life was better with her in it than it had been without. His brother even said so. Over a beer, Luke had joked about her piss-taking, how she seemed to bring out the best in David, commenting that he'd never known him so happy. Stone had been on the verge of telling him that he was the reason for that, not her; that being home and in touch meant more to him than anything. He'd held back at the last moment. Luke never could take a compliment.

Stone sat down and made a list of actions he wanted to discuss with Frankie before they met with the parents again, wondering if the couple had managed any sleep. He was betting they hadn't. For someone with a missing child, a few minutes without news must be torturous – never mind a few hours.

Despite Frankie's opinion of Tim Parker, Stone didn't want to read too much into the fact that he hadn't reported Daniel missing right away. As a rule, the public tried not to waste police time. Few parents liked to be seen jumping the gun or being made to look foolish when their offspring arrived home none the worse for wear, having forgotten the time, got involved in some activity or, God forbid, got lost. David was more interested in exploring the relationship between the boy and his stepfather, and that would necessitate talking to Alex and Justine first. The au pair was a good bet. She was due into the station in less than an hour. He was hoping she'd have insight to share.

Frankie arrived, two steaming mugs in her hand. She set one down on his desk and pulled up a chair. 'How d'you want to play it this morning?'

'I'll take Justine Segal. You tackle the football coach.'

'Makes sense, given that I've already had the pleasure.' She rolled her eyes. Another yawn. 'Or not, depending on your point of view.' Frankie checked her watch. It was eight o'clock. 'That doesn't give us long.'

David cradled his cup, wondering how long it would take her to tackle him about going AWOL last night, figuratively speaking. He felt guilty for having dumped her with the delicate stuff. Telling a mother that her son was missing was a hell of a responsibility. She'd handled it with sensitivity and compassion. He wanted to share that thought, except it would lead to a conversation he wasn't ready to have.

11

Stone spotted Justine Segal's clapped-out green Renault Clio enter the station car park below his office window. He checked his watch. She was ten minutes early. He observed her from above as she got out and sauntered toward the entrance. Seconds later, the phone rang, the front desk announcing her arrival. He gave Frankie the heads-up and left the office, heading for reception.

On his way to the ground floor, the DI considered taking Justine out for a chat – somewhere less formal than the station. Witnesses often went into defence mode at the first sight of an interview room. He decided against that for two reasons: he didn't want her thinking he had the time to take a stroll with Daniel Scott missing and experience had taught him that difficult questions were best handled at home or within a professional setting, especially in cases where there was every likelihood of people getting upset.

Fortunately, the interview suite was quiet.

'Please have a seat.' He closed the door behind him.

The room was warm. Justine took off her navy linen jacket and sat down. The DI loosened his tie, pulled out a chair and sat down opposite his interviewee. Close up, the au pair looked pale and drained. He was relieved that she hadn't witnessed his lack of composure the previous evening. At least with her he could pretend he was on top of his game, even though he was far from it. It was high time he got a grip and did his job.

Justine fiddled with a small silver cross hanging round her neck, eyes scanning the basic, windowless room. She was not as confident as she first appeared to David through the window. Her posture was tense – stiff upper body – hands fidgety, subconsciously projecting her anxiety across the room.

Maybe that walk would have been the better option after all.

'Thanks for coming in,' Stone said. 'I won't keep you long.'

'Thank you.' Justine was visibly relieved to hear it. 'Alex needs me. In fact, I'm not sure why I'm here. I've told your colleague all I know about Daniel's disappearance. I have nothing more to add.'

Yup . . . defensive. He could see her point of view, though. She was miles from home, caught up in a family drama and feeling partly responsible. Nevertheless, her upset seemed genuine.

'All the same, I'd like to go over it again.' He explained why it was important to get the details right. 'I need some background from you.' Justine nodded her consent and he carried on, taking notes as he went. 'I understand you've not worked for the Parkers for very long.'

'Six months. Tim took me on when Alex came out of hospital. She lost a child, right after Christmas. It was stillborn, a little girl. Horrendous experience for everyone. They've been through so much. Daniel's disappearance . . .' She paused, taking a deep breath, struggling to get her words out. 'It will kill them, Inspector. Tell me what I can do to help.'

'I believe there was some disagreement over who was supposed to collect Daniel from football training? Mr Parker was under the impression that you were doing it.'

'So was I. He said he'd be tied up, but when I got to the school Daniel had already left. I called Tim. He didn't pick up. I left a message and then drove straight home. Daniel wanted to put balloons up for his mother's homecoming and I wanted to get it finished.'

The image of that welcome home sign popped into Stone's head. He wasn't ashamed to say that he was as affected by it as anyone else. It seemed to mock him as he entered the

64

house. 'I listened to the voicemail you sent Tim, Justine. You sounded very angry—'

'I'd had a wasted journey. Wouldn't you be?'

'I'm not so sure I'd have been so vociferous about it with a relatively new employer.'

'I was worried.'

'Even so, having met Mr Parker, I'd say you were chancing your arm, speaking to him that way.' If Stone had been asked to describe Justine, he'd have said she was anguished. She dropped her head, prompting a further question: 'Was it only the misunderstanding over who was collecting Daniel that made you angry, or was there something else you'd like to tell me about?'

Lifting her head, the au pair took in a deep breath. 'You are very perceptive, Inspector. Normally, I try to get to training ten or fifteen minutes early. I like to watch Daniel on the field. We have this thing we do. A challenge. If he scores a goal while I'm watching, I take him to the cinema and pay for popcorn. If he doesn't, he pays. Last night, I was running late. I knew he'd be disappointed that I'd let him down. We both love the movies.'

'Sounds like a lot of fun.' Stone said. 'Has he ever paid up?'

'Not yet.' It came out like a sob.

The DI tried to regain her attention with another question. 'Do you normally act as taxi driver when Daniel needs a lift?'

'Of course, if he has football or golf and his parents aren't available – that's my job. They're busy professionals, often away from home. Plus, I love spending time with him. Is it relevant?'

'Only in as much as you might have seen the vehicle we are now trying to trace,' Stone explained. 'Did you speak to Daniel's football coach when you got there?' His witness drifted off someplace else. He gave her a gentle nudge. 'Justine?'

'Sorry. What did you say?'

'Mr McCall? Did you speak with him at the training ground?'

'Yes. It was Roger who told me that Daniel had gone. I assumed Tim had picked him up.'

'How come you were late?'

'Traffic was bad – an accident that took a while to clear. I arrived at the school at five past seven.'

'I see.' The lack of punctuality explained her distress when he'd seen her at the house surrounded by the search team. She was undoubtedly shaken, unable to settle, avoiding eye contact with Tim and Alex – a guilty look witnessed by Frankie too. Stone didn't dwell on it . . . but he would if he had to. 'What would Daniel normally do if you were late?'

'I'm never late!' She bridled. 'And it's normally a few minutes after seven when they leave.'

'Would Daniel wait if you weren't there?'

'Yes, he'd been told he must stay with Roger.'

'And Mr Parker doesn't know you were delayed?'

Justine shook her head, guilt eating her up. 'It was cowardly of me, but I couldn't bear to tell him it was my fault. Inspector, you must find Daniel. I can't live with myself, knowing that I might have prevented his disappearance.'

The DI tried to placate her. 'You weren't to know there would be an accident.'

'That's what I keep telling myself, but it hasn't helped. And it won't until you find Daniel and return him to us.' Stone felt sorry for her – she clearly cared for the boy. A tear appeared on the bottom lid of her right eye, a sparkly balloon, like a miniature of the ones that were hanging in the Parkers' hallway the night before. It clung on to Justine's lashes for a moment before the weight took it over the edge. It dribbled down her cheek and she wiped it away, her bottom lip quivering as she tried to regain composure. 'Will you tell Alex?'

'Not unless she asks me directly. Though if I were you, I'd mention it. If the search goes on for any length of time, it's very likely that she'll broach the subject. And then, whatever the consequences for you, I'll have no choice but to level with her.'

A pair of brown eyes were begging him not to.

Stone imagined her panicking over her lateness, the relief she must have felt when McCall told her that Daniel had already been collected and was on his way home, her anger that his stepfather had caused her unnecessary distress. To some extent, those mixed emotions explained her attitude to her employer on the phone. Letting off steam was human nature after a shock, however minor, but this situation was serious.

He wanted more from Justine Segal.

'What exactly did Roger McCall tell you?'

'That Daniel had already left.'

'Nothing more specific?'

'I'm not sure what you mean.'

'Did you ask him if he'd seen your employer pick up his stepson?' Clearly, she hadn't. Stone made her sweat for a beat. 'You assumed it?'

'It didn't occur to me—'

'Really?' He eyeballed her. 'It surprises me that you made that assumption. Did it not strike you that something more sinister might have happened?' He could have added the words 'to a child left in your care'. He didn't. 'If I were you, my imagination might have gone into overdrive. Other scenarios may have crossed my mind, however fleetingly.'

'You're a policeman—'

'And you are a registered au pair.'

Justine began to weep at the implication that she'd failed in her responsibility.

Stone didn't let her tears waylay him. His job was to find the truth. The timing of the offence and who said what to whom was crucial. Get that wrong and it would throw everything else out of kilter. 'Even if I weren't a policeman, the very least

I might do is ask other parents to corroborate Roger McCall's account. Did you do that?'

'I couldn't. They had all left by the time I arrived.'

'All of them?' The DI paused, wondering if her five-minute delay was nearer ten, or even fifteen. 'There were no stragglers getting changed? No kids collecting footballs, helping the coach out? Children do that, don't they, put the kit out and collect it afterwards?' It's what his brother's kid used to do.

'There are no changing facilities available in the evening,' Justine explained.

'Isn't the school site also an FA facility?'

'Yes, but it's something to do with insurance, health and safety, I think. The school board – is that what you call it? – won't allow it. The premises aren't covered for every child who wants to play football, so they leave the pitch dirty and get washed at home. It's always been that way, ever since I came to work here.'

It was time to push her a little further. 'Justine, timing is vital when we're dealing with missing persons. Is there any possibility that it was later than you thought when you arrived at the playing field?'

'No, my eyes were peeled to my watch the whole time I was driving. I told you why I was late.'

'And presumably worried—'

'Daniel is my responsibility. Look, I did panic, if it makes you feel any better. I checked my phone immediately and noticed the message from Tim saying he'd collect Daniel. That's why I was angry with him. He can be a little selfish sometimes. No, not selfish, inconsiderate. Not on purpose. He's a busy man.' She wrung her hands and changed the subject. 'Your colleague asked me to send a screenshot of the message. May I ask why?'

'It was important to have a record of it.'

'Is that all?' Justine waited. 'You're not the only one who is intuitive, Inspector.'

Stone watched her carefully as he delivered a blow he knew would knock her sideways. 'Mr Parker claims he never sent that message.'

'He did!' She was adamant.

'Yes, I know. And I'm sure we'll get to the bottom of it when we see him later this morning. If you wouldn't mind, I'd like it if you were not at the house when we do this.'

Justine nodded her consent. 'I have some errands to run for Alex.'

'Perfect. We should be done by around midday so, if you could delay your return, I'd be grateful. And please . . . do not speak to either of your employers until after we've had the opportunity to interview them.'

'I understand.'

Stone's phone signalled an incoming text.

'Excuse me a second.' He took the device from his pocket. The message from the PolSA team leader was short and to the point: *School grounds searched: negative result.* Pocketing the phone, he carried on with the interview. 'Did you know Alex or Tim before you went to work for them?'

'No.'

'How did you get the job, if you don't mind me asking?'

'Through a specialist recruitment agency,' she explained. 'I was living and working in London when my host family moved to Saudi. It wasn't a place I wanted to go, nor does it suit my lifestyle, so we parted company.'

Stone made a note to check her references. 'I assume you stand to lose your job if this gets out—'

'I'll never work with children again if Mr Parker is blaming me for Daniel's disappearance.'

'I'm sure that's not the case. You couldn't invent that DM, could you?'

'So why is he saying he didn't send it?'

It was a question Stone didn't have an answer to. He wanted her off the subject. 'What are the Parkers like as a couple?'

'They're lovely.'

'Is that the loyal answer or the truthful one?'

She thought for a moment. 'They've had a lot of sadness in their lives lately.'

Stone wondered how far that sadness extended, if the marriage was sound, if behind closed doors in their palatial home the couple were not as happy as they appeared to those looking in – more importantly, if the state of relationship had anything to do with Daniel's plight. 'Are they good to you, the Parkers?'

'Very. I live in their annex. I get an OK wage and a little time off. Not much, but I'm learning about your culture and Daniel is learning about mine. His mother is keen that he's fluent in languages. On her instructions, we speak only in French. His parents treat me like a member of the family and that's why I feel so guilty now. You must find him.'

'What's he like?'

'Daniel? He's a wonderful, thoughtful child. Never any bother. Any suggestion that he took a detour on the way home is nonsense. If he got into a car, he knew the person who was driving. Please, you must believe me. I spend a lot of time with him. I refuse to believe that he wandered off or ran away. He's never done it before. He wouldn't worry us like that. It's not in his nature. Besides, he was desperate to see his mother. Excited to be staying up late to welcome her home.'

Stone noted the 'us', and wondered if Daniel was closer to Justine than to his parents. A lot of kids were like that. There was a time when his brother's son would do anything to spend time with him rather than his father. Luke was persona non grata, Uncle David a hero in Ben's eyes; they did everything together, a thought that needled him years later. The lad was now eighteen; as he grew up, he changed – and not for the better. Uncle and nephew were now estranged.

His loss.

Mind back on the investigation, Stone pressed on, reassuring Justine that his team were doing everything possible to find Daniel. 'Can we go back to your aborted attempt to pick him up? I'd like to show you something.' The DI pushed an A4 sheet of paper across the table. 'Can you indicate on this map where exactly you parked your Renault?'

She looked slightly bewildered.

'I saw you drive in,' Stone explained. 'There are several exits from the school grounds.' He pointed them out to her. 'The same can be said for parking places: a school car park here, a lay-by here, and grass verges where cars pull in to wait for pupils leaving school.' The sketch had been supplied by one of the uniforms who'd been out to the scene.

Justine pointed at a location near the school gates. 'I park here if I can.'

'Is that where you parked last night?'

She nodded. 'By the time I arrived, there was plenty of room.'

'Thank you. To eliminate parents from our enquiries, I'll be asking everyone collecting children to pinpoint their position. Daniel was last seen walking towards a car we've not yet traced.'

'Yes, Alex told me. What kind of car?'

'Our witness wasn't specific.'

'Then you must ask him again.'

'I didn't say it was a man.'

Justine shrugged. 'I assumed—' She stopped short, realising she'd made one too many assumptions already.

Stone let it go. 'Justine, did you call Mr Parker right away?'

'As soon as I saw his message. As you heard, I was angry.'

'And feeling a little guilty?'

'Yes.'

'What time did you make the call?'

She held out her phone.

The DI took it from her, confirming Frankie's account that

the au pair called Parker at seven ten. If, as Curtis suggested, his meeting ended before six thirty – and Parker didn't arrive home until seven thirty-five – even taking account of a twenty-minute ride home, it begged the question: where had he been?

12

They left Wallsend at ten, heading north-west on the A19. Traffic was heavy as they passed through the industrial heartland of North Tyneside, the landscape improving once they turned on to the Berwick Hill Road. In the village of Ponteland they took a right on to the A696 where it was prettier still.

Stone glanced at Frankie. 'How did it go with McCall?'

'I told you, he's a waste of space.'

'No further forward?'

'He hasn't a clue of make or model of the car. I questioned him on where exactly he last saw Daniel. He said there's a metal gate at the western edge of the football field. After training, the lad climbed over it to exit the field. The vehicle was waiting on the other side.'

'That's interesting.'

'Because?'

'Justine parks her car on the north side, close to the school entrance. She insists that she always parks there, even if there's no space in the lay-by. She bumps it up on the kerb. If Daniel went the other way, it would suggest he'd made specific arrangements.' He didn't wait for a response. 'Did McCall say anything else?'

Frankie shook her head. 'He's not the attentive type: wasn't able to give a description of the driver; couldn't decide whether there was a passenger in the front seat; has no idea if the car belonged to another parent. He's certain that Daniel got in the rear though. Whoever picked him up had several options. Local officers took McCall to the scene at daybreak to pinpoint exactly where he saw the car. They described it as a gateway into the field.'

They exchanged a worried look, David voicing his concern

that choosing an unauthorised parking spot might have been a deliberate attempt to avoid official entrances and exits – and more importantly the scope of CCTV – a thought not lost on Frankie.

'McCall reckons he's a coach, not a babysitter. He said he can't watch all the kids in his team. As far as he's concerned, training ends and they take off. She quoted McCall in a derisory tone: "It's the parents' responsibility to be there when I blow the final whistle. So what if Daniel nipped over the fence? How was I to know that it wasn't his old man picking him up—"'

'His old man? Did you ask—'

'If he meant Daniel's biological father? Yes—'

'And did he?'

'No, "old man" was a figure of speech. The only father McCall is aware of is Timothy Parker. McCall claims Daniel got in and the vehicle moved off. That's all he knows.'

'Without delay?'

'Yes. Door slams shut. They're gone. End of.'

'Which way was the car facing?'

'South.'

'Anything on CCTV yet?'

'No, I had a word before we left.'

David went quiet. It was hard to second-guess the choices an offender makes: an unpremeditated pick up was one thing, a planned abduction entirely another matter – options of where to park were largely determined by escape routes. Then there was the victim: was Daniel a random choice, a carefully selected child or had he met someone on the Internet? If the kid went willingly it would suggest familiarity, in keeping with the vast majority of abduction cases. The name Charlie Dawson gnawed at Stone. All parents would be quizzed on the matter and Daniel's iPad was being examined as a matter of urgency to see if the name cropped up. There were many unanswered questions but it *was* possible to draw conclusions that he may have known the person he took off with after football – Justine Segal had said as much.

'We should check out the school again.' They had stopped by briefly in the early hours of the morning in poor visibility. 'We need to see it in the light of day,' Stone said. 'And I want every parent who parked within the vicinity of that school spoken to by close of play. Hone in on specifics: Did they see Daniel? Did they see the car McCall described or any vehicle they hadn't seen before? I know we've kind of ruled him out, but I'd like to know if anyone has misgivings about McCall. Remind them of the need to be discreet. I know you'd strip him of his licence for not escorting every player off the pitch, but realistically that's never going to happen and this is the guy's livelihood we're on about. Quick as you can. Oh, and see if there have been reports of suspicious vehicles or individuals on the force-wide incident log within the last twelve months.'

'You think there's been some grooming going on?'

'Just covering the bases. Action it, Frankie.'

She was already on the phone.

Stone listened as she relayed the actions to personnel at their base. She swivelled in her seat to face him, placing her phone on the dash, her face set in a scowl. 'We've had confirmation that there's no Charlie Dawson at Daniel's school, parent or child, male or female. I was hoping there would be.'

The implication was clear.

'Any hits on the PNC?'

'Loads: Charlotte Dawson, Charlie Dawson, Charles Dawson.'

'Any child abusers among them?'

Frankie shook her head.

'Anybody at all worth checking?'

'Not at this stage. I've got a couple of people working on it.' Frankie glanced out the window. She didn't want to speculate on who might have taken Daniel and what they might have done to him. Quickly, she changed the subject. 'How was Justine Segal when you spoke to her?'

'In a bit of a state.'

'Figures. She's close to Daniel, according to the lad's parents.'

'That's not what I meant,' Stone said. 'Turns out she arrived five minutes late to pick the boy up, an accident that blocked the road. I know these things happen. I find it odd that someone of her calibre and experience wouldn't factor in enough time to meet her ETA.'

'Her calibre?'

'She's registered with a top-notch recruitment agency in London. I gave them a bell earlier. Justine was with her previous family for seven years. Never put a foot wrong. They had nothing but good things to say about her. She's screened and vetted by the International Au Pair Association, very well thought of. And yet she took McCall's word on trust last night, albeit briefly.'

'What do you mean?'

'She never questioned the identity of who drove him away,' Stone said. 'Shocking, isn't it? Allegedly, it was only when she checked her phone and discovered the DM from Parker that she knew for sure, or thought she did.'

'Bet she was relieved.'

'Yeah, but not for long . . .' Stone gathered his thoughts for a moment. 'If Daniel was gone when Justine arrived but McCall was still there, it puts him in the clear. Unless his story is a complete fabrication and the boy was in the boot of his own car . . .'

'He wasn't.'

Stone narrowed his eyes. 'And you know this how?'

'I was going to talk to you about that.' Frankie pressed her lips together, feigning contrition. 'You're not going to like it when I tell you.'

'What have you done?'

'I already searched his car.'

'When . . . and on whose authority?'

'It's called taking the initiative, David.'

He stared at her. 'When, Frankie?'

'When you were contemplating whether to take the case; when I had a spare half hour; when it seemed like a shame not to. Is three whens enough or shall I keep going?' Frankie had to think on her feet. Her explanation hadn't cut it with her boss. 'I heard Control on the radio reporting a misper. What was I supposed to do? I was in the area. It would have been a dereliction of duty not to give it a whirl. McCall runs more than one training session. He takes the ten- to thirteen-year-olds early in the evening, has an hour off, then coaches the senior team from eight till ten. He was about to leave when I got there.'

'And how did you get into the boot of his car?' Stone fixed on her guilty face. 'Scratch that. I don't think I want to know.'

'David, don't be like that. I asked him nicely . . . like my dad told me to.' She didn't stop for breath. 'And before you ask, I took a friendly CSI bod along, so we've got samples if we need them. It's OK, I didn't spend any money.' She made a crazy face. 'In my book, that deserves at least two Brownie points. I wasn't waiting around until he torched the car to get rid of evidence, if there was any, was I?'

'Does this friendly CSI have a name?'

'He does . . .' She put one finger on her chin, thinking. 'I swear my head's a sieve lately. I'm sure it'll come to me.'

Stone laughed. 'You're a piece of work.'

They had reached the picturesque village of Belsay.

Stone changed down, indicating his intention to turn right. As they passed Bolam Lake, shards of sunshine streamed through the trees edging the water, the view taking their minds off the dodgy road surface. As the car negotiated a hairpin bend, Frankie shifted in her seat to face him, a thought crossing her mind. 'An RTA is a convenient excuse to be late. Did you check out Justine's claim?'

Stone nodded. 'It's legit. Control received a 999 call just after six thirty – around the same time she left the house. Some idiot ran off the road while texting. Ended up in a ditch with two broken arms. He was well over the limit, driving whilst disqualified with no insurance. He's now on bail facing another ban.'

'What's she like – Justine?'

'Pleasant enough.'

'Ouch.' Frankie raised an eyebrow. 'You have doubts about her?'

'No! I felt sorry for her. She's nice.'

'You really know how to flatter a girl . . .' Frankie laughed. 'Who the hell wants to be *nice*?'

'You know what I mean. If you ask me, she has more to give. She didn't admit that she was late in picking Daniel up until I pushed her. That's understandable in her position, I suppose. I don't know, I got the impression she was holding back. Time will tell if she has something else to hide.'

'Like the fact that she's screwing her employer?'

'Oh, c'mon!' Stone said. 'That's a cliché if ever I heard one. She's only been working for Parker for a few months.'

Frankie put a hand on her chest, acting as if she were about to faint. 'David, I'm crushed that you'd even suggest that I stereotype people. If you'd had eyes for anyone but Alex last night you might've noticed an exchange between Tim and his au pair when we first walked into the house. It was fleeting – not destined for my eyes or his wife's – but it was there, as plain as day.'

Stone glanced at her. 'You don't miss a trick, do you?'

Frankie laughed. 'My extra-marital sensor is as good as any.'

He appreciated her intuition as much as her honesty. Turning right on to the Otterburn–Elsdon road, he drove on through open countryside. A few miles further, yon side of the village of Scots Gap, he pulled into the Parkers' driveway and took in the house in all its glory. In the cold light of day, it was simply stunning – and that was only the stable block.

13

Alex looked out from Daniel's window over the lush green countryside at the rear of her property. It was a world away from the bleached Majorcan landscape she'd shared with Kat less than twenty-four hours ago. Their holiday seemed a distant memory now: the sun, the pool, the wine, long conversations. Alex had no inkling of impending doom or that her life would change in an instant – from bliss to horror in a few short hours. Ordinarily, the sight of her slice of Northumberland – a tapestry of woodland, forestry and agricultural land – would lift her spirits, but not today. Today, the remote location did nothing of the kind. The stillness and lack of movement merely accentuated her isolation from the rest of the world. Not only had her life changed – she had changed.

A ring on the doorbell startled her.

Letting go of her hand, Tim shot out of the room as if he were on fire. He knew Justine wasn't there to answer the door. Alex checked her watch, wondering what was keeping her. She'd asked her to stop at the chemist on her way home to pick up some paracetamol and expected her before now. Laying Daniel's clean pyjamas on his pillow, she placed Wolverine on top of them and smoothed them flat before following her husband from the room. He was letting Stone and Oliver through the front door as she entered the hallway. A morose shake of the head from the detective sergeant. Without greeting them, Alex turned away, leaving the detectives to Tim. If they had no news, she was in no rush to speak to them.

In the kitchen, Alex threw a switch on the kettle. It had been boiled twice already, if only to give her something to do as she awaited the arrival of the police. She laid her hands flat on the bench, using it as a prop, and threw up in the sink, then washed and dried her face. She made a pot of coffee and was filling a milk jug when Tim arrived by her side, fussing over her as he had done all morning, making sure she was OK, which of course she wasn't.

'Don't fuss,' she said. 'I'll be there in a minute. Take care of our guests.'

'They're hardly guests.' His tone was disparaging.

'Visitors then. Don't split hairs, Tim. They're here to help.'

'Yeah, well they're not, are they? I may as well go out and find Dan myself for all the use they are.'

She gave him hard eyes. 'Why don't you then?'

Frankie was closer to the door than Stone. She could hear the couple talking, muffled voices through the kitchen door. They sounded like they were arguing. She hated this part of her job, witnessing potential victims of crime turn against one another, that gradual deterioration in relationships that seemed to come at times of stress. Often as not, there was an element of blame involved, neither party willing to accept responsibility for a missing child.

Alex turned, leaning against the counter, observing her husband. They had talked long into the night, interspersed with periods of melancholy, until they were so exhausted they had fallen into bed. Alex had lain awake, his strong arms around her, conscious of him slipping away, his breathing slowing into a steady rhythm, and then his grip relaxed and he was gone. How could he sleep?

'Why didn't you return my text last night?' she asked.

'What?' The question had thrown him.

'You heard me. What was so important that you didn't answer?'

'Alex, the police are here.' He spread his hands in a gesture of incredulity. 'Does it matter?'

'It matters to me.' She stared at him, hating him for what he'd done. 'I was excited to be home, looking forward to seeing you and Daniel. Have you any idea how much I missed you guys? I was counting the seconds until we could all be together, the three of us, especially you and me. I wanted to go back to the way we were before . . .' Alex bit down so hard, her jaw almost locked. She simply couldn't say the name of the child she'd lost: Beth.

A dark shadow crossed Tim's face. He drew her towards him and gave her a hug. Her body was limp against his chest, the strength sapped out of it. There were no tears from either of them. 'Sweetheart, I would do anything, *anything*, to put this right.' He stroked her hair. 'You know that, don't you?'

She pulled away. 'Haven't you done enough!'

'Alex, this is not my fault—'

'Whose fault is it then?'

'I'm sorry. Please . . . don't shut me out.'

'I can't . . .' She fended off an attempt to draw her close. 'Don't touch me!'

'We'll talk later. We can't do this now. The detectives are waiting.'

'Let them.' Alex stepped away. 'You haven't answered my question.'

'I couldn't text you. The policewoman had my phone.'

Frankie picked up the lie instantly. 'Did you hear that?'

Stone was frowning, shaking his head.

'He just told her that he couldn't text her last night because I had his phone. That's a blatant lie. When I checked his phone, I handed it right back. At no time was it out of his possession. That's twice we know of that he's misled people. Wily bastard, isn't he? If he's lying about that, what else is he lying about? More to the point, why is he?' Frankie put a finger to her lips, her head on one side, straining to hear the rest of what was being said. There was a pause in the conversation. Frankie whispered, 'She's not happy.'

Alex entered the room first, Tim following behind with a tray of coffee. He invited the detectives to move through to the adjoining room. They all sat down around a dining room table that seated twelve, five chairs on either side, a carver at each end.

'How are you holding up?' Stone's focus was Daniel's mother.

She threw a question back at him. 'Has there been *any* progress?'

'House-to-house enquiries are being carried out in and around the location where Daniel was last seen. Ponteland High has also been searched. As you know, the football pitches are located at the western end of a split site shared with the Middle School. I had a chat with Justine this morning and Roger McCall has also been re-interviewed.'

He nodded to Frankie, her cue to take over.

'Early this morning, McCall was escorted to the scene. He's given a clear indication of the position of the car that Daniel was seen climbing into after training. Voluntarily,' she added. 'At this stage, we have no evidence to suggest that he was taken against his will.'

'That's a relief,' Parker said.

'Is it?' Alex snapped her head around to face her husband. 'I'll be relieved when he walks through that door and not before.'

'Me too, but—'

'But what, Tim?'

'Alex, calm down! He got in willingly . . . I mean, it sounded like he wasn't being manhandled. That's all I meant by it.' Realising that he was putting himself in the firing line, Parker met Stone's gaze across the table, a plea for help almost, an attempt to fend off a further attack and put his wife's mind at rest. 'That's good news, isn't it, DI Stone?'

'For Christ's sake!' Alex said. 'Listen to yourself! Did he have to go into that vehicle kicking and screaming to satisfy you, Tim? Does that somehow let you off the hook? My boy is out there and you think that's OK?'

Parker was wounded. 'Our boy,' he reminded her.

She didn't respond.

There was an awkward moment while husband and wife regarded one another, a moment too of remorse and reconciliation. Frankie wondered what had gone on during the night, whether they had played the blame game. What had been said; more importantly, what had been left unsaid. Would that she had been a fly on the wall.

Stone filled the silence, his focus on Alex. 'We've managed to locate your ex-husband locally. He's in Heaton.' The area he was referring to was a residential suburb two miles north of Newcastle, around twenty miles from Scots Gap. Handy for a quick knock on the door when Rob Scott was least expecting it.

Alex looked surprised. 'That's news to me. As I said, I've had no recent contact with him.'

'We intend to visit the school,' Stone said. 'Then he'll be our next stop. Mr Scott has no idea we're about to pay him a visit. It would help to know what kind of reception we might get.'

'That rather depends on how drunk he is.'

'You don't believe we'll find Daniel there, do you?' The question had come from Frankie.

'Not a hope in hell,' Alex said. 'He wasn't interested in our son when we were living together. There's no chance that he'll be interested now.'

'Even if Daniel wished it?' Frankie asked.

Alex shot her a disparaging look. 'Even then.'

'Still, we need to check it out.'

'Absolutely,' Tim said.

Another dark face-off between husband and wife.

'DS Oliver has a point,' Stone said. 'We must consider all the angles, including the possibility that Daniel somehow managed to get in touch with his biological father or vice versa. You said last night that he had a weekly allowance, that he was a saver rather than a spender, unlike your ex. You seemed to suggest that money is important to Mr Scott. That he uses people to get his hands on it. Maybe he saw an opportunity and took it.'

Alex considered his words carefully. 'I hear what you say, but since Daniel was old enough to count, I've instilled in him the need to be careful where money is concerned. He chooses wisely when he wants something. I can't believe he'd search for his father, let alone actively seek him out after the appalling abuse he doled out when we were with him.'

'But you concede that it might have worked the other way?' Stone said.

'Absolutely. Rob would stop at nothing to get his hands on my cash, however indirectly. He doesn't like me these days, Detective Inspector. Not since I slapped a restraining order on him before we went to court to determine custody. He likes the police even less, so watch yourselves.'

'He has no visiting rights?'

'Not on your life!'

'Then maybe he nurtured a secret relationship with Daniel—'

'I don't think so. A child would cramp his style with the ladies. You'll know what I mean when you meet him. Mind you, wait a few years and that might change, particularly if our son makes something of himself, especially if he manages to accrue any funds; then Rob will come crawling out from whichever stone he's hiding under with a sob story that would make an adult weep. If there's one thing he's good at, it's manipulation. He'll play the son-needs-a-father card, no question. If that doesn't work, he'll try common or garden emotional blackmail, so maybe your theory has some credence. By all means, check him out.'

Stone moved on.

There was a huge discrepancy between key witnesses, not to mention a message on Justine's phone that Parker denied sending. That fact was uppermost in David's mind and he couldn't wait to get started.

14

Frankie kept quiet as Stone explained to Alex that a formal interview with her current husband was required before tackling her ex and that such an interview could take place at the family home or at the station. In either case, it would have to be conducted in isolation, by which he meant not in her presence. Nodding her understanding, Alex pushed her chair away from the table, an apprehensive glance at her husband before leaving the room.

As the door closed quietly behind her, Tim Parker poured more coffee, draining the pot, suggesting he replenish it in case they needed more.

'We're good, thanks.' Stone was having none of his delaying tactics. Parker was understandably nervous and that's right where the DI wanted him. Placing his mobile on the table between them, the voice-memo facility switched on, he began the interview: 'Mr Parker, I'd like to take this chronologically if I may.'

Way to go, David!

Frankie was itching to see how far Stone intended to push a witness who was fast becoming her number one suspect, although she was prepared to hold that thought for a moment longer. She wasn't the only one in the room who'd noticed the formality creeping in. Daniel's stepfather was no longer 'Tim' but plain old Mr Parker, whose nod was a signal that Stone should carry on. And continue he did, with equanimity.

'I understand you had a meeting with your business partner, James Curtis, at your place of work yesterday, in the early evening.'

'Correct,' Parker said.

'And that's why you couldn't pick Daniel up?'

'Indeed.'

'You told DS Oliver that after the meeting you immediately checked your phone and found a voicemail from Justine. Could you give me the gist of what was said?' Stone pointed at his phone. 'For the record.'

'Yes, of course.' A film of sweat had begun to form on Parker's forehead and upper lip. He was a man under pressure, continually tapping his right foot on the floor, unaware that his body language was under scrutiny as he recalled the conversation. 'Justine was very upset that I'd collected Daniel from training. This threw me, as I'd done nothing of the kind. I panicked, naturally, and drove straight home, by which time she'd climbed down. Unfortunately, her good mood didn't last. As soon as she realised I didn't have Daniel with me, she freaked out again. You know what the French are like.'

'No.' Frankie saw red. 'Why don't you tell—'

Stone cut her off before she could let Parker have it with both barrels. 'I found Miss Segal very pleasant,' he said. 'She's deeply traumatised by Daniel's disappearance. I think she can be forgiven for being a little cross, don't you?'

Parker ignored him, switching his focus to Frankie. 'As I said last night, I thought Daniel and Justine were playing games. He's a practical joker at times – and often involves her in his escapades – but I soon realised that it was not so on this occasion. In retrospect, I should've known better. Daniel wouldn't be that cruel.'

'What time did your business meeting end?' Frankie studied him closely. Having found him out, she was dying to hear which way he'd jump.

The entrepreneur dropped his head, then raised it, eyebrows knitting together as if he was trying to recall the exact time. He was in no rush to supply an answer. 'Around seven, I think it was.'

'Are you sure it wasn't earlier?' Stone asked.

He shrugged. 'It could have been a few minutes either way, I suppose.'

Frankie caught Stone's nod – it was almost imperceptible – a sign that she should hit Parker with the unpalatable truth. He was keen to push on with other lines of enquiry.

'I've been reliably informed that your meeting ended at around six thirty,' she said.

Parker raised an eyebrow, a casual gesture. 'Perhaps I'm mistaken. I thought it was later.'

He was cool. She'd give him that. 'The thing is, it couldn't have been – if, as you say, you checked your mobile immediately after the meeting ended. Justine didn't call you until well after McCall had blown the final whistle on Daniel's training session at seven o'clock. It was ten past when she left the voicemail, a fact verified by her phone and yours.'

'Then clearly I was mistaken.'

'This morning, officers checked the CCTV at your business premises. It shows you leaving the boardroom at six thirty-three p.m. You drove away two minutes later, so you couldn't have been at the office when you received Justine's voicemail, could you? Where were you, Mr Parker?'

'I told you, I drove straight home.'

'With your mobile switched off?' Stone asked.

'My mobile is never off. Like you, I'm a busy man.'

Frankie got in quick. 'Too busy to answer Justine's call, it seems.' Or your wife's later on in the evening, Frankie was thinking but didn't say.

'The device was on silent mode during the meeting, as I'm guessing yours are now. Interruptions are tiresome in any transaction, don't you find? Clearly, I hadn't switched it back on when Justine's call came in.'

Stone challenged him. 'But she claims that you arrived home at around seven thirty-five. If you drove away from your place of work at six thirty-five it stands to reason that you stopped on the way. DS Oliver timed that journey on the way here. It takes precisely twenty-two minutes. That leaves around forty minutes unaccounted for. I'll ask again: where were you?'

Parker said nothing.

Frankie wanted to punch the air. She hadn't timed their journey and guessed that Stone had googled the information before they left the station. It was a good ploy, one that put Parker on the back foot. His chest rose and fell, a deep intake of breath he couldn't hide. Between them, they had got to him.

'Let's return to Justine for a moment,' Stone continued. 'You said she'd calmed down by the time you got home. What did you mean by that?'

'What I actually said was *climbed* down.' He pointed at the mobile on the table. 'Check your recording.' He was being pedantic, putting the DI in his place. It was a stalling tactic while he tried to second-guess what was coming next.

Frankie was surprised by his superior attitude, the way he spoke to Stone as if he were some thick Geordie boy who wouldn't know his arse from his elbow.

The DI wasn't playing his silly games.

'Answer the question,' he said.

'Justine told me that she'd found my DM.'

'What DM was this?' Frankie asked.

'I have no idea. I never sent one.'

'And yet we have a screenshot of it,' Stone said.

Frankie was urging him to go for the jugular. Her boss kept his cool. They had very different styles. Parker might now be a man under immense pressure, but he was apparently well connected. Not a pillar of society exactly, but respected among the business community, on the board of more than one charity, a member of the Round Table and so on. On the face of it, he wasn't making much sense. In fact, he was looking downright guilty. As the step-parent of a missing child, Parker needed careful handling. If Parker was innocent of any wrongdoing, it would look bad for the police if they placed him under arrest.

'I never sent a message, I swear it.' He pointed at Frankie. '*She* examined my phone. Ask her.'

'*She* has a name and a rank,' Stone said calmly.

'And *she* doesn't believe a word you're saying,' Frankie added.

Stone cut her off. 'Let's move on . . .' His focus was back on Parker. 'You spent a week with your stepson while his mother was in Majorca. How did you get on?'

'Very well.'

'Were there any disagreements between the two of you that might be relevant to his disappearance? Stepchildren can be difficult sometimes.'

'No. And, for the record, Daniel isn't at all difficult. We may not be blood relatives but he and I enjoy a close relationship, as good as any father and son.'

'In that case, why did it take you two hours to report him missing?' Frankie asked.

Parker hesitated, clearly tired of all the questioning. 'It was important to establish that he *was* missing. I made a few calls. I spoke to McCall. These things take time, as I'm sure you're aware. Then I drove down to Wallsend. That's twenty-five miles from here. Unlike you, I don't have a flashing blue light. It took me three quarters of an hour to get there. These days police stations are not conveniently placed for easy access, are they? It took me ten minutes to work out which bloody station would deal with a case of this nature, a few more to find the one that covers my area. Can you imagine how frustrating that is, given the circumstances?'

Neither detective could argue with that. The public were up in arms about the level of cover, particularly so in rural areas where you'd be hard pressed to spot a uniform and, when you did, they were never on foot. It was a bone of contention among the rank and file.

'You could've phoned,' Frankie said.

Parker was beginning to lose his rag. 'I didn't want the Control Room. I wanted to speak to a human. Someone who would understand the urgency of finding Daniel before his mother arrived in the UK. I was frantic. How do you think I felt?' He was so slick. He had an answer for everything.

A shadow crossed the room.

Parker looked toward the window.

Alex was in the garden, head down as she walked.

Her husband turned his attention to the detectives, his face set like granite. 'If there are no more questions, I need to be with my wife.'

'No, sir,' Frankie said. 'Forgive my bluntness, but you need to start telling the truth. You lied about what time you left the office yesterday. You lied about driving straight home and where you were when you accessed Justine's message. You lied to Alex about why you didn't answer her text when she landed at Newcastle airport last night. I heard you myself. You are very close to being arrested, so start talking.'

Parker glowered at her.

She held his gaze. 'You want me to get the cuffs out? I'm quite happy to. A child is missing. Your wife's only child. For God's sake, man, you're not being honest and it's making you look bad.'

What Frankie didn't say was that Parker was fast becoming a prime suspect in his stepson's disappearance. There was no need. He'd worked that out all by himself.

15

'You're mental.' Frankie slammed the car door. Pulling her seat belt across her left shoulder, she glared at Stone as she clicked it into place. 'David, you're making a big mistake. He's not being straight with us. We both know that. If it were up to me, he'd have been in the back of this car and so would I. Jesus! Last night you were off your game. Today you've really lost the plot. We had Parker on the rails and you decide to walk away? What the hell were you thinking?'

Stone started the car. 'I'm thinking I'm going to have to rein you in.'

'Don't you dare make out that I'm being overzealous—'

'Aren't you?'

'No! Far from it. I'm following the evidence. I thought we both were.'

Stone turned left towards Scots Gap, then took a right towards Bolam, keen to get to the crime scene at Ponteland in one piece. As the car sped along the undulating, winding country lane, Frankie continued her rant. He'd never seen her so enraged. A few miles on and there was no let-up.

'Look,' he said eventually, 'just because you don't like Parker, doesn't make him guilty. I don't doubt that he has some explaining to do, but we're not ready to make a move on him yet. A lot of that in there was bravado! You said he was upset at the station. Anyone who cared to look would see he still is. He's under pressure—'

'So would you be if you'd killed your kid.'

'You don't know that.'

'And, with respect, neither do you.'

'It was my call to make, Frankie.'

'Well it was the wrong one.' She went quiet.

Stone's relief didn't last.

'Oh, I get it,' she said. 'He's a big cheese, so we must lay off, is that it? What is he, a hand-shaker and therefore untouchable?'

'You know me better than that.'

'What are you worried about then? That he might make a complaint or sue for damage to his precious reputation? Let him! Daniel's safety is what's important here, not some egomaniac here-today-gone-tomorrow fucking entrepreneur who thinks he's God's gift. He's a good-looking nowt with a chip on his shoulder the size of the Baltic Flour Mill.'

'Did it occur to you that he might be innocent, that he's deflecting his anger on to us because he can't cope with the responsibility for what's happened? If your stepson was missing, what state would you be in?'

'We're not talking about me – and he wouldn't have gone missing because I wouldn't have been late.'

'*He* wasn't late, Justine was. Frankie, stop! You're going overboard here. You must bear in mind that this is a borderline case, only being handled by us at your insistence. It would be different if a kid had been lifted from a pram.'

'You said that already.'

'And I'll say it again until you start listening. It's great that you have an inbuilt early warning system in the case of missing children – I love that, I do – but there are other considerations here.'

'Such as?'

'What will it do to Alex Parker if we cart her husband off in handcuffs?'

'She'd be better off without him.'

'I agree with you. I'm only making the point that she's been through enough already. And don't question me. I've made my play and you'll have to live with it.'

'What is wrong with you, David? He went AWOL for almost an hour and he's unable or unwilling to explain why.

Without an intense sit down, shut the door cognitive interview, we'll never get at the truth. We need him in the station, sweating like a bastard, with a damn sight more to lose than his reputation. We need to establish exactly where he went or we're not going to be able to pin him down.'

'Are you finished?'

'Not even close.'

'People tell lies for all sorts of reasons, Frank. You've been in the job long enough to know that. Show some finesse, why don't you? You said earlier that you thought he was having an affair with the au pair.'

'I'd put money on it. I saw the looks between them.'

'OK, then maybe he broke it off with her while Alex was in Majorca. She was royally pissed off on that call. Maybe her beef with him was more than the fact that he'd sent her on a wild goose chase. If she'd been dumped, she could've been giving him a hard time over it. Maybe he stopped on the way home for a beer, rather than face going home for an ear-bashing. I could do with a drink myself.'

Frankie pulled a face at his sarky remark. 'OK, give me one good reason why he would send her a DM, then delete it from his phone and lie about it – because that's exactly what he's done, in my opinion. Assuming my opinion counts for anything.'

'Of course it does! If you're right about them, maybe he was getting rid of incriminating evidence of an affair before his wife got home, deleting all Justine's messages from his phone, rather than a particular DM, unaware that it would come back and haunt him.' Stone glanced at her. 'Surely that makes sense, even to you.'

Frankie looked away – and he knew he'd finally managed to persuade her.

16

Tim Parker was ill at ease. DI Stone he could cope with. DS Oliver was a different animal altogether: wild, wilful, unafraid to say her piece, the kind of police officer you should never cross. *Shame.* If he were being honest, she was also his type: petite, brunette, able to hold an intelligent conversation, locking on to her target as he would in a business meeting, keen to get the upper hand. She wasn't exactly hot, but she had obvious potential, nothing a trip to a spa and a good hairdresser couldn't fix. Had they met in any other circumstance they might have hit it off. He'd like to think he'd have impressed her too, except the enigmatic cop had her sights on him for other reasons. Well, she wasn't the only one with a grouse . . .

Or a game plan . . .

Tim had done his homework. He'd scanned the Internet and found various documents dealing with the police's response to missing persons, management protocols for the recording of information, a continuum of risk from zero to high, the latter requiring immediate deployment. Daniel – while not in the lowest category by any means – wouldn't fall into the bracket of *the* most vulnerable. Stone would undoubtedly have carried out an initial risk assessment and appeared to be taking his stepson's abduction seriously, offering family support, but how hard was he really looking? As for that bitch Oliver: her radar was way off if it was pointing at him. Of the two, it was her Tim was most wary of. If she'd had her way, he'd be in the cells right now. The difficulty he faced was how to influence the investigation when he was caught in the middle of it.

It was time to use his contacts.

He'd no sooner taken his mobile from his pocket to do that when the sound of a key turning the lock caught his attention.

Justine was letting herself in. He'd been waiting for her, keen to quiz her about her police interview. It was obvious that she'd been crying. As their eyes met across the hallway, her expression took his breath away: pure, unadulterated hatred was the only way to describe it. Tim swore under his breath. The last thing he wanted was another fight, another scene. He was about to go to her when Alex arrived from Daniel's room. She'd heard the front door closing and had come to investigate.

'Thank God!' she said. 'Justine, where have you been?'

'At the police station.' A flash of guilt crossed the au pair's face.

Tim was immediately on his guard.

'I was worried about you,' Alex said. 'The detectives have been and gone already, though why they had to drag you to the station makes no sense to me. They could have interviewed you here.'

'They had their reasons,' Justine said.

Tim steeled himself for the bombshell that would follow. It didn't come. Alex hadn't picked up on Justine's comment. All she seemed interested in was her painkillers. Tim relaxed as their au pair searched her bag and handed over a small package.

'I'll make you a drink,' she said to Alex.

The two women moved into the kitchen, Tim following to keep an eye on Justine and gauge her mood. Her eyes flitted nervously between her two employers as she brought a glass of water to the island in the centre of the room where Alex had parked herself on a high stool. Justine was clearly unhappy, on the edge of something. Tim had an idea what it was and that it spelled trouble.

Alex had noticed too, and was gearing up to interrogate her. 'Justine, what's wrong?'

'Ask your husband.'

Alex almost choked on the tablet she'd swallowed, confused

by the sudden formality. Justine had been on first-name terms with the family from day one. She was avoiding eye contact. Tim was suddenly fascinated with the garden. 'For God's sake! Will one of you please tell me what's going on?'

Justine glanced at Tim. 'Are you going to tell her, or will I?'

Alex shifted her attention to her husband. 'Tell me what?'

Tim's mouth dried up. His world was about to change in ways he could only imagine. Knowing what was coming was like watching a car crash about to happen and being power-less to stop it. As a rule, he'd have had a plan B, but for once in his life he hadn't a clue how to handle the situation. Things had moved so fast since last night. There had been no time to formulate a proper response. Oliver was right. Didn't matter how he put it, whatever he said would make him look guilty.

'The reason I didn't pick Daniel up was because Tim sent me a message to say that he'd do it,' Justine said. 'He denied this to police, even though I have proof of it on my phone. They questioned me about it this morning. It was awful, Alex. I felt like a criminal.'

Tim lost his bottle as his wife glared at him and then focused her attention on the au pair. 'Justine, I don't understand. Why on earth would Tim send a message and then deny sending it when it could so easily be proved that he had?'

'I don't know.' Justine looked like she was about to cry. 'All I care about, the *only* thing I care about is your son and that you know it wasn't my fault that he went missing. I love Daniel. I'd never do anything to harm him. Alex, please . . . tell me you believe me—'

'I do!' Alex turned on her husband. 'Tim?'

Alex and Justine were waiting for an explanation.

Tim had none to give. He'd already gone through it with Oliver – and nothing bad had come of it – but he wasn't look-ing forward to round two with his wife and their au pair. This was so unfair. He was every bit as driven to find Daniel as the police – more so. 'I didn't send the message, Alex.'

Justine flew into a rage, yelling like a woman possessed. There was no way he was shifting the blame for Daniel's disappearance. She'd get a lawyer if she had to. Her reputation was at stake. The slightest hint of any impropriety and she'd be out on her ear, her CV worthless, her career prospects rendered null and void. 'Alex, I'd give all that up to find Daniel—'

'And you think I wouldn't?' Tim's voice was harder than before. 'I'm as clueless as the police seem to be – I. Did. Not. Send. That. Message. I swear to you.'

Justine's expression screamed: *Liar!* She accessed her phone in seconds and showed Alex the DM to prove her point.

Alex kept her cool in a way that scared her husband. 'It's right here, Tim. I'm calling DI Stone—'

'No, Alex. I told him the same thing, I promise you.'

'Tell me now or I make the call.'

'This is crazy. You can't be serious!'

She looked right through him, then pulled out her phone. 'OK, OK, I wasn't entirely honest with Stone . . . I deleted the message.' White noise filled his head as Alex and Justine tried to make sense of what he'd said. Their faces wore the same expression, a mixture of horror and doubt, a million questions on their lips. He knew it made no sense and was already regretting his decision to come clean.

17

In Ponteland, Stone turned right into Callerton Lane. A little further on, on the left-hand side, the car passed a sign: *Ponteland Middle School and Ponteland United*. A green strip underneath proclaimed: *Premier League and The FA Facilities Fund*. Behind it, there was an advertising board for a children's nursery: *Henry's Hut*.

Stone parked up and got out.

Frankie followed, trying to forget their row in the car. She didn't have time to dwell on that or the fact that Parker had dodged an arrest, despite her best efforts. She stood for a while, the warm sun on her back, surveying the windows of the houses opposite. They had a good view of the front entrance but, at Stone's insistence, house-to-house enquiries were being conducted further down the road.

'It's as well we came in daylight,' Frankie said, pointing across the road. 'Whoever picked Daniel up is too savvy to have done it in full view of that lot. The FA facility behind us caters for juniors up to nine years old. Did I mention that McCall's training is nowt to do with them?' She didn't wait for a reply. 'His son used to go to the school. He got involved in extracurricular activities, like a lot of parents do, and never gave up. Despite what Parker may think of him, and my assessment that McCall is a terrible witness, his work is voluntary and the kids love him, Daniel included. Training for the older kids takes place on yon side of the school.' She thumbed over her shoulder. 'That way.'

Stone was nodding. 'Let's walk.'

They set off in a westerly direction, passing a second entrance to Ponteland Community High School and Ponteland County Middle School, their school badges proudly displayed alongside their names. A white van pulled up on the grass verge before a set of traffic lights. The sight of it made Frankie shudder. Her heart began to thud as she fought to keep calm. She turned her head to the side so that Stone wouldn't notice her reaction.

Breathe, breathe.

Recovering quickly was a skill Frankie had developed over time, learned behaviour that came with a little help from the force psychologist. She forced herself to focus. Mind on the job, she couldn't help thinking that whoever had taken Daniel had first completed a recce of the street. Traffic lights were a potential hazard to an abductor. A clean getaway was essential. If the lights were against them; STOP and they might get caught, GO and they would certainly draw attention to themselves.

No brainer.

The offender they were after was taking no chances.

Realising that Stone had uttered a total of two words since leaving the car, Frankie made polite conversation. 'I didn't know that was a specialist language centre, did you?' She flicked her eyes to white lettering on a brick building to their left.

'No.' Uninterested, Stone kept walking.

Frankie practically had to run to catch up with him. 'Three words. I suppose that's progress.'

He glanced at her. 'Excuse me?'

'I said you're up to three, boss. If we're really lucky we'll squeeze four before we make it to the roundabout.'

Stone ignored her sarcasm, his eyes inspecting the ground beneath their feet. On the side of the footpath, there was very little grass. The surface was churned up in places, deeply rutted with tyre tracks, evidence that parents had used the verge to park and collect their kids from school.

'This is where Justine usually parks,' he said. 'She told me this morning.'

They stopped walking.

On their side of the road was a thick hedge. On the other, a row of bungalows. On the west side of the school buildings were playing fields: rugby posts clearly visible over the top of the hedge, football pitches further away. They continued down the road, Stone making the odd observation.

Frankie assumed he was in a huff, hadn't yet forgiven her for her tirade in the car.

A toddler on a bike rode beside his jogging mother, his little legs pumping away, his face beaming as he tried to keep up. The occupants of a panda car waved to Stone and Oliver as the vehicle passed by, part of the house-to-house team on their way to knock on more doors. At the roundabout, the detectives turned left, ignoring the sign for Darras Hall, a smart housing estate, for want of a better phrase, catering for those with salaries she could only dream of.

Seconds later they arrived at a six-bar metal gate.

Frankie checked her phone. 'This is the gateway where McCall saw the car.' She turned her phone to show David. It wasn't a proper pull-in, just a bit of tarmac leading to the playing fields beyond, the gate providing a barrier between them and the road.

Stone glanced at the image on display, comparing it with what he could see with the naked eye. There was space for only one car, unlike the proper lay-by up ahead that could take three or four, or even five vehicles at a push, a thought that was fast dawning on Frankie.

'It was planned, David. This is not some random stop. Do you agree?'

'Yeah, but unless he or she parked right in front of the metal gate, the car wouldn't be seen through the hedge.'

'I guess it did then. Partially obscured, McCall said.'

Frankie's eyes flew over the hedge in question. Across the playing fields, in the distance, she could see the airport control tower. She turned her back on the open countryside, commenting that the gateway wasn't overlooked. The houses across the road were hidden behind an equally verdant hedge. A glimpse from an upstairs window was the best they could possibly hope for.

As far as exit routes were concerned, the possibilities were many. That didn't bode well for Daniel: straight up and a car would reach the A69 within minutes for an escape route west; down the A696, past the airport, a stone's throw to the A1 north and south; the Throckley Fell road or through Ponteland and out the other side. If Frankie was depressed when she arrived, she was more so now. Daniel could have been taken anywhere.

18

The ringing tone seemed to go on and on. Alex imagined her sister in a yoga position, as she'd been for much of the week, blaspheming at the intrusion, only this time it was the phone and not the Spanish goats she'd be complaining about. In the car on the way from the airport last night, Alex had ignored her text and two calls this morning. She couldn't hold off indefinitely.

'Kathryn Tailford Irwin.' She sounded out of breath.

Alex held back.

Yesterday they had shared a glass of wine on the terrace at Casa Pegueña, clinking glasses and toasting the future, putting the past behind them, neither having had much to celebrate going into 2016. They had made a pact not to dwell on the past, to concentrate instead on all that was good in their lives. Right now, Alex couldn't think of a single thing that fit the bill. There was, it had to be said, a lot they would both rather forget.

'Speak now or the phone goes down,' Kat said. 'Whoever you are, you should know that I'm not into long-distance heavy breathing.'

'It's me, Kat.'

'About time! I treat you to sun and sangria and this is how you repay me? Alex, hang on. I'm just in from a run and left the door open in the rush to answer the phone.' The receiver went down on a hard surface. There was a short pause, then she was back. 'It's bloody glorious out there. The tan is glowing. Hope it's the same at your end of the country. How's everyone?' A pause. 'Alex? Are you there?'

Alex *was* there, poised to break the news. Kat was the last person she wanted to talk to but it had to be done. 'It's Daniel,' she said.

There was a tremor in Kat's voice. 'What's happened?'

Alex didn't answer.

'Is he OK?'

'He's missing . . .'

'Since when?'

Alex waited a couple of beats for the information to sink in. 'A detective waylaid me at the airport when I stepped off the plane. Someone picked Daniel up from training last night before Justine could get there. Tim was frantic. He spoke to Daniel's coach and rang everyone he could think of: Dan's mates, the parents of kids he plays footy with, even the hospitals. There were no admissions and no one's seen him since he walked off the pitch around seven o'clock.'

'Oh fuck! I'll be on the next train—'

'No, Kat. Stay put. You can't—'

'The *hell* I can't! I'm coming up. No arguments.'

'I don't want you here.'

There: it was out.

Alex hadn't meant to reject her quite so vociferously, even though she'd anticipated her sister's offer to drop everything and head north to take charge, but what she'd said in reply was the plain, honest truth. Kat's presence would add stress to an impossible situation, not take it away. Alex had her hands full as it was. She didn't want Kat's help, much less her sympathy.

She'd gone quiet.

As a kid, she could sulk for England.

Alex apologised immediately for the hurtful way her words had come out. 'I know you mean well, but you'll be in the way if you come. The police are all over us.'

'You won't even know I'm there, I promise.'

'No.' Alex heard frenetic tapping on a keyboard.

Kat's voice hit her ear again. 'The three-thirty train gets in at quarter to seven.'

Alex raised her eyes to a ceiling hand-painted with the

Orion's Belt constellation. She and Daniel shared a love of astronomy. He'd lie on his back for hours looking at it. She rubbed at her temples, trying to think of a good excuse to put her sister off.

'No need to pick me up,' Kat said. 'I'll get a cab. I should be there by half past seven, latest.'

'It's not happening, didn't you hear me? I meant what I said—'

'I know what you said but I want to help. Alex, don't shut me out.' She was almost begging. 'We've spent far too long apart in the last decade.'

'And whose fault was that? You hardly know Daniel.'

A long, painful silence.

'Don't do this,' Kat said. 'Please . . . let me help.'

'You've done enough already—'

'The holiday was nothing.' Kat paused for breath. 'Oh, I get it. Tim's against me landing on you, is that it? He's not my favourite person and I'm not his, but we're family. We need to stick together now. We can put aside our differences. I'll hold my tongue around him, I swear. I'll go out and look for Daniel myself if necessary. All that's important is getting him home.'

'It's not Tim, it's me.'

'What?'

'I want to be alone. Surely you of all people understand that.' Kat would remember all the times when Alex reached out to her and was knocked back. Rejection was painful. It was high time she understood that. Alex stalled: 'I can't cope with you right now – or anyone. The place was crawling with police last night. They were here until the early hours. They searched the house with sniffer dogs and questioned Justine this morning – Tim too.'

'Of course they did! They'll interview everyone who's seen Daniel in the past few days. You can't read anything into that. They adore him.'

'I know . . . but something's not right, Kat.' Alex glanced at the bedroom door, dropping her voice a touch. 'DI Stone, the guy in charge of the investigation is very supportive, but his DS is wary of Tim, I can feel it and . . . to say Tim's not himself would be a gross understatement.'

'When has he ever been?' Kat knew she'd said the wrong thing and took it back. 'I'm sorry, I didn't mean that.'

'Yes, you did. And that's why it wouldn't be a good idea for you to stay with us.'

'Then I'll book into a hotel.'

'Drop it, will you!' Alex was almost yelling.

'Look, you said yourself, Tim's frantic. It's hardly surprising, is it? The police will soon realise he wouldn't harm Dan. The idea is ridiculous.'

'Yeah, but he's acting weird.' Alex dropped her voice a touch. 'It's not the drugs this time, Kat. It's . . . I don't know what it is, but I get the feeling he's hiding something. Before the police left, I overheard the female detective threatening to arrest him if he didn't tell the truth.'

'About what?'

'I don't know. They asked me to leave the room while they questioned him.'

'They actually said that?'

'Or words to that effect. Stone is the SIO. He's switched on, I trust him. I had no choice but to comply with his request. Clearly he had his reasons for not wanting me there. Make what you will of that.'

'Is Tim in custody?'

'No, he's at home—'

'There you go then. You must have misheard. Or picked up the wrong end of the stick.'

'I don't think so.'

The door to Daniel's bedroom opened and Tim walked in. He looked exhausted and Alex could see he'd been drinking – or worse. 'Here you are,' he said. 'I've been looking all over for you.'

'Just give me a minute,' Alex said.

He didn't move. 'Who's on the phone?'

'Kat. She has a right to know what's going on.'

He rolled his eyes and turned to go. As he retreated, Alex told Kat everything: all about the mix-up over who was doing what; the fact that Tim had waited two hours to file a report; about the DM that Justine had received from him; and his confession that he'd deleted the message from his phone before walking into the police station.

Kat was astonished. 'Why on earth would he do that?'

'He panicked, or so he said.'

'Doesn't sound like him.'

'He begged me to believe him.'

'And do you?'

'Yes, no . . . I'm not sure.'

'Unless he intended deleting the message from Justine's phone too, it makes no sense. I mean, why would he lie about sending her a message in the first place?'

Alex cut her dead. 'That's what is so peculiar. He admits deleting it, but is adamant that it didn't come from him. Kat, maybe you were right about the two of them. I know I wrote it off when we were in Majorca, but now I'm not so sure . . .' Tim was back. 'Call you later, I've got to go.'

19

Alex Parker's first husband, Rob Scott, only lived nine miles away in a decent street in Heaton, a two-bedroom mid-terraced house with no garden to speak of and a small rear yard. The house needed a lick of paint. The front door bore signs of a recent break-in, the wood freshly splintered where a jemmy had been used to prise it open. The windows hadn't been cleaned for years but flickering light from a TV screen was visible from the street.

Stone rang the bell and got no answer. He rang again and heard yelling from within but still no one came to answer the door. The sound of breaking glass was ominous, putting both detectives on alert.

'Where's the Kevlar when you need it?' Frankie said.

Stone wasn't laughing. 'We better get in there before they kill each other.'

Frankie pushed the bell harder, keeping her thumb on it. No joy. 'I'm not sure if it actually works, David. I hope that's not Daniel he's yelling at.'

'Really? I was thinking the opposite.'

She knew what he meant.

Despite Alex Parker's insistence to the contrary, they were half-hoping they would find Daniel safe and well inside, none the worse for a night spent with the man Alex had dubbed 'a pathetic excuse for mankind'. Being taken from his family by a belligerent biological father with a score to settle – whether the boy had gone willingly or not – was markedly preferable to being abducted by a stranger.

Frankie's guts were churning.

Stone looked on as she used her fist to hammer on the door three times. The din from within ceased. At the bay window, an indistinct figure looked out from behind greying net curtains, then moved away. Moments later, the door was yanked open by a man mountain, rough-looking, with a shaved head and dark eyes. He'd been drinking and was wearing a T-shirt with the words *We're All Screwed* written across it.

'If you're selling Jesus, I'm not fucking interested.' He began to retreat.

'Mr Scott?' Frankie stuck her foot over the threshold, the sole of her shoe upturned against the weather strip, preventing closure. On the way there, they'd decided that Frankie should take the lead. Female officers were often used to interview combative men, lowering the temperature, lessening the possibility of an aggressive face-off between two alpha males. Even drunks would think twice about squaring up to a female cop, especially one half their size.

'Who's asking?' Scott opened the door a little wider.

'We are.' Frankie held up ID.

Despite the bad shape Rob Scott was undoubtedly in – unwashed, unshaven and reeking of beer – Frankie could see how attractive he might once have been to Alex Parker: powerful physique, chiselled features, strong jawline. Now on his uppers, with bleary eyes hardly able to focus, this giant of a man had let himself go.

'I'm DS Oliver. This is my colleague, DI Stone. Can we come in?'

'No. Piss off.'

She tried again. 'We'd like to talk to you about Daniel.'

'Daniel who?'

'Your son, Mr Scott.'

'You're 'aving a laugh, darling—'

'No, I'm deadly serious.'

Scott made a show of checking the street. 'What is this, Candid-fucking-Camera? What's the little shit done? Run away from his cow of a mother, has he? I'm impressed. Didn't think the wimp had it in him.'

Frankie pointed inside. 'Can we talk?'

'I'm busy.'

'Too busy for your son?' She got no reaction. 'That's unfortunate. Perhaps you'd prefer to accompany us to the station. Say the word and that can be arranged. We'll have a squad car here in minutes. Your call . . .' She waited. The stand-off didn't last. 'Thought not . . . Now let us in.'

'What do you want?'

'To search your property.'

'Certainly, if you have a warrant.'

'We can get one.'

'When you do, let me know—'

'C'mon, Rob. Where's your community spirit? Don't let the lack of paperwork stop you from inviting us in. I can smell dope from out here. But lucky for you I'm not interested in your recreational habits. No need to panic. You can even get wasted while DI Stone and I have a quick look around.'

'Makes you think I've got him?'

'You were unhappy with the court's decision and made some threats after the custody hearing. It's a matter of record.'

'I'll tell you what it's a matter of. That cow blocked access to my son!'

'That must be very difficult for you. If Daniel is here, you're in violation of a court order.'

'I told you, he's not.'

'And once we've established that, we'll be on our way.' Frankie gave her word on that. 'Now, are you going to let us in or do I call the Drug Squad?'

Scott stepped aside, mumbling under his breath as Stone and Oliver entered a house that was better kept on the inside than it was on the out. And that was saying something. The reason for that was sitting on the sofa in the living room, Scott's waiflike girlfriend. Alex had warned them that he used women as slaves almost. In his mind, shagging and tidying up was all they were good for. Frankie was hopping mad. Had this moron run out of women of means and graduated to vulnerable girls half his age?

Stone bent down beside her. 'You OK, pet?'

'Eh?' The girl's pupils were dilated.

'How old are you?'

'Eighteen.' She went back to her rollie.

The DI clearly didn't believe her. While he couldn't prove that the girl was underage, if Frankie was any judge, he'd alert social services at the earliest opportunity. He stood up, a sour look transferring his anger to the homeowner. 'I'll check upstairs,' he said. 'If that's OK with you, Mr Scott?'

'Knock yourself out and don't make a mess,' Scott yelled after him. The irony.

'Nice place,' Frankie said, an attempt to divert his attention into the living room and away from Stone, who would be looking for signs that the girl lived there as well as for Daniel. Scott's home wasn't the festering shitpit they were expecting. If it wasn't the drugs, the way he treated women and the age of his current squeeze, she'd have no squabble with the tenant. 'Have you seen or heard from Daniel recently?'

'Not since Alex pissed off, no.'

'You've not sneaked off to watch him play football?'

'She lets him get dirty? Class! Hear that, Trace? My lad plays footy.'

Tracy looked up, spaced out from another joint. 'That's nice.'

'Nice? I'm one proud motherfucker me.'

Frankie wasn't finished. 'Do you have a vehicle, Mr Scott?'

'Yeah, five . . .' He mimicked Alex Parker: 'Check the garaaage.'

Tracy snorted.

Scott laughed like a hyena.

Frankie wasn't amused. She knew he didn't have a car – not one registered to the address, anyway; Stone had already checked – but Tracy might. There was a banger parked right outside, though it was red, not grey. Maybe the girl was telling the truth and she really was eighteen.

The couple continued to knock back alcohol, chain-smoking cannabis, neither giving a toss that police were on the premises. After half an hour of searching, nothing of interest had been found; a bit of booze, more drugs, but no sign of Daniel or proof that he'd ever been there. As Stone gave the signal to leave, Scott began to let his mouth go, threatening to swing for Tim Parker if the boy wasn't found soon. Suddenly he was playing the loving parent.

The DI had a quiet word, advising him that if anything should happen to Parker he'd return to lock him up. 'It's inadvisable to make threats to kill in front of two police witnesses.'

'Says who?'

'Step away,' Stone said.

'Or what?'

'Calm down! We're doing all we can to find your boy . . .'

During the altercation, which David was handling without help, Tracy had fallen asleep. Frankie took her photograph in case she was a runaway from her parents or local authority care. Technically, without her permission, it was against the rules. Frankie would worry about that later. It might help ID her or even save her life.

She was about to put the phone back in her pocket when it rang in her hand: *Andrea*.

Frankie was instantly on her guard. Andrea knew she was on duty and the nature of the case she was dealing with. She wouldn't call unless it was important. Frankie moved into the hallway to take the call, leaving the door open in case Rob Scott kicked off again.

'Andrea, what's up?'

'Can you talk?'

In the living room, Scott was still trying it on with Stone, refusing to sit down. Demanding answers. Effing and blinding, playing the big man.

'I can,' Frankie said, 'but that might change.'

'I can hear the commotion. You in trouble?'

'No, but if I go offline send the cavalry. I'm at 125 King John Terrace, Heaton.'

'Are you with Stone?'

Frankie leaned against the wall, one eye on the two men in the next room. 'Affirmative. Why?'

'There was an RTA on the A19 (A189/Annitsford junction) involving his brother, Luke. It happened an hour ago. Luke asked me to get a message to David, which I thought might be better coming from you. The thing is . . .' Andrea paused. 'He didn't make it, Frank.'

'Fuck!'

Frankie turned away from the set-to between Scott and her boss. For a second, Andrea's voice was drowned out by Frankie's thoughts, all the spiteful things she'd said to David earlier crowding in on her. She wanted to take them all back, to be on the very best of terms with him when she broke the news, but what was said could never be unsaid. As senior accident investigator in Traffic, Andrea was right to call. Frankie caught snippets here and there: '. . . paramedics worked on him at the scene . . . it took us a while to trace his son, Ben . . . the lad freaked out and won't ID the body.'

'Where is he now?'

'Cramlington.' Andrea meant the Northumbria Specialist Emergency Care Hospital.

'OK, leave it with me.'

'Sorry to lay this on you. If there was any other way—'

'I know.' Frankie thanked her and hung up.

In the next room, oblivious to the unfolding drama, Stone seemed to have got the better of Scott, who was now slumped in a chair, a beer in one hand, another spliff in his mouth, a chimney of smoke clouding above his head. All Frankie knew about Luke Stone was that he was a little older than David and that he had a son the DI was once close to. How close they were now she didn't know. She was about to find out.

20

It was baking outside, a blast of heat hitting the detectives as they climbed into their vehicle. Conscious of Rob Scott and Tracy peering at them through the grubby net curtains, Frankie let Stone drive away. She couldn't tell him with an audience gawping at them. He turned right on to Heaton Road and then indicated left and made the turn into Jesmond Vale Lane, skirting Armstrong Park. Feeling a heavy pressure in her chest, for once in her life, Frankie had no words.

'You're very quiet,' Stone said.

'Can you stop here a minute, David.'

'What? You call me worse than a pickpocket and now you want ice cream?' He grinned at her, his kindness making her feel even worse than she did already. Up ahead there was an ice cream van, a crocodile of children lined up beside it waiting for their Saturday treat. 'Kidding!' he said. 'What flavour? My shout. I could do with one myself. It's like a sauna in here. You want monkey's blood, sprinkles or both?'

Frankie felt physically sick.

She shifted in her seat to face him. 'I don't want any.'

'You sure? We're here now, I'm having one.'

'No wait . . . there's been an accident.'

The smile slid off his face, the colour draining from him. Instinctively he knew she didn't mean any accident. This one was serious. Worse than that: it was personal. His voice broke as he asked: 'Who?'

'Luke.'

Frankie knew what it was like, going about your business normally – in his case handling Rob Scott – then receiving such unexpected and devastating news. Her boss was crumbling already, broken by what was to come and terrified to know more.

Wiping his face with his hand, he took a deep breath. 'How bad?'

She shook her head. 'I'm so sorry. He was in collision with a lorry. Traffic investigators managed to locate his son. David, they need an ID. Ben doesn't want to do it.'

'Where did they take Luke?'

'Cramlington Hospital . . . Let me drive you.'

Stone dropped his head, his knuckles turning white on the steering wheel as he clung on to it, fighting to hold on to his emotions. The sound of children's laughter filled the car, their smiley faces as they walked by a bizarre contradiction to the mood inside the vehicle. Frankie rested a hand on David's back. He hadn't said a word and she didn't know what to say to him. She had given the death message before but never to a colleague. And not to one she cared as much about.

He sat up suddenly, turned the engine over and pulled out into the traffic. Once clear of the ice cream van, he put his indicator on, head-checked the road, pulling hard on the wheel. U-turn complete, he put his foot down. Unlike the journey from Scots Gap to Ponteland, there was no discussion or analysis as they sped down the Coast Road. He'd talk when he was ready.

David appreciated her support and her silence. She'd never know what it had meant to him to come home after years of living in London, catching up with Luke, walking down Memory Lane over a pint in the pub, laughing over their antics as kids growing up in Northumberland. As an expat for the last fifteen years, he'd made biennial pilgrimages to Tyneside, his trips starting with a walk across the Millennium Bridge, stopping in the middle to catch his breath, a sight that made his heart swell. And when he finally made the break, his homecoming was everything he'd dreamed it would be.

He drove on autopilot, his thoughts all over the place as he tried not to imagine his brother's body in the morgue. Luke had lost his wife to cancer a few years ago. He and Ben had never recovered from it. Instead of bringing them closer, Ruth's death had pushed them apart. Ben had gone astray and Luke had struggled as a single parent. Now he too was gone.

They had reached the hospital. Stone parked his vehicle as close to the entrance as he could, slapped a POLICE sign on the dash, keen to get inside and find his nephew. As he reached for the door, Frankie put a hand on his forearm.

'I'm coming too,' she said.

'Don't feel you have to, Frank. I'll be fine.'

'Just till you locate Ben . . . I could sit with him while you make the ID. Please, I'd like to help.'

He nodded in lieu of thanks.

If she'd said anything on the journey, anything at all, he'd have summoned a panda to take her back to base. She hadn't. Experience had taught her that it would take a while for him to get his head around the overwhelming news and begin the grieving process. She was so quiet in the car, he'd almost forgotten she was there. In a strange way, for reasons he didn't entirely understand, he wanted her along. He wouldn't shut her out. With Luke gone, David's police family were on the bench to take over, Frankie first in the queue to fill that gap.

They found Ben alone in a quiet room reserved for bereaved relatives. He stood up as they entered and burst into tears. David put his arms around him. They embraced each other for a moment and then the DI stepped away. The lad was in shock, naturally. Physically, he was in bad shape. He looked like he'd slept in his clothes. His ashen face reminded Frankie of Scott's undernourished girlfriend. And, like Tracy, Ben reeked of booze and cannabis. Frankie had seen homeless, neglected youths in better condition.

This would not please Stone.

'This is Frankie,' he said. 'Wait here with her, will you?'

Frankie sat down as he left the room and gave Ben her condolences.

There were signs of a minor injury to Luke's head, but otherwise he looked for all the world as if he were sleeping. David took his right hand, squeezing it gently. It was cold to the touch. The last time they had met, that same hand had punched his arm, a conciliatory gesture. A little over five weeks ago, on 11 May, Stone's beloved Newcastle United were relegated to the Football League Championship as Luke's team Sunderland won 3–0 against Everton.

David lost it then, weeping for a future he and Luke would never share, wishing he'd come home more often to visit. With a bit of effort, he could have. Regretting his decision to leave in the first place would not bring Luke back. In the privacy of the morgue, Stone let go of everything: their plans to spend more time together, their memories, their brotherhood . . . thank Christ his parents were dead already. The shock of losing their firstborn would've killed them for sure.

David confirmed the ID and walked down the corridor wondering why his brother came to be on that fateful stretch of road so far from home. Luke had moved to Wearside to work shortly after Stone had left for the Met. He pulled out his phone and rang Control. They would have been the first to receive the call.

Half an hour later, he pulled up outside Ben's digs, a traditional Tyneside flat in poor condition, probably bought by a greedy landlord for the sole purpose of renting out to the city's student population. Money for old rope was the cliché that sprung to Frankie's mind as the DI got out of the car and took Ben inside. When he emerged a few minutes later he appeared more angry than sad. He didn't say why as he got in and started the engine and Frankie didn't pry. She guessed it was the state of Ben that troubled him . . .

Maybe the condition of his home was worse.

'I'm going to need time off,' Stone said. 'Just a few days, until I get my shit together. You saw Ben, he's next to useless, so it's down to me to make the funeral arrangements.'

Frankie was nodding. 'No problem. I'll cover for you.'

'Thanks. If you find you can't manage on your own, use Mitchell.' He was referring to Ray Mitchell, a DC destined for promotion: capable, reliable, if a little green.

'You want to go for a drink? You could probably do with one.'

'Maybe later. I have stuff to do.'

'Stuff? Can I do it?'

'No. I'll drop you at base so you can pick up your car. I need to clear time off with the Super anyway.'

'That I can do for you.'

'You sure?'

Frankie gave a half-smile. 'The least I can do. If Windy thinks you're swinging the lead, I'll send him the accident report. That'll shut him up.' Windy was the nickname for their guv'nor – Superintendent Gale – a third-rate, self-important, useless piece of shit she had no time for. 'You're entitled to seven days of compassionate leave.'

'Seven?' Stone gave her questioning look. 'You sure?'

'Rule 2 in the Frank Oliver Handbook of Dos and Don'ts: Know your rights. Rule 3: Keep in with your Fed rep.' She grinned. 'Take your due, David. You've had an awful shock.'

'I won't need that long.'

'Book yourself the whole week in case you do.'

At Northern Command HQ they parted company. Frankie watched him drive away, a mixture of emotions competing for space in her heart and in her head: sorrow for Stone, joy for her – an opportunity to prove her worth at last. Many a detective had made their name stepping in at times like these.

Taking charge of a major incident had always been on her wish list. She had never figured it would come this soon. The truth was, she didn't want it, not like this. A life was too high a price to pay.

21

With Stone incommunicado, Oliver cleared his leave with their guv'nor and checked in with her team. Still no progress on Charlie Dawson, whose name she could only visualise in Daniel's tidy handwriting. She'd no sooner got up to speed and told Control and DC Mitchell that she'd be fielding all calls in the Daniel Scott case, when his mother rang in unexpectedly, her anxiety reaching the detective sergeant down the line. She wanted to talk in person, but not at home. Frankie was intrigued, keen to facilitate a conversation that Alex Parker was so desperate to have.

They agreed to rendezvous at The Blacksmiths Coffee Shop in Belsay village, seven miles south-east of Scots Gap. The café closed at five. Frankie reckoned, with a bit of luck, she could make it with a little time to spare. It was like the Third World War had broken out on the way there, a convoy of army vehicles heading in the opposite direction, presumably from the Otterburn firing range, an MoD training facility a few miles further north, a vast wilderness, almost two hundred and fifty square kilometres in size.

Despite it being the weekend, Frankie expected customer numbers might have died down by the time she reached the café. She was wrong. The place was heaving, the only available table a few yards from a counter crammed with home cooking that made her stomach rumble and her mouth water. Suspended from a beamed ceiling, blackboards listed all manner of food to tempt her, every item guaranteed to stem the strongest hunger pangs.

Frankie ordered a tuna sandwich to go and a pot of tea for two, asking the waitress not to bring the brew until her guest arrived and to leave her sandwich on the counter for her to collect on the way out.

She took a seat facing the door, concerned that she was meeting Alex in such a public arena with sensitive matters to discuss that might be overheard. For a moment, she considered taking a table outside in the garden, but the sound of cutlery being placed in the dishwasher out back and the general hum of conversation suggested that she was worrying unnecessarily. Customers were deep into their own business, taking little notice of anyone around them.

It had been years since Frankie had been inside the old forge. The main area hadn't changed much. An extension had been added to the rear of the property, doubling the size of the place overall. A black Lexus LS saloon pulled up outside the front door. Alex was either talking to herself or on the hands-free. By the time she came inside, the waitress had taken her cue from Frankie, arriving with the tea.

'Thanks for meeting me.' Alex took off her coat and sat down, glancing over her shoulder and then at the detective sergeant. 'Is DI Stone not coming?'

'No, I apologise, he's been called away and can't join us.'

Frankie couldn't fail to notice how appalled Daniel's mother was by her reply. As a rule, she wouldn't disclose a single thing about a colleague's personal circumstances; but it seemed appropriate to let her know that he hadn't simply dropped the investigation in favour of something deemed more pressing. 'Sudden death,' she explained. Then, realising how that might sound to a woman whose son was missing, clarified her statement in case Alex read into it something that wasn't there. 'Close family member. Rest assured, the work goes on. Daniel is the only thing on our minds. I will, of course, be taking my lead from my boss.'

'Thank you, I appreciate it. Please pass on my condolences.'

'I will.' Frankie picked up the teapot and began to pour.

Alex didn't hang back. 'I overheard you threatening my husband this morning.'

Frankie stopped what she was doing and looked up.

Alex raised a placatory hand. 'I'm sorry, I'm not accusing you of improper conduct, Detective. Let me put it another way. You were suggesting that he was being less than truthful. I wasn't listening at the keyhole, I promise you. I happened to be walking by when you raised your voice. Look, whatever you know, or even suspect, however bad it is, I want you to share it with me. Daniel is my son, not Tim's.'

'I understand,' Frankie said. 'And I'll be straight with you. Had it not been for my DI, I might have – would have – locked your husband up. The truth is, he was being deliberately evasive. He failed to give clear answers to straightforward points we raised with him, not least of which was the DM he denies sending to your au pair telling her he'd pick Daniel up.'

Alex's mobile rang as she was on the brink of disclosure. She checked the screen and ignored the call. 'My sister, Kat. She's been calling constantly. I'll call her later.' She seemed irritated by the interruption.

Frankie knew the feeling. 'Alex, if you have information I should know about, no matter how insignificant you think it might be, you must tell me. We can't operate with our hands tied.'

'That's easy for you to say.'

'Yes, it is.'

'I love my husband.'

'I'm sure you do . . . but if you know something. . .' She let it hang there.

Alex was wary of sharing whatever was on her mind. 'With respect, you're not the one who'll be accused of betrayal if I tell you what is bothering me.'

'No, I'm not.' Frankie locked eyes with her. 'If you want honesty you have to be prepared to give it in return. I can see how this might hand you a dilemma – it's never easy being a whistle-blower, especially when the person you're informing happens to be your partner.'

Alex wasn't about to be rushed.

'Trust me,' Frankie said. 'Anything you say—'

'Will be used in evidence,' Alex interrupted quietly.

'If it comes to that, yes.' Frankie held her gaze. 'I won't lie to you. You've asked for openness and that's exactly what you'll get from me. What I was going to say was, anything you say will be investigated in the strictest confidence. I will only act on it if it has a bearing on the case or will hamper my efforts to find your son. If I'm to make any progress, we're going to have to trust each other.'

Alex wavered for a moment, then leaned in, dropping her voice. 'When Justine arrived from the police station she was very upset with Tim. Completely understandable, given Daniel's disappearance and her responsibility for him – the two are very close. She told me about the DM and I then threatened my husband that I would contact your DI unless he came clean.'

Frankie was on tenterhooks. Of all the things Alex might've said next, what she came out with left the DS dumbstruck.

'Tim deleted the DM before reporting Daniel missing,' she said.

Before Frankie had time to respond, a waitress appeared at the next table with a birthday cake, a Victoria sponge, a single lit candle at its centre. The women sitting there began singing Happy Birthday. Other customers, including four skinny octogenarian cyclists dressed in fluorescent Lycra, followed suit. It was a bizarre intrusion both women could've done without.

Frankie asked, 'What explanation did he give for deleting the message?'

'*He didn't*. Well, that's not strictly true. Aware of my imminent arrival from Majorca, he claims he was overwhelmed, in a panic, having lost Daniel. Don't be fooled by the signals he gives out. He likes to think he's good under pressure. He's not. Never has been. He's been under a tremendous amount of stress since we lost our baby.'

'That must've been tough for both of you.'

'Worse for Tim. He wants to be a father, more than anything.' Alex sighed. 'He's really not thinking straight. He begged me not to tell you about deleting the message. I tried explaining that it was ridiculous not to, that you'd find out soon enough, but he wouldn't listen. That's why I asked to meet you here.'

'You did right to tell me.'

'I know, or I wouldn't have come. You might wonder why I seem to be pointing my finger at him. I'm not. The idea that he could have harmed Daniel is ridiculous. He adores him.'

'Maybe he sent the message, then forgot he was supposed to pick Daniel up. If that was the case, Justine's subsequent voicemail would act as a stark reminder. I imagine it would throw most people into a spin. But why lie to cover it up?' Frankie didn't add that if it had been her, she might have contacted McCall to ask him to hold on to the lad. Tim Parker hadn't done that. She'd already checked.

'No, you misunderstand.' Alex was showing signs of frustration. 'When I said "he didn't" before, I wasn't referring to the fact that he didn't lie. I meant he didn't send it.'

Frankie raised her right eyebrow. 'Are you telling me he deleted a DM he didn't send?'

'That's exactly what I'm telling you.'

'Well, if he didn't send it—'

'Someone else did,' Alex cut in. 'It's the only plausible explanation. Unless you still think he's an inveterate liar, I'd say his account has been hacked.'

Stone had come to the same conclusion.

Nevertheless, Tim Parker had a lot to answer for.

'If your husband had been upfront with us this morning, we might have known more by now. He's done Daniel no favours by keeping quiet, Alex. Wasting police time is an offence. For your sake, I'll give him the benefit of the doubt until I make further enquiries. In the meantime, thank you for confiding in me.' Their conversation was over.

22

Exhausted though she was, physically and mentally, Frankie drove to Parker's place of work with the intention of catching his business partner before he knocked off. James Curtis was in conference with a junior associate, according to his PA. The detective sergeant sat down to wait for the meeting to end, that half-eaten tuna sandwich worming its way into her head. With the sun streaming through her car windows, it would be like toast by the time she got back to it.

Bored with inactivity, her thoughts turned to her DI. His brother's death would have triggered emotional and psychological trauma for sure. Thinking about that brought her own experience flooding back: feeling disconnected, out of sync with her surroundings, unable to eat or sleep, wanting to hide from others and yet resenting their tendency to withdraw from her because *they* couldn't handle the situation. She was in a fog for weeks, unable to think straight, wanting the world to slow down while she caught up. Years later, those waves of grief still hit her unexpectedly.

Poor David.

With a heavy heart, expecting an outright rejection from her boss, she pressed his number on her mobile, lifting the device to her ear. It rang out for quite a while before he picked up.

'Stone.'

'Boss, it's me, how are you doing?'

'I had a brother this morning and now I don't.'

By the sound of him, he'd probably been drinking since she'd left him. In general, he didn't indulge. Now was as good a time as any to increase his intake she supposed. If he wanted to dull his pain with alcohol, who was she to argue? When she lost a sibling, had she been old enough to partake of the hard stuff, she'd have grabbed at the opportunity.

'Don't tell me you ran into trouble already,' he said.

'No, I thought you might like some company. I could swing by the chippy if you like, or grab a lamb bhuna and bring it round.' She nearly added: 'Before you drink yourself into oblivion,' but it would be harsh under the circumstances. His silence was as overt a knockback as she'd ever get. 'Can't promise you wall-to-wall scintillating conversation,' she added. 'We could watch TV and hang out. You know how I love a movie night.'

'Most of my stuff is in London, Frankie.'

'My granddad's got the *Likely Lads*, *Auf Wiedersehen, Pet* and the entire collection of *When the Boat Comes In*—'

'Seen 'em all.'

'Scratch that then, but don't give me the brush-off, David. You're not the only one who needs company. Billy No Mates was named after me. Ask anyone.' The lie arrived fully formed. 'Actually, I wasn't being entirely honest with you before. I could do with your advice on something.' Asking for help was the only way he'd agree to see her.

Thank fuck for leverage.

'Make mine veggie rice and you're in.' He gave her the postcode. 'Don't expect tidy.'

'I'll keep my sunnies on and promise not to peek.' His village was only fifteen miles inland from her own home, a thirty-minute drive. 'If things change and I can't get away, I'll ring you.'

'Yeah, whatever.' The dialling tone hit her ear.

There was nothing worse than indifference. While David didn't seem arsed whether she called on him or not, he probably wouldn't eat if she didn't go and feed him. She hung up too, feeling glum.

The male PA sitting at the swish reception desk grinned. 'You should work on your delivery,' he said.

'And you should wind your neck in unless you're asked for an opinion.' She gave the cheeky git the thousand-yard stare.

Affronted, he backed off, dropping his head in his work, hiding his shiny blue eyes under a long floppy blond fringe. His internal phone rang. He picked up, listening for a second or two before speaking. 'Yes, she's in reception . . . Right away.' Replacing the handset on its cradle, a pair of wary eyes found Frankie's. 'You can go in now.' He pointed to his left. 'Second door on the right. Would you like something to drink?'

'Gin . . . make it a double.'

'I didn't mean—'

'Coffee is fine,' she sang the words over her shoulder – her turn to grin.

'What can I do for you, Detective?' James Curtis stood up as Frankie approached. They shook hands and introduced themselves properly. Communicating via email was never as good as seeing the whites of someone's eyes. Since her rendezvous with Alex, Frankie had been wondering if Tim Parker was lying to absolve himself of the responsibility for his stepson's disappearance or not. What she needed was more background information.

'I've just come from a meeting with Alex Parker.'

'How's she coping?' Curtis pointed out a carafe of water and clean tumblers in the centre of the vast table. 'You want some water, tea?'

'I'm good, thanks; a) I'd never reach it and b) your receptionist already offered.' Frankie noticed he hadn't asked after Tim. 'Alex is very concerned for Daniel's safety, naturally, but she's not a woman given to hysterics. That helps. When people lose it, it makes our job more difficult.'

'It must be very hard for her. Daniel's a great kid.'

'So I hear. I gather you've met him?'

'Many times. Is there any news?'

'None.'

Curtis was around forty years of age, relaxed, casually dressed, wearing jeans and a navy Thom Browne polo shirt, a complete contrast to his Mr Uptight-but-Impeccable business partner, Timothy Parker. Personality-wise, the two men were very different, an implausible union. As for Curtis, he even smelt better than she did after a long day at work.

His mobile rang.

Snatching it up, he apologised to Frankie and spoke harshly to the person on the other end about not wanting to be disturbed, then apologised again and left the boardroom. Frankie glanced at her watch. It was getting on for six.

Young Daniel had been missing for twenty-three hours.

Lack of sleep was taking its toll. Frankie got up and stood by the open French door. Outside, there was high-end patio furniture. A transparent windbreaker, so spotless it was hardly visible, with a view over the dramatic, jaw-dropping Northumbrian landscape. Whoever designed the place had done so with the sole intention of impressing visitors. This was the best view money could buy, a world away from her own soul-destroying, energy-sapping working environment; a claustrophobic incident room.

Alex's voice arrived in her head: *Unless you still think he's an inveterate liar, I'd say his account has been hacked.*

Frankie couldn't rule the theory out. By her reckoning, there were limitless possibilities. She counted them off in her head: an unknown source had done it remotely for any number of reasons; someone closer to home might have tampered with the account – Justine, Daniel himself, Laughing Boy in reception – though she doubted he had the bottle; Curtis was a good bet too. As close to the entrepreneur as anyone, he'd have both means and opportunity. It was easily done: a phone left unattended, a computer left logged on with the Twitter app open, a password indiscretion, a criminal fleecing him for all he was worth. But as Stone had already pointed out, there had been no ransom demand. Maybe, whoever it was, they were making him sweat. The computations were endless, but her money remained on Parker himself.

Curtis was back, a worried expression on his face. What he said next completely felled her. 'Excuse the interruption, DS Oliver. Did Tim tell you that the company is in trouble? That's why I'm working late.'

'No, he didn't. What kind of operation do you run here?'

'Recruitment and HR managed services providing temporary and permanent staff to a wide range of industry sectors. We were on the Fastest 50 list last year, would you believe.'

'Fastest Fifty?'

'Industry leaders in the north-east. One of the fastest-growing companies in the region. It's a list compiled by St Chad's College, Durham — part of the university's business school. We've gone from hero to zero in twelve months and spent a lot of Alex Parker's money.' He swept a hand across the boardroom. 'All this? We're merely keeping up appearances.'

That was the first Frankie had heard of it. She was certain it would be news to Alex, too.

23

Frankie checked in with Mitchell at the office and briefed the dayshift uniform inspector on stuff she wanted the late shift made aware of. There was as yet no word from Twitter, which seemed odd in the age of instant communication. She rang them again, demanding a response at the earliest opportunity before finally heading home, brooding over Daniel, increasingly worried for the boy's safety. The first twenty-four hours were critical. Beyond that . . .

She didn't want to go there.

The fact that his stepfather was in trouble financially (especially if his wife didn't know) gave credence to the fact that he was a man under immense pressure and not thinking straight. There were no outward signs of a cash-flow problem at home or at work. The Parkers had the fuck-off house, several high-end motors, the classy business premises most company owners would die for. Frankie wondered how long it would last if Curtis's revelation was correct. She could think of no reason why he would lie about the state of the business and couldn't help wondering just how much of Alex's inheritance the two men had parted company with.

It would be nice if one of them would tell her.

Frankie had to concede that the threat of bankruptcy might have resulted in Parker taking his eye off the ball. He flat-out denied sending Justine a message. And would a man of his standing really be stupid enough to delete such a message when the chances of being found out were high? The worst-case scenario was that he had a dark secret. That he was concealing his true nature beneath the veneer of respectability, exploiting his wife with a view to abusing her son.

Frankie sighed.

Sadly, she could cite too many cases where it had happened. While child deaths from homicide were on the decline, abuse was on the rise, the need for protection greater than it had ever been. In those incidents she'd come across, where the perpetrator happened to be a close relative, no distinction had been made between a birth parent, step-parent or adoptive parent; they were lumped together in statistical analysis that would make a sane adult's eyes bleed.

One death was one too many.

Was Parker capable of such a betrayal of trust, she asked herself. If so, had he harmed Daniel? And, in turn, had the child threatened to rat on him to Justine or his mother on her return from Majorca? Maybe Alex's imminent arrival to the UK had triggered a need to keep the lad quiet. Permanently. Those questions and others floated in and out of her head as she let herself in to her flat.

David was getting used to the hiss of the ring-pull as he opened his beer. The sun had gone in and it was already getting chilly in the living room. He stared at a pile of yellowing newspapers, a small sack of kindling and full log basket next to the wood-burning stove, as if somehow it would jump into the fire and light itself. Given her need to look after him, the least he could do for Frankie was warm the place up.

He lit the fire, made sure it was away and sat down to finish his beer. He could feel his grandmother's presence in the tiny room. She was a Northumberland Fusilier's widow at twenty-four, her husband having died during World War II, one casualty among many who had lost their lives on 20 May 1940, attempting to delay the German advance at Arras, France.

Through bleary eyes, David looked across the room, imagining her in her fireside chair, the flickering fire lighting up her eyes as she sat reading, her default position. The wonky bookcase in the corner was crammed with her books, historical and contemporary; memoirs and autobiographies among her favourites. Those she didn't own she'd borrowed from the library in Alnwick, an Aladdin's Cave of literature that had kept his erudite ancestor company until the day she died in 2014 at the grand old age of ninety-eight. The house had been empty since.

It seemed warmer when she was there.

Soothed by thoughts of his beloved nan, the glow from the fire, and another couple of cans of beer, David was getting drowsy. He laid his head back, shut his eyes, and thought about the lumpy bed he and Luke had shared as boys, a hand of bony fingers pushing through his hair, then smoothing it down, a whisper – *Goodnight, you two* – as he lost consciousness.

24

The phone was ringing as Frankie got out of the shower. Grabbing a towel, she ran into her bedroom, sweeping her mobile from the chair where she'd left it: *DC Mitchell*. Swearing under her breath, she took the call. 'Ray, if this is going to come between me and the takeaway I ordered, you're paying for it.'

'It might.'

Frankie caught her reflection in the mirror on her bedroom door. 'If you could see me right now, you'd know how idiotic that statement is.'

'There's been a development.'

Frankie's heart sank, the news knocking her for six. The phrase Mitchell had used was police speak for a death or something equally catastrophic. Stone couldn't cope with that, not on the back of his brother's accident. This would tear him apart. Telling Alex that her son was missing had been an agonising task. Giving her the death message would break her for sure. It was a mother's worst nightmare.

'Why didn't you call me? I'd have come in—'

'The guv'nor said you'd been up half the night and that I should deal with it.'

'Yeah, right,' Frankie said. 'Windy hated my old man and he's shafting me.'

'It's not working,' Mitchell said.

'Damn right. Where was Daniel found?'

'Sarge?'

'Daniel, where was he found?'

'He was never lost.'

'What? You're not making any sense!'

'He was returned home thirty minutes ago—'

'Oh God!' Frankie's mood lifted instantaneously. 'Don't you *ever* do that to me again, Mitch, or you'll be the one getting a development.'

'What does that mean?'

'It means a kick up the arse.'

'What did I do?'

'You . . . oh, never mind. Stop buggering about and tell me what you know . . . in plain language.'

'Yes, Sarge.'

'Where are you anyway?'

'Outside the house. Daniel was unharmed and accompanied by his friend Harry Price and Harry's father, Paul. The lad is perfectly well and, like Price, he's nonplussed by all the fuss. Price has a caravan near Keswick and goes down there most weekends. He claims he offered to take Daniel along – company for his lad – and Parker agreed. And when Price suggested a pickup after footy training, Parker was OK with that too. Harry and Daniel play in the same team. That's why our bods didn't get an answer at Price's door when they were making enquiries. He brought Daniel home early because he was dying to be reunited with his mum. As you can appreciate, she's ecstatic. I have no bloody idea what's going on with her other half. If you ask me, the man is unhinged. That or he's got some bloody awful advanced Alzheimer's thing going on.'

'Was this arrangement made on Twitter?'

'How did you guess?'

'It's a line of enquiry I've been following,' Frankie said. 'There was no correspondence on Parker's device about these arrangements last night, I checked it thoroughly. Did you examine Price's phone?'

'Give me *some* credit. I looked at both.'

'And?'

'Same as with Justine Segal: the messages are on Price's mobile, missing from Parker's.' Mitchell paused. 'The guv'nor says you and I need to drop this now, pick up Stone's case files and get on with them while he's on compassionate leave. He doesn't want you going off on one of your crusades – his words, not mine. Be warned, Frank. He thinks you and Stone have been time-wasting on a uniform job.'

'What does Windy know about police work?' she said. 'Do me a favour, Mitch. Before you leave Scots Gap, nip in and tell Alex Parker I'll be round to see her in the morning.'

'You'll have to be quick about it.'

'You giving the orders now?'

Mitchell chuckled. 'No, Sarge . . . Remember the burglary reports that came in last week?'

'What about them?'

'They've been upgraded to aggravated. There were two more last night. The homeowners were tied up and gagged. One had a heart attack and had to be airlifted to the Freeman Hospital.' Mitchell filled her in on the details. 'Suffice to say, the guv'nor wants us to crack on with that.'

'And we will . . . when I've seen Alex.'

25

Justine hadn't been able to get near Daniel since he'd arrived home. Alex had been with him the whole time, feeding him, chatting with him, hugging him. It was comforting to watch the two of them. Though, if she was honest, Justine felt a little resentful and, deep down, pushed out. She got that way sometimes, forgetting that her charges were on loan and not for keeps. Daniel was a kid you warmed to instantly. His disappearance had unglued her. The fact that he was safe assuaged her guilt and filled her with joy.

Like his parents, her relief was heartfelt and profound.

Until now, Justine hadn't realised how much the boy meant to his mother. Alex wasn't interested in explanations from the man who'd brought him home, only that he was back where he belonged, unharmed and blissfully happy that she was back from Majorca. Tim was less accommodating. He'd given Paul Price a mouthful at the door, unable to hide his rage. When Price suggested that Tim was party to the arrangement – that he'd agreed via DM that he could collect Daniel from football training and keep him overnight – her employer went into meltdown.

Tim emerged from his study, a drink in his hand. Justine ignored his foul mood, turning the other way, approaching the living room cautiously, half-expecting to be sent away and told that her services were not required for the rest of the evening. She pushed open the door. Alex and Daniel were nowhere to be seen. Both sets of French doors into the garden were wide open. Seconds later, they came into view.

'May I have a moment with Daniel before he goes to bed?' Justine said.

'Of course! He's tired now, anyway.' Alex turned to face her son. 'Daniel – you should be in bed, young man. Get changed and Justine will come and say goodnight. She missed you, darling. We all did.'

Justine tapped gently on Daniel's bedroom door. He was sitting on his bed, pyjamas on, a book in his hand. She took in the delicate contours of his face, his doe eyes, the awkward embarrassment of a ten-year-old who was glad to see her but didn't want to show it. She loved that about him.

'Have you cleaned your teeth?'

He nodded, then grinned at her raised eyebrow, knowing that he'd been found out. They had an arrangement: clean teeth or no treats. As he walked into his en suite bathroom, Justine smiled. She'd once caught him out. His electric toothbrush had been on, nowhere near his mouth, and she'd sent him back for a second try. After that, he hadn't tried to pull the wool over her eyes . . . until tonight.

He climbed into bed and she sat down beside him.

'I was worried about you,' she said.

He almost snorted, a half-smile covering the fact that he thought all adults must be deluded. He was such an innocent child. He hadn't understood the wrangle over his homecoming and skirted the subject when Tim began to interrogate him at the door, until his mother put a stop to it.

'I thought you were putting up balloons?' he said.

'I did,' Justine said, 'but I had to take them down again.'

'Did Mum see them?'

'Yes, and she liked them very much, especially your brilliant banner.'

He gave a beaming smile. 'I didn't want to go to the Lakes but Harry really wanted me to. He was dead excited when he came to footy. Tim told his dad that Mum wouldn't mind. She didn't, did she?'

'No, of course not . . . well, maybe a smidge.'

'Mr Price said I didn't have to stay the whole weekend.'

'And you didn't.' Justine winked at him. 'You missed me too, eh?'

'A bit.'

'Well, you're home now, Dan. That's all that matters. Do I get a hug?'

He put his arms up, turning his cheek, wanting a kiss but making out that it was such a chore. Her heart swelled as she put her arms out for a hug he fell in to. He'd never know how important it was for her to embrace him after the trauma of the past twenty-four hours. She read to him but within minutes he was gone, the face of an angel, his long eyelashes twitching as he sank deeper into the safety of sleep. Justine kissed his forehead as she did at every opportunity, covered him up, and quietly left the room.

26

The front door was slightly ajar. Frankie looked around her – no one there – pushed it open and peered in, adrenalin pumping, a sense of dread eating its way into her gut. Her concern was unwarranted. The door led directly into the living room. David was curled up on an old-fashioned, two-seater sofa, one leg over the edge, foot resting on the floor, the other leg bent at the knee to fit a piece of furniture far too small for him and probably purchased in the fifties. He was sleeping soundly, head cradled in one hand, a beer can in the other. A dribble of brown liquid had spilled out on to his shirt. Frankie counted five squashed-up beer cans on the coffee table, three more on the threadbare carpet.

She'd seen better-looking crime scenes.

It was cold in the room and the fire was dying. She opened the door to the stove, threw a log in, put her Indian takeaway on the top plate to keep it warm, then stepped into a kitchen her grandma would call a scullery, with no room to swing a cat. The tap squeaked as she turned it on to fill the kettle, the water spluttering out through ancient plumbing, the insight into David's private life making her feel like the worst kind of voyeur. Whatever she was expecting, it wasn't this.

'I see you found everything.'

'Needs must.' Frankie didn't look round. 'Your burglar appears to have fled the scene.'

'Hey! I tidied up.'

'What bits?' Now she turned to face him, a wry smile on her face. 'Nice of you to sober up for my visit . . . Crack open another, I have news worth celebrating.'

There was a small folding table in the living room and two chairs. David extended it for all the little cartons and so they could sit comfortably. He found a couple of forks and sat down beside her. They ate hungrily, Frankie relaying the information Mitchell had given her, some unanswered questions still niggling at the edges of her brain. She didn't bother Stone with them and he didn't seem to want to talk about Luke either, which she considered slightly worrying.

When they had finished eating, David left the table, stoked the fire again and headed for the sofa. Frankie made coffee, the one item he did have in his otherwise bare larder. 'Just because this village is called Pauperhaugh, doesn't mean you must live like one,' she said as she walked into the living room, a mug in each hand.

'This is my nan's place,' David said.

'Yours now, I take it.' She handed him a mug. 'Did she raise you?'

'Have you been nosing around while I was asleep?'

'Force of habit.' She pointed at the mantelpiece, more especially to the framed photos of two little boys lined up there. 'I figured that was you and Luke.' She let her hand drift around the room. 'And those . . . those and those.' She laughed. 'Even my grandma doesn't have *that* many embarrassing images on display.'

'She did a damned sight more than raise us, Frankie.'

Frankie took a seat. She knew his parents were both dead but not the circumstances in which they had died. She felt guilty for not having pressed him on the subject. They had talked about her parents often enough, her old man especially. She seemed to remember mentioning his when he arrived on the scene. He'd sidestepped her questions and she'd backed off, assuming he didn't want to talk about them. Not everyone was lucky enough to get on with relatives.

'What happened to your mam and dad?'

'They went climbing in Glen Coe and never returned. The accident made the national news when it happened. I was six at the time, Luke eight.'

'And your nan stepped in?'

A smile. 'Woe betide anyone who'd suggest otherwise.'

'She did a good job, David.'

'She was great. You'd have liked her.'

'Is that her?'

He followed her gaze to the mantelpiece and nodded. 'That photo is mine. I'll take the others down when I get around to it. It never seemed important until now. I need to move on, Frank. Can't live in the past for ever, can I?'

'Did you see her much after your move south?'

'Not as often as I'd have liked.' Another smile.

'Did I miss something?'

The smile turned to a grin. 'I'd been planning my last trip for months. Under three weeks to go and I'm carrying on like a big bairn waiting for Santa to hoy himself down the chimney. I loved coming home. It was always a laugh. She had such a great sense of humour, essential if you live here—'

'It cracks me up, that's for sure.' Frankie made a show of looking round the room.

'Sorry, I shouldn't have let you come with the house in such a state.'

'I'm pleased I did.'

'Why? I'm shit company tonight.'

'Tonight?' Frankie grinned. 'Joking! Give yourself a break, why don't you? You've had a massive shock. Have you checked on Ben?'

'Not since we dropped him off.'

Frankie stared at him. 'Don't you think you should?'

'He's not my responsibility.'

'He's your nephew and his father died. You don't need to like him but, given your history, you above all people would understand what that feels like.'

She fell silent and studied him for a while, keen to know more about his past, wanting to ask him why he'd quit the Met and come home; what it was that had prompted the move

144

south in the first place; and what had triggered a meltdown when he first set eyes on Alex Parker.

Anticipating a further exploration into his private life, David changed the subject. Work was always a safer bet. 'You mentioned Twitter before. What did they have to say?'

'Nothing. They didn't get back to me. At the time, I thought it was worth a shot. Makes no difference now Daniel is home. Windy told me to drop it and get on with something else. I'll have Mitchell cancel the action in the morning.'

He sat back studying her. 'What was it you wanted my opinion on?'

Frankie had to think on her feet. 'Windy's up in arms. Wants to know why we've been poking our noses into uniform business. Mitchell said he wants us to reference off the misper job. He's ordered us to stand down. There's been a string of serious house burglaries he wants us to investigate. Remote premises. Telephone lines cut. Organised crime, by the sounds of it. Offenders were tooled up, balaclavas, the whole nine yards. They care less if people are at home when they walk in.'

'Sounds nasty.'

'It is.' Frankie checked her watch. 'It's also late, I'd better get going.'

Stone stood at the door waving as she drove away, Frankie watching him in the rear-view mirror. No sign of maudlin. He was going to be all right.

27

Price was so convincing. Tim wanted to put him against the wall and beat the living shit out of him until he told the truth. What the fuck was going on here? There would be questions from Alex today, he could count on it. He'd watched her and Daniel fawning over one another while they got reacquainted, swapping stories of the week she was away, giggling their heads off, whispering conspiratorially, ignoring him. Even Kat got in on the act, calling her nephew, expressing her delight that he was home. Since she'd heard that he was missing, she'd been constantly on the phone. On one occasion, Alex lost her rag, telling her to back off, promising to call her the minute there was news.

Tim couldn't help feeling left out on a limb, resenting the fact that, for everyone else, the drama was over. For him, it seemed, the nightmare would go on. Using his hands as a vessel, he splashed cold water on his face, trying to shake off the drowsiness he was increasingly feeling. The reflection in the bathroom mirror didn't please him. He was showing signs of age, losing his looks as well as his grip on reality. He couldn't remember the last time he'd felt on top of his game.

Their GP had prescribed them both benzodiazepines to get over their loss. Superwoman had only taken hers for a few days to help her sleep, whereas he'd carried on to the point where he became dependent, physically and psychologically. When the doctor wouldn't give him more, Tim took another course of action and found a man who would. He'd been knocking back pills with alarming regularity ever since, more so in the past six months. Even he could see that his anxiety disorder was out of control. The more he took, the more he needed, until he was doubling up on a combination of drugs and alcohol just to take the edge off.

Despite Alex's rejection of drugs this time round, he'd been slipping them into her drinks undetected since her trip to the Balearics. They seemed to be working too. No histrionics from her. She was Ms Cool 'n' Collected, exactly the way she liked it: with Stone, that bitch Oliver, Justine and Dan. The only one getting the thick end of the wedge was him, now that Golden Boy was home. Tim could swear she didn't believe a word he said these days.

He glanced across the hallway into Daniel's bedroom.

What in God's name did Alex think there was to smile about? When she'd lost their baby girl, she'd been upset, but not on the same scale as losing Daniel temporarily. The difference was startling . . . and hurtful. Understandable on one level: Daniel had a personality, a shared history with his mother that Tim's child didn't have. Daniel was a real person, not the idea of one she could forget in a few months or so.

Daniel was her world.

The dizziness hit Tim again. He couldn't concentrate and his coordination wasn't what it should be. After his difficult interview with Oliver yesterday, he'd increased his intake. A big mistake. Good thing it was Sunday. He'd never make it to work. Had it been a weekday, he'd have made an excuse and taken a taxi. Curtis would have spotted his odd behaviour for sure. He wanted to wind up the company, blaming Tim for making bad financial decisions.

He wasn't having that.

He had to focus, lay off the drugs and booze, despite the impulse to do the exact opposite. He almost jumped out of his skin when his phone bleeped. Taking it from his pocket, he glanced at the screen. Not an email or iMessage. His skin began to creep, the full focus of his attention Twitter's signature bird logo.

He was terrified to tap on it.

147

There were seven general notifications and a tiny number 1 on the DM envelope. His finger hovered over it for several seconds before he plucked up the courage to access it. The picture of a close friend he'd not seen for a year or more was at the top of the column of followers listed there. The blurry words seemed to dance in front of his eyes:

Thanks for the invite, Tim. Great to hear from you. ETA around three. Debbie and I can't wait to catch up with you guys.

Thanks for the invite?
What the fuck?
The doorbell rang.

Frankie pressed the bell again and waited. The windows were open and she could hear classical music playing inside. Uplifting. She couldn't identify the piece – Mozart, possibly – but she loved the clarinet. One thing she was certain of: this was a very different house to the one she'd visited yesterday.

Alex arrived at the door seconds later. She'd chilled out since they had met at the café, a wide smile on her face reaching her eyes as she invited Frankie in. All was well in the Parker household. Despite instructions from her guv'nor to lay off, Frankie wasn't standing down until she was satisfied that the boy was safe and well. Mitchell had already seen and identified him, but she couldn't help herself; she wanted to sign off on the investigation properly, to be sure that nothing untoward had happened to him and that no offences had been committed.

'Could I have a word with you and Tim before I see Daniel?' she asked.

'Yes, of course. Wait here, I'll get him.' Alex disappeared along the corridor.

From her position in the hallway, Frankie could see into Daniel's room. The boy was lying on his bed, head in a comic book as if nothing untoward had happened and they had all been panicking unnecessarily. He was the spitting image of his mother, fair-haired, bow-lipped with the clearest skin she'd ever seen on a kid heading for puberty.

Alex was back, Tim in tow.

'Will this take long?' she asked. 'I'm sorry, but Tim's feeling under par this morning.'

'I'm not surprised,' Frankie said. 'It's been a difficult few—'

'Don't justify yourself to her!' Tim shot his wife a black look, adding one for Frankie. 'For the record, DS Oliver, I'll be fine – as soon as you get out of my house.'

What was his problem?

Despite the early hour, Frankie could see he'd been drinking – or worse. She cut out the small talk and got straight down to business. It didn't take long for her to feel confident that everything was as it should be. 'Well, if you're both satisfied that nothing untoward has gone on, I'll close the case,' she said. 'I want you both to know that if anything like this ever happens again, or if there's something I can do for you in the future—'

Parker cut her off. 'As I told your young colleague yesterday, we're not interested in what the police think. All we ever cared about was getting Daniel home.'

'Tim!' Alex was livid.

'It's right, isn't it? Our precious boy is home and nothing else matters.'

'How dare you! Excuse my husband's rudeness, DS Oliver. I don't know what's come over him.'

Parker glared at Frankie. 'Now you mention it, there is something you could do . . . for me anyway. Alex has what she wants. Why should I be any different?'

'Name it,' Frankie said.

'I want a formal apology.'

'For what, sir? Doing my job?'

'She's right, Tim.' Alex switched her attention to Frankie:

'As far as I'm concerned, you have nothing to apologise for, Detective. We're both grateful for all you've done. And please extend our thanks to DI Stone when you see him. There's no need for a post-mortem—'

'Figuratively speaking,' Tim interrupted. 'Unfortunate choice of words, dear.'

His condescending tone infuriated Frankie. It hadn't been directed at her and it wasn't her place to rise to it. She kept her focus on Alex. 'There are some practical steps you might consider taking: changing passwords on your devices being one; perhaps supplying Daniel with a mobile telephone so you can keep in touch with him.'

Alex was nodding. 'That sounds very sensible.'

'If either of you are concerned about anything, no matter how small, please get in touch.' Another glance into Daniel's room. 'I've got one quick question for your boy.' She was gone before either parent had time to object. If they wanted another domestic, she'd rather not play referee. She gave Daniel's door a tap and stuck her head in. 'Hi, Daniel . . . I'm Frankie, one of the detectives playing hide and seek when you weren't lost.' She grinned.

'Hi.' He gave a little wave, a smile developing as she stepped over the threshold.

Frankie pushed the door to, shutting out the hushed, angry voices that could be heard from the hallway. No wonder the boy spent so much time alone. 'I'm pleased to meet you. I hear you've been missing your mum.'

'Yeah.' The lad's eyes lit up when she handed over his iPad. Technical Support had finished with it. There was nothing on it, only games and stuff, no mention of Charlie Dawson.

She had to know.

Daniel got up and put the device on charge. 'Mum's taking me with her next time.'

'Bet you didn't miss her as much as she missed you. She was very worried about you, but the mystery is solved. These things happen sometimes. A misunderstanding. No one's fault.'

'So why are they arguing?'

She looked over her shoulder and leaned in. 'Adults do that sometimes. They don't need a reason.' Her smile was returned and she changed the subject. 'I have one question for you, is that OK?'

He nodded, keen to know what it was.

'Who is Charlie Dawson?' His enquiring reaction demanded an explanation. 'When we were looking for clues as to your whereabouts, your mum found a piece of paper with the name written on it.'

The lad appeared slightly embarrassed. 'He's a policeman.'

Frankie's chest tightened. 'And how do you know him?'

Daniel giggled, eyes sparkling with delight. He held up his story generator. 'I'm writing a detective story. Charlie's the main character. You can read it if you like.'

28

One minute the jogger was running in the sunshine, listening to her favourite playlist, the next her arms had stopped pumping and she was no longer moving forward. She was pinned to the tarmac by her own dead weight. She lay motionless, though she didn't know whether she'd lost consciousness and, if so, for how long. The pain in her head was immense. The fingers of her right hand twitched involuntarily as she attempted to move, the vibration travelling up her arm. A sob left her throat as she felt the movement, the grit like kitty litter beneath the palm of her hand a sign that she wasn't paralysed from the neck down. With heroic effort, she managed to inch her fingers a little further to the left, a change of texture . . . no gravel . . . here the tarmac was raised and smooth.

The white line . . .

This unnerving information caused her to cry out. The only markings on this isolated stretch were unbroken lines down the centre, ensuring no overtaking on the bends. She was in the middle of the road, disabled, physically and mentally compromised.

Roadkill.

Just then, the wind took her hair, whipping it across her face, covering one eye. The realisation that she had a finite time to get up and save her life hit her like a brick. Crippled with fear, expecting a car to come racing around the bend at sixty miles an hour, was a premonition like no other. Even the tallest four-by-fours wouldn't see over the hedgerow. They would be upon her before she knew it. And still her limbs refused to budge.

Her eyelids were heavier now. Forcing them open, she had an impression of blue to her left and grey straight ahead, a hint that she was on her back, head turned to the right, but with no sensory perception to uphold that point of view.

Her unrestricted eye saw movement . . .

There it was again, no more than a dark shadow in the distance. She froze momentarily, unable to trust her eyesight, panic taking hold, squeezing what little breath she had left in her lungs. The shadow moved closer. It wasn't a car, lorry or, God forbid, a tractor. It was tall and thin, a human closing in, someone running to her rescue. Help had arrived. She cared less that it might be the person who'd knocked her down. In whatever form it took, she'd take it. In her alternative world, the fact that she wasn't alone was all that mattered.

She could hear the heavy breaths of her rescuer, her right earplug having been knocked out. Then she was grabbed by the wrists and manhandled, hauled across the road surface like a sack of spuds. As she was carted away, a warm trickle of what she assumed was blood ran down and pooled in the hollow of her neck. She was powerless to stem it, incapable of resisting, unable to *do* anything. She wanted to beg whoever was aiding her, explain that they were causing injury, that they should leave her be and call for assistance from a professional. But she couldn't formulate words.

Then suddenly she was still.

The glaring sunshine had disappeared, an ominous darkness taking its place. A summer storm broke overhead, rapid and violent, the distant rumble of thunder, followed by a crack of lightning that lit up the sky. A splodge of rain hit her eyelid, followed by another crash of thunder, much closer now, warm torrential rain hitting her skin like knitting needles. She felt cold, so very cold, her breathing increasingly shallow.

The darkness was winning. She couldn't tell if she was losing consciousness, fading into a coma, or something worse. A voice broke through the soundtrack playing loudly in one ear, muffled as if being transmitted through a sodden blanket. The words seemed strange and faraway. Oddly familiar. She made a final valiant attempt to keep her eyes open. A blurred figure passed in front of her. She strained to focus on the indistinct silhouette hovering above her head. Whoever was standing there was crying too. It took enormous effort to raise a hand and grab at them but her grip was weak and ineffective. The figure unpeeled her fingers and walked away.

She *was* alone.

29

Due to a violent and unnatural death from a road traffic accident, an inquest had been opened and adjourned, the coroner delaying her decision to release Luke Stone's body for burial until further enquiries were made. Unable to hack it at home while he waited to say his final goodbyes to his brother, David Stone returned to work to assist with the aggravated burglaries Windy was so keen to resolve, the offences carrying a hefty sentence – a good collar, if they could find those responsible. It wasn't the first time that country houses, stately homes or castles had come under attack by organised thieves on their turf. In the nineties, Frankie's old man had been involved in Operation Border Reivers. Weeks of surveillance and intelligence-gathering on both sides of the Scottish border had led to the arrest and detention of a gang who'd been stealing to order, local and prolific career criminals prepared to risk lengthy terms of imprisonment to make a buck.

At Stone's request, Frankie had leaned on an informant who'd tipped her off that a gang were planning an imminent hit on Alnwick Castle this time around, the seat of the Dukes of Northumberland and their families for seven hundred plus years, made more famous by the creation of Alnwick Garden by the current duchess; even more so as J. K. Rowling's fictional Hogwarts, School of Witchcraft and Wizardry.

Frankie smiled.

Someone at the briefing had told her to get on her broomstick and head over there, moaning when she handed him the graveyard shift. Everyone laughed, including Stone. He'd ordered immediate, round-the-clock surveillance of the castle until further notice.

Stone and Oliver were double-crewed. They had been sitting in the car for hour upon mind-numbing hour, keeping observations in Alnwick market town. Working with detectives from across the force area, they had grafted for days without a lead, hoping to spot suspicious characters, or better yet, the dual-coloured, blue transit van with a bad paint job Frankie's snout had told her they were using. There was no offence more upsetting than invading people's homes, making them feel anxious in a place in which they should feel safe. If Stone had his way, he'd throw the book at them, but first he had to catch them.

'How trustworthy is your source?' he asked. 'I'm bored now.'

Frankie's eyes never left the windscreen. 'He's a conniving, dishonourable little shit, but he's never given me a bum steer up to now. The syndicate he's ratting on aren't finished yet.'

'I hope you're right.'

'So do I . . .' Frankie glanced at him. On her say-so, covert officers had been posted on all routes, an expensive operation. He wasn't happy about it. 'You'll get no sympathy from me, boss,' she said when he complained. 'You ignored my advice to take your full entitlement to compassionate leave. You should've stopped at home.'

During periods of inactivity, he'd talked about Luke quite a bit, making Frankie laugh like a drain at how they had fought, man and boy, over the beautiful game. Football was in her blood too. There had been many a row over it in her own household. All the same, she couldn't pass up the opportunity for a sarky remark about him being related to a 'Mackem' – the slang for a native of Sunderland and supporter of their rival team.

The radio crackled into life: 'Control to Hermes.'

Stone rolled his eyes at Frankie for the daft operational name their guv'nor had designated to the recent spate of organised crime littering his desk. Windy liked to think of himself as a bit of a scholar. Everyone else thought he was something unrepeatable in polite company, Frankie's description of him even worse.

Putting his burger on the dash, Stone licked the grease from his fingers and pressed to receive. 'Go ahead, Control.'

'Urgent message from Superintendent Gale,' the controller said. 'Stand down and return to base ASAP.'

'You're kidding!' Frankie didn't fancy foot patrol. She continued noshing her lunchtime carbs and spoke between chews. 'He needs to make up his bloody mind. Either he wants his name in the papers, his face on the news, or he doesn't. He can't have it both ways.' Windy would get a big pat on the back from HQ if they were to detect a series of offences targeting art and antiquities in the hands of the upper class.

'Did he say why?' Stone was asking.

'Not to me,' Control said. 'But I sent you a link to the force-wide incident log at his request.'

'OK, I'll check it out. Anything else?'

'He wants DS Oliver too, sir.'

'Yeah,' Frankie snorted. 'To make the tea.'

The controller laughed and ended the transmission. Like everyone in Northumbria force, he knew there was bad blood there.

Stone picked up his lunch. 'Does it bother you?'

'Does what bother me?'

'The way the guv'nor routinely hands you all the shit jobs.'

'I'm impressed you noticed.'

'It's hard not to.'

Now she looked at him, a wry grin appearing. 'Rule 4 in the Frank Oliver Handbook: Never let the bastards grind you down. That's not original but it'll do. I have mates who'll bend over backwards to lend a hand if I'm stretched, David. What does Windy have?'

'The more offences you crack, the more he seems to resent you.'

'Comes with the territory. Rule 5: Avoid joining a force where your old man and his old man before him have made enemies. It's my fault, David. My dad tried telling me to join Durham Constabulary. I wouldn't listen.'

'Well, the guv'nor has every detective in CID roped in on this one.'

'Yeah. If this is a new job, it must be decent or he wouldn't be pulling us off. We should go. Can't believe our targets will show their faces in daylight, can you? They're not that stupid. They'll have done their homework long before now and will send a numpty in to recce the place, a drive-through. If they think they've been rumbled or suspect a stake-out, they'll be on their way until the heat dies down. They can't risk running into a police roadblock with a stash worth millions on board.'

'You're right. Let's get out of here.'

Frankie pointed at his phone. 'Want me to view the link while you drive?'

'If you would.' He started the car, indicating his intention to leave his parking spot. A grey BMW flashed him out and he stuck a thumb up to show his appreciation.

Frankie tutted, a gesture of frustration. 'Control must've sent the wrong link. This is about an RTA.'

'Doesn't matter.' Stone found the outside lane. 'We'll check it out when we get to HQ.'

To kill the tedium of another journey to base, Frankie read on. 'Or maybe not,' she said, eyes scanning the text.

Her serious tone of voice had Stone intrigued.

He glanced at her.

'Pathologist isn't happy,' she said by way of explanation.

Stone was asking for details she'd rather not share. One fatal road traffic accident was enough for him this week; she didn't want him traumatised by another so soon after the first.

'Well?' He waited.

'Says here the casualty was already lying in the road when she was hit.'

'Nasty . . . What the hell was she doing there? And why are we getting involved?'

'She has an inconsistent injury—'

'Which is?'

'You sure you want me to go on?'

'I'm fine, Frankie.' He seemed irritated by her concern.

'The car ran straight over her. Catastrophic crush injuries: collapsed lung, ruptured spleen, broken bones. It missed her head entirely and yet – and this is the important bit – she has an injury to the back of her skull that bears no road debris. The pathologist believes it was sustained before the accident, not during, incapacitating but not killing her. He has it down as suspicious.'

'Then it's a job for the Murder Investigation Team.'

'Not if the injured party happens to be someone we already know.' Frankie turned to face him, a grave expression on her face. 'You've been put in charge of the outside enquiry team, David – the IP is Justine Segal.'

30

At Northern Command Headquarters, Superintendent Gale was wound up, barking orders at anyone who'd listen, according to the front desk. Despite his obvious dislike of Frankie Oliver, he needed his best team on a suspicious death linked with a family who'd only just been reunited with a missing son.

Stone knocked on the door, a sideways glance. 'Ready?'

'Anytime,' Frankie grinned.

David poked her shoulder playfully. '*Don't* wind him up.'

'Me?' Simulating horror, Frankie straightened her face and opened the door, throwing Windy her best smile as she entered his office, a glance at the clock on the wall behind him. 'Afternoon, sir. The desk sergeant said you wanted to brief us right away. We didn't keep you, I hope. I know you like to get a wriggle on, it being Wednesday afternoon. Your mid-week tee off is at four, isn't it?'

Stone cut her off. 'What Frankie means is it's a long way from Alnwick, sir.'

Windy was irritated about more than Frankie's barefaced cheek. 'Why wasn't I told that Timothy Parker – the stepfather of your recent misper – is acquainted with the Chief Constable?' He didn't wait for a response and none was forthcoming. 'I'm not sure how and, to be perfectly frank, I'm not keen on finding out. Suffice to say, he's in a foul mood now the family au pair has come to grief. Will one of you tell me what in God's name is going on?'

'We were rather hoping you'd tell us,' Frankie said. 'If Parker knows the Chief, he didn't say anything to us. And, with respect, it wouldn't have made any difference if he had.'

Windy ignored her. 'DI Stone?'

'Frankie has been fielding calls left right and centre on the way down the A1. I'd like to speak with the senior traffic investigator before I comment, sir. The officer in question is due to go off shift. She's standing by to speak to us. It's also crucial that I liaise with the pathologist before he leaves for the weekend. He's also waiting.' It was a heavy hint that they were needed elsewhere.

'Very well, I won't keep you . . .' Windy stood up, pulling his jacket from the back of his chair. 'I want a comprehensive report in my inbox by close of play.'

The senior accident investigator met them as arranged directly outside the morgue. From their greeting, it was clear that she and Frankie knew each other well. Stone liked Inspector Andrea McGovern instantly. She was straightforward, no airs and graces, a woman who seemed overly pleased to meet him for some reason and yet a little wary perhaps. He felt an instant affinity to her and couldn't fathom why.

'I told Andrea all about you,' Frankie said.

'Did you now.' Stone narrowed his eyes.

'None of it repeatable,' McGovern said. 'Though I'm open to a bribe if you're desperate.' Her handshake was solid. 'Good to finally meet you.' She paused, her smile fading. 'I'm sorry for your loss. I did all I could for Luke.' She swallowed hard, another awkward pause. 'As soon as he mentioned that you were a copper, I realised who you were and that you worked with Frankie.'

'Was it you who—' Stone broke off.

'Yes, I was first on the scene . . . If it would help to sit down and chat sometime, I'd be happy to.'

'I'd like that.'

Now Stone understood. His connection with Andrea McGovern extended beyond the fact that they were police officers. She'd comforted his brother in his darkest hour. He'd never be able to tell her how much he appreciated the gesture, the attempt to make him feel better. He held back from asking what exactly had been said or finding out if his brother knew how critically injured he was. He had so many questions. None he could ask now. They would talk again . . . when he was less raw.

Frankie came to his rescue in the nick of time. 'Shall we go in?'

Paul Mason, the Home Office pathologist, was a man in his fifties with a dark complexion and a silver head of hair that contrasted with the growth on his chin where it had already turned white. There were signs of premature ageing around kind, intelligent eyes that looked out through a pair of thin-rimmed, titanium specs, and the worst cauliflower ear Frankie had ever seen. She'd called ahead to warn Mason of their arrival and to ensure that it was a convenient time for them to view the body and discuss his findings. The injuries to Justine were no more and no less than either detective was expecting.

Mason lifted the sheet covering her body. Over and above the marks of a recent post-mortem, there were catastrophic injuries to the torso, bruising where the wheels of a car had run over her as well as multiple lesions.

'I'd like to start with Inspector McGovern if I may,' Stone said. It was important to review all the facts relevant to the investigation. 'Andrea, can you give us the rundown on the incident from your point of view?'

'The call came into Control at 15:05. Paramedics and two Traffic vehicles were dispatched. Our guys got there first, established a perimeter and questioned the drivers of the two cars directly involved. They had been heading towards each other on the humpback bridge that crosses Hart Burn on a bend in the road, an Audi A3 travelling south, a Ford Focus travelling north. It's a blind summit for any vehicle approaching from the north side. When the Audi was flashed by the oncoming car, the driver assumed it meant go, put his foot down and carried on. The driver of the Ford meant stop, not go. The victim was lying in the road. Powerless to do anything to prevent what happened next, the Ford driver looked on as the Audi mounted the brow of the hill and ran right over her. Ms Segal took the full force and was pronounced dead at the scene.'

Stone almost shuddered. 'I believe you told Frankie that the scene gave no cause for concern initially?'

'I wasn't there myself,' McGovern said. 'But that is correct, yes.'

'They must've had some cause for concern or they wouldn't have called out Mr Mason.'

'That's right. The most likely scenario, based on what the scene was telling them, was that Ms Segal had either tripped and fallen or become ill whilst running – a heart attack perhaps – and was subsequently hit by a car, the driver having little chance of avoiding her as she was hidden from view. Two things struck them as odd: firstly, the age of the IP – she was relatively young, athletic build – fit looking, anyway; secondly, she was lying directly across the middle of the road, arms and legs outstretched, as if she'd lain down or been placed there carefully, the whole thing staged. It was an unnatural position if she'd merely fallen, an observation echoed by Joanna Brent, the driver of the Ford. Mr Mason raised the alarm following the post-mortem. In view of what he told me, I suggested we meet up at the scene. I had the road re-examined forensically – no easy task in torrential rain.'

'Visibility was poor at the time of the accident?' Stone wanted chapter and verse.

'Very. It's been chucking it down all afternoon. The weather not only hampered our efforts, it seems to have affected the two drivers involved at the time.'

'Would that account for the lack of communication between them, in your opinion?'

'Absolutely,' McGovern said. 'I'd like a quid for every time a flash of lights has led to, rather than prevented, an accident. The Audi driver, Trevor Taylor, saw the flashing of headlights but not the Ford driver's frantic attempts to flag him down. Both were shaken up, the witness in Ford especially so. She saw the whole thing. Poor sod woke up this morning with no idea that this was the day her love of driving would come to an end. I very much doubt she'll be getting in her car any time soon. She was so shaken by what she'd seen, one of my lads had to take her home.'

'It must've been awful,' Frankie said. 'I cringe if I hit a rabbit or pheasant.' She received a dark look from McGovern. 'Shit, David I'm so sorry, I didn't mean—'

'Relax, Frankie.' Stone's focus was McGovern. 'Has Justine's family been informed?'

'Not yet,' she said. 'French police are trying to trace them.'

'I might be able to help in that regard,' he said.

The investigator looked at him oddly.

'I was recently in touch with the recruitment agency she worked for. The kid she looks after went missing. He's back now but we were covering the bases.' He looked at Frankie. 'Get on to them for a home address. We don't want her parents finding out from the press.'

'I'll sort it,' McGovern said. 'Looks like you have enough on your plate.' There was a split-second non-verbal exchange between the two women. No one liked giving the death message. Frankie was thanking McGovern for saving Stone the pain of having to do it himself.

'Are you sure?' Stone said.

'Positive. And if there's anything else my team can do to help, just yell.'

The DI voiced his gratitude. 'What about Justine's employers, the Parkers? Have they been informed?'

'Yes, I did it myself. They're completely devastated. I believe their son Daniel is very close to the victim. He hasn't been told yet,' McGovern added. 'I thought you should know.'

'How was Justine identified?' Frankie asked. 'If she was wearing running gear, would she be carrying ID? I don't when I'm running.'

McGovern raised an eyebrow in astonishment, a humorous retort on the tip of her tongue she decided to keep to herself. 'It didn't take long for traffic to build up on either side of the bridge post-accident. A local girl had seen Justine earlier in the day and knew she worked at the big house along the road.'

Stone thanked her for the information and turned to the pathologist, who'd been waiting patiently. 'Mr Mason, could you give us your findings now.'

'I'd be happy to.' He glanced at the body briefly and then at the police officers. 'I can tell you with absolute certainty that this young woman was healthy before today's events. She had no disease of heart, lungs or liver that would have accelerated her death or caused her to collapse before she was hit by the vehicle, neither had she suffered any life-threatening episode: coronary thrombosis, stroke, heart attack.' He returned Stone's gaze. 'I understand you knew her?'

'Not personally,' he said. 'She was a witness in a recent case that may or may not be linked with this one. I interviewed her last week.'

'Might that be a motive?'

'Anything is possible.'

'Well, despite severe haemorrhaging, this young woman survived beyond being struck. She may not have been fully conscious, but she was alive at the point of impact.'

This was so difficult for Stone. For the second time in a week, he'd been forced to view the remains of someone he knew. He could feel the gaze of Frankie and Andrea like lasers on the side of his face. In Frankie's case, she might present as a hard-nosed copper but it was all a front. She'd been watching over him all week, making sure he was off the drink and feeding himself properly. He simply didn't know how he would have coped without her.

'DI Stone?' Mason waited. 'I'm sure you have questions for me.'

'Yes, sorry. You mentioned an injury to her head.'

'It wasn't evident during the prelim. The victim was on her back. The injury only became apparent when I did the post-mortem. Luckily, she was the only fatality and I was able to conduct the PM as soon as she arrived here. I should also tell you that Inspector McGovern and I found no item of the shape and size that might have been responsible for Ms Segal's head injury, on or near the bridge.'

'Any idea what kind of weapon was used?' Frankie asked.

'Hard to tell,' Mason said. 'Some sort of heavy tool, although the indentation isn't one I've seen before.'

'Are you able to suggest what may have happened?'

'Guesswork is not my bag, as well you know, DS Oliver.'

'OK, so you're a scientist and I know better than to ask. Give us your observations based on your examination.'

'I'm certain that Ms Segal was struck from behind with some force. There are scuffs to her hands and knees as you might expect if she'd fallen. Her Lycra running gear is torn, as if she'd been dragged across the tarmac on her back.' He nodded to his assistant who showed them the clothing and turned Justine over. Mason thanked him and carried on. 'As you can see, she has substantial scrapes and scratches to her back, buttocks and legs that correspond to the damage to her clothing.'

'Might she have been caught by a car and dragged along?' The question had come from Stone.

Mason was shaking his head. 'I'd expect these injuries to be more severe if that was the case.'

'I agree.' Andrea had seen more than her fair share of those types of accidents since she'd joined the Traffic department.

'How would the offender know a car wouldn't come from the south side?' Stone asked.

'Maybe they had local knowledge.' All eyes were on Andrea.

'Traffic at the time the incident occurred is notoriously bad from the north on a weekday as families drive to pick up their children from school. I was told repeatedly that drivers heading south avoid that stretch of road like the plague.'

'So, to recap,' Frankie's eyes were on Mason. 'You're saying that someone whacked Justine over the head and then dragged her to the lea side of the bridge where the offender knew she'd be run over as an attempt to cover up the assault, knowing that she was likely to die as a result?'

The pathologist's nod drew an ominous line under the proceedings.

31

Having established that they were dealing with a murder, Stone and Oliver debriefed in the car on the way to base, the DI voicing his concerns over Justine Segal's death. 'I'm wondering if it could be connected to Daniel's disappearance. Our money was on Tim Parker for the abduction that wasn't, right? The missing messages . . . His evasiveness . . . Even you and Alex were coming around to the idea that his Twitter account may have been hacked, that he might have been the target of some cruel prank—'

Frankie agreed. 'There simply has to be a link.'

'The question is, were we looking in entirely the wrong direction?'

'You mean Justine was the victim all along and not the parents?' Frankie met his gaze. 'That's a tantalising theory.'

'And a worrying one. We know absolutely nothing about her beyond what she told me in interview – and that wasn't much. She claimed she left London because she didn't fancy Saudi. We only have her word for it—'

She eyed him with interest. 'You think her past is catching up with her?'

'Maybe . . . relatively speaking, she's new to Northumberland. I wouldn't imagine she has that many friends, living with the Parkers as she did, although I gather she received a small allowance and time off occasionally. We need a full background profile. Speak to her girlfriends – and boyfriends too if she has any.'

'Which brings us to Tim Parker,' Frankie said. 'I'll bet you dinner that they were having an affair. If it were up to me, I'd send forensics in to examine Justine's annex before the Chief's new bestie gets rid of the evidence. Parker can't object to that now, can he? If he did, it would make him look more than a bit suspicious.'

'Put them on standby,' Stone said. 'I want to interview Parker first. I want to know if he's ever been inside that annex since Justine moved in.'

As Frankie made the call, Stone took a right-hand turn and headed for Scots Gap. It wouldn't hurt to delay crime scene investigators while they interviewed Parker. Frankie was right: he'd be ill-advised to make a song and dance about examining the place now that his au pair had drawn her last breath.

They drove on in silence, leaving the city behind. Northumbria force area was so diverse: a patch that included a party city that had undergone widespread regeneration in recent years, the windswept Northumberland countryside, stunning coastline, villages and market towns, a landscape unchanged for centuries. The land was as much a character as the locals.

'Andrea's nice,' Stone said.

'She's great.'

'Known her long?'

'Oh yeah, we go way back. We were at training school together, roommates too. We're practically sisters. She's a great laugh, a good copper too. Even my old man thinks so, though half the time he's only saying that to wind me up. You know what dads are like: someone else's offspring is always cleverer, funnier, more exciting. No wonder I feel like the poor relation. You should hear him: Andrea this, Andrea that.' Frankie stuck her fingers down her throat, making Stone laugh.

'She's a pro,' he said.

'Is that a euphemism for seriously hot?'

'No!' Stone could feel himself blushing. 'I meant what I said. If her team had been content to log Justine's death as an accident, we'd be whistling for witnesses now. As it is, they had the good sense to record vehicle licence numbers and take note of everyone arriving on the scene, by car or on foot. We'll have to speak to them all, starting with the two drivers directly involved.' He glanced at Frankie. 'Did you two ever work together?'

Frankie shook her head. 'After our probationary period, she applied to be a motorcycle cop, where she remained until the bike fleet was scrapped on grounds of health and safety – the worst day of her life, to hear her tell it. Years on, she mentions it at every opportunity.'

'I should have thought bikes were an essential resource. They were in the Met. We relied on them for a quick response.'

'I agree. To add insult to injury, a few days after they were decommissioned here, Durham motorcycle riders were utilised to provide outriders for a visit by Gordon Brown to the region. Andrea was furious.'

'Where did she go?'

'Oh, she remained in her motor patrol unit, then worked her way up to lead her present team. She's been there ever since.' An email alert interrupted Frankie in full flight. 'Ha! How spooky is that? It's Wonder Woman. She's sent photographic evidence from the crime scene.' Frankie checked the accompanying text. 'Witness statements will be uploaded on HOLMES before the day is out.' She grinned at Stone. Andrea McGovern was the real deal.

32

The phone had been ringing off the hook for what seemed like hours to Alex: one mumbled condolence message after another, more sympathy than she could reasonably stomach. Since he'd got home from school, she'd coaxed Daniel into the living room, sat him down in front of their smart TV with a bowl of snacks, where there was less chance of him over-hearing the conversations she was having with local people and, more importantly, with Tim.

'Do you think we should be worried for our safety?' she whispered, keeping one eye on her son. She ran a hand through her hair, holding it off her face for a second before letting go. 'I mean, first Daniel, now Justine, what next?'

Tim looked at her oddly. 'What do you mean?'

'You heard Inspector McGovern. Justine's death is "unex-plained". What she really meant was suspicious. You know how people talk, Tim. It's all over the village. Jesus, Justine was a foreigner in our care and now she's dead. I can't imagine what her family will think of us when they're told.'

Her husband was unresponsive.

He'd been showing signs of acute stress lately – and now it seemed he'd lost the plot. On the back of losing their baby, Daniel's disappearance had hit him hard. Even since they got Daniel home and the detectives had gone away, Tim hadn't managed to relax, let alone return to normal. And McGovern turning up, asking to come inside, had only served to make matters worse. He simply hadn't been able to cope. He was spiralling out of control, drinking anything he could get his hands on, acting weird.

She tried again. 'You haven't upset anyone, have you? At work, I mean?'

'What? No!'

'Don't look at me as if it was a ridiculous question. You're hardly opposed to a bit of sharp practice, are you?'

He smirked. 'You taught me well.'

'If you're looking for a scapegoat,' Alex said. 'Try your friend, Curtis. That slug inveigled his way into your firm and you stood by and let him. Something's going on between the two of you, I can feel it. If you have reason to suspect it has *anything* to do with what's happening to us, have the guts to share it so we can tell the police. I won't have Daniel put at risk.'

'Oh, it's all about him, isn't it? Let's not upset our precious boy—'

'You spiteful sod! Would you feel differently if he was your kid?'

'Fuck off!'

A brief glance into the living room from Alex. 'Will you keep it down?'

'Relax, he can't hear a thing.'

The words were hardly out of his mouth when Daniel glanced over his shoulder, his noise-cancelling headphones far too large for the size of his skull. He'd sensed the tension going on behind him and was very protective where Alex was concerned. She managed a smile which he seemed to accept before refocusing on *The Good Dinosaur*, the movie animation he was watching.

Alex dropped her voice. 'Do you think we're in danger?'

He glared at her. 'That's right, pile on the agony. Things are bad enough. I could do without your pessimism. We are well covered. This place is like the Bank of England vault. You insisted, remember? State-of-the-art security because of the isolated location, you said. No one will get past that, you said. We'll all be safe here, *you* said. What do you want me to do? Sit at the front door with Daddy's shotgun?'

Alex gave him hard eyes. It was a hurtful thing to say and

well he knew it. She adored her parents and they her. Tim took it back immediately, tripping over himself to apologise. They were both distraught. Fighting with each other wasn't helping. He drained his beer, then opened another can.

Alex gave him a derisory look.

'What's that for?'

'Please stop . . .' She pointed at the glass in his hand. 'I don't want you drinking to excess in front of Daniel during the day. You know how nervous it makes him.'

'That wasn't what you were going to say—'

'You're right, it wasn't.'

'Go on then, spit it out.'

Alex hesitated. 'I was wondering if our high security explains why Justine was attacked outdoors. If they couldn't get to her here, that might explain why they killed her elsewhere.'

'They? Who the fuck are "they"?'

'I don't know . . . I'm scared, Tim.'

'Don't be such a drama queen.' Her husband was angry now but also on edge, psychologically traumatised by recent goings on. 'And who said anything about Justine being attacked? The police said she was run over. Will you listen to yourself? You're making the facts up as you go along. Your interpretation of "unexplained" is based on local gossip and innuendo by village idiots who have nothing better to talk about. You surprise me, Alex, you really do.'

'You're wrong,' she said. 'There were witnesses—'

Tim froze, taking the glass away from his mouth. 'Says who?'

'Marjorie, the old dear who lives in that row of cottages on the main road. The police told her that Justine was lying in the road on her back, unconscious, when—' Alex convulsed at the thought of what happened next. Her eyes flew to the door as a shadowy figure arrived. Someone was standing right outside.

33

Frankie grabbed Stone's arm as he raised it to ring the bell, pulling him away from the door. 'Mind if I take him and you take her, guv? Parker is wary of me, I can feel it.' She rolled her eyes. 'It might be because I had my hands round his neck when we last spoke, figuratively speaking. That's no bad thing. I had him on the rails and that's exactly where I want him.'

'This is not a game, Frankie.'

'Did I say it was?'

'He may be innocent.'

'Of screwing Justine? Not a chance. I saw lingering looks, even if you didn't, and we both heard her voice message. That was nasty, an exchange between two people who know each other intimately in my opinion. Parker is a looker, he's also rich and powerful, thanks to Alex's money – an attractive combination to some. I reckon he turned on the charm and the au pair fell for it. Whether he killed her or not is another matter . . .'

Alex opened the door and peered out, narrowing her eyes against bright sunshine. Stone gave his condolences, asking if they could come inside and talk. He registered her surprise. For a moment, she stood there motionless. She was probably expecting McGovern, who'd informed them of Justine's death earlier in the day.

'We'd like to speak to you regarding Justine,' Frankie explained. 'DI Stone and I are looking into the circumstances surrounding her death.'

Alex opened the door wider, inviting them in.

'Could we adjourn to my office?' She quickly head-checked the living room. Daniel was engrossed in his film. 'Daniel has no clue of what's happened. Do you mind if I check in on him first?'

Stone nodded and she left them for a moment to speak to her son. Seconds later, she showed them into a large room off the hallway, the walls of which were lined with books – most, though not all, to do with public relations. Several, Frankie noticed, Alex had written herself.

Tim Parker hadn't said a word since they arrived. It looked like the couple weren't on speaking terms and the detectives wondered why. If Alex had shed a tear over the sudden death of her au pair, it didn't show. That wasn't surprising. Her husband was a complete mess, though, no help to her whatsoever. When kids were in the house, someone had to hold it together. Still, as family dramas go, this was seismic, the second in a week.

'It might be wise to tell Daniel of Justine's death immediately.' Stone was looking at Alex. 'As his mother, this must be your decision, of course, but do bear in mind that he'll find out what's happened on the news, in the local press, from kids at school . . . My advice would be to get it over with now.'

'We'll tell him when we see fit,' Tim snapped.

'Sir, it would be a mistake to leave it.'

'Why so?' Alex asked.

'The pathologist has ruled out accidental death. We're now treating the incident as murder.' The DI's comment drew no reaction from Tim or Alex, barring an exchange of glances. 'Daniel is a bright boy. He'll guess something is up. He'll be angry if he finds out from a third party. They were close and you won't want him hearing it from someone else.'

Frankie took Tim Parker into the dining room next door, Stone and Alex remaining in her study. A switch was thrown in David's head as soon as the door was closed. Once they were alone, Alex dropped her coping routine. Tears misted her eyes, that same beseeching gaze, a desperate plea for help. She appeared as shaken by Justine's death as her husband. Their stoicism seemed unnatural. Maybe they were both scared witless.

Stone was mesmerised by Alex Parker and, for a moment, couldn't speak.

Alex opened French doors leading into the garden and locked them into place. When she came inside, she moved towards the drinks fridge, took out two bottles of rose lemonade Stone happened to know was botanically brewed in Hexham, twenty miles away.

She handed him a bottle and a tumbler, then pointed through the open door.

'Shall we?'

'I'd as soon talk to you here,' the DI said.

'As you wish.' She took the seat nearest to the door, unscrewed the bottle top and poured the liquid into her glass. Ignoring his, Stone took a notebook from his inside breast pocket in case he wanted to jot anything down. He hadn't come to get pally.

'When did you last see Justine?' he asked.

'At around two, two thirty, maybe a little after. I was working on a presentation. She came in to make sure that I was happy to pick Daniel up from the RGS. I said I was and she left.'

'You knew she'd gone jogging?'

'I assumed so: she was dressed for it, though I never saw her leave. I wouldn't necessarily – she has her own front door.'

'She wasn't working today?'

'No, I'd given her the week off. In view of the shock we had over Daniel, I wanted to collect him from school myself and spend time with him before I return to work. I took him swimming and then out for tea at Francesca's in Jesmond, his favourite pizzeria.'

'So, it was unusual for Justine to have a Wednesday afternoon off?'

'Yes, it was. I thought she might go home, but her parents are away somewhere. Her half-day is normally a Monday when Daniel has a violin lesson after school. I pick him up myself on my way home from work. I have an office in the city by the law courts. We usually do something together if Tim is away and we don't have to rush back.' She paused, a worried expression. 'Do you have any reason to suspect that Justine was followed from here?'

'Not if Wednesday was a break from her normal routine. Why do you ask?'

'Why do you think? I don't believe in coincidence. Do you?'

Stone didn't answer. He could see where she was heading. Alex Parker was no fool.

'I'm afraid we're being targeted,' she said. 'I was saying the same thing to my husband shortly before you arrived. Naturally, I'm concerned for our safety. Are we in danger, in your opinion?'

'I wish I could give you a definitive answer,' Stone said. 'I don't want you to worry. I think it more likely Justine was the target, not you. All options will be investigated thoroughly.'

'Thank you, Detective Inspector.'

'Did Justine jog much?'

'Every other day. She was training for a half-marathon.'

'How would she normally spend her days off?'

'We never saw her for dust. On the one hand, she was quite studious. She used to read a lot, go to the cinema, with or without Daniel. On the other, she wanted company of people her own age, I expect. She was always on her phone. She'd built up a big circle of friends down south, I believe. Her former employer was more generous than we are regarding time off . . . not that she ever complained.'

'And here?'

'You saw her, Inspector. She was a magnet.'

'An extrovert would you say?'

'Absolutely.'

'Strange, that's not how she came across in interview . . . If anything, I found her a little closed off. Did her friends ever come to the house?'

'Not that I'm aware.' Alex looked uncomfortable.

'Well, did they, or didn't they?'

'No. Socialising here was not something Tim and I encouraged. We work from home sometimes. He made that quite clear when he interviewed her for the job. She seemed not to mind. I think she would've said so if that had been the case.'

'Can I ask you where you were at around three o'clock today?'

'I was here.' Tim Parker relaxed in his chair. He lifted his can to his lips, studying Frankie over the top of it. Even through beer goggles he didn't like her and he'd made up his mind that the feeling was mutual.

Frankie lifted the nib of her pen from the pad she'd been scribbling on. 'A day off?' she said.

'In a manner of speaking.' He raised his can. 'Unfit for duty, ma'am. Guilty as charged.'

Well, he was right about that. It had Frankie wondering why. Three scenarios played out in her head. One: he *was* being targeted by person or persons unknown – a creditor, perhaps – was scared to death and had chosen booze as a coping mechanism, an attempt to dumb down his anxiety. If that was the case, it wasn't working. Two: Justine had threatened to tell his wife about their affair, he'd lost his temper in drink, followed her from the house and done for her. Three: stone-cold sober, he'd murdered the au pair to cover up their affair, and his abuse of alcohol was driven by guilt.

Frankie never took her eyes off him. 'Can anyone verify that?'

'My wife . . . until she left to pick up Daniel.' Frankie was about to ask at what time she left when Parker volunteered the information. 'It must have been at around three, perhaps a little later.'

'Did you actually see her leave?'

A nod. 'She came in to say she was off. I was in my study.'

'It must've been a shock to hear of Justine's death.'

'Of course.'

Frankie noticed the flicker of sadness in his eyes. For a moment, she thought he might lose his cool. He recovered quickly, taking another long pull on his beer. He was trying to give the impression of cooperation but was seething underneath. He'd rather have been interviewed by Stone. Too bad, Frankie thought. I'm in the driving seat. She continued: 'Justine lived in the annex, didn't she?'

'Yes. She was very happy there. It gave her, and us, some space. Had she lived, we expected her to stay with us for very long time. She was fantastic with Daniel and a great help to us, like her predecessor, Maria.'

The Parkers' former au pair had come up in conversation when Stone and Frankie were discussing who might have taken Daniel. Who better than a disgruntled ex-employee who loved the boy? Daniel's return home had meant this line of enquiry had been abandoned, but with Justine dead, Maria would now be asked to give an account of her whereabouts and, if she couldn't do so, would be investigated as a possible suspect.

'Maria?' She wanted a surname.

'Friedman,' Parker said.

'German?'

He shook his head, her mistake amusing him. 'Maria was the quintessential British nanny, not a continental au pair. She'd been with Alex since Daniel was born, long before I came on the scene.'

'What was she like?'

'An employee.' Registering Frankie's disgust, he continued

unperturbed: 'Don't get me wrong, she was very nice and good with the child, but I'm not in the habit of fraternising with the hired help.' He was taking the piss, putting Frankie in her place.

She didn't bite. 'Local woman?'

'Yes, unless she's moved away. You'll have to ask Alex.'

'They kept in touch?'

'Again, you'll have to ask my wife.'

'Can we return to Justine for a moment? Specifically, to her living arrangements.' Frankie was building up to the six-million-dollar question, his jugular in sight, if not in striking distance. 'Was the annex exclusively her domain?'

'Yes.'

'Have you ever visited her there, sir?'

'Why should I?'

'It's a simple enough question.'

'And an impertinent one,' he said. 'As I told you a moment ago, childcare is Alex's domain, not mine. I have little to do with the domestic staff.'

Frankie kept up the pressure. 'A simple yes or no will do.'

'No then.'

'You have never visited her there?'

He sighed. 'That's what I said.'

'I thought I'd give you the opportunity to reconsider.'

'I've never so much as set foot inside the place. That should be clear enough, even for you.'

Frankie took her time making a word-for-word note of what he'd said. 'So, just to keep it open and above board, you two were not having an affair?'

'No, we were not.' Despite the air conditioning, Parker was sweating. 'Why would you ask me that?'

'It's what I'm paid for. What about her Renault?'

'What about it?'

'Have you ever been inside that vehicle?'

Parker stroked his chin. 'I believe so. She gave me a lift to

180

the garage once to pick up my car when it was in for a service.'

'They didn't have a courtesy car?'

His eyes were like lasers. 'As I recall, there wasn't one available.'

Frankie wrote down his answer. 'Forensic officers found a number of different sets of fingerprints in her vehicle. I'm going to need your prints and a buccal swab for elimination purposes – and Daniel's too, for the same reason.'

'Why?'

'Alex said Justine transported him all over.' Frankie performed the procedures, marking the containers with Parker's details and an exhibit reference, placing the samples in evidence bags which she then signed and dated. She held up the samples. 'Please don't concern yourself about these, they'll be destroyed afterwards.' She stood up, telling him she had all she needed for now.

Parker hauled himself off his chair looking smug, like he was home and dry. He couldn't look any more pleased had he won the lottery. As he followed Frankie out, she stopped short of the door.

'Oh . . . ' She turned to face him. 'I almost forgot. A team of crime scene investigators will be arriving shortly to examine Justine's rooms. DI Stone and I apologise for any inconvenience this may cause.'

34

Andrea McGovern kissed Frankie on both cheeks as she stepped through the door. Dumping her bag on the floor, Frankie gave her a hug and traipsed along behind her into the living-dining room where the table was set for three, complete with pristine white linen napkins, candles and a bottle of Argentinian Malbec breathing in the centre.

'Shall we sit outside?' Andrea said.

Frankie nodded, her eyes drifting around the living room as she wandered out on to the balcony. She loved Andrea's style. So tasteful. She'd done it out nicely, each piece of furniture carefully chosen to complement the rest. The flat was in the historical market town of Morpeth with a magnificent view over the River Wansbeck, guaranteed to take the temperature down after a day of policing. No wonder so many coppers lived here.

Frankie slipped on her sunglasses.

Andrea arrived with a glass of wine, kicked off her flip-flops and sat down, crossing her long legs. The sun, low in the sky behind her, lit up her short-cropped, spiky blonde hair. They were about as close as two women could be, kindred spirits, well suited to a career in law enforcement.

Frankie leaned into her chair and shut her eyes. She was exhausted, hungry and grateful not to be cooking tonight. 'Dinner smells divine . . .' she said, stifling a yawn. 'You spoil me.'

'You can't live on take-out alone.'

'Yes, Mum.' Frankie's peepers were still shut.

'And talking of divine dishes . . . How's the Northern Rock?' It was the station nickname for Stone.

'He was busy in the incident room when I left. Paperwork,

nothing that concerned me, he said. He's a stubborn bugger sometimes. Practically ordered me to leave. I'm no good to him burned out, apparently.'

'I think it's a bit late for that, don't you?'

Frankie was grinning. 'You're supposed to say, "You look amazing, Frankie . . . I don't know how you do it, Frankie . . . You have such energy, Frankie . . ." or words to that effect.' She opened her eyes. Another gaping yawn. 'I suspect David will do anything rather than go home to his place, such as it is.'

'You've been there?'

'Right after Luke died.'

'You didn't say.'

'Why would you be interested?'

Andrea raised an eyebrow. 'I'm nosy.'

'He was in a bad way,' Frankie said. 'His cottage even worse. It looked like a bomb had dropped – and that's before the ceiling fell in.'

A third yawn was unstoppable. Frankie glanced over the balcony. The river beneath them was dead calm. Ducks floated silently downstream. An old couple were enjoying an evening stroll as the sun sank beneath the horizon. So peaceful.

'Have you seen the Parkers yet?' Andrea asked.

Frankie gave a nod. 'We interviewed them earlier.'

'Anything interesting come up?'

'My fist . . . almost. If nothing else, Timothy Parker is guilty of being a prize arsehole. Honestly, he's so condescending. I wanted to punch his lights out. He deliberately rubs me up the wrong way. I'm trying to keep an open mind, but you should've heard him—'

'You should have put him in his place—'

'I did. It'll take more than him to rattle me.'

'So, what's the story?'

'Not sure yet. Daniel Scott is absolutely devastated.' Frankie met Andrea's gaze. 'Stone wanted him processed and told before a forensics team arrived. Can you believe his mother asked *me* to break the news about Justine? She was with me to pick up the pieces. Even so, I think it would've been better coming from her. That said, she didn't have much time to prepare or practise her delivery. You'd think working in PR, she'd have found the words.'

'It's not the easiest thing to do though, is it?'

'No, I suppose not. By the way, thanks for telling Justine's parents. Stone really appreciated that. We both did.'

'The least I could do. Where were the Parkers at the time of Justine's death?'

'In the house, allegedly. They alibi each other, though the timing is tight.'

'You still think Justine was having an affair with her employer?'

'Yeah, but he denied it.' Frankie loved that she could talk to Andrea away from the office and bounce ideas around, use her as a sounding board in complete confidence that anything she said would go no further. 'He's a slippery bastard. He claims he's never been in her flat – she lives in a separate annex. So it's a provable lie if he has.'

'Maybe he hasn't.'

'I'd put money on it.'

'What about her vehicle?'

'He admits to that. Alleges she once gave him a lift, so if his prints and DNA are found there, he has a good excuse. Different if our bods find anything in her digs—'

'You sure about that?'

Frankie took her glass away from her lips. 'Depends where we find his DNA. I asked the Murder Investigation Team to fast-track samples taken from the annex and the laundry room in the main house. There were unwashed bedsheets in the dirty-linen basket and I wanted them tested. The SIO wouldn't bite. He's sent some samples off and is holding on to others to see if we get anywhere.'

'That's frustrating.'

'Tell me about it.'

'You don't think you're being optimistic?' Seeing Frankie frown, Andrea explained her thinking: 'Even if you find his DNA in the annex, technically it's his house. You'd expect to find it there, wouldn't you?'

'So why lie about it?'

'I'm only saying. Any good lawyer . . .' She didn't need to finish the sentence and moved on to another. 'How did you swing it? A forensic sweep is a big deal.'

'Not in a murder investigation. Victim's home is the starting point. Stone backed me up. He trusts my intuition.'

'Big mistake.' Andrea grinned.

Frankie laughed.

It was an in-joke between them.

When they there were young in service, Andrea had been invited to the Olivers' home several times: for dinner, festive occasions, any excuse for a party. Clan Oliver loved a blowout. Over time, Frankie couldn't move without her tagging along. She began to feel claustrophobic, as if she had a permanent shadow that didn't belong to her. Misconstruing Andrea's motivation as a desire to elevate their relationship to something more than friendship, Frankie sat her down one day and told her to back off. Andrea had laughed until she cried, and the reason for that had just put her key in the front door.

'Hey!' Rae Oliver's smile lit up her face as she joined them on the balcony. 'What a lovely surprise, I didn't know you were coming!' She landed a kiss on Frankie's cheek. 'One for you,' she said. 'And . . .' She almost leapt on Andrea. 'One for my girl.' The embrace was passionate and reciprocated.

'Put her *down*,' Frankie faked disgust. 'You don't know where she's been.'

It hadn't been her that Andrea was interested in all those years ago. It was her big sister, Rae. Hence the jibe about her intuition, or lack thereof. It had taken her parents a while to accept their same-sex relationship, but accept it they had, wholeheartedly – and so had Frankie. Rae and Andrea were out and proud, very much in love, civilly partnered for the past nine years. They enjoyed the kind of relationship Frankie wanted when the right person came along.

Rae excused herself and left the room to grab a drink.

Andrea took the opportunity to quiz Frankie further on her first murder case. 'You were about to tell me what the story was.'

'There isn't one yet . . .' Frankie said. 'Although Justine's diary makes interesting reading.' Rae reappeared and they stopped talking.

35

The minute hand moved forward a notch, the grandfather clock striking the eleventh hour. After an early swim, Alex and Tim had gone to vote, a big day for everyone in the UK, potentially a life-changing event, the referendum affording the nation the opportunity to influence Britain's future. But as soon as they returned from the polling station, Tim had hit the drink, all day and into the evening. As the hours ticked by, he'd become more and more combative and was making little sense. One minute he was raging about Daniel's disappearance, which he kept insisting was not his doing, the next lamenting Justine's death, a blow that seemed to have knocked him for six. Currently, he was rambling about other odd events, occurrences he was unable to explain, a long-winded account of old acquaintances giving him a wide berth, sending him private messages in reply to ones he'd never sent – abusive, most of them.

Tim was beginning to doubt his own sanity. He was leaking friends left, right and centre, not to mention clients, and the police didn't believe a word he said. Alex had suggested that he change his password, send a note to everyone in his address book, private and personal, letting his contacts know that his account had been hacked. 'You must nip it in the bud before it gets out of hand,' she'd said. 'You can't bury your head, hoping it'll go away. You need to get a grip.' Didn't the stupid cow think he knew that? His anger had flared and she'd backed down. He was painfully aware that something had to be done, but that bitch Oliver thought he was guilty whatever he said. She had him in her sights and had made it clear that she was gunning for him.

Alex had no sympathy for Tim. How could he blame DS

Oliver for suspecting him? He'd done himself no favours, bad-mouthing her the way he had, taking a swipe at her at every opportunity, belittling her. It should come as no surprise if the detective gave him a hard time. He needed to show some respect. When Alex told him that, he'd waved her away dismissively, asking her what the hell she was staring at. She'd kept her voice low, determined not to engage; she'd be wasting her breath when he was in such a black mood. At one point, he was yelling so much, she thought he might wake Daniel. She'd been forced to tell him to keep it down.

Glancing across the room, she studied her husband. He looked a mess: dishevelled, unshaven – a five o'clock shadow giving him a sinister appearance. It wasn't like him to let himself go. He was a far cry from the person she'd married three years ago. As far as she was concerned, his confusion was self-inflicted. She'd seen him popping pills when Stone and Oliver left the house last night, and again this morning, and had challenged him on it. He denied it, of course, but she suspected that he was too far gone to stop. He was beginning to act as if the whole wide world was against him – including her – and seemed hell-bent on making himself ill. Feeling under pressure from the police was only part of his mania.

Tim turned to face his wife. She looked dreadful. He reached out to her and then took his hand away, guilt eating him up. Her expression spoke volumes. Through the fog of booze and pills, he imagined her comparing him to Rob Scott, the creep she was once shacked up with, a drunk who used to climb into bed stinking of booze and expect her to respond to his advances. If he didn't get his way, he'd become abusive. And, if that didn't work, he'd turn violent. It pained Tim to think that she was now frightened of him. If Alex was drawing parallels with Rob Scott, Tim could see her point, but did she really think he'd done something wrong, something so terrible he might even kill for it?

With that worrying thought lingering in his mind, he

turned away, the thought making him flip. Telling Alex to go to bed, he poured himself another stiff drink. As he picked up his glass, he caught sight of himself in the blackened window, his reflection looking malevolently back at him. Justine's ghost stirred . . . Her voice forcing itself upon him: *Are you going to tell her, or will I?* That's what she'd said on her return from the police station, having been questioned over Daniel's disappearance. Standing there in the hallway, exposed and fearful, Tim had failed to hide his horror as Alex turned to face him.

Things had gone from bad to worse when Justine blurted out the DM revelation in front of his wife, accusing investigators of making her feel like a criminal. Tim had felt the ground shift beneath his feet. What choice did he have but to come clean? For a moment, he'd thought the au pair was going to say more – something he didn't want Alex or anyone else to know – then bottled out at the last minute. His world began to tilt . . . It was only a matter of time before it would collapse.

36

Frankie made numerous calls while waiting for Stone outside Newcastle Civic Centre where he was meeting the coroner. Her mind was in turmoil. Everything Andrea had said about the two drivers on either side of the humpback bridge checked out in terms of detail, though her assessment of the psychological effects of the 'accident' were way out. Audi driver, Trevor Taylor, was in a terrible state, according to his wife. He'd suffered delayed shock over the weekend, already undergoing treatment from his GP. Ford driver, Joanna Brent, on the other hand, had come to terms with what she'd seen and was in far better shape than Frankie had been led to believe she might be when they spoke on the phone.

Like any Monday morning, the city was busy, people rushing about their business, in and out of the local government offices and to Northumbria University opposite, students and lecturers laden down with books and heavy bags. To pass the time, Frankie had been rereading copies of Justine Segal's diary and address book, her father's mantra like an earworm inside her head: *Understand the victim; understand the crime.*

Digging into the victim's lifestyle was paying off. She'd learned things about the au pair that pointed to motive and she couldn't wait to share her findings with Stone. She glanced at her watch, wondering what was keeping him. He'd gone off to see the coroner in the hope of persuading her to release his brother's body for burial. He was desperate to get the funeral over and done with, for Ben's sake as much as his own. Though Frankie didn't know the details, Andrea had completed the accident investigation and submitted her report to the coroner, so why the hold-up?

Frankie was about to go back to her reading when the DI

appeared at the top of the steps. He shook his head as he walked towards her.

He'd drawn a blank.

'What's taking so long?' Frankie was irritated by the cruel delay.

Stone shrugged. 'Some issue with Luke's medical records.'

'What? That's ridiculous – he died in a car crash over a week ago.'

'It's not that simple.'

'Well, it should be.'

'The coroner is almost there, so stop worrying. I'd rather she got it right. There will be an insurance claim from Ben. As a student, he's dependent on his father for financial support. Now it's gone . . . well, I don't have to draw you a picture.' Stone took off his jacket, loosened his tie, suggesting they take a walk. They had a big day ahead of them, a briefing with the Murder Investigation Team already scheduled. He wanted a clear head.

'Has the lorry driver been charged?' Frankie had to know.

'Not yet.'

'Drunk?'

'Sober. But he's claiming a momentary lapse in concentration. However – and this goes no further – one eyewitness claims he was driving erratically, asleep at the point of impact, and there were no skid marks on the road, which would seem to back that up.'

'That's more like it.'

Stone stopped walking. 'Did you know that already?'

'No.'

'Andrea didn't say?'

'No. She didn't have to – it was obvious.'

'Not to me . . .'

Stone missed her indignation.

'For the record,' she said. 'Andrea has more integrity than that.'

Her boss had his hands up.

She waved away his apology. 'Did you complain about the adjournment?'

'No point. It's not the coroner's fault. As I said, there's an outstanding issue with Luke's medical records. She must satisfy herself that he didn't have any pre-existing medical condition that might have added to his plight. His GP has submitted a report to that effect, but the paramedic who treated him at the scene has since gone on leave. She wants a full dossier and, to be honest, I do too. They're chasing him today.'

They took a short ride to Jesmond Dene, a dense wooded valley packed with indigenous trees and shrubs. A continuous path led from one end to another – a distance a little over three kilometres – that crossed beautiful bridges and fast-flowing waterfalls, gifted to the city by philanthropist Lord Armstrong in 1883. It was one of Frankie's favourite escapes. Only a stone's throw from the city centre, it offered peace and tranquillity, a quiet haven for anyone who cared to visit.

They parked the car.

Stone made no move to get out.

He pointed at the papers on her knee, the pages of which were well-thumbed. He knew what it was. He'd asked her to skim through them while he was with the coroner. She hadn't wanted to bother him with it on the way into town and planned not to mention that she'd been up half the night going through them. She wanted to make him look good when he fed back to the Murder Investigation Team later.

'Are you any further forward?' he asked.

'I've not been idle, boss.'

'Did I say you had? I could hear the cogs turning on the drive here. And now you're smiling like a village idiot, so I'm guessing it must be good news. Your expression is verging on smug.'

She tapped the pages. 'The more I dig, the more convinced

I am that Justine's lifestyle led to her death. It's not the first time that it's got her into trouble either. Shall we grab a coffee and walk? I have a story to tell that'll blow your mind.'

While she went to fetch the drinks, Stone sat down on a bench at Pet's Corner, eyeing animals in pens, birds in the aviary. A lump formed in his throat as two little boys ran toward the cages and peered in, his nan's voice arriving in his head: *Keep your mitts out, they might bite!*

David took out his phone, checking his inbox for important information. He found none. No intelligence had come in that would progress their investigation. Forensic results would be a few days yet, so he hoped Frankie's input would give the MIT something to smile about. He looked up, watching her chatting to a couple she'd met on the way out of Millfield House Café, the dene's tearoom. Wherever she went, she seemed to bump into someone. In the office too, a crowd always gathered around her.

Would that he was as popular.

En route to Jesmond, Frankie had confided that morale was low among the outside team – those engaged in carrying out external enquiries on behalf of the MIT – the perception being that the case might turn out to be protracted, a depressing thought, given that budgets were stretched. Overtime was non-existent. In this period of austerity, Windy had an iron grip on the purse strings. He'd made it clear that he expected thrift from his new DI, regardless of his poncey new job.

Frankie arrived by his side, handing him a coffee in a paper cup. 'What's wrong? You were OK a moment ago. Now you've got a face like a slapped arse.'

He didn't react.

She was dying to share her news.

'Shoot!' he said.

'Before we get to Justine's journal, I had a very interesting conversation with Lady Veronica Knight while you were busy—'

'Justine's former employer is titled?'

'Yes – don't interrupt.' Her eyes sparkled with excitement. 'All that stuff Justine spouted about not wanting to go to Saudi is bullshit. She had an affair with Sir Geoffrey Knight and then tried putting the bite on him by threatening to tell his wife. He didn't give in to her demands. Instead, he confessed to his missus, sacked the au pair on the spot and resigned from the Foreign & Commonwealth Office, fearing a kiss-and-tell. The family hightailed it to Western Asia to lie low.'

'That's not what they told me or the agency.'

She glanced at him. 'Would you want to wash your dirty linen in public if you were that important?'

'I am that important!'

'Only to me.'

Stone flushed up.

Frankie stifled a grin. 'No wonder Justine wanted to keep her job. She had a nice little sideline going.'

'How did you get Lady Knight to cough?' Stone stepped aside to allow a group of joggers to pass by. 'Presumably she didn't volunteer information likely to be aired in future proceedings.'

'A minor irritation. She was prepared to talk, but off the record, David. I said I'd treat her as an informant.'

'On whose authority?'

'I called Windy.'

'And he agreed?' Stone was amazed.

'You know how he likes the landed gentry. You weren't around to ask and I needed to act. As soon as Lady Knight knew the information was safe and wouldn't be disclosed in open court, I couldn't shut her up.'

'So, what's with the worried face?'

'She threatened to have my warrant card if it ever gets out. We need to protect our source, David.'

'We? I wasn't there.' He was teasing her. 'Relax, Frankie. The worst that could happen is we both go down for contempt.'

His playful expression turned into a perturbed one. 'What were Sir Geoffrey and Lady Knight doing at three o'clock on Wednesday afternoon?'

'Boarding a Saudi Airlines flight out of Jeddah, which landed at London Heathrow at 17.40 BST, by which time Justine was already dead. I verified this with LHR passport control.'

'Why? Lying low, you said.'

'Wimbledon starts today. They have Centre Court tickets.'

'Nice. I assume you told them it's safe to stay?'

Frankie nodded. 'It wouldn't surprise me if they haven't already moved in. She detests it over there, apparently.'

Stone stopped walking. The Ouseburn was fast-flowing at this point and he stared into the bubbling water for a moment, then turned to face her. 'So what did you find out about Justine?'

'Um, first I think you owe me an apology.'

'For what?'

'You practically accused me of stereotyping when I suggested she was having an affair with her employer.'

'I did, didn't I—'

'Will I book the table, or will you?'

'Don't be too hasty. You need corroborating evidence.'

She took the papers from her shoulder bag. 'Knight isn't the only one in Justine's address book. Which brings us full circle . . .' What she meant was, her money was still on Parker, although his business partner, James Curtis, was also on that list. Suddenly, her case was hotter than Stone and she hadn't even got to the good bit yet.

37

DCI Gordon Sharpe, the Senior Investigating Officer in the Murder Investigation Team, had called a full briefing at Northern Command HQ, summoning all officers to attend. The incident room was packed, detectives and civilians paying full attention, everyone keen to find Justine's killer, remove a danger from the streets and eliminate the possibility of anyone else getting hurt.

At six foot five, Sharpe towered over those seated before him. He was an officer with many years' experience in his field of expertise, a detection rate any officer would be proud of. Calling for order, he assumed his position at the front of the room, taking a moment to introduce his guests who were standing by to update the squad. 'Many of you will know DS Frances Oliver,' he began. 'I used to babysit her as a kid. She was a pain in the arse then and I hear she hasn't changed much . . .'

A chuckle went around the room.

'These days she answers to Frank or Frankie but never Fran. So, those of you who want to keep your teeth, be warned.' The SIO smiled at Frankie before moving on. 'On her right is Inspector Andrea McGovern, Senior Accident Investigator, and, on *her* right, is DI David Stone who is handling the outside enquiry team. If any of you are wondering why, he's been investigating an alleged abduction involving Daniel Scott, the child Justine Segal was employed to look after. DI Stone recently transferred in from a Met murder squad, so we're lucky to have him assisting us.' Sharpe looked along the line. 'Welcome, all of you.'

'When was the abduction attempt?' a female DC asked, eyes on Stone.

'Daniel went missing on Friday, June seventeenth. His

disappearance may or may not be related to Justine's death.' Stone went on to explain. 'There was no attempt to grab the boy as such, more a misunderstanding – or so we're led to believe. The child was returned home safe and well the following day, the case written up as "No Further Action", *but* . . .' He stressed the word *but*. 'Given Justine's death, we're now keeping our options open. At this stage, we're undecided as to whether it's the boy's parents, Tim and Alex Parker, who are the targets, or the victim herself. Frankie will have more on that in a moment.'

Satisfied with his account, the SIO moved on. 'We have a lot to get through. Andrea, would you like to kick us off?'

'Yes, guv.' McGovern got to her feet and scanned the room. 'My input into your briefing sheet gives details of the incident we're dealing with. I don't propose to go over it. I can confirm that we are happy with the accounts given by both drivers at the scene and that their vehicles were in good condition. The drivers themselves, Trevor Taylor and Joanna Brent, were routinely breathalysed. We found nothing that would give us cause for concern, no drink or drugs, and they gave very similar accounts when questioned. My guys are at your disposal. We've done some house-to-house on your behalf, such as it is. There are only three small cottages nearby: East, West and Middle Cottage.'

'I wanna work in the sticks,' someone muttered.

'Don't we all,' a colleague added.

'East and Middle cottages were empty at the time of the incident,' McGovern continued. 'Both tenants were at work. That has been verified by their respective employers. However, the third tenant in West Cottage, Mrs Marjorie Smith, a lady of retirement age, is of interest to us. She claims to have seen a jogger pass her house shortly before patrol cars and paramedics arrived at the scene. She was unable to estimate how long before. It could have been ten, fifteen or even twenty minutes.'

'Are we sure this is our jogger?' Sharpe asked.

'Well, she was female, wearing a baseball cap and the same colour Lycra. Mrs Smith is definitely worth another knock in case she's remembered anything else we need to know.' McGovern nodded to the uniformed officer waiting for her signal. Using a remote, he activated a PowerPoint presentation on the wall behind the main speakers. An aerial image of the crime scene appeared on screen, allowing her to resume her delivery. 'Mrs Smith's cottage is south of the humpback bridge where the incident took place. The farm track to the north, on the opposite side of the road, leads into dense woods, as you can see.' McGovern turned back to her audience. 'The witness was at pains to point out that the clearing in the centre of the woods is frequently used as a lovers' rendezvous point. She walks her dogs there. Years ago, we would've expected local intelligence on this location. Nowadays there are so few patrols in rural Northumberland, the local copper who covers this section had no idea of this meeting place and therefore has no information to give. Not his fault. Ours is a vast county. He's too stretched to recce it all.'

Stone interrupted, his focus on Sharpe. 'Sir, it might be worth putting a couple of would-be lovers in the car park for a couple of days to keep observations – for reasons that will become clear when Frankie gives her feedback.'

The hands of several volunteers shot up.

The SIO told the assembled squad to behave.

Stone's smile was a cover for deep restlessness. Having once worked in a Major Incident Team, he missed the camaraderie of such a close-knit unit. It wasn't the same in general CID. It had its moments – and Frankie made it bearable – but he longed for a position where he could utilise the skills he'd developed in the Metropolitan Police. He'd been well-regarded down south, respected as an asset. His last case as a murder squad DCI was one he'd never forget. The sight of Alex Parker had brought it all flooding back.

'Can I just point out that I was not one of the first respond-ers,' McGovern continued. 'My involvement began when cause of death was determined as suspicious. The Home Office pathologist, Paul Mason, believes that an injury to the back of the IP's head is inconsistent with having been run over. The alarm was raised and I attended the scene, together with Mr Mason. Neither he nor I found anything that might have inflicted the injury to Justine's head and the PolSA team have yet to recover a weapon. The witness on the south side of the bridge, Joanna Brent, was very clear that Justine was lying in such a way that was unnatural had she fallen, as if she'd been placed there deliberately to ensure that she was run over. When my officers attended, they found the victim fatally injured. She had a set of wired earphones on her person, with no phone attached.'

'We need to find that mobile,' Sharpe said.

'Guv?' Frankie raised a hand. He gave her the nod to say her piece. 'If Justine's body was placed across the road to cover up a murder, why would the offender take her phone?'

'She has a point,' Stone said.

'Maybe it just hasn't been found yet,' the SIO suggested.

'I very much doubt that,' McGovern said. 'The search team were thorough. It's highly likely that Justine was dragged across the road for some distance. Her clothes were badly ripped and, although it was raining cats and dogs at the time she was attacked, we have since found a small amount of skin on the opposite side of the road that hadn't been washed away. We've yet to confirm that it's hers. I expect it's only a matter of time.'

'There is another explanation,' Frankie said. 'Her mobile may contain information the killer is trying to protect.'

Stone nodded in agreement.

'Sounds reasonable,' Sharpe said. 'Anything else, Andrea?'

'That's it for now, sir.' McGovern sat down.

'OK,' Sharpe said. 'I'd like to move on, if I may. Frankie,

the main thrust of the enquiry will now focus on information you've brought to the table, so the floor is yours.'

It was her cue to stand, her big moment.

'Has anyone not seen the briefing sheet . . .?' One hand went up and she passed a copy to the officer concerned before addressing the whole team. 'Your guv'nor tells me you can all read so, like Andrea, I intend to cover only what's not on it. The SIO is now in receipt of the victim's diary and an address book CSIs found in her bedroom. I've had a chance to study it. Taken together, the documents are illuminating. Justine had an interesting private life that included multiple and simultaneous sexual relations with men. Whether she used the woods Andrea referred to for her clandestine liaisons, we don't yet know, but it's a convenient location, very close to home.'

'We'll put someone in there,' Stone reassured everyone. 'We need a clearer picture of Justine's movements to add to her profile. Let's get one thing straight from the get-go: this information goes nowhere; it does not get discussed away from the incident room, in the staff canteen or anywhere else. I'd like you all to put away any personal opinions you will undoubtedly have on victim lifestyle. If the press get hold of it, they may take the view that if you lie down with dogs, you get up with fleas. Such prejudice has no place in a murder enquiry. Justine Segal deserves justice, no matter how many men she was shagging. Your only priority is to find her killer. Is that clear?'

There were no dissenters and he asked Frankie to carry on.

She waited for conversations to die down. 'Following our enquiries, we have reason to believe that Justine was prepared to use blackmail for monetary gain. We have it on good authority that she's tried this before.'

'The motive was to shut her up?' one detective asked.

'Possibly. She was sacked by her former employer for making demands with menaces—'

'I thought she had no form,' the SIO said.

'That's also correct. The offence never came to light as it was never reported to police. Her target dealt with the matter privately. He came clean to his missus and sacked Justine from his employ.'

'Justine didn't kiss and tell?'

'No, she upped sticks and moved north to work for the Parkers.'

A hand went up on Frankie's left. 'The briefing sheet mentions Daniel's former nanny, Maria Friedman. Are you going to be talking to her?'

Before Frankie could answer, Stone did it for her. 'Not at this stage,' he said. 'If something has equal importance then I'd put a team on each. If something is absolutely in your face, you drop everything else, take the baton and run with it. Justine's personal life appears to be key, so I'm interested in that, her digs, her car, the crime scene.'

'Frankie . . .' The SIO cut in. 'I want a quick result from the crime scene investigators. Can you chase that up?'

'Yes, guv.'

'Anything you'd like to add, David?'

'Only that, having had her hands burned once, we have no evidence to suggest that Justine tried it on a second time. The names on the list you are about to see were found in her address book. They correspond to entries in her diary. It's crammed with telephone numbers, mostly men. Frankie has worked her socks off in preparation for this meeting. She's had illuminating chats with one or two of them. This needs further investigation. Justine was a bit of a ladette on the sly. She liked to sleep around, got her kicks wherever she could find them. Any one of these men could potentially be the person we're looking for.' He uploaded the list on screen so everyone could see Frankie's diligence in black and white . . .

Gary Hamilton (building contractor)

James Curtis (employer's business partner)

201

Jan Eriksen (literary translator)
Marcus Shelby (restaurateur)
Robson Wise (solicitor)
Informant (subject to blackmail threats – eliminated)
Timothy Parker (current employer)

The list went on.

'Sir,' Frankie faced the SIO. 'Of those listed, two are extremely significant: Timothy Parker, Justine's current employer, and James Curtis, Parker's business partner. Either one could've received a blackmail threat, though neither has made a complaint. Curtis worked out of the office on Wednesday and has no alibi as such. Parker was off work too – which gives them both means and opportunity – though in *his* case, his wife has given him an out. She claims they were both in the house at the time. How reliable that alibi is, we're not sure.'

'And the others?'

'All have alibis apart from Wise and Hamilton. Wise met Justine in a pub in Stamfordham. He can't account for his whereabouts at the time of her death. Hamilton had done remedial work on her annex shortly after she moved in. He's the only manual worker among those on the list. Chronologically, he was her first northern conquest and she was still seeing him.'

A comment from the back. 'She must've liked a bit of rough.'

Frankie gave the officer a disparaging look and carried on. 'Justine rated her boyfriends in her diary. Gary scored a perfect ten, Parker eight, Curtis nine. Wise had a line crossed through him. She hasn't seen him since March.'

'Good work,' Sharpe said. 'Frankie, what do you propose to do next?'

'That's up to you and DI Stone, sir.'

'Put some pressure on the four you've identified. Start with the locals first, but bear in mind that anyone on that list may have more to tell us. We make no move until we're certain we have enough evidence to make an arrest and ultimately to charge.' Sharpe extended his thanks to Andrea, Frankie and Stone for such a comprehensive update. 'Final comments, DI Stone?'

Stone stood. 'There seems little doubt that the IP's death is in some way connected to a colourful private life.' He jerked a thumb at the list on screen. 'As you can all see, we have an informant who has since been eliminated from this enquiry. She is the wife of our blackmail victim. I intend to raise actions for everyone on that list. These men are now an absolute priority. Please bear in mind that those affected may not be willing to talk to us. It's up to you and your interview technique as to how much information we obtain from them. I don't care how long it takes. We need to know how many of her admirers experienced the nasty side of Justine Segal.' The meeting disbanded.

38

Detectives had worked solidly for two days, the SIO requesting an extension of his budget to take account of the wide line of enquiry Stone and Frankie had uncovered and agreed to undertake on behalf of Northumbria's Murder Investigation Team. Progress was painstakingly slow, but a picture was emerging of Justine's private life. She was a woman who simply enjoyed sex with no strings. Between consenting adults, there was no law against it.

No evidence had come to light to suggest that she was doing anything other than having fun and Frankie began to wonder if threats to her former employer were true or merely a figment of Lady Knight's overactive imagination. There was no doubt that her husband was in the air when Justine was struck down but Sir Geoffrey had point-blank refused to answer any questions. He declined to talk to Frankie and was rude when she got in touch, threatening to get his lawyer involved if she didn't stop harassing him. His attitude created a dilemma for the police, who needed to corroborate his wife's account, even though her evidence would be given under the radar. Although Lady Knight had agreed to have a word with her husband, Frankie had little faith that he would budge. Now his blackmailer was in the morgue, why would he?

Frankie took herself out for lunch, a short drive to the seaside town of Tynemouth. A brisk walk along the Longsands always did the trick; an opportunity to stretch her legs, important thinking time. This time Stone tagged along. They parked on the steep incline beside Crusoe's Café and walked north towards Cullercoats, the spire of St George's beautiful nineteenth-century church in the distance. They strolled along the shoreline in silence for a time, the sun warm on their backs, the thorny issue of Sir Geoffrey's refusal to cooperate sticking with Frankie despite her surroundings. It wouldn't surprise her if Lady Knight's motivation to tell all was driven by an ulterior motive. Maybe divorce papers were pending, in which case her disclosure was bound to increase any financial settlement; if Sir Geoffrey shared his misdeeds with the police, his wife could prove adultery.

Stone patted a dog whose owner was trying to get him to come to heel. Frankie looked on as it bounded away, then turned her attention to her boss. 'Can we compel Sir Geoffrey to tell us what he knows?'

'No point, is there? Besides, you're treating his wife as an informant—'

'And if she withdraws her statement?'

'We'll worry about that when the time comes. You didn't expect transparency, surely? Sir Geoffrey is no different from any of the other men we talked to. The married ones are bound to want to protect their relationships—'

'Then they should keep it in their pants.'

The DI didn't argue. 'Anyway, what Lady Knight said is no more than a hint to Justine's lifestyle. It points to a possible motive. When push comes to shove, we might not even use it. It would look bad for us if we blackened a victim's name unnecessarily. Justine didn't deserve a violent death, no matter how she got her kicks.'

Frankie wondered if David had ever been involved in a full-blown relationship, if a woman was his reason for moving south to join the Met. She'd had her moments with men. Never anything she could call serious, on the scale of Rae and Andrea for example, a relationship she'd watched develop from a deep and meaningful friendship. They were so well suited. Theirs was real commitment, the type Frankie was after, not some brief encounter she'd end up regretting a few months down the line.

Stone stopped walking when his mobile rang. As he went for his pocket, Frankie parked herself on a nearby rock, her face turned towards the blinding sun, the North Sea crashing to land behind her, a white foaming curl of power dissipating before vanishing into glistening sand. Stone was facing her, eyes on the horizon as he pressed to receive the call.

'Stone.'

'Detective Inspector David Stone?' A female voice.

'Who is this?' He'd not answer to his name and rank without knowing who was on the line.

'My name is Kathryn Tailford Irwin – Kat. I'd like to talk to you about my sister, Alex Parker.'

'In that case, give me a few moments and I'll call you.'

The DI hung up, telling Frankie who'd been in touch. He called the incident room. It was important to check this woman out, to establish that she was who she said she was. A crafty journalist might be playing games. As the English philosopher, Sir Francis Bacon, once said: knowledge is power.

The ringing tone stopped.

Stone identified himself. 'I need the mobile number you have on file for Kathryn Tailford Irwin . . . no, I'll hang on . . .' The office clerk was back in seconds. As she reeled off the number, he checked it against the one recorded as the last to call his mobile. Satisfied that it was the same, he thanked the clerk and dialled Irwin's number. As it rang out, he checked that no one was within hearing distance, beckoning Frankie closer. She shot to her feet, joining him as he tapped the loudspeaker so she could listen in.

'This is DI Stone, Ms Irwin. Please go ahead.'

'Thanks for returning my call, Detective Inspector.'

'No problem. How can I help?'

'I wouldn't have troubled you if it hadn't been important. I realise you must be extremely busy. The thing is . . .' She paused. 'This is delicate . . . Ali hasn't been altogether honest with you.'

'Ali is a pet name for your sister, I assume.'

'Yes, sorry. I had a terrible lisp as a child. Ali slipped off the tongue and it stuck.'

'In what way is she not being honest?'

Stone's eyes met Frankie's, a flicker of interest igniting into a full-blown fire. Secrets were gold to any detective. Informants prepared to break a confidence, even more so.

'You may be aware that we were recently on holiday together in Majorca,' Kat said. Stone confirmed that he was. He was beginning to lose the will to live and wished she'd get to the point. Finally, she did. 'One night we'd had a bit to drink. Ali made a confession that, I must say, didn't surprise me. She told me that when she was pregnant with her second child, she had her suspicions that Tim was cheating on her.' She paused. 'They lost the baby . . . I'm not sure if you knew.'

'Yes; I did.'

Kat Irwin hadn't taken a breath. 'Ali blames Tim for it. She said the stress was too much. She was terribly upset when I suggested that he and Justine might be taking advantage, carrying on behind her back. As drunk as she was, she refused to believe it, never mind accept it, even though I could see her wavering.

'And what was her response?'

'She said I shouldn't go making allegations without foundation.'

'That's good advice.'

'Yes, well, can we speak off the record?'

Frankie was nodding frantically, keen for the next instalment.

'Yes, of course,' Stone said.

Again, the woman hesitated. 'I have a friend who knows Parker intimately. He's a serial philanderer, Inspector. I warned Ali not to marry him, but would she listen? I suppose she told you about the other gold-digger she fell for. Tim may be more suited to her class-wise. Believe me when I say he's no different from Rob Scott, not really. I think Tim was at it with the housekeeper and I suspect he's lying about the DMs he sent to Justine and the family who kept Daniel overnight. Not to put too fine a point on it, I believe that my brother-in-law is playing games. I think he made my nephew disappear to punish Ali for the death of their child. He clearly resents Daniel.'

'Have you any proof of this?'

'None.'

'Then I'm afraid I can't help. These are very serious allegations—'

'I know . . . I also know how well-connected he is up there.'

'I hope you're not suggesting that he'll receive preferential treatment, Ms Irwin, because I can assure you that his status is immaterial. We are running a murder enquiry. In case you are in any doubt, that means no holds barred, no turning a blind eye and *no* mercy if it turns out that Parker is responsible for Justine Segal's death. Am I making myself clear?'

It seemed bizarre to have this damning a conversation in such surroundings. Frankie watched a couple of giggling kids race down the beach, their father chasing them into the water. One fell over and began to cry. The sea looked inviting but it was bloody cold.

Kat Irwin was back. 'We have different priorities, Detective Inspector. Ali is mine. She may appear as if she's coping but believe me when I say that she's falling apart at the seams. She needs your help. I'd come up, but she won't let me. Tim and I haven't always seen eye to eye, I'll admit that, but only because I know he's not right for her. She's afraid that my presence will make matters worse and neither of us wants that. To be honest, she's been avoiding my calls.'

'I'll talk to her, Ms Irwin.'

'Look, I know it sounds crazy – and I wouldn't blame you for writing me off as a crank. I'm extremely worried. Tim is microdosing LSD. Who knows what it's doing to him? I have a horrible feeling that he may be responsible for Justine's death. Ali won't thank me for dropping him in it but I'd never forgive myself if I didn't speak up and anything happened to her. And, in case you're wondering, I'm mindful of the fact that what I said also gives *her* motive for Justine's death. That's a chance I'm prepared to take, Detective Inspector. I love my sister. I know her better than anyone. She wouldn't hurt a fly. I'm not so sure about Tim. I think Ali and Daniel need your protection.'

She hung up, her final words echoing in the detectives' ears.

That meal Stone had offered Frankie was almost on the table.

39

'David, hang on a minute!' Frankie followed Stone off the beach and up the hill to their vehicle. 'We should take Kat Irwin's wild allegations with a pinch of salt. Far be it from me to defend her brother-in-law, but Justine didn't stop working for the Knights until the week before Christmas, days before Alex was due to give birth. If Parker was having an affair, it must've been with someone else.'

'Unless they were carrying on in London,' Stone peered at her through his Oakley sunglasses. 'Tim and Alex both have business in the south. They're regular commuters to the capital. Justine told me she'd met neither before she came here. She could have been lying. Maybe it wasn't the party city that drew her north, maybe it was Tim. I want you to study that diary forensically and find out exactly when she first mentioned him.'

'I'm on it. But don't you find it odd that Kat Irwin fingered her brother-in-law for Justine's murder – and her own sister, for that matter? The woman sounds poisonous.' Frankie raised a cynical eyebrow. 'She has "a friend who knows him intimately" – well, we've all used that one. I don't buy it, do you? OK, we know Parker was having an affair with Justine, but what if she's not the only one he's been taking to his bed?' She let the implication hang a moment. 'You said, he has business in the south. What if Kat Irwin was that business, or part of it? He certainly had the opportunity to be carrying on behind his wife's back. If Kat was messing with him too and was dumped for the au pair, it also gives her motive.'

'Make some enquiries, Frankie. We need to know her movements.'

Satisfied, Frankie climbed into the car.

Stone did likewise. Clicking his seat belt into place, he found reverse gear and pulled out of his spot to let a waiting beachcomber in. The female driver waved her thanks and threw him a beaming smile that gave Frankie the impression that she'd like to know him better. There were so many kids in the rear seat, the detective lost count.

As Stone's car reached the T-junction, Frankie's mobile rang.

She swore. 'Why is it always lunchtime when people want to talk?' She struggled to get the device from her pocket and didn't recognise the number. Curious to know the identity of the caller, she said, 'Mind if I take this?'

'No, you go ahead.' Stone turned right, heading for Northern Command HQ.

'DS Oliver?' A male voice.

'Who is this?' Like Stone, Frankie never confirmed her identity to strangers.

'It's Gary Hamilton. We spoke the day before yesterday, about Justine Segal.' He was the workman one of the guys back at base had called 'a bit of rough.'

'Aah,' she said. 'Your call is fortuitous. As it happens, I was about to give you a bell. I think it's time we had another chat about where exactly you were on the afternoon of Wednesday, June twenty-second.'

She mimed the name *Hamilton* to Stone.

'That's why I'm ringing,' Hamilton said. 'Remember I told you I was grafting in Gretna that day?' He sounded upbeat, excited almost.

Frankie readied herself for the alibi he'd had plenty of time to rehearse and hated herself for being so cynical. On the other hand, she didn't want the suspect too relaxed. 'There's nothing wrong with my memory, Mr Hamilton. In fact, I have total recall. You told me it was an empty property and that you were working alone with not one witness to verify your whereabouts.'

'I forgot, didn't I?'

'Forgot that you had someone working with you?'

'No. I'd filled up at the Gulf petrol station. I found the receipt in my van this morning. That's the God's honest, I swear. Do you know the garage?' He was too desperate to wait for her answer. 'If you're coming from the M6, take the first turning to Gretna, follow the signs to the Gateway Retail Outlet. You can't miss it. It's on the roundabout, Glasgow Road junction with the B721. I'm well-known in there. Ask anyone.'

'With respect, Mr Hamilton, I need more than a till receipt. You could've asked a friend for a favour, picked it up off the roadside or many a thing. On its own, it doesn't prove that you were miles away when someone was mowing down a defenceless woman on a lonely country road, does it?'

'The manager has CCTV showing my van entering the garage at two fifteen. He copied it for me. I tried to hand it in up there – the polis station is only a few hundred yards away. They wouldn't take it. They're Police Scotland, so I guess they have a point. Anyway, it has your name on it. It's as plain as day, I promise you: clear-cut proof that I was where I said I was when . . . when Justine died. All you need to do is pick it up. Cameras don't lie.'

'Unless they've been tampered with,' Frankie said.

'Gimme a break.'

'OK, Mr Hamilton. I'm prepared to give you the benefit of the doubt for now. Thanks for doing my job for me. Right now, I need all the help I can get.'

'You'll check it out?' He sounded hopeful.

'I will indeed. Where will you be this afternoon?'

'At home in Carlisle. You already have the address.'

'Fine, send me a jpeg of the receipt and hold on to the original. It might be your passport out of our investigation. One of my officers will be in touch with you and the garage.'

'Thanks.' There was a beat of time. 'DS Oliver?'

'No, Mr Hamilton. I won't say a thing to your other half. No letter will be sent to your home address.' Frankie wished she had a quid for every time she'd said that this week. 'I assume you have email so I can get in touch?' She scribbled it down as he reeled it off. 'If your receipt corresponds with the timing on the petrol station's CCTV, you'll hear no more from me. I have one further question: has your new-found alibi jolted your memory any? If you're out of the frame, you can be honest. Don't be shy.'

'I hate to speak ill of the dead.'

'Oh, go on. Everyone else has.'

Hamilton paused a second, as if uncertain whether Frankie was being serious. 'Justine was great, don't get me wrong, but she was always pleading hard up, wanting me to bring her stuff, tip her a few quid. I reckon it may have got her into trouble.'

As soon as he was off the line, Frankie made a call, putting the job out to one of her team, then turned to face Stone. 'It seems we're down to three.'

'Yeah, I heard. Who do you fancy seeing next?'

'Let's give the loser a whirl.'

The loser?

'Not-So-Wise.'

Robson Wise was understandably nervous about meeting the police. They met him in the Bay Horse public house in the quiet Northumberland village of Stamfordham, around eleven miles west of Newcastle upon Tyne. Ironically, it was the same establishment where he'd met Justine for the first time, allegedly. He was sitting waiting when they arrived, his expression downcast. A solicitor by profession, married for fifteen years, father to three children, he looked nothing like Frankie imagined he might. The man was unshaven, casually dressed in jeans and a pink polo-shirt. At forty-four years of age, it had to be said, he was not wearing well.

Stone took soft drinks over to where he was sitting, introduced himself and took the lead as bad cop. 'Mr Wise, when you and I spoke on the phone, you indicated to me that you'd met Justine Segal in this very pub purely by chance.'

His nod was almost imperceptible. 'That's correct.'

Stone sat down. 'Are you sure about that?'

'Yes.'

'Well, that poses a problem for us. Before we continue, let me give you a piece of advice. Don't be wasting our time. This is a murder enquiry we're dealing with. We're extremely busy and haven't the energy for games.'

Wise glanced at Frankie, prompting her to intervene.

'Mr Wise, we're coppers. It's not the first time we've come across men in your predicament in our line of work. For that reason, we understand where you are coming from. It's only natural for you to be secretive when it comes to your private life. DI Stone and I are willing to listen, but we require honesty and it's clear you've not told the truth so far.'

He didn't answer.

Stone tried again, this time more forcefully. 'If you were a criminal lawyer rather than one concerned with property, you'd understand that detectives have ways of finding things out. My colleague here,' he nodded in Frankie's direction, 'is about as good a detective sergeant as I've come across. Within seconds of talking to you the first time around, she discovered that the oldest of your children attends the same school as Daniel Scott, the young man Justine Segal was employed to look after, so my question to you is: who was stalking who?'

'What?' Wise was horrified by the suggestion. 'Listen, I'll put my hands up to having a brief encounter with Justine, but stalking? No. You've got this wrong. If anyone was doing the stalking, it wasn't me.'

Frankie had never seen a man so taken aback and, for reasons she didn't entirely understand, she believed him. It was time to play the sympathy card. 'Robson – can I call you Robson?'

He nodded.

'Stalking is perhaps too strong a word. I think what Detective Inspector Stone means is, your meeting in this pub was engineered. One of you made it happen. We really need to know which one.'

'Not me!'

'Was Justine here when you arrived?' Frankie asked.

'No, she followed me in. We got chatting at the bar and . . . well, you know the rest.' He looked away, embarrassed. When he turned to face them, there were tears in his eyes. 'I only saw her the one time, I swear.'

'That much we are prepared to accept,' Stone said.

Wise was visibly relieved.

'It fits with what we know,' Frankie explained. 'We examined Justine's diary.'

'To be perfectly honest, I wish I'd never set eyes on her.'

'But you did,' Stone said. 'So, let's start again, shall we?'

Wise took a deep breath, hesitating as someone passed their table. 'OK, I'll be straight with you.' He kept his voice so low it was hardly audible. 'Justine was nice to me. I was flattered. She let it be known she was up for it. In a moment of weakness, I let my guard down. That makes me sound like such a dickhead. You'll have heard it a hundred times but I've never done anything like this before in my whole life. I love my wife. My children, too. It will destroy my kids if this is made public.'

'Why didn't you tell us this before?' Frankie asked.

'Because if I admitted seeing Justine, I'd have been forced to offer an alibi for the time of her death. I was with my wife for the period in question and I knew you'd have to corroborate my account with her. I couldn't bear the misery that hearing it from you would cause her. I have since told her the truth and she's heartbroken.'

215

'I see,' Stone said.

'No, I don't think you do. My wife, Margaret, is terminally ill, Detective Inspector. She has months rather than years to live. My confession has hurt her terribly. I knew it would, which is why I didn't tell the truth initially. I couldn't have you going to the house without giving her some warning. God knows I owe her that much. I don't suppose it matters now I've finally plucked up the courage to tell her myself. If you must see her to verify my story, I beg you to make it as painless as possible.'

'You said you were with Margaret when Justine died,' Frankie said. 'Were you at home?'

'No. Margaret had an appointment with her oncologist at the RVI. I went along. It wasn't good news I'm afraid.'

Frankie's stomach took a dive. 'What's his name?'

'Stanley . . . that's a surname.'

'Then maybe we could get him to corroborate your alibi and not bother your wife.' She glanced at Stone.

He was nodding his approval.

Wise thanked them, his relief obvious to both detectives. 'If you could do that, I'd be forever grateful. Perhaps then she won't think I'm a murdering bastard as well as a total sleazebag.'

'Did Justine make any demands on you?' Stone asked.

'In what respect?'

'Money . . . favours?'

'No, as I said, I only saw her the once.'

There was a flicker of something behind his eyes that was upsetting him. The entries in Justine's diary popped into Frankie's head – his name crossed through. She'd taken that to mean that he wasn't a good screw, that he couldn't get it up and Justine was writing him off as a no-hoper. Or maybe that wasn't it. Frankie exchanged a brief look with Stone. She was going off-piste and didn't want him to interrupt.

'Where did you have sex with Justine, Mr Wise?'

216

The solicitor blushed. There was fear there too. He was dying of acute embarrassment and clearly didn't wish to answer. He wanted Frankie to stop. He hadn't figured on such an in-depth line of questioning. He'd had sex with a woman who was not his wife and now he was paying for it. What more was there to say? What did she want, blood?

'Robson?' Frankie waited.

'In my car.'

'In what location?'

He hung his head, then raised it again, terror in his eyes. 'A quiet spot she knew, close to where she was killed. I *swear* I was not there on the day she died.'

'And then you drove her back here?'

He nodded. 'Her car was parked right outside.'

'Was there any chat between the two of you?'

There it was again, that same despairing look. He turned his head away, blew out a breath. 'I got upset after we'd, y'know . . . To be honest with you, I was distraught, feeling like a shit for having cheated on my dying wife. I shared that with Justine. When we arrived, she just got out of the car and walked away.'

And crossed him off her list.

40

It was getting on for three o'clock. Frankie called the incident room, asking someone to contact Margaret Wise's oncologist urgently, then hung up and put the phone on the dash. Her thoughts were with the victim as Stone drove towards Parker's business premises. He and Curtis could both be there – only one, or neither. The element of surprise was what the detectives were after. As the countryside flashed by, Frankie shut her eyes, feeling the cool draught from the vehicle's air-conditioning caress her skin. It was one of the hottest days of the year so far, set to reach the mid-eighties in Northumberland. The rest of the country was experiencing a washout, as it had done for most of the month.

Crazy.

'What's going on in that head of yours?' Stone asked.

'Currently, it's a toss-up between the weather and Justine.' Frankie opened her eyes, turned the fan up to maximum, directing the stream of cool air to her upper body. 'It's too damned hot to think.'

'What about Justine?'

'She's a split personality, don't you think? Leaning on weak married men by night, using her sexuality to get what she wants. A fun-loving, caring au pair by day, adored by the children she helped raise, liked by almost everyone with whom she came into contact, except you – I know you had your misgivings.'

'Did I?'

'"Pleasant enough" were your exact words, as I recall. What woman, or man for that matter, wants *that* written on their tombstone? You may as well have called her invisible—'

'That's deep for you, Frank.' He reached across and placed

218

his left hand on her forehead, his brow creased in concern. 'You sure you're feeling OK?'

Frankie laughed.

It was good to see him on form, no easy task given that his brother's funeral hung over his head like a dark cloud. The thought made her sad, even though she'd never met Luke except in conversation with David. She thought she'd have liked him a lot.

'You've gone all melancholy,' Stone said.

'Have I?'

'Justine isn't the only woman of two halves I've encountered recently.'

Frankie acted as if there had been no break in her thought pattern. 'Don't you find it fascinating the way she crossed Wise off her list, just like that, as if the man was of no consequence?'

'Nice sidestep!'

She ignored the remark. 'He was an obvious target. Dying wife. Sex-starved. A worried man who needed, if not tenderness, then the physical release she was able to provide. He was easy pickings, David. Justine could've been in there had she played her cards right, and yet she chose to walk away. There was a lot of good in her, don't you think?'

'You make her sound like Maria to his Captain Von Trapp. You'll be breaking into "Edelweiss" next. I prefer Knopfler myself.'

She punched his arm. 'You're a cheeky git sometimes.'

'I had no idea you were so cerebral.'

'Er, what does that mean again?'

James Curtis didn't seem surprised to see a police presence at his business premises, or that they were double-crewed. His office overlooked reception. Even through the reinforced glass wall, Frankie could tell that he was nervous. The lad with the floppy hairstyle took one look at her and decided not to argue. He glanced over his shoulder, a hint to his boss that his attendance was required. The executive got to his feet. Seconds later, the door opened and Curtis walked through it, confirming that he'd see Stone and Oliver without an appointment.

Big of him.

The alternative was worse.

'I was expecting you.' Curtis shook hands with both officers. 'Come through.'

They all took a seat in the boardroom, Frankie taking care of the introductions. This was the first time that Stone had met Parker's business partner. For a moment there was silence, two professional males checking each other out, forming impressions, getting ready to do battle, or so she thought. What happened next was gratifying. Life was good sometimes.

'I assume you're here about Justine Segal?' Curtis said.

'Yes,' Stone said. 'And we expect your full cooperation.'

'And you'll have it.' Curtis linked his hands in front of him, elbows on the table. For a man under suspicion, he appeared relaxed. 'I began seeing her in February. Once a week, once a fortnight. Nothing heavy. What can I say? She was fun and unattached. I was neither of those things.' He caught Frankie's bored expression. 'Don't concern yourself, DS Oliver. I won't trot out the sob story that my wife doesn't understand me. She understands me perfectly – if that's what you're worried about.'

Frankie held his gaze. 'DI Stone and I are grateful for your honesty, Mr Curtis. It makes our job easier.'

The man sighed. 'I was saddened to learn of Justine's death, of course. More so when I read in the newspapers that it was murder. I knew you'd get to me eventually, given that I couldn't account for my whereabouts at the time of her death. Fishing is a solitary pursuit mostly. No CCTV on the riverbank that would let me off the hook. No pun intended.' He smirked.

'A woman died,' Frankie said. 'There's no room for humour here.'

Stone cut her off. 'What was Justine like?'

'Didn't you meet her while investigating Daniel's so-called disappearance?'

'Yes, but not in the same context. I never saw, shall we say, the side of her that you did.'

'She was unlike any woman I've ever come across.' In terms of eye contact, Curtis was favouring Frankie. 'She understood the difference between raw sex and commitment. I liked that she wasn't needy and felt safe in the knowledge that she wouldn't grass me up to my wife. Justine was after a good time, not love.'

Ignoring his rhetoric, Frankie said, 'Think carefully. Are you absolutely sure of your dates?'

'Of course, or I wouldn't have said so.'

Curtis had no idea where Frankie was heading or, if he did, he didn't show it. Stone's words arrived in her head: *I want you to study that diary forensically and find out exactly when she first mentioned him.* He'd been talking about the possibility that Justine had met Parker before she came north to work for him. That theory could equally apply to the man they were interviewing now. There was no evidence to that effect in her diary. Her enquiry needed answering.

'Perhaps I'm asking the wrong question,' Frankie said.

'Only you would know.'

'When did you first meet her?'

'Sometime in early January, shortly after she began working for Tim.'

'Are you certain about that?' Frankie wanted to know. 'We have a strong suspicion that she may have chosen to come north for more than employment with your business partner. I thought perhaps it might have been you.'

'It wasn't.' Curtis dropped his hands into his lap. 'Though I'd have been flattered if that had been the case.'

Frankie ploughed on. 'Were you aware that she was seeing other men?'

'I'd be surprised if she wasn't. I never asked and she didn't tell me. It was not my business.'

'She never talked about it?'

'Why would she? There was nothing complicated about Justine. When you were with her, life was simple. She had the knack of making you feel like you were the only man in the world. Our meetings were about freedom of expression: good food and wine, sparkling conversation, great sex.'

'In the woods in the back of a car? Do me a favour.'

Curtis's lip curled.

The arrogant prick thought he was so cool. Frankie wasn't buying his bullshit. Even in clandestine relationships, there would be something about the other party that got up your nose, if only occasionally. She needed to exert pressure on the businessman but wasn't entirely sure how to go about it. As he carried on talking, she listened. It was all too pat, as if he'd rehearsed it over and over. Well, Frankie wasn't into amateur dramatics.

Time to rip up the script.

'Why were you so sure she wouldn't grass on you?'

'I knew, that's all.'

'She told you that, did she? And you believed her? With respect, Mr Curtis, before February she was a perfect stranger to you. Regardless of the simplicity of your relationship, you couldn't have known that she wouldn't change her mind and drop you in it. And yet it was a chance you were prepared to take?'

'I told you, she was a free spirit.'

'And that didn't worry you?'

'Not for a nanosecond. I trusted her.' Curtis picked up the jug of water Floppy had just brought in. 'Hassle-free is the way I roll.'

'Will there be anything else, James?' the receptionist said.

'No, thank you.'

Floppy disappeared.

As Curtis poured himself a glass of water, Frankie exchanged a look with Stone. He'd sat quiet for much of the interview, studying the suspect, allowing her free rein. He pulled his phone from his pocket. When he looked up, she saw a flicker of excitement in his eyes but had no time to dwell on what might have occurred.

She turned to face the businessman. 'Did Justine ever ask you for money?'

'She wasn't a prostitute.'

'That's not what I asked.'

'It's what you implied.'

Frankie waited.

'Then no,' he said. 'Though I got the distinct impression that money was important to her. She liked the idea of wealth. So do I, so let's not hold that against her. It buys the best tables in restaurant, the best seats at the theatre—'

'But not the best men.' Frankie was taking the piss, letting him know what she thought of the egomaniac, hoping to provoke him into saying something he might regret. Curtis was too clever for that. 'So,' she moved on. 'You were entirely confident that you would get away with your extra-marital affair—'

Curtis smirked. 'You're not married, are you, DS Oliver?'

'That's beside the point.'

'Is it? Do you have any idea how many married people, men and women, have affairs? If you asked them all why, you'll get the same answer. It was a risk they were prepared to take. We're a naïve bunch. It never occurred to me that Justine would blow the whistle. Most single women who play the game like to keep quiet about it, for obvious reasons.'

'So, if I was to ask your wife about your infidelity it would come as a shock?'

At last, a reaction.

Frankie one – Curtis zero.

She hated arrogant men. Curtis was degree standard. That didn't bother her. Interviewing suspects was what fired her jets. Nothing else came close. In a battle of wills, he'd never win.

'What is it you want, Detective?'

'The truth.' She allowed a beat of time to pass. 'How did it sit with your business partner that you were seeing his au pair?'

'I'm not sure what you mean.'

'It's a simple enough question. Presumably, you told him about it.'

'No. Why would I?'

'You really expect me to believe that?'

'Believe what you like. It's the truth.'

'There was no banter between you over how good she was in bed, in the back of the car, in the woods, wherever it was you were screwing her?' Frankie wondered how many names had been taken by the surveillance team the SIO had deployed in the woods. She didn't believe that Justine was the only person who used that spot as a meeting place. 'C'mon, Mr Curtis. I work in a male-dominated organisation. I've witnessed the male ego first hand. Women have been handed the gossip label, but I know how much guys like to talk.'

'Sorry to disappoint. That's not my style.'

'Did you ever visit Justine at her annex?'

'No, never.'

'OK.' Stone took over. 'Let's move on.'

Frankie tried not to show her frustration. She'd barely started. Her DI's intervention had been swift and, she suspected, triggered by Curtis's denial. Stone wouldn't wish to dwell on the fact that they were waiting on DNA results. He'd put in a fast-track request but Frankie wasn't hopeful. Like Windy, Detective Superintendent Sharpe was being frugal where his budget was concerned. He wasn't tight, but neither was he generous. It was the taxpayer's money he was spending after all.

Curtis was clever enough to know that if the detectives had evidence against him, he'd be on his way to the station for questioning. It was only a matter of time before they would establish if he'd been telling the truth. It was important to keep up the momentum.

Stone fired off a question. 'When DS Oliver interviewed you the first time, you said that your company was in financial crisis. Can you elaborate on that? The reason I ask is that Alex Parker seems to have no idea whatsoever that your business is in trouble.'

Curtis bridled. 'With respect, what has that got to do with Justine?'

Stone stared him down. 'I'm asking the questions.'

'As you wish. I've examined the business accounts and discovered that a lot of money is missing – a regular payment going out to an offshore account I had assumed was owned by Alex.'

'Who signed off on it?'

'Tim did.' Curtis hesitated. 'We had an arrangement to repay her stake in our business and I didn't question it until we got into difficulty.'

'And now?' Stone asked.

'That's a matter for me, Tim – and our legal representatives.'

'OK, we'll leave it there.'

As they walked away, Stone pulled out his mobile and showed it to Frankie. Sharpe had been in touch. Wise was in the clear. His wife's oncologist had confirmed his attendance at the hospital while he delivered some devastating news. The couple were captured on CCTV at the main entrance to the RVI fifteen minutes before the appointment. That left Parker, Curtis and Hamilton still in the mix.

41

Alex was suffocating, something damp and heavy pinning her down. She sensed her parents before they came into view. They looked blissfully happy but their joy was short-lived. Their smiles faded as she approached. Alex watched them drift away. An attempt to follow was thwarted by something tangled around her feet, preventing her from breaking free. She stopped struggling when she lost sight of them. A crowd appeared in their place, no more than dark blobs in the distance, getting closer. That's when the whispering began, the voices multiplying the nearer they got, all talking at once.

'Stop!' Alex yelled.

You'll NEVER leave . . .

'Get away from me, Rob! Daniel, come to Mummy.'

He's no good for you . . .

Alex snapped her head around. 'Mind your own business, Kat.'

Daddy and I are delighted for you, darling . . .

'Mum? You came back!'

Are you going to tell her, or am I?

'Tell me what, Tim?'

Alex recoiled as a hand touched her shoulder, squeezing gently, then it was gone. A dark, forbidding shadow whipped across her face, blocking out the light, but not the heady scent of jasmine and patchouli. Sensual. Deliciously overpowering. Familiar and yet not so.

The shadow returned, hovering over her.

'Justine? What are you doing there?'

Her flowing red dress fluttered upwards in the breeze, exposing shapely legs, like the fifties image of Marilyn Monroe's iconic flying skirt. A wide smile lit up Justine's happy face.

With outstretched arms, she began to fly, soaring like a bird across deep blue sky. Alex wanted to join her. She couldn't move. Kicking out didn't help. Her shackles held fast, then suddenly she was free. The red dress was gone – Justine along with it.

A peculiar sensation enveloped Alex, a drug-induced coma-like state where she could see and hear but was power-less to manoeuvre any of her limbs. She felt weightless, cast adrift in the space between slumber and wakefulness, almost there but not quite. She floated in the confusion between the loathsome reality of consciousness and the safety and security of sleep, a feeling of desperation creeping over her. A warm tear rolled down her cheek. Her eyes blinked, open and shut, drawn to a pinprick of light on the horizon. Every step closer to the shiny star produced two backwards. The darkness was strangely comforting, whereas the luminosity stung her eyes, like piercing shards of jagged glass.

Alex rolled over, senses on high alert, intensely aware of danger. Something was wrong. Drenched in sweat, she slid a hand across the mattress. Tim was missing, his side of the bed cold. Lifting her head from the pillow, she craned her neck to see the blue digital display on his clock-radio: 05:57.

More whispering, closer than before . . . this time real, not imagined, a threatening tone, muffled through her bedroom door.

Alex turned to face it, propping herself up on one elbow, straining to hear what was being said – and to whom. It was impossible to make it out. She tried not to panic. Tim had always been a light sleeper. This morning, she understood why he might be up and about early: James Curtis had called him at midnight, off his face and ready for a fight, ranting on about Stone and Oliver's appearance at the office earlier in the day. The main thrust of his call was to tell Tim that their partnership was over. No longer interested in rescuing the business, he was suggesting they file for bankruptcy. The row lasted a good half-hour, Curtis wanting to throw in the towel, Tim dead against such a drastic course of action. They were bulls locking horns . . .

Her husband's fury arrived in Alex's head, albeit a one-side conversation, what she could remember of it: *Over my dead body! Are you fucking crazy? The courts will sequestrate our assets. We'll lose everything. The credit-rating we've spent years building up will be wiped away in an instant. You and I need to talk, James. You do nothing, you hear me, nothing until I return from London.*

Alex rolled over on her back. She agreed wholeheartedly with her husband's point of view. What Curtis suggested last night was insane, bankruptcy a very last resort. There were alternatives the two men should consider first. Never had she seen Tim so livid. And when she tried to advise him, a gentle tug on his arm to attract his attention, he'd pushed her away, telling her to keep the hell out of his business. It was the first and last time he'd lay hands on her.

Then, as now, it made her think of Rob.

When Curtis hung up on Tim, her husband had flown into a rage, throwing his whisky tumbler across the room where it smashed against the wall. As Alex bent to pick up the pieces, she'd asked him when he was planning on telling her about his financial problems. *I wasn't*, was the answer he gave, then he rounded on her, yelling at the top of his voice: *That fucker's been raking off money left, right and centre and he's not getting away with it. I was handling it without worrying you—*

But she was worried: about Daniel's future, her marriage, her beautiful house. Tim had reassured her that they wouldn't lose it. The way things were going, a small villa in Majorca was all they would afford. Eventually, Tim calmed down, apologising for his behaviour. To make amends, he got down on his hands and knees to help her clear up.

It'll be OK, Alex.

It didn't sound OK.

The row beyond the bedroom door continued. For the first time since she'd fled from Rob Scott, Alex's future looked bleak. Since Majorca, her perfect life had disintegrated. Bizarrely, what was happening was even more frightening to her than physical abuse.

Her nerves were frayed by it.

She crept out of bed and tiptoed to the doorway. As she leaned towards it, her husband raised his voice, a threatening nasty tone that was increasingly becoming the norm. Before she could identify the target of his aggression, the alarm on her bedside table went off. She shot back to bed and shut her eyes as the door creaked slowly open.

42

Alex wasn't the only one who was disturbed; Stone was too – by his own emotional rage. His relationship with his nephew had never been good. Now it was even more strained and uncomfortable. David was childless – the way he liked it – and Ben had thrown a grenade into the room. A bit of emotional blackmail when his uncle's guard was down. Well, it wouldn't wash, family or not.

He waited for the lad to stop his whining. 'You've got a neck, asking for bed and board,' he said. 'I have neither the time nor the inclination to listen to you. Neither do I have the space to put you up, which you might have found out, had you ever visited your great grandmother for longer than the time it took for her to open her purse. How long did it take you to spend your inheritance, Ben? A week? A fortnight?'

'I'm not asking to live with you. I just need a crib till I get myself sorted.'

'It's a bit late for that, isn't it?'

'Uncle Dave—'

'Drop it, son. You're wasting your breath. I'm running a murder enquiry here and you're tying up a very busy phone line. I suggest you bunk in with one of your university mates. Believe me, you'll have more in common with them than you do with me.'

Stone looked up from his desk. Frankie had a face like thunder. She'd be giving him earache over this later but he couldn't help that. She wasn't his mother – although she acted like it sometimes – and she only had half the story. He and Ben had history, the kind the DI could do without. The lad was a selfish, self-opinionated waste of space who didn't give a shit about anyone but himself. He'd made the last years of his father's life a misery and Stone wasn't about to hand the lad the opportunity to do the same to him. Luke had been so worried about his son he'd resorted to asking advice on how to handle him. Together, the brothers had dug Ben out of many a hole, only to discover that he'd found a new hole to plunge into the minute their backs were turned.

Ben was muttering down the line.

'Speak up,' Stone said. 'I can't hear a word you're saying.'

'I said I can't move in with them.'

'Why doesn't that surprise me?'

'Please, Dave—'

'I told you already. No one likes a loser, least of all me. And while we're on that subject, you show an appropriate level of respect to your father this afternoon or I'll have something to say about it. You dress up, you hear me? Suit, black tie, clean shoes.'

'I'm not in the fucking army.'

'I'm warning you! You turn up wasted and, believe me, Luke won't be the only one they put in the ground.'

'Boss!'

A black look shot across Stone's desk like an Exocet missile, stopping him in his tracks. Frankie flicked her eyes towards a huddle of detectives, a heavy hint that his uncharacteristic loss of control had drawn, not only her attention, but the entire team's. He slammed the phone down, got up and walked out.

So, Mr Cool had left the building. Frankie was horrified by what she'd heard. Stone was bigger and better than that. How could he be so cruel, turning his nephew away when his father hadn't yet been laid to rest? The boy was an orphan who needed help and Stone, his next of kin, the only close family around to offer it. Frankie glanced at the door. The temptation to charge out of the room and confront him was overwhelming. It was also dangerous.

Still . . .

231

She got to her feet, pushing her chair away from her desk, gathering up her mobile. She wandered over to a nearby desk. 'If anyone asks, I'm incommunicado.' She was about to leave the room when her internal telephone rang. Trotting to her own desk, she snatched it up.

'Oliver.' It came out like a bark.

'Blimey, Frank! Did someone slap you with a complaint?'

'Have you got something for me or not, Mitch? Because if you haven't, piss off and bother someone else.'

'Yes, Sarge.' Mitchell wound his neck in.

'C'mon then, out with it.'

'I've been out to see Marjorie Smith, the retired lady who lives at West Cottage, near the crime scene. She's not sure about the jogger she saw. It could've been Justine. Equally, it could have been someone else. She's sure it was a female and the clothing she described fits. She also remembered seeing a cyclist that no one else seems to have spotted.'

'Any update on the missing phone?'

'None, although her service provider confirmed it's not been used since the morning of her death.'

'Did you check on her bank account like I asked you?' When Curtis mentioned large amounts of money leaving his business account, it had Frankie wondering if Justine had set up an offshore account for the sole purpose of fleecing her men friends. It was a long shot, but the detective sergeant needed a break.

'Her agency has only one account listed for her at a West-minster branch of Santander.'

'Did you call them?'

'Yeah.'

'Let me guess, they fobbed you off?'

'Quite the opposite. The manager was very cooperative now that her customer is deceased. There have been no trans-actions from Justine's account to an offshore bank or any other foreign financial institution since she started banking there ten years ago. The account was opened in her hometown in France. They're sending us a printout with all the details.' Mitchell paused. 'Can you hold a minute? Gaynor just walked in. I'm worried.'

'Why?'

'She has a smile on her face.'

Frankie laughed, her dark mood slipping away.

Gaynor (who half the shift called Gloria) was the office gopher who never cracked a smile unless there was a cream cake or an almond Magnum on the go. A lovely girl but with little or no sense of fun. Mitchell had moved the phone away from his face. Frankie could hear them talking.

'You're welcome,' Gaynor said in that sulky voice of hers that made it sound like she was being ironic. She walked away, high heels click-clacking on the wooden floor.

Mitch was back: 'I swear, every time I see that woman "I Will Survive" is like an earworm in my head. As it happens, it was worth it today. She brought good news, Sarge. I now have in my possession a very late forensics report.'

'Well, get cracking and tell me what's inside.' She heard Mitchell shuffling papers. There was a long pause while he scanned the document. 'Looks like we're on! Five sets of prints in the IP's annex and a couple of partials. We've got a match with Daniel Scott and Timothy Parker in her digs *and* in her car.'

'Yes!' Frankie punched the air.

Life was good sometimes.

'Hang on, Mitch.' Frankie lifted the papers on her desk, searching for a plan of Justine's living quarters. 'C'mon!' she whispered under her breath. 'Mitch, where in the flat were the prints found?'

'On both sides of the architrave of the door adjoining Parker's home. The prints are high up. It's as if he's stood in the doorway, arms at head height, hanging on to both sides. And there's more in her bedroom.'

Frankie glanced at Stone as he re-entered the incident room and went on with her call. 'Where in the bedroom?'

'On a mobile phone charger and on a small bedside cabinet.'

Frankie found the plan she was looking for and opened it out on her desk. It showed the annex. Her eyes located the bedroom. 'Which cabinet? There are two.'

'On the east side of the room.'

'Furthest from the door, then?'

'That's the one.'

'Any DNA?' Frankie held her breath.

'Give us a sec.' Mitchell turned the page.

Her half of the conversation prompted Stone to wander over and join her. She wasn't ready to talk to him and pretended that she was listening to her caller. Picking up a pen, she drew a cross on both sides of the door and a little box representing the phone charger on the relevant bedside cabinet, scribbling the word PRINTS next to them as Mitchell's voice arrived in her ear.

'There are multiple – unidentified – samples in the vehicle, including semen. There's a DNA match to Parker in her bed, not in her car.'

'Semen?'

'No.'

Frankie pencilled a big cross in the centre of the bed and wrote *Parker's DNA – no semen* for Stone's benefit. It wasn't enough to get him or her excited. 'The boss is here now. Is there anything else we need to know?'

'There's a handwritten note attached: the SIO has ordered an urgent forensic report on the unwashed sheets taken from the laundry in the main house.'

'About time,' Frankie said.

'We should have a result on that soon.'

'Scan and email the results you have.'

'Doing it now.'

'Thanks.'

Frankie hung up.

Stone looked at her. 'We've got him?'

'We've got him for lying about being in the annex, boss.'

'What's with the formality, Frankie?' A wry expression crossed his face. 'Anyone would think you were angry with me.'

'I think you're a prize twat, but that's beside the point.' Frankie didn't stop for breath. She was cross. Not only with him. 'Sharpe has fast-tracked the remaining samples we retrieved from the Parkers' laundry. I don't think we should interview the suspect without all the facts to hand. If it were my call, I'd wait for the results. There's not one shred of evidence linking him to the murder.'

That suited Stone. He had a funeral to attend.

43

It was freezing in the crematorium as David Stone climbed into the pulpit under the scrutiny of a sizeable congregation, gathering his resolve. Ben was as smart as a button in the front pew – as he'd asked him to be – if in a mess emotionally, ill-equipped and far too young to come to terms with the death of his remaining parent. Knowing what it felt like to lose both of his – in David's case at the same time – an unspoken message of empathy passed between them. Regretting their row earlier, David had resolved to draw a line under their difference of opinion and help him. Frankie hadn't said anything about his loss of control at the office, probably deciding that it was unwise to intervene where family were concerned. He appreciated that.

He needed an ally, not an enemy.

His eulogy was heartfelt and amusing in places, delivered with pride and love for a brother taken long before his time. 'He was a great guy,' David said. 'The best brother anyone could wish for. When our parents died, our nan took us in. For years, we shared a bed in her tiny cottage. As kids, we were inseparable, aspiring to become policemen when we grew up. They were happy days . . . Playing detective in nearby woods . . . Inventing bodies to find . . . Using our nan's magnifying glass to examine imaginary crime scenes.'

Stone faltered momentarily.

He couldn't go on . . .

He must.

'Later in life, Luke's future took a different turn when he met Ruth and became a proud father to Ben. Ruth was the love of his life and he was devastated to lose her. We remember her today . . .'

A sob took his attention.

His eyes flew in the general direction.

Luke's sister-in-law, Ben's aunt, had travelled from Australia to pay her respects. The arms of those flanking her gave comfort. There were tears and stoical faces among the congregation. Some had already spoken about Luke's popularity. He was outgoing and gregarious, not a loner like David, someone said.

David moved on to mention his migration south: 'It was the best and worst time of my life, a period when I got sidetracked, locked inside my own little bubble, paying less attention to my family than I should . . .' His voice broke, a big lump forming in his throat. 'Luke was always there for me. He never put pressure on me to come home, though I knew he wanted it . . . I only needed to hear his Geordie accent and I'd be booking the next train home, if only for a few days . . .' Some mourners chuckled. Mostly local, they knew exactly what he meant by it. The pull of Northumberland was strong. 'And when I finally did, it meant everything to me. The past few months will live with me forever . . .'

A single tear dribbled down David's cheek.

When he mentioned Luke's joy that *he* was back on Geordie Mean Time, David saw Frankie wiping her eyes, remembering how mercilessly she'd ribbed him about what he'd missed: the county, the music, the people. Apart from Luke, she alone knew what it meant for him to be back where he belonged.

Their eyes met briefly.

She was standing with Andrea. It was probably his momentary loss of control that had upset her. Having done his brother proud, David was on the move. There was not a dry eye in the crematorium, including his own. It was only when people filed from the chapel that he really caught the sadness in Frankie's eyes. She gave him a hug and walked out into brilliant sunshine.

*

Finally, the family were free to exit the chapel, released from the excruciating agony of extended commiserations, a tradition Frankie had never fully understood. The occasion was hard enough to bear without adding to it. Andrea left immediately, a duty call. Frankie hung around on the fringes of a dissipating crowd: heading to work, heading home, some walking off through the archway of the central clock tower and into the Garden of Remembrance, taking a moment to remember Luke, Ruth and others who'd gone before.

There would be no tea and sandwiches. No sherry or cake. David wanted the service over and done with as quickly and as painlessly as possible so they could all move on. Frankie didn't disagree. She was about to approach him when she noticed Ben heading in his direction. Sensing his urgency, she stepped away, sheltering from the sun under the shadow of a tree.

As the two males came face to face, David embraced Ben warmly, a gesture of reconciliation, then stepped away. They didn't see her but Frankie was close enough to earwig their conversation. She was so proud of David for reaching out to him inside the chapel. Then it all went tits up . . .

Ben's tears had been replaced by bravado. 'Do I measure up then?'

David didn't rise to the provocation. It was obvious to Frankie that he didn't want to engage in round two. Not here surrounded by bereaved relatives. Ben lit a cigarette. He took a few drags, blowing smoke high into the air. Frankie could smell weed. The dynamics between man and boy changed instantly.

Jesus! The stupid sod had just blown any chance of harmony. What the hell was he thinking? Frankie was about to find out.

David's friendly eyes turned cold. 'Must you?'

'Yeah, I must.'

'Put it out!'

'Or what?'

David glared at him.

Fine!' Ben threw the cigarette on the ground, stubbing it out with his foot, hell-bent on being a dick.

'Pick it up,' Stone said.

Ben thought better than to argue, slipping the roach end into his pocket. 'So, what happens now?'

David had no time to respond.

A straggler arrived, hunched over, walking with the aid of a stick. A brief respite. More sympathies. The woman was old. Frankie would be surprised if she hadn't already received her telegram from the Queen. David bent almost double, embracing her warmly, a benevolent hug, a sympathetic smile.

It was a poignant scene to witness.

A young man drove up and got out of his vehicle, apologising for the time it had taken him to get out of the car park. He shook hands with David, took the lady's arm and led her towards his waiting vehicle. The DI watched them drive off before turning his attention to his nephew.

'I still need a bed,' Ben said.

'Not my problem. I told you, it'll never work.'

'And I told you I can't bunk in with mates.'

'Why not?'

'I dropped out.'

'Well, you'd better drop back in and sharpish!' David's attitude was confrontational now, his tone scathing. 'Were you born clueless or are you trying really hard? When your compensation case goes to court – because it will – you'll be expected to prove your commitment to your university course or you'll get bugger all in terms of a settlement from the arsehole who was driving that lorry.'

'I'm finished with uni—'

David was livid. 'Pat yourself on the back, son. Your dad would be real proud. You finally got what you wanted.'

'What's that supposed to mean?'

'It means you're on your own.'

David walked toward his nephew and leaned in. 'Listen to me, you piece of shit! Of the many bad moves you've made in your relatively short and aimless life, this one takes the biscuit. Have you *any* idea how much your mother wanted you to get a proper education? How much your father sacrificed to put you through university?'

Ben didn't answer.

'No, I didn't think so. What exactly is it you want from me?'

'You said you'd sort out probate.'

'Give me one good reason why I should.'

'You're family—'

'Not any more.'

If Ben thought David was finished, he was sadly mistaken. The DI was building up to something, Frankie could tell. As if he sensed a presence, he glanced in her direction and seemed surprised to see her standing there. Clearly, he'd forgotten that she'd driven him to the crem. Without breaking his rhythm or changing stance, he turned to face his nephew. 'Your dad's place is worth a few quid. It should make you a tidy profit and you'll be sorted. Is that the plan?' He narrowed his eyes. 'You're a property tycoon now, right? *Wrong.*'

Ben's cocky stance fell away. 'What's that supposed to mean?'

'It means you should check in with your solicitor before you book that cruise.' David was readying himself to leave.

'I'm his next of kin. He can't do that!'

'He can and he did. It's his last gift to you, Ben. All legal and above board, signed in the presence of his brief, i's dotted and t's crossed. Any provision he made for you comes via me from now on, when or *if* you play ball. So, I suggest you get your arse in gear and buckle down. If you do that, you'll get the exact same allowance your father was paying you. Except, unlike your dad, I'll be checking on your attendance every week . . . No show, no dough.'

'Fuck off.'

'That I can do.'

David walked away. Frankie followed at a safe distance. She wasn't looking forward to the journey back.

44

Stone took a moment to view the wreaths that had arrived with his brother's body and those sent to the crematorium by family and friends unable to attend. Then he and Frankie moved towards the exit in silence. The car park was full, the next cremation already taking place. They tried very hard here but, as far as Frankie was concerned, it was no more than a dumping ground. A human waste disposal unit. A conveyor belt of grief that brought her little comfort. The place held nightmarish memories from childhood. They had faded over time, but even now she hated being here.

They had reached her car.

The lights flashed as she pressed her key fob, a blast of heat escaping from the interior as she opened the driver's door. Stone hesitated, glancing towards the path that ran between the west chapel and the crematorium's waiting room where he'd been arguing with his nephew. Frankie followed his line of sight. Ben hadn't moved. He was smoking another illegal cigarette now his uncle had moved away. His head was bowed and he was talking to someone on the phone. Wondering if he was calling a taxi, Frankie tried to catch Stone's eye. It was fixed on his nephew.

'David, go back and offer him a lift,' she said.

'Let him walk.' Stone opened the passenger door and got in.

Frankie climbed in beside him. 'I heard everything you said to him.'

'And I suppose you have a point of view—'

'You know me, boss. My mouth won't stay shut if I have something that needs saying. If you want my honest opinion—'

'I don't.'

She ignored him. 'It was unforgivable, treating him like that. Ben is eighteen! He needs help. If his dad put you in charge of the purse strings, all well and good, but the lad's going to need psychological support as well as a helping hand with finances. You must see that. You can't turn him away. It wouldn't be right.'

'Right?' Stone looked ready to explode. 'I'm not his legal guardian. Now, are you going to drive me or do I call a cab?'

'Suit yourself.' Frankie had never seen him so morose. He'd had his dark days recently, but this was something else. She put her key in the ignition, turned the engine over and pulled away.

'Turn right,' he said.

She drove through the gates on to the West Road. 'Where are we going?' It was the opposite direction from her preferred route to the office. 'David?'

'Home! My home – I need to pack my stuff.'

She glanced at him. 'To go where?'

'I've had enough. With Luke gone, so is my reason to stick around.'

After all he'd said inside the chapel, the impression he'd given that being 'home' was important to him, she was horrified. An image of his cottage arrived in her head, photos of his nan, the wonky fireplace, the old bookcase, threadbare furniture and rocking chair – all of it wrapped in a history of love, its thick walls riddled with nostalgia. The thought that he was prepared to kiss it all goodbye made her want to weep.

Pulling hard on the steering wheel, she turned left at the Denton roundabout, then immediately right on to the fore-court of the Jet service station. Yanking on the handbrake, she turned to face him. 'That's it?' she said. 'You're telling Ben he shouldn't quit and you're going do exactly that?'

'Maybe I don't have it in me to live up to your high expectations, let alone match up to my predecessor—'

'Don't you ever think you're not as good as he is. You are.

Every bit as good, but I don't intend to stroke your ego, so get a grip and stop being such a drama queen. What about Justine? Whoever killed her is still out there. Doesn't she count? Andrea promised her parents we'd find whoever's responsible for her death. You can't up and leave like this.'

'Watch me.'

'Aren't you tired of running, David? It cost you a rank last time. If you keep going like this you'll end up as a uniformed PC on traffic detail. Is that what you want? I never figured you for a loser.' She got out of the car, slamming the door.

The middle of a murder investigation was not a good time to go AWOL. Luckily for Stone and Oliver, there was no reason to return to the office that evening. Aware that Luke's funeral was taking place, the SIO had released them for the rest of the day and agreed to wait for the second forensic report before tackling Timothy Parker again. Mitchell would ring the minute it was in, but he'd been told not to expect it until morning.

In one way, the impasse was opportune. In another, it was disastrous. Stone was shitfaced by eight o'clock and being obstreperous all over again. There had only been two good developments: he hadn't yet packed a bag and he'd agreed to see the case out. Having eaten very little, Frankie was half-cut on one glass of wine. She'd decided, against her better judgement, to kip on his sofa rather than drag Andrea out to drive her home, insurance against her boss doing a runner in the middle of the night.

Let him try.

Frankie smiled inwardly. She'd hidden his car keys in a place he'd never find them and taxis were non-existent in the sticks. If he tried to leave, she'd knock the stupid bastard out if she had to. Taking her life in her hands, she entered the kitchen. As she'd suspected, Stone's fridge held only alcohol. She looked up at the unsafe plasterboard and gaping hole in the ceiling, then down at the pathetic white plastic bag dangling from her right hand.

Jumping out of the car at the Jet service station had been advantageous. She'd done it to get away from Stone, because she couldn't bear to breathe the same air as someone so intrinsically perverse. As she stood rigid and seething on the forecourt, taking time out, she had suddenly become aware of the curiosity of an attendant at the payment desk who'd witnessed her anxiety through his viewing window, all this captured on CCTV.

When the attendant's eyes shifted to Stone, his enquiring expression morphed into one of concern. Fearful that he might misconstrue their odd behaviour as a probable threat to the contents of the till, she'd glanced at her vehicle. Her petrol tank was full, so she marched inside to put the guy's mind at rest, bought a few provisions and apologised, telling him that she was having a serious domestic with her bloke. The half-truth seemed to satisfy him. It wouldn't be the first time he'd witnessed a couple at each other's throats.

She cleared away a space on the kitchen bench big enough to cobble something together with what she'd managed to purchase at the petrol station to force down her boss. Cooking had never been her thing and her efforts tasted foul, a far cry from his nan's home cooking, she imagined. Nevertheless, he ate the lot and didn't complain.

As she refilled her wine glass, she chanced her arm. 'The issue of Ben is not going away, David. Mark my words, if you don't deal with him now, as his trustee, it may come back and haunt you. He might try and drag you into court, attempt to change Luke's will.'

'He won't win—'

'Do you really want the hassle?'

'No.'

'Then why don't you try working *with* him rather than against him—'

'Why don't you leave it out?'

'You'll thank me one day.' She grinned.

Her attempt to lighten his mood didn't work. Stone got up, grabbed another beer from the fridge and slumped down on the sofa facing the fire. Frankie followed suit, choosing his nan's rocker, hoping it might somehow add weight to her argument.

'I'm really not trying to wind you up,' she said.

'Then don't . . . please.'

She remembered the mood swings and angry outbursts at home, the loss of self-control, her parents' inability to intervene without causing their firstborn to bolt from the house. Without talking about her own experience, how could she explain how much support Ben needed to get him on track, why it was so important to be there for him, no matter how difficult a task it might prove to be.

'Teenagers can be a pain but they're also extremely vulnerable to the influences of others,' she said. 'Ben comes across as rude and hostile – I'm not denying that – but underneath that cocky exterior, he's lost. A sullen teenager trying to make his way in difficult circumstances. He needs a guiding hand . . . Yours.'

For a moment, Stone let his silence do the talking. 'His problems are of his own making,' he said eventually.

'Are you sure about that?'

'Absolutely.'

If he thought she'd drop it, he was sadly mistaken. 'David, he's provoking you, can't you see? He's asking the earth, knowing or even expecting you to reject him, reinforcing the fact that he's unworthy. I bet you a month's pay that he wasn't like that as a little boy.' Frankie was trying to get him to see sense. If Ben had been a kid lacking discipline, she could understand his uncle's attitude. If the opposite was true, she might gain some sympathy for a lad who, in her opinion, had experienced a disproportionate amount of sadness compared to his peers. Was it any wonder he'd gone off the rails? 'Well?' She tried lightening the mood. 'Was he a difficult rug rat or a little angel?'

Stone warmed a little. 'He was OK.'

'Then it stands to reason that something happened to make him lose it.' Except Frankie knew that wasn't always the case. Some kids got lost all by themselves with no apparent trigger. However, she had to try to hit the right note. 'Losing his mum must've been very difficult for a start.'

'It was for all of us.'

'I'm sure it was, but he's not much more than a kid! There is a difference. Don't you think that might explain his reliance on dope?' Frankie was convinced that Ben's antisocial behaviour was a cry for help. She was worried that he might sink even lower, get into difficulty and end up in serious trouble, possibly on harder drugs, harming himself or even those around him.

'You want him to end up in Durham jail? Think of Luke—'

'I am! My brother is a pile of ashes because of him! He was racing to hospital to collect *him!* Want to know why? I'll tell you, shall I? That little toerag had been on an all-night bender. Luke told Andrea that he'd received a call from one of Ben's mates. He'd collapsed and was rushed to A & E after taking a cocktail of drugs and alcohol. Luke ended up in the same hospital and only one of them walked away. The wrong one.'

Frankie didn't know what to say. Quietly she said, 'I understand but—'

'Do you, *really*? I doubt that. Who have you ever lost?'

Frankie looked away. He had absolutely no idea.

45

Frankie drove. Forensics were in and she couldn't wait to get to Northern Command HQ. Stone was a mess, marginally better than when they'd passed each other on the way to the 'torture chamber' in his nan's house. The goosebumps on her body were mammoth when she got out of the shower; they would have been less so had she bathed in an Alpine stream. The radio was full of the political fallout from Brexit, as it had been for days. The EU referendum had gone the wrong way. Both detectives had been stunned by it. Since then, the newspapers, radio and TV had been full of it. Brexit had divided the country and what was done could not be undone. This was democracy in action. Scotland and Northern Ireland had voted to remain, but overall the public had chosen to leave the European Union. The headlines were depressing. Cameron had resigned. Britain was in turmoil.

Frankie sighed. 'No matter how many times I hear it, I still can't believe it. I hate to think what will happen further down the line.'

Stone killed the radio.

He was in no mood to go there.

He crashed through the door to the incident room. Mitchell was on his feet, heading in their direction, a mug of coffee in his hand. Stone walked past him without so much as a by your leave. He wasn't feeling particularly chatty this morning. The funeral was bad enough, his row with Frankie more than he could handle. He hadn't budged an inch regarding his nephew – not yet anyway – although at the crematorium he'd gone some way to resolving their differences until Ben went off on one. For now, the subject was off limits.

'Where is it?' Frankie asked Mitchell.

'On his desk.'

'Anything else come in I should know about?'

'No, Sarge. To be honest, we're not getting very far.' Mitchell glanced over his shoulder in the direction of Stone's closed office door, the venetian blinds drawn. He might as well have written LEAVE ME THE FUCK ALONE and hung it on the door. The DC turned to face Frankie. 'How did it go yesterday?'

'As well as it ever can.'

Mitch held up his mug. 'You want me to fix you up with one of these, strong and black?'

'Anyone would think you were a detective.'

The DC smiled. 'Want a bacon buttie to go with it?'

'I'll pass, thanks, but get one for the boss. In fact, make it two: brown sauce, not ketchup. He hates the stuff.' She looked around the incident room and then at Mitchell. 'Any sign of the SIO this morning?'

'Not yet.'

'If you happen to bump into him, tell him we're in conference. If the boss feels as bad as I think he might, he'll want a couple of hours to get his head in gear before consulting with Sharpe. We don't want him thinking we're not up to the job.'

'You can't tell behind those.' Mitch pointed at her sunglasses.

'You did!' Frankie said. 'I'd better get going.'

Stone was already reading the forensic report when she entered his office. His expression was enough of a hint that the findings were of interest. He passed it over his desk for her to get up to speed. Mitchell arrived with breakfast before she'd finished scanning the document. Stone wolfed his food down so quickly it hardly touched the sides. Only when he was done did they get down to business.

'The first forensic report found Parker's DNA in Justine's bed,' he said. 'No semen. His prints were lifted from three separate locations in her room, even though he denies ever being in there, but this . . .' he tapped the follow-up document, 'is gold. Alex Parker identified the unwashed bed linen crime scene investigators took from the washing machine as her own and yet Justine's DNA is all over it.'

'She's the au pair,' Frankie said. 'She makes the beds.'

'Yes, and we'd expect to find it there, but this is not any old DNA, Frankie. It's bodily fluids. Looks like I'm buying you dinner after all.'

'Don't get your credit card out yet. It's not news that Justine liked to sleep around. Those samples only prove that she was there. She could have been screwing him, screwing Alex, or both together. You never know what goes on in rural Northumberland . . .' She made a crazy face. 'Except in Pauperhaugh, where absolutely nothing happens.'

Stone laughed.

She did too.

'Maybe they're a couple of swingers, she said. 'Mind you, if that was the case, you'd expect them to do their laundry more often.'

'Except Justine had the week off.' Stone paused, considering the implications of the forensic report, a theory forming in his mind. 'So, Justine and Parker have it off in the marital bed, which was supposed to be changed before Alex got home from Majorca. Justine shoves the linen in the washing machine before she goes to collect Daniel – at which point all hell breaks loose. She's so distraught, she totally forgets about it. Once she's off duty, nothing jogs her memory. We might have copped some good fortune here.'

Frankie agreed. Tim Parker was back at the top of her list.

46

They briefed the Murder Investigation Team SIO at 11 a.m. Given Timothy Parker's antipathy to Frankie, it made sense for her to conduct the interview. This time it would take place under caution at Northern Command HQ, not on the entrepreneur's home turf. They finally had evidence. He'd lied about his association with the murder victim. Sharpe wanted him under pressure and talking. It was time to shake him up.

'You OK with that, David?' the SIO asked out of courtesy.

Stone nodded, a wry smile. 'Frankie has the ability to get a rise out of most people.'

Her response was directed at Sharpe. 'You should see what I can do with a baseball bat, sir.'

'I'll pretend I never heard that,' he said. 'I take it you're happy to lead?'

'Are you kidding? My dad would have had the cuffs on by now. My granddad would've had him in the dock.'

Sharpe and Stone both knew there was some truth behind the joke.

They met Parker off British Airways flight BA1335 from Heathrow. It landed right on schedule at 19:30 in the pouring rain. Stone intercepted him as he made his way to the arrivals hall, much as he had done to his wife at passport control a fortnight before. The entrepreneur made a song and dance about his car being in the short-term car park, the fact that it would be towed away if it ran over the maximum period, so Frankie had driven his vehicle back to base, Stone taking their suspect in his car.

The interview was ten minutes in. Frankie had been chipping away at Parker, little by little. For every point she raised, he concocted a story to fit. He was well-schooled to answer only the questions put to him and never volunteered information. It was hard going.

'Mr Parker, as I stated at the beginning of this interview, finding the person or persons responsible for Justine Segal's murder is a top priority for us, so let's go over it again, shall we? You have admitted entering her accommodation. Are you now willing to concede that you plugged your phone into the charger in her room, even though your study is closer?'

He made no comment.

Frustrated by his noncompliance, Frankie made a meal of examining the plan of his home, then looked up. 'Your phone charger is here, in the hallway of your house.' She pointed to the relevant spot. 'Did it not occur to you to use that, rather than squeeze yourself around the side of Justine's bed to reach her device?'

'Obviously not.'

'Do you really expect us to believe that? It's twice the distance. Isn't it the case that you were planning to have sex with Justine and that's why you used her charger. Your prints were found on it, man. And on the cabinet on which it stands. You must've expected to be there a while.'

No response.

'OK, what if I told you that we found your DNA on her bed.'

'You would do. I sat down.' Parker's steely eyes gave nothing away.

'Sitting on someone's bed is a very personal thing to do,' Frankie said. 'I wouldn't do it unless I was intimately involved with that person, yet you chose to do so and lied about it.'

'You caught me out, DS Oliver. I'm embarrassed and I apologise unreservedly. I'm a married man. I'm sure you can appreciate why I didn't come clean initially about entering her room. It doesn't look good, does it?'

Frankie never took her eyes off him. 'You lied unnecessarily in my opinion. It's your house. We'd expect to find your DNA in most rooms. On June twenty-second, I specifically asked you if you had ever been inside Justine's annex—'

'It's actually *my* annex.'

Frankie ignored the interruption. 'You said, quote: "I've never so much as set foot inside the place," unquote. That's a fairly strenuous denial.'

'It wasn't semen then?'

Cleverly worked out.

Frankie thought of the positioning of the prints, particularly those found high up on the architrave of the door. She imagined him standing there, a hand on either side of the doorway before crossing the threshold, invited or not. 'Why did you enter her room?'

'I can't recall.'

'Oh, c'mon. Give it a go.'

'I looked in. We had a chat.'

'You did more than "look in" though, didn't you, Mr Parker.' She flipped open her file, eyes dropping to the notepad in front of her. 'Can you outline to me exactly how you came to look in on her?'

'I think her door was open. She spoke to me. It would have been impolite to ignore her.'

'That's not the truth and you know it.' He failed to respond and Frankie carried on. 'Mr Parker, people who tell lies about small things are usually prepared to lie about big things. I need your honesty now: a yes or no to a straightforward question. Have you ever had sex with Justine Segal . . . *anywhere*? Are you clear about what I'm asking?'

'Perfectly.'

'Then I'd like an answer.'

Parker rubbed at his forehead. 'No.'

'You are denying a sexual relationship with your au pair?'

'Categorically.'

He waited for the next question, knowing it would make

her share what little evidence she had. He was making a good fist of the interview, giving away as little as possible. He knew he didn't need to tell them anything at all. It was up to them to build a credible case. He was very astute and, so far, Frankie had nothing concrete to tie him to her murder case.

'You will recall that forensic science officers entered your premises on Friday, twenty-second of June following Justine's death. They processed her room, recovering several personal items. What you may not know is that they removed bed linen from her bed and some found in the washing machine in the laundry room. The latter items had been stripped from your marital bed. Your wife has confirmed that.'

Parker's expression was inscrutable.

'Your sheets. Your bed.'

'And your point is?'

'We believe they were removed by Justine prior to your wife's return from holiday. Did I mention they hadn't been washed?'

'You have now.'

'Well, they have now been examined,' Frankie said. 'Traces of your semen and bodily fluids from Justine were found on them. Do you have anything to say about that?'

If he did, Parker kept quiet about it.

'The positioning of these samples would suggest sexual activity. Justine didn't get the chance to wash them because everyone's focus was on Daniel at the time. She was worried about his disappearance. If you recall, when he was returned home by Mr Price, she was given the week off by your wife. The dirty laundry must have slipped her mind. And yet you sit there telling lies like a bloody schoolboy.'

'DS Oliver has a point,' Stone said. 'We're not interested in where you put your semen, Mr Parker. Only that you continue to evade the truth. You have lied repeatedly. Every time we prove that to you, you change your story to fit. Fortunately for you, it is not a criminal offence to lie to us.

Had it been so, your name would already be on a charge sheet. Perverting the course of justice or wasting police time is another matter entirely. Mark my words, if I feel at the end of this enquiry that you are guilty of either offence, you *will* be prosecuted.'

Parker's eyes were back on Frankie. 'Did you find any other bodily fluids?'

The interview was being recorded. She had to tell the truth. 'Yes, we did. They belong to your wife.'

'Then has it occurred to you that *she* may have been having a relationship with Justine in our marital bed?'

Frankie came straight back at him. 'I can assure you that we've examined all the angles, Mr Parker, including that one. Are you guessing or do you have reason to suspect Alex of impropriety? I think it an unlikely contrivance myself. I'm sure that a woman as classy as your wife would have washed the sheets before taking another woman into her bed.'

'I'm sure that's true. Maybe she rushed off on holiday before she could wash them and, as you say, Justine didn't do her job properly. How was I to know that the sheets were not fresh? A man has to do what a man has to do when his wife is away. Three people. Three samples. Makes sense to me.'

'Oh, c'mon! That is rubbish and you know it. Maybe Mrs Parker could shed more light on it than you.'

Parker was angry . . . More than angry.

Frankie had seen the involuntary muscle movement in his face. What's more, he knew it. It was as if a switch had been thrown. She'd been in the job long enough to recognise the signs – in suspects and in colleagues. Given the right stimulus, she possessed it too. There was a part of it in everyone, an inner rage most right-minded folk could suppress. For a small percentage of individuals there was no off switch. Parker was one of those. For a moment, she thought he'd play right into her hands, then the clever bastard wrong-footed her again.

'You said you wanted elimination prints for Justine's car,' he said. 'Not for her living quarters and certainly not for mine.'

'Please don't raise your voice, Mr Parker. Correct me if I'm wrong, but you'd already ruled yourself out for the annex.'

'You also said the samples taken would be destroyed—'

'And they will be,' Frankie said. 'At the end of this case.'

Parker began to flap. 'I did not give my consent for anything other than her car.'

'Calm down.' Frankie didn't mean it. The more agitated he became, the better she liked it. 'It's perfectly acceptable for us to use these samples in relation to this matter. We didn't need your permission. This is a wide-ranging murder enquiry. It would be a dereliction of duty if we didn't look at the evidence we've collected in its entirety—'

'You have harassed me from the moment Daniel went missing, DS Oliver. You can count on a call to the Chief Constable.'

'You're being paranoid, sir. It must be all the steroids you're taking.' Her eyes locked on to his. 'What are they for? To combat ageing or to enhance your sexual performance?' She didn't expect or receive an answer and had to work very hard not to smirk. 'As far as making a complaint goes, that is your right, of course. I can assure you that I have acted in accordance with the law.'

Parker glared at her across the interview room. He looked more worried than ever before. Frankie was keen to capitalise on his loss of self-control. She was in no rush. The longer she waited to pose another question, the more frustrated he became. 'You are a pathological liar, Mr Parker. You've been caught out and we want the truth now. Are you aware that you have something of a reputation?'

'In what respect?'

'A witness has come forward.' Frankie glanced at Stone. 'We didn't even have to go and look for her. She approached us, entirely voluntarily you understand, very keen to give you a character reference. She described you as a serial philanderer. Not a very flattering label, I grant you. However, there may be some truth in it. We never write off a statement if we agree with it.'

'I demand to know the identity of that witness.'

'Is it true?'

'No. And by definition, "serial"' – he used his fingers as inverted commas – 'requires a string of affairs and you've put forward no evidence of that.'

'I was never any good at maths or English. Detecting is my only skill—'

'Get to the point!'

There it was again: that switch.

Frankie hoped the CCTV trained on him would pick it up. She'd make time to watch it later, slow the footage down and discuss it with Stone. The longer the interview progressed, the more anxious Parker became. His non-verbal communication was giving him away: hands never still, an inability to maintain eye-contact. This middle-class druggie needed a fix.

Parker took a deep breath. 'What are you accusing me of exactly?'

'Remember we discussed Daniel's former British nanny, Maria Friedman? You omitted to tell me that, since she left your wife's employ, the two of you have engaged in a sexual relationship. She's prepared to make a statement to that effect. Do you deny it?'

'No.' He was cornered.

'At last you've admitted your infidelity. That wasn't so hard now, was it? Are you going to be as upfront about your relationship with Justine?' The silence was deafening. 'Mr Parker? I'm sure you want to hold on to your wife, if only for financial security. We happen to know that your company is in difficulty and have learned that there have been allegations and counter allegations as to who is responsible for the debts you are now facing.'

He looked away, sweat visible on his brow.

'Can you tell us about that?' Frankie knew she had him.

'My business finances are private and irrelevant to this enquiry.'

'Fair enough. Let's move on then—'

'Look, I'm holding my hands up here. I had a thing with Justine. Very briefly. Nothing serious. Naturally, I didn't want Alex knowing about it. But I didn't kill her, I swear. Now you have what you want, I'd like to go.'

'I'm sure you would. But why should we believe you when you've clearly been lying to us?'

'Because it's the truth.' The guy was practically hyperventilating. 'On its own, your forensics won't be enough to charge, let alone convict me. We both know it, so I think we're done here.' He pushed his chair away from the table and got to his feet. 'Charge me or I'm leaving.'

Frankie looked at Stone.

Parker was right. They didn't have enough to hold him. The interview had provided proof of infidelity and systematic lying they believed was motivated by a need to hang on to a wealthy wife. In that respect, Kat Irwin had been spot on: he was no different from Rob Scott.

'Mr Parker, we are far from done . . .' Even in her own head, Frankie sounded supremely confident. 'A murder investigation is a marathon, not a sprint. We usually get there in the end. You will be bailed to return to this police station in a month from now.' She handed him a sheet of paper. 'This is a complaint form. Be sure to spell my name right: Detective Sergeant Frances Oliver. You are free to go.'

47

Three floors up, Frankie watched Timothy Parker leave the front entrance of Northern Command HQ. As he strode across the car park towards his high-end motor, he looked up, his pace slowing, a smug expression on his face. He opened the door and climbed in. Scooping his driving specs off the dash, he put them on, a last glance in her direction. He was gone in a flash. In Frankie's eyes, he had few redeeming features. During the interview, they had both given away more than expected. But, in real terms, he'd probably come out on top. What niggled her most was that he knew it.

Stone arrived at her shoulder. 'Don't take it too hard, Frank. You did a good job.'

'I'm not.' She turned to face him. 'I can't deny that I'm disappointed. He's an objectionable prick who'll shag anything that moves but, deep down, I don't think he killed Justine Segal. I'm sorry, David. I'm just not feeling it. To be honest, I don't know if he's got the balls. We have absolutely nothing that ties him to her death.'

'His only alibi is his wife,' Stone reminded her.

'You think she's protecting him?'

'I really don't know. She was certain that he was in the house when Justine was killed. She was less sure on exactly when she left to pick Daniel up from school. I was banking on a little wriggle room, hoping her timing was off. Maybe that's wishful thinking on my part.'

'If Alex found out he has more respect for her cash than he does for her, she might think harder.'

Despite the DI's kinds words a moment ago, Frankie could tell his head was down. Looking around the office, she could see that the rest of their crew weren't faring any better. The fact that Parker had walked without charge had come as a bitter blow. They were trying hard to hide their disappointment.

It wasn't working.

'Where do you want to debrief?'

'My office,' Stone said. 'This lot look like they're going to cut their throats.'

'Then we'll have to give them something to smile about. Rule 6 in the Frank Oliver Handbook: Low morale is strictly forbidden. Rule 7: No one goes home until I say so.'

'Yeah, let's push on.'

They withdrew from the window, grabbed a bottle of water from the vending machine and sought the privacy of his office, telling the team they didn't wish to be disturbed. The SIO would not be happy and they were both under pressure to come up with a credible suspect.

It wasn't happening.

Stone settled in his seat. 'Parker's not out of the woods yet – agreed?'

'Agreed.'

'Then the way I see it, there are only two scenarios in play here. Either we're on the right lines and this *is* to do with Justine's diary – in which case we keep digging – or we're missing something vital, some local intel in the months leading up to her death—'

'Our lads did a thorough check on that,' Frankie said. 'Nothing happened in that area that's relevant to us. There were no break-ins, no assaults or moving traffic offences. You saw it up there. It's a sleepy hollow that hasn't changed for centuries. If a pig farts, it's headline news. You're a thug if you don't say please. Nothing goes on, believe me. Nowt nasty, anyway. Until this . . .'

'Then we're back to that list,' Stone said.

'That's down to me. The receiver couldn't have done a better job on Justine's diary, I promise you.'

'I'm not suggesting otherwise.'

'Aren't you? Other than the four I originally mentioned to the SIO, the others have been corroborated one hundred per cent. I double-checked them myself.'

He eyed her across his desk. 'This investigation reminds me of one I was involved with down south. On the face of it, the victim was the perfect wife and mother, but scratch beneath the surface and there was a femme fatale at work. The woman had a whole other life. We uncovered multiple relationships with men and women: mènage á trois, bondage – you name it, she was into it. The husband, a strong suspect, was arrested for her murder. We figured he'd uncovered her interesting lifestyle but later binned that theory and let him go. He knew nowt, nor did any of the people she worked with. The real killer was an ex-plaything she didn't rate any more. She was blackmailing him and it backfired.'

Frankie thought for a moment. 'There is Alex, of course. If she knew Parker was having an affair with Justine, then that gives her motive. Kat Irwin planted the seed while the two were on holiday, remember.'

'And she refused to believe it,' Stone said. 'I'll be honest with you, Frankie. I have my doubts about Kat Irwin's motivation for that phone call. She was quick to point the finger at Justine and, at her own admission, has never got on with Parker. Maybe she's a poisonous troublemaker, like you suggested.'

'Why though? There must be a reason.'

'Who knows? Some people are perverse. Of the four you couldn't rule out initially, Wise is gone. So if it isn't him, let's concentrate on the others and see where it takes us.'

'Curtis is still a candidate in my view.'

'Agreed. What about Hamilton, the guy working in Gretna?'

'Also ruled out—'

Stone saw red. 'Says who?'

'The SIO.'

'How come I don't know about it?'

'Police Scotland made the enquiries at the garage, David.

They passed it directly to the Murder Investigation Team. I've not seen it myself but I was told that the SIO was entirely satisfied.'

'Then there's your starter for ten, Frank. Sharpe has gone on leave for two weeks. I'm acting SIO now, which means we to cross-check every piece of evidence, even if the MIT have referenced him off. But be discreet around his team. If Sharpe is right and they think you're questioning his authority, it'll piss them off. If he's got this wrong, it might do us some good.' He left her to it.

48

Slipping her warrant card into a slot on her computer, Frankie logged on with renewed enthusiasm. Clasping her hands behind her head, she replayed her conversation with Stone, specifically his suggestion that they were missing something vital. *Perhaps some local intel in the months leading up to her death.* David was wrong about that. DS Dick Abbott, a trusted colleague, had carried out those enquiries. A detective of twenty-five years' service, he'd made sure that it was done properly. There were detectives she'd never doubt.

Abbott was one of them.

No sooner had that certainty arrived in her head than it was pushed aside by a more dispiriting thought. Since she'd joined the CID, things had changed drastically. A reduction in staff across all departments meant that there was no longer an opportunity to speak to a local beat officer who'd know his or her patch, inside out. No longer were they on speaking terms with members of the public in the community they served. Nowadays that didn't happen. A receiver or statement reader would issue actions to detectives that were explicit and pertinent to an investigation. Once those instructions were carried out, the job was written off, the action complete.

It was a case of: in, out, move on.

The fact that detectives had lost the luxury of spending time with witnesses – as they would have in her father's time – was a sore point for Frankie. Her dad had impressed on her the fact that such discussions often produced a nugget of information that could turn an investigation on its head. A fighting chance was all she wanted.

Was that too much to ask?

With that depressing thought lingering, Frankie pressed a

few keys on her computer and waited for the page to load. When it did, she found that no follow-up action had been issued in respect of East, West and Middle cottages. She noted that Andrea's enquiries with Marjorie Smith at West Cottage were marked as complete. Mitchell's were ongoing but, to be on the safe side, Frankie went over them carefully, finding nothing that sparked her interest. Maybe there was nothing to find. She scanned text relating to the remaining tenants. None had reported any visitors to neighbouring properties that might have been the offender she was seeking. A single man, Barry Hall, lived in Middle Cottage. He was a computer programmer, aged sixty, whose business premises were in Hexham. East Cottage was occupied by a married couple, Teresa and Jerry Dixon, who both worked for Newcastle City Council at the Civic Centre. The initial statements from all three were similar: out at work; never saw or heard a thing.

Bugger.

Frankie switched to the force-wide incident log, typing in the code for the area of interest, entering the date of Justine Segal's death. The murder incident was a mammoth item with everything listed, including all personnel involved, from first responders through all departments, including Traffic and the dog section. Literally everything about the job was outlined in meticulous detail.

It made for grim reading.

Her eyes travelled down the screen. Offenders returning to the scene might be a joke in crime fiction, but there were isolated incidents where it had happened for real. She wanted to make sure that no one had been sniffing around her crime scene since Andrea had completed the house-to-house. The area was now flooded with officers making enquiries, asking about parked cars, strangers in surrounding villages and in woods being used as a lovers' lane. Often, a vehicle might belong to local or national press; a rubbernecker or merely an innocent traveller passing through. If they existed, all would need further investigation. One new item hit her in the eye that hadn't been there last time she checked:

Burglary: other than dwelling.

The details underneath the item gave her cause for concern. Hackles rising, she picked up her phone, speed-dialling Stone's mobile. The ringing tone stopped. 'I found something,' she said. 'You need to get in here.'

Seconds later, his office door opened and he walked through it, his expression a mixture of curiosity and optimism. 'Don't tell me you cracked the case single-handedly. My ego couldn't handle it.'

Her grin was infectious.

Other detectives joined in – a momentary pressure release. The buzz and banter took a moment to die down. Frankie waited for Stone to grab a spare seat and haul it over to her desk. By the time he'd sat down, the team were all ears.

'Ignore your phones,' she said. 'You lot need to hear this too.'

Stone was wary. 'Don't tell me we missed something glaringly obvious—'

'No, Dick handled this. Everything was done by the book, boss. We were, however, concentrating on what was going on prior to Justine's death. I decided to look at what might have happened since, and I struck lucky. On Wednesday the twenty-ninth of June, Jerry Dixon who lives in East Cottage reported a burglary to his shed.' She glanced at Stone. 'You think his name is Jeremiah, boss? I'm surprised you haven't been round there to introduce yourself.'

Everyone laughed.

Any self-respecting Mark Knopfler fan knew that the name appeared in the opening line of 'Sailing to Philadelphia' – a song that had been repeating in Frankie's head since she first saw Dixon's name on the log.

She stopped ribbing her boss, got up and crossed the room, asking everyone to pay attention to a blown-up image pinned to the wall, part of an Ordnance Survey Map that showed the crime scene, the row of cottages she was referring to, the humpback bridge, the woods on the south side of the small country lane and surrounding farmland.

All eyes had followed her there.

Using her forefinger, she indicated various points on the map as she spoke. 'As you can see, Marjorie Smith lives here on the western end of the small terrace, Barry Hall in the centre, Teresa and Jerry Dixon on the eastern end, closest to our crime scene. Hold that thought, guys. It may well be significant. It just so happens that the Dixons' shed was broken into at some point between Monday, June twentieth – two days prior to Justine's death – and Wednesday, June twenty-ninth when Dixon went out to mow his lawn and found the lock on the shed door broken. A pedal cycle and a wrench had been removed. He reported the theft at four p.m. that day.'

'MO?' Stone asked.

'Unsophisticated: break lock, gain entry, steal from within.'

'You think Justine saw something on her run and got whacked for it?'

'I don't know is the honest answer, but if that missing tool caused the injury to the back of her head, the offender may have used the pedal cycle to make a quick getaway.'

'Sarge?' Mitchell had his hand up.

Frankie's nod was his cue to carry on.

'The cyclist Mrs Smith caught a glimpse of at around the time of Justine's death bothers me. She hadn't mentioned it to Andrea when first questioned and was a bit vague when I pushed her on it. There's some dispute over whether she saw it on the twenty-second or mistook the date. Because of that, I double-checked with every car driver approaching the humpback bridge from either direction.'

'And?'

'None of them saw a bike.'

'That's good to know. It could well be significant.' Frankie addressed them all. 'Look, there's been a lot of rural crime lately, so I could be wrong. Assuming for one minute that I'm right about this, once the person responsible for assaulting Justine dragged her across the road and on to the bridge, he'd have been shitting himself, wouldn't he? If I were him, I might have ridden off-road into the woods, dumped the bike and legged it cross-country. So maybe Marjorie wasn't mistaken.' Frankie caught Stone's eye. 'This is a new line of enquiry, boss. We need to get on top of it.'

'Volunteers for working the weekend?'

Several hands shot up, Abott's among them.

'Dick, you know the score. First thing tomorrow morning, I want you out at those cottages. I want war and peace on this burglary. Re-interview all tenants, not only the Dixons. Find out if they saw or heard anyone lurking on or near their properties in the weeks prior to Justine's death; we need details of that bike – make, model and distinguishing features. If Dixon has photographs, all the better. I want pictures, SOCO and detailed descriptions of the shed and its contents. If there's anything else missing, let me know. Go to town on it. That's your only reason for breathing tomorrow. Mitch, go with him and don't come back empty-handed. Frankie, widen the search area for the murder weapon, the bike and Justine's phone. I want it circulated force-wide with a warning marker: leave in situ/preserve for forensic examination/contact the incident room immediately.'

Detectives were already rising to their feet.

The team dispersed for the day.

49

Multiple messages poured in as Tim Parker finally dared to turn on his mobile phone: texts from Alex, Carole, James . . . and one or two from his Lloyds Bank manager, Arthur Conrad. Fuck him. Fuck 'em all. Carole was different. He'd just come from there. Where else would he turn at a time like this? She was loyal and made few demands. She knew how to enjoy herself and was about as far from Alex as it was possible to be. One drink had led to two . . . two to three . . . and, before he knew it, they were indulging in LSD at gone midnight.

Carole had begged him to stay over. As wasted as he undoubtedly was, Tim had to face Alex and find out what had been going on in his absence. He'd misjudged the acid, though. Thought he had time to get home before the full effects entered his system. He was tripping already, his head in a spin, his concentration draining away as he tried to keep his car on the road without drawing attention to his erratic driving, creating panic among other road users.

He needed a Traffic cop like a hole in the head.

That would please Alex.

Tim's head was spinning. Why should he explain himself to her? He'd messed up. What of it? He wouldn't beg forgiveness from her or anyone else. It was partly her fault that he was in this mess. The baby. It all started with his baby. Then there was Daniel . . . his failing business . . . and now Justine. It was all too much.

Tim wiped sweat from his brow, wondering what Stone and Oliver had told his wife. More importantly, what she'd told them. There was only one dead cert in play here: she'd be waiting up, wanting answers, demanding them.

Another pill . . .

Another swig of whisky.

Tim's left hand was tingling.

Taking it from the steering wheel, he examined it closely. His wedding band shone, revolving like a lighthouse beacon around his finger, a beam of light so strong he was forced to look away. The road ahead morphed into a technicolour highway. Street lamps flashed by, headlights and taillights reflecting on the wet surface becoming brighter and more pronounced, a kaleidoscope of light trails shooting off in every direction.

Weird . . . but cool.

The dials on his dashboard danced like stars. His own personal universe. He felt bigger than ever before. The mini he was following suddenly blew up into a monster truck, and bigger still, until it blotted out the night sky. Seeing the giant vehicle, Tim had an urge to race it along the sparkly superhighway.

Pulling into the outside lane, he floored the accelerator, his speedometer climbing . . . sixty . . . seventy . . . eighty miles an hour. Unable to see properly, he felt the jolt of self-preservation, the possibility of insanity or death. Either was preferable to his current reality. He pulled hard on the steering wheel. Miscalculating the distance to the nearest lay-by, he hit the brakes with such force that the car skidded on wet tarmac, the vehicle glancing off the kerb at the back edge of the pull-in. The inertia threw him forward. His safety belt – the only thing preventing serious injury – almost snapped his collarbone.

He fumbled for the handle.

The door wouldn't open. Pushing hard made no difference. His car was lodged against a rubbish bin as tall as a house. Slamming the vehicle into reverse, he backed up. Behind him, a horn screamed a warning that he'd overshot the broken white line. The rear of his motor was now on the main car-riageway – half on, half of the road, at an angle – putting him in imminent danger from passing traffic. Approaching lights in his wing mirror were lightsabres reaching out to him, closing fast. He dropped his head on one side and stared at them.

He'd never seen anything so exquisite.

Another horn . . .

Yeah, yeah.

Selecting 'Drive' Tim pressed the accelerator. The car shot forward just in time. Somehow, he managed to manoeuvre the vehicle into a parallel position in the safety of the stopping area. He tried the door again. This time it worked. A gulp of fresh air . . .

Finally.

Stumbling out on to the grass, Tim bent double. He threw up so violently, vomit splashed on his shoes and strides, a pungent mixture of bile, alcohol and drugs. He reeked of the stuff but he was high and this crazy trip was brief respite from a horrible reality. His perfect life had fallen apart: his marriage, his company, his relationship with Daniel – Tim could no longer look the kid in the eye. Her perfect boy was all Alex could think of. What about *his* kid?

His poor, dead baby . . .

Tim wanted *her.* A child he could see daily. His own flesh and blood. And if he couldn't have her, he wanted no one. A tear ran down his cheek, seeping into his mouth, warm and salty. Drugs were all well and good but what had begun as a daily pick-me-up had fast become an addiction. Even he had to admit that this was a trip too far.

Tim wept.

He'd been out of control for weeks, heading for disaster. Tonight, by the skin of his teeth he'd managed to keep it together. Stone and Oliver's presence at the airport was the last thing he needed. To call it a shock was a gross understatement. He had to admit, it had shaken him to the core. Embarrassing didn't cover it . . .

Not even close.

Had he managed to hide his anxiety from the police, or was he kidding himself? He was sure he'd kept his cool but then, as now, his heartbeat had become irregular. That walk from Northern Command HQ to his vehicle was the longest he'd ever take with the heat of Oliver's gaze bearing down on him from above.

Tim took a deep breath, his temperature rising, his most vital organ kicking a hole in his chest from the inside as he climbed into the car. His mobile was lying on the front passenger seat. He stared at the screen, his whole body shaking. It bleeped an incoming text from Alex, the fifth since he'd turned the phone back on. The words grew bigger and indistinct the more he looked at them. . .

The police were here.

Are you OK?

Call me.

A x

Five words was all he managed to type:

They think I killed Justine.

Did you?

Tim dropped the phone and held his head in his hands, elbows on the steering wheel, then sat up straight as more lights lit up the car. His eyes drifted to the roof of his vehicle, then to the rear-view mirror. A car had pulled up behind. No one exited the vehicle. The driver lit a cigarette and so did he. Was he under surveillance? Were they watching his every move? Oliver was right: he was paranoid. Had they let him go to see what he'd do next? What *would* he do next?

50

Saturday morning: 8 a.m. Stone had the SIO's office to himself, an opportunity to carry out a mini-review of his case. He liked days like this, time to concentrate without the distractions and constant interruptions of his normal daily routine. Phones were never silent in a murder incident room but call-takers wouldn't bother him today unless something vital came in. Then it would be game on, all systems go, calling staff back on duty if warranted.

Through his office door, David could see Frankie working away at her desk. When she'd stuck her head in earlier, she was a very different person from the one who'd left the night before. Fresh and well-rested. Her motivation was up and it showed. It was her commitment he valued most, that and a keen sense of justice, a drive to collar the bad guy and lay the victim to rest.

He felt it too.

Changing priorities were commonplace in any murder investigation. By their very nature, such cases were complex; it was often necessary to alter direction at a moment's notice. Unravelling these appalling tragedies was challenging but also immensely satisfying. It's what drew them both to the job, made them consider all the angles and kept them on their toes. Stone was hoping she was right about the burglary they had discussed last night. Time would tell if they would get a lead from it.

God knows, they could do with a break.

Sensing his gaze, Frankie stood up and approached his office door, checking her mobile as she walked, presumably for news. As she peered through the glass, he beckoned her in. 'I've widened the search area,' she said. 'I bloody hope that the East Cottage break-in is connected, otherwise I'll have blown a substantial amount of our budget on fresh air.'

'It's a chance I'm prepared to take,' Stone said. 'We need that murder weapon.'

'Hopefully Dick and Mitch will have something for us later. It's a bit early to expect anything yet. I'll cross everything and leave you to it.' She turned to leave.

He spoke as she opened the door. 'Have you got a minute, Frank?'

'Sure.' She remained in the doorway.

'Take a seat.'

'I'm fine standing.' She was staring at him, a little wary. When he failed to explain what he wanted, she closed the door and came closer, a concerned expression. 'Am I in trouble?'

'Why? Have you done something wrong?'

'No, but you don't look very happy.' She bit the inside of her cheek, curiosity getting the better of her. 'If I had to guess, I'd say that, whatever it is, it has Windy's name written all over it. Parker is well connected. Don't tell me his complaint reached the Chief already.'

Stone was shaking his head. 'Even if it had, he hasn't a leg to stand on. It won't come to anything, I promise you. Any grievance will be written off . . . along with all your others.'

'There aren't *that* many.' Frankie knew he was pulling her leg. 'Besides, who's counting? I have more commendations than reprimands and that's good enough for me. A detective with no complaints isn't trying hard enough, according to my old man. He should know. He had plenty. How about you?'

'Only the one.' Stone felt his stomach tighten. He hoped she wouldn't ask about the investigation into his conduct. He'd spent the best part of a year trying to put it behind him. The fact that he'd been absolved of all responsibility didn't make him feel any less of a disgrace. In his eyes, he was culpable. No matter how many times they said that he had nothing whatsoever to reproach himself for, he'd always be guilty. Preservation of life was the fundamental duty of any police officer.

'From the look on your face, I'm guessing it was a full-on disciplinary matter,' Frankie said. 'What did you do? Lamp someone who didn't like Ant and Dec?'

David's grin never made it to his eyes.

Frankie bridled. 'Do you and I have a problem?'

'No.'

'Do you?'

He knew what she meant. 'No.'

'Well, my bullshit detector just went off the scale.' She sat down . . . it was time to get serious. 'David, what is it? I get the impression that I've stepped in something very painful. Boss, we all have our demons. Is it something to do with your homecoming?'

'Yes.'

'Then get it off your chest. There's no one around and we're waiting on developments. I'm not being pushy, but if you feel the need to share, now's as good a time as any.'

'Drop it, Frank.' Stone shifted focus. 'We're not waiting anyway. There's been another armed robbery. Kelso this time. A hundred grand's worth. Occupants tied and gagged. This organised crime needs sorting.'

'Not our patch. Not our problem.'

'Except Windy is offering cross-border cooperation.'

'Wonder where he found that in the manual.' Frankie turned to face him. 'You'll be OK. As acting SIO, he can hardly pull you off the job.' The implication was clear. She looked crest-fallen. She'd worked hard on the investigation and wouldn't want to give it up before bringing about a resolution.

'Don't worry, Frank. You know too much about this case. You instigated the search for Daniel. To be honest, the explanation given for that bothers me. We have no idea if it is or was in some way connected to Justine's death. I want you on it with me. You have local knowledge I may need to tap into.'

'So does Dick. In case you haven't noticed, Windy likes him.'

'You're my DS.'

'And if Windy doesn't play ball, I'll be out on my ear.'

He knew she was right. 'I'll argue our case if and when that happens – I can be persuasive when I have to be. You want a drink?'

'No, I'm good thanks. Any thoughts overnight?'

'Plenty,' he said.

'You still want me to re-examine Hamilton's alibi?'

'I think so, don't you?'

'Absolutely. We know his vehicle pulled on to that garage forecourt in Gretna and that his credit card paid for the fuel.'

'It's definitely his van?'

Frankie nodded. 'The time and date on the receipt match up too, but I had a look at the CCTV. The blown-up image of who gets out isn't great. Sharpe might have been happy to eliminate Hamilton but, I have to say, I'm not convinced.' She pointed at his computer monitor. 'I'd like your opinion, if you wouldn't mind giving it the once-over.'

Stone logged on and brought up the image.

Seconds later, he looked up. 'I agree, it's not great quality. We – or should I say you – need eyes on Hamilton. We're kicking our heels until Dick and Mitch return with the results of their enquiries. Find out where Hamilton is today. Carlisle is only sixty miles away. If he's not there, Gretna isn't that much further. You can be there and back by lunchtime and it means I'll have more to throw at Windy, should he start making his mouth go.'

Frankie was already halfway to the door.

51

She left Northern Command HQ immediately, filling her police vehicle up before leaving North Tyneside. She took the A1 south, then turned right on the A69, the road that would take her west to Carlisle, a little over an hour's journey. Gary Hamilton had done well for himself. He lived in an elegant Grade II listed house in Stanwix Village, north of the River Eden, less than a mile from Carlisle city centre.

Building work was obviously a lot more lucrative than policing.

According to his other half – a lovely woman who introduced herself as Lucy – Gary was working the weekend at the same Gretna address Frankie knew about, a renovation project that, as a sole trader, would take him months to complete.

Lucy tucked her hair behind her ear. 'Is this about the accident?' she asked. 'Gary told me all about it. Terrible business. I think he was quite shocked by it.'

Frankie wouldn't collude with him by lying to her. 'I need a quick word with him, that's all.' She looked up. There was not a cloud in the sky. 'It's a lovely day. I quite fancy a run up to Gretna. Saves me having to head to the station. I have something I need to show him.' At least that part was true.

Lucy held on to the door. 'I'll call and let him know you're on your way.'

'No, please,' Frankie said. 'Don't put yourself out if he's busy. There's no point interrupting him twice.'

Lucy wasn't buying it. Frankie had no way of knowing if she'd call Hamilton to tip him off and had no power to stop her. Who could blame her? She was probably beside herself, wondering what had really brought the police to her door and exactly how her bloke was involved.

*

As she left Carlisle, heading north, Frankie thought about the interview with Tim Parker and his threat to contact the Chief Constable or, God forbid, the IPCC, an option he might well choose if there was even a remote possibility of damages. She wasn't overly concerned. She was well within her rights to retain Parker's DNA and fingerprints. Even so, it was good to know that Stone had her back when complaints were on the table.

Thinking of him made Frankie sad. Whatever was bothering him, whatever disaster had befallen him in London, her boss wasn't ready to disclose it yet. Perhaps, like her, he never would be. Some things were too painful to repeat, even verbally among close colleagues. She had the distinct feeling his bête noire was one of them.

The northbound M6 was busy.

Frankie turned on the radio for the ten o'clock news. Police and marshals were gearing up for a mass demonstration march in London against Britain leaving the EU. The word Brexit made her shiver. She switched channels. The reception wasn't great so she selected 'media' to access her most recent playlist. The rest of her journey was a blur.

Gretna wasn't the most picturesque Scottish border town Frankie had ever seen, but she wasn't stopping long. She was keen to find out if Dick and Mitch had made any progress with the burglary of Dixon's shed, near her crime scene. The renovation project Hamilton was working on was a two-storey Victorian villa with a large front garden. The house was clad in scaffolding and a rubbish chute led from an upstairs window into a skip below. The windows were open and she could hear music playing. A blue van was parked on the driveway, white lettering on the side: *Hamilton Building Services – Domestic and Commercial – ihandson.com – a family business.*

'Can I help you?'

Frankie turned to the voice. A man was sitting on the wall

to her left, covered in white dust: jeans, no shirt, tight pecs, a six pack. Frankie tried her best not to take an interest. It wasn't his well-developed physique but the dangerous-looking hammer dangling from his leather tool belt that had drawn her attention.

It wasn't a wrench but as good as.

'Gary Hamilton?'

'Who's asking?' The man stood up, took a last drag of a cigarette, flicking it away as he walked towards her in the sunshine, his body glistening with sweat.

Frankie held up ID. 'DS Oliver. Nice to meet you finally.'

'A bit off your patch, aren't you?'

'I made a special trip.'

'I thought we'd cleared the matter up.'

'I have one or two more questions.'

'Would this not do?' Hamilton pulled out his phone and held it up. 'How did you know I was here?' If his attitude was anything to go by, Lucy hadn't called or had failed to get through. From the look on his face, he'd made the jump before Frankie had time to answer.

'Your lass is under the impression that you were a witness to an RTA,' she said. 'I wonder where she got that idea?'

'You said—'

'Relax, Gary.' Frankie held up a hand. 'I don't break promises. I didn't enlighten her, and I won't, unless I'm forced to. So, now we've established that I'm trustworthy, let's see if you can say the same. Are we OK to have a chat?'

'Fire away.'

'My SIO is entirely satisfied that your van entered the Gulf petrol station at the time you indicated. He's even happy that a credit card registered in your name paid for the fuel. We're less sure about this . . .' She reached into her bag, pulled out an A4-sized photograph and held it up. She already knew the answer to the question she was about to ask. 'It's a grainy image, it has to be said. Is it you?'

Hamilton took it from her. His untroubled expression morphed into one of horror. Either that or he deserved a BAFTA. He raised his eyes slowly, the realisation dawning.

His alibi was in the wind.

'I swear to you that this is a genuine mistake,' he said. 'Look, I can explain. I saw the receipt and assumed—'

'Who is it, Gary?'

'My brother, but I wasn't trying it on—'

'Is that him?' Frankie pointed toward the house. Someone was clashing about inside, clouds of dust pouring from an upstairs window. 'I'd like a word with him, if I may.'

'Is that really necessary?'

'I think you already know it is.'

Hamilton sighed. Joining forefinger and thumb, he stuck both digits in his mouth and let out a shrill whistle. A head wearing a reflective hard hat popped out from the top-floor window, another ashen face, a protective mask hanging loose around his neck.

'Ian, get down here!'

Moments later, the lad emerged from the front door, the same stamp as Gary, if a little younger. Similar in build with hands the size of shovels. Leaving his hard hat on the front porch, he walked towards them, stuffing rigger gloves inside his utility belt, pushing safety goggles on top of short-cropped hair, the only part of him free of plaster dust that made Frankie think of Stone's missing ceiling.

Before the builder reached them, Frankie gave Gary Hamilton some friendly advice. 'Do yourself a favour and keep it shut. Leave this to me.'

'Something I can help you with?' the lad approaching said.

'I'm DS Oliver, Northumbria Police. And you are?'

'Ian . . . Hamilton.' He stuck his hand out. Realising how dirty it was, he withdrew it, wiping it on his jeans. His hands were full of callouses, fingernails bitten to the quick.

Frankie pointed at the vehicle on the driveway. 'Do you ever fill this van up with diesel, Mr Hamilton?'

'Aye, occasionally.'

'When was the last time you did that?'

He glanced at his brother. 'Dunno. A week, maybe.'

'Did you pay by card or cash?'

'Card. We have an account there.'

'We?' Frankie kept her focus on Ian but felt Gary's head go down.

Ian waved a forefinger between himself and his brother. 'Me and him.'

Frankie showed him the photo she'd just shown his brother. 'Can you tell me who this is?'

'It's me.' No hesitation.

Taking a crumpled pack of Marlboro from his pocket, he lit one and offered them around. Gary accepted. Frankie declined.

'Are you absolutely sure?' she asked.

Ian spoke with the cigarette hanging from his mouth. 'Positive.'

'Am I to assume that you're in business together?' They both had to think about that one. 'No? OK, maybe I got that wrong.' Frankie moved on. 'Is this the only vehicle you have?'

'No.' Gary Hamilton knew what was coming. 'Our other van is in the body shop. Bit of a prang on the roundabout. An old lady leaving the Gateway shopping centre shot out of there like Lewis Bloody Hamilton – no relation, more's the pity – took out my wing mirror and put a nasty dent in the side.'

He volunteered the registration.

Frankie wrote it down and turned to face his brother. 'Ian, you've been a great help. I won't keep you any longer. I just need another word with Gary before I leave. Would you mind?' She waited for him to move away before turning to face her witness. 'You told me that you were working alone on Wednesday, the twenty-second of June. That's not true, is it?'

He shook his head.

'Well, if Ian was with you that day, why the hell didn't you say so? I'm curious to know why you didn't give yourself an alibi when you could've done. Or was your brother grafting his arse off here while you were sixty miles down the road in Northumberland doing away with Justine Segal?'

52

The journey to North Tyneside was interesting. As Frankie crossed the Scottish border into Cumbria, her mobile rang. Dick and Mitch had returned to Northern Command HQ with news that Stone couldn't wait to deliver. Frankie's easygoing DI was suddenly on fire. 'Strangest burglary they've ever come across, apparently. There was some expensive kit in that shed, including a lawnmower worth over a grand: brand-new, motorised, a starter key left in the ignition, the whole works. Dick said he'd have given his right arm for it.'

'Not a random burglary then?'

'Not a chance. Our offender wasn't after what he could get, Frank. He was after that bike and a wrench.'

'Which begs the question, was he local?'

'That's what Dick said. He reckons whoever took the bike knew it was there. The shed was locked but they had no trouble getting in. The lock was still attached to the hasp. The wood was old, the door easily kicked in. Jerry Dixon supplied us with the bike guarantee, so we have make, model and serial number, should we ever find it—'

'We'll find it, David. Even If I have to look for it myself.'

'Dixon is meticulous about putting his tools where they belong. He's got one of those shadow boards with shapes cut out. Every damn tool was there except the wrench.'

Frankie braked as a slow-moving tractor emerged from a field on her left. She pulled out into the climbing lane that allowed eastbound vehicles to overtake on the hill. The A69 might be the major route linking north-east to north-west – or in her case, the other way around – but it could be a bummer if you wanted to get somewhere in a hurry.

'Did they get a photographic record of the shadow board?' she asked.

'Yup. They were very thorough.'

'We need to get it to the pathologist and try to source the exact same tool.'

'It's already on my desk,' Stone said. 'Dick's idea. Mitch did the legwork.'

'Did they question Marjorie Smith?'

'Relax, Frankie. They questioned everyone. It was a great idea to catch them on a Saturday morning. All four tenants were in. None of them saw or heard anything suspicious in the last month, but Marjorie had a good think and is adamant she got the day right regarding the bike. She saw the jogger first, then the cyclist.'

'How come she's so sure?'

'She remembered wondering why people run when they can ride.'

'You can see her point. It's hard work. Did the lads ask about direction of travel?'

'Mitch said she got a bit muddled at that point. First, she said it was heading away from the crime scene, then changed her mind. That's the only thing she's unsure of. Either way, the person could easily have diverted into the woods as you suggested last night. The rider was wearing Lycra and a dark baseball cap. The bike was moving too fast to establish gender.'

'What self-respecting burglar would turn up at a target property without a vehicle in which to transport his stash?' It was a rhetorical question from Frankie. 'The area is off the beaten track, not a major route. It's not likely that our man woke up after a night on the hoy and needed to get home, is it? Nor is Scots Gap a place you'd visit without a reason to.'

'Unless Justine arranged to meet someone, either at the house or along the road and it went horribly wrong. Although, you'd expect him to have wheels if that were the case, and we didn't find any abandoned cars.'

'Exactly. Public transport is dire in the sticks.' Frankie wound her window down, rested her arm on the sill and slowed down, frustrated with her lack of progress. 'Private transport sucks too sometimes. I'm stuck in traffic a mile long with some bugger up front doing forty in a sixty limit. WHY?'

'There's no rush to get back, Frank. Enjoy the sunshine.'

'Doesn't look like I have a choice,' she moaned.

David chuckled. 'How did you get on with Hamilton?'

'It was worth the trip. There are two Hamiltons, not one. Gary took over his father's business when he died. He has a younger brother on benefits who, as far as I can tell, is as fit as a flea.'

'He's working for Gary under the radar?'

'Yup. The black economy is alive and well in Gretna it seems. I showed them the photograph independently. They both coughed that it was Ian straight away. Gary swears he wasn't trying to mislead us and that the mix-up was genuine.'

'And you believe him?'

'Not a word. He claims that when he saw his vehicle registration on CCTV, he assumed it was him. He's too sharp for that. I think the daft sod found that receipt and saw a way of covering his arse without dropping his brother in it with the social. He might be capable of bending the truth but, if you're asking if he killed Justine, I'd have to say no.'

'That's good enough for me, Frank.'

'Yeah, well we're running out of suspects.'

'Or homing in. Cup half-full, Frankie.'

'That's another way of looking at it.' Traffic was moving again. 'Any news from the search team?'

'Not yet. I hate to say it, but they're not hopeful. Dick reckons that bike and the wrench will be in Bolam Lake.'

'I agree. We need to drag it.'

'We can't afford that.'

'Who said anything about money? Leave it with me, boss. I'll make some enquiries.'

'Into what?'

Frankie was the one with all the contacts locally. She'd been in the job long enough to know that when budgets were tight there were ways of getting what you wanted without it costing the earth. It was a question of utilising her connections, tapping into them. If she was good at one thing it was currying favours from those she'd assisted in the past. There were alternatives to explore. A means of expediting matters to her advantage.

She could do this . . .

'Trust me,' she said. 'I know what I'm doing.'

'You do *nothing* without prior consultation, is that clear? I can't have you swanning off and trashing the SIO's budget.'

'I thought you were the SIO—'

'Don't split hairs.'

'There's no point being SIO unless you act like one, David.' Frankie grinned. 'Hello? David, are you there? Reception is really bad . . . I'm losing you.'

'Pull the other one, Frank. I've used that one too. It won't wash.'

She cut him off.

53

Stone looked up as Frankie entered the incident room two hours later with a grin as wide as the Tyne. Worrying. He was almost frightened to ask what had taken her so long. The word scheming sprang to mind. On the one hand, he didn't want to know. On the other, he was desperate to find out where she'd been – who with – and how many she'd roped into her plans.

She took off her jacket and sat down. 'You will *not* believe what just happened.'

'We already don't,' Stone said.

Frankie placed a hand on her chest, feigning innocence. 'I'm crushed that you think so little of me.'

Stone raised an eyebrow. 'Where have you been, Frank?'

Dick and Mitch were all ears. Whatever Frankie had been up to, they knew she wouldn't have been wasting her time.

'Where?' Stone asked again.

'A short detour through the Tyne Tunnel to Jarrow. Don't panic, I paid the toll with my own pocket money. It won't come out of your precious budget. I know how stretched you are.'

'Get on with it then.'

'The Marine Unit have a new intake. They want to do a training exercise and they'd like to do it at Bolam Lake. They want me to assist as pretendy SIO and issue instructions. Isn't that exciting? It means I get to play for half a day, if that's OK with you?' She was looking directly at David. 'What's more, they'd like to start this afternoon.'

Dick was shaking his head, a big smile. 'How the hell did you manage to swing that?'

'I told them the boss just returned from the Met and that he's a keen Sunderland supporter. Couldn't stay away apparently—'

'What?!' Stone almost choked on his coffee.

'The sergeant is a Wearsider. I had to tell him something! You've got a friend for life there, boss.'

Bolam Lake Country Park was beautiful, a tranquil nature trail in the heart of Northumberland's stunning countryside, an area teeming with wildlife that had open woodland and grassland on which to picnic. The destination was loved by walkers, anglers and families alike. Frankie's favourite was Pheasant Field where her parents used to take her as a kid. She arrived at the lake before the Marine Unit's underwater search team, a chance to look around and plan her operation. The lake itself was bordered on two sides by unnamed minor roads. She drove the route. There was little traffic and a few places where a car might stop unnoticed. She pulled into West Wood car park, noting the lack of CCTV, then did the same at the main car park at Boathouse Wood.

Abandoning her wheels there, she set off on foot.

The lake was only three-quarters of a mile long. She walked the circular path, anticlockwise, recceing every possible location where a vehicle could park close to the water's edge. In the end, she decided that a savvy killer wouldn't choose one of three public car parks where they might be recognised or seen acting suspiciously by a canny eyewitness. By the time she'd completed the circuit, her Marine Unit colleagues were unloading their kit from their cargo van: Sergeant Stan Burnett, seven of his officers and one technician.

'Thanks for doing this,' Frankie said. 'I really appreciate it.'

'Happy to help.' Burnett's Wearside accent was strong. 'Have you had long enough to formulate a plan?'

She nodded. 'I've driven and walked the route.'

'Great. Where do you want us to start?'

'There are three locations I'm interested in, for no other reason than it's where I'd dispose of a bike if it was hot. Our theory is that the offender we're after used a wrench to commit a serious offence and a bike to get home and then disposed of it later. Working on that assumption, it has to be a place where a car might stop for long enough for our offender to lift a pedal cycle the weight and size of Jerry Dixon's from a vehicle and lob it with enough force to reach deep water.' She pointed at the shoreline. 'As you can see, it's pretty shallow near the edge.' An afterthought: 'That's assuming they had a car and didn't ride here.'

'And if they didn't?'

'Then we're screwed. If they came on the bike the items could have been disposed of anywhere along the water's edge and we/you have no resources to drag the whole lake. I can only hope that's not the case.'

Frankie had half-inched four leaflets from a dispenser on the wall outside the visitor centre, illustrating the lake and surrounding area. She took them from her pocket. On each one, she'd marked three locations in blue biro and numbered them in order of priority. She gave Burnett three copies for his team and kept the last so she could explain what she was after. He was both impressed and grateful.

The Marine Unit were drawing a crowd. They were a friendly bunch, well used to public attention as they donned dry suits. They chatted away to day-trippers, explaining that they were on a routine training exercise in a search-and-recovery-style operation. One diver was allowing kids a sneak peek of their equipment van, another issuing a gentle warning of the dangers of playing even in shallow water as he pulled on breathing apparatus.

Burnett and Frankie moved out of earshot.

'My number one choice is on the south-west side where the road is nearest to the lake,' she said. 'There's a pull-in there with direct access to the water's edge. In my opinion, location two on the south-east side is risky but doable, depending on visitor numbers.' She looked at Burnett. 'It was tanking down on the day we're interested in, so maybe not that many people were about, unless they were anglers who like to get wet.'

'How long ago was this?'

'June twenty-second. Why d'you ask?'

'It was closed season until a fortnight ago,' he said. 'So, there may well have been quite a few anglers about. Even if there weren't, people like to sit in their cars and read, have a picnic, or even something more personal on a rainy day.'

'Exactly.' Her eyes were on the map. 'As you can see, number two is closest to the car park where we're standing, which also happens to be the busiest. See this . . .' She moved her finger. 'A lone parking spot on the south side of the road with easy access via stone steps to the shoreline. Once up the steps and over the wall, the location is hidden from the road by rhododendron bushes. A good spot in which to hide and pick your time. Assuming the bike and weapon were dumped here, our offender would have good vision in all directions and would hear anyone coming a mile off.'

Burnett was way ahead of her, studying the map closely. 'Location three is risky in my view. The jetty on the south side is useful to lose the bike in deeper water, but it's much less secure. It can be seen from other areas by walkers who don't mind the rain. It only takes one pair of eyes and you'd never be aware of them from that distance if it was chucking it down. The jetty would be visible to anyone sheltering on the northern bank.'

Frankie agreed.

'Tell me about the weapon.' Burnett waited.

'It's a wide-jaw adjustable wrench. Pretty heavy.'

'Make?'

'Holden: fourteen inches long.'

The Marine Unit sergeant scribbled down her description. 'Don't hold your breath on that score,' he said, looking up.

'Thrown with some welly, it would go a damned sight further than a bike. We might never find it. To be honest, if it was me, I'd have chucked the items in separately. Less chance of being found that way, assuming your offender was thinking straight at the time.'

Burnett glanced at his watch. It was almost six. His team were ready to roll. Frankie watched them huddle together for a quick briefing. They climbed into a transit van and set off in the direction of the West Wood, leaving their spectators behind, Frankie included. She went to her car to wait, then got out again. She couldn't settle.

The wind was picking up. After a beautiful day, the sun had gone. A darkening sky hinted at more rain. After pacing up and down for half an hour, her phone rang: *Burnett*.

Mentally, she crossed her fingers. 'Oliver.'

'Location one is a negative, Frank. No bike or wrench.'

'Damnit!' She tried not to sound downhearted. 'Tell your lads the beers are on me if they find either.'

'I offered them curry.' Burnett chuckled. 'Isn't that what Saturday nights are for?'

'You're on.' Frankie had no plans for the evening beyond calling on her dad. The thought that marine officers might have private business pricked at her conscience – she hoped she wasn't trashing their arrangements or wasting their time.

'We're moving on to location two,' Burnett said.

'I'll meet you there in ten.'

He ended the call.

Wildfowl bobbed up and down on choppy water and swans took shelter in the shallows as Frankie made her way on foot to meet them. A canoe sailed by as she arrived, the kids inside craning their necks to see what was going on. A diver Burnett had introduced earlier as PC Gail Rickerby disappeared beneath water that was gunmetal grey, the canoeists moved on by dive buddies holding her safety line. There were always more officers above the surface than below.

It was starting to rain.

Frankie was a little claustrophobic. She couldn't imagine how cold it was in the murky water, groping your way through mud and debris with nil visibility and the constant danger of entanglement. The Marine Unit would never have suited her. With one eye on the operation, she called Stone. Reception was poor. He was in transit, probably making his way to his dilapidated cottage in Pauperhaugh. Right now, she'd give anything to be sitting in his nan's rocking chair in front of a roaring fire, a glass of good malt, the prospect of a night of television ahead of her.

'Sorry not to have good news,' she told him.

'Keep at it, Frank.'

'We don't even know that Bolam Lake is the dump site.'

'You should have thought about that.' He was joking. 'Don't give up. Your intuition has been right so far.'

*

Twenty minutes later, a bike emerged from the depths of the lake, held aloft by Rickerby. Burnett raised a thumb and took a photographic record of the diver standing there with her find. Frankie waited with bated breath, hoping that the pedal cycle was the one she was looking for and not someone else's. Photo shoot over, the bike was transported from the water, covered in sludge.

More photographs . . .

More detail . . .

A Marin Muirwoods 29ER, matte black with reflective graphics.

Accessing the Notes app on her mobile, Frankie knelt beside the Marin, pulling on a pair of nitrile gloves. She wiped a small amount of muck away from the serial number, checking it against the entry as Rickerby arrived by her side. Frankie's smile was all the confirmation the officer needed that her job was done – half of it anyway. If she could find the wrench, they would hear Frankie scream from Northern Command HQ.

A familiar voice shouted: 'Good work!'

Frankie stood up, turning to the voice.

Stone was right behind her, sheltering from the rain, a Sunderland FC football scarf hanging loose round his neck. She burst out laughing and so did Burnett.

'I told him you're a Toon supporter,' Frankie said.

Stone handed Burnett the scarf, any rivalry between them melting away.

54

The search at Bolam Lake went on, Burnett insisting that he'd use the remaining daylight hours to locate the wrench, assuming it was there. He suggested that Stone and Oliver leave his team to it – now that the bike had been found the detectives had much to discuss. Frankie wasn't having that. Dragging them out on a Saturday night weighed heavily on her mind. The least she could do was feed them. Her old man's weekly bulletin would have to wait.

Cancelling her plans to visit him, she texted instead:

Still grafting, Dad. It's nice for some!
Any point keeping you some bait?
None. I'll be hours yet.
Stay safe. x
xx

Frankie pocketed her phone. Her father would be disappointed. He loved their special time together when her mum was playing bridge. If Rae and Andrea were there too, all the better. Policing had been her father's life. Since his retirement, he'd found it hard to switch off. Stone opened the car door and climbed in.

He saw her sad expression before she had to time hide it.

'Everything OK?' he asked.

'Couldn't be better,' she lied.

She'd miss her dad tonight.

Starting the car, she left Boathouse Wood, turning right towards Belsay, then left on the A696 to Ponteland – a village eight miles south. According to Burnett, the team had binned the idea of curry in favour of Cantonese. The New

Rendezvous restaurant had a fantastic takeaway menu, especially for groups as big as theirs. He'd called the order in and was told it would be ready in an hour, enough time for Stone and Oliver to slip into the Diamond Pub next door for a swift half and a chat before collection.

They took their drinks outside. It had stopped raining and the sun had come out. The seats were wet, so they stood in the sunshine, neither of them saying much. After all the excitement of recovering the bike, Stone began to question how far it would take them. 'Have you considered the possibility that this burglary has sod-all to do with our investigation?'

'Several times . . . but there hasn't been a burglary in that area for moons. It's practically a crime-free zone, David. I told you, it's like your place – nowt happens there.'

'You're not selling it to me, Frank.'

'Don't be daft. Your cottage is divine. All I'm saying is, Marjorie Smith has lived in her house for fifty-plus years and has never known trouble, let alone a break-in.'

'Then it's well overdue.'

'I don't think it's a coincidence. Do you? Really?'

'No.' He was buzzing.

Frankie took a sip of lemonade. 'If it was only the bike, I might consider it. Linked with a tool identical to the one used on our victim, no. That is a coincidence too far. It must be connected. There's no other way to read it, in my view. You heard the pathologist. Justine's injuries are entirely consistent with the wrench we sourced, even down to the size of the worm screw and adjustable jaws. It all fits. That's why we need that weapon.'

She paused, checking her phone, her face set in a scowl.

Stone's eyes were asking if there had been any developments. She shook her head and he carried on as if there had been no interruption. 'Deep down, we both know that weapon came from Dixon's shed. It's a question of whether the burglary was random or not: ancient shed; stolen wrench; Justine in the wrong place at the wrong time. Or . . . and this is important . . . was the wrench stolen to facilitate her murder?'

He let the sentence hang.

In any murder case, the possibilities were endless. Frankie was mulling it over, trying to fit it all together in her head. It was the first time that he'd properly looked at her. She was tired and yet undeterred. She would debate the whys and wherefores all day long if it resulted in putting away the sick bastard that struck an innocent jogger, incapacitating her, dragging her on to a bridge to face certain death. It was an action beyond cruel. Frankie wouldn't rest until someone was behind bars.

'Maybe there's another question we should be asking ourselves,' she said.

'Like what?'

'If the burglar kicked the door in knowing exactly what was inside, maybe they're trying to pull a fast one by pointing us in the wrong direction. We have one eye on Parker, right? Me, more than you, probably . . .' Stone didn't argue. Frankie wasn't done. 'He lives close to our crime scene *and* admits to being home—'

'He had no choice. He was seen by Alex.'

'But why stay home if he was guilty? If he *is* the culprit, wouldn't he make damn sure he wasn't there? I would. The fact that he was home draws, rather than deflects, suspicion.'

'You've changed your tune.'

'Hey! I called as I saw it. What was it you said? Just because I don't like him doesn't make him guilty. Rule 8: If you've made an arse of yourself, front up.' She pulled a silly face. 'I'm more than happy to be wrong if someone is trying to shaft him, David.'

Traffic lights outside the pub changed to red. In seconds, there was a long line of cars waiting in both directions. It gave Frankie an idea. 'There were many men in Justine's life. Maybe one of her admirers is trying to frame Parker for reasons unknown to us. Curtis, for example. His convenient fishing trip worries me. And another thing . . . if Justine knew her assailant, that could explain how they got close to her. That person may even have parked in the woods opposite—'

Stone shook his head. 'Why would they need the bike if they had a car?'

'Hear me out. Our search team didn't go into the woods until hours later, *after* Marjorie Smith pointed out that it was a regular rendezvous. Andrea said there was a tailback of traffic immediately after the incident. If the assailant's exit route was blocked, that could account for the bike theft. We're assuming both items were lifted at the same time. We don't know that for sure. If Justine's attacker was blocked in, they may have doubled back to Dixon's shed to steal the bike as a means of escape, or maybe Jeremiah knows more about this than he's letting on.'

Her comment entered Stone's head in the shape of a question mark. Another theory, another avenue to explore. He was almost frightened to ask where she was heading. Burnett's intervention meant he didn't have to.

55

Against the odds, the Marine Unit had found the wrench and retained it in a tray in their utility vehicle. It wasn't unprecedented, but it was unusual for underwater investigators to process evidence at the scene. It would be transported to the laboratory for forensic examination. No bagging was necessary. Leaving it to dry in ambient temperature would preserve it, giving scientists half a chance of success. Immersion in water destroyed most things. Frankie hoped they would get lucky.

The wrench was rusty, its surface pitted with age. That would aid the pathologist to determine if it was the actual murder weapon. It was unlikely to help the investigation beyond that. Nevertheless, there were high fives all round, well-earned thanks as well as sincere congratulations extended to every member of the dive team, a big pat on the back for Burnett, without whom the operation would never have taken place. With goodwill and no funding, his unit had gone above and beyond a duty call.

Stone proffered a hand. 'This won't be forgotten.'

'He's right,' Frankie said. 'We owe you, Stan.'

'And you will pay.' Burnett had half an eye on the takeaway. 'Anything in those bags will do. Get 'em open, Frank. My crew are ravenous.'

She dumped the Cantonese on a picnic table, telling everyone to dig in. No one held back. There wasn't room for everyone to sit so she and Stone grabbed some food and parked themselves on the tailgate of her car. In fading light, the divers ate enthusiastically – and so did they – until David's mobile pierced the peace and tranquillity of Boathouse Wood. After such a long and taxing day, Frankie was irritated by the interruption.

'We're not in,' she said. It wasn't like her to be grumpy.

'If only that were true,' Stone told her. Theirs was the age of constant interruption, when every police officer was contactable round the clock. He checked his mobile and was visibly apprehensive.

Frankie was instantly on her guard. 'Who is it?'

'My old boss.'

'Could be worse.'

'No, it couldn't.'

She laughed. 'I was thinking Professional Standards.'

'That's not remotely funny.' It was out of his mouth before he could stop it.

Frankie was taken aback. He'd gone from jubilant to irritated in the blink of an eye. She wanted to apologise, retract her comment and explain that she hadn't meant anything by it, but no words would remove the wounded expression on his face. She couldn't fathom what had triggered his angry outburst when they were in such a bloody good mood.

Burnett looked over in their direction, a concerned expression. Frankie smiled, covering her distress. He returned to his food and she relaxed. He drank with her old man and she didn't want him telling tales out of school. If her dad thought Stone was giving her a hard time, there would be hell to pay. She was a big girl now, capable of fighting her own battles. And still Stone was procrastinating.

As far as Frankie was aware, this was the first time anyone from the Met had been in touch with him. Now she came to think of it, that was odd. The police family were famous for maintaining contact. She only needed to look across the car park to the picnic table to witness the camaraderie. You didn't last long in their job without the support of fellow officers. Fighting crime was the glue that bound them together. Watching each other's backs came as second nature. They trusted each other instinctively. If one was hurting, they all were. They didn't forget or lose touch.

So why now?

Stone was in two minds whether to answer. Frankie wondered if the persistent caller was the reason he'd fled the south in such a hurry. She was convinced it was something to do with a woman. She couldn't keep her mouth shut when it came to her old boss but David had never once spoken of his. This contact represented a major trauma for him, as had his initial meeting with Alex Parker. Like a rabbit caught in headlights, he'd frozen, and that bugged her. The time had never been right to tackle him on the subject . . .

Luke dying had put paid to that.

'Go on!' She tried to make amends. 'Maybe you won the force lottery.'

Reluctantly, he pressed to accept.

'Sinead?' He cleared his throat. 'Great to hear from you.'

His expression told another story. It was blatant lies. There was nothing great or even good about this call. Whoever Sinead was, she represented a memory too painful for him to share, even in loose terms: old boss, girlfriend, mate? In all the time Frankie had been working with him, the name had never once come up.

Unless Sinead was THE woman?

'Yes,' Stone appeared on edge. 'I spoke to her quite recently . . . last Wednesday, why? . . . What? . . . No!' He was getting more and more tense the longer the conversation went on. He listened for what seemed like an age. By the time the caller paused for breath, he'd lost his appetite. 'Yes, of course . . .' His food hit the bin. Frankie's followed soon after. His eyes gave nothing away as he hung up. 'We need to get to the Parkers' house now.'

56

Of all the scenarios conjured up in their heads on the way to Scots Gap, what greeted Stone and Oliver was unexpected. As they turned off the main road, the driveway was crammed with high-end vehicles, lights on in every room in the house, a party going on, inside and out. As they got out of the car, music drifted in the air from the garden, the smell of a barbecue, the sound of chatter and laughter. No one came when they rang the bell, so they walked round the side of the house.

The garden was stunning, lights twinkling from every tree, guests spilling out of a marquee with champagne and canapés, staff in uniform walking round with trays of fizz and more food. Alex and Tim Parker were in the centre of the lawn, clinking glasses with another couple, his arm around her waist. A picture-perfect scene, the first time that either detective had seen the couple genuinely at ease in each other's company. No one noticed the detectives standing in the shadows.

'Jesus!' Frankie said. 'Talk about making our job more difficult.'

Stone nodded to the patio doors. 'Go inside. Clear the house so we have somewhere to take them. This is going to be hard enough without an audience.'

Frankie left him.

Less than a minute later, she emerged from the house, moving curious guests outside. Stone gave her the nod. Independently, they made a beeline for the Parkers. Over her husband's shoulder, Alex caught Frankie's eye as she strode across the lawn. Daniel's mother was instantly on her guard. Like the first time they had met, another moment of menacing clarity passed between the two women. Whatever had prompted the detective sergeant's visit was not news Alex Parker wanted to hear.

Making her apologies, she drew Tim away from their friends, a look of trepidation wiping away the joy Frankie had witnessed on her face moments earlier. Tim Parker wasn't keen to leave his conversation until he saw Frankie. When he clocked the DI approaching, his reaction was one of disdain. He was angry that the pair had the effrontery to visit in full view of his posh mates.

Before he could create a scene, Stone politely asked them both to step inside.

They went into Alex's study, closing the door behind them, less chance that someone might stumble in there unaware that the detectives had come to deliver yet another death message. Stone invited them to sit. The couple declined. Their hands came together, a show of solidarity in the face of they didn't know what. Someone had turned the music off outside, the jungle telegraph informing guests that Tim's fortieth birthday party was over.

Frankie waited for Stone to begin.

He hesitated.

She chanced a quick glance in his direction. His body language was rigid, eyes fixed on Alex. To anyone who didn't know him well it was impossible to detect. Frankie knew that he'd come apart at the worst time possible.

She had to cover for him . . . yet again.

'Alex, I'm so sorry,' she said. 'We've been informed by the Metropolitan Police that your sister Kathryn Tailford Irwin was found dead in her apartment yesterday.'

'Ohmigod, no!' Her hands flew to her face. There followed a moment's silence. 'I don't understand . . . Was there some kind of accident?'

'We believe that she died at home sometime in the afternoon. Detectives in the south are treating her death as suspicious. Her little girl is safe and with the childminder.'

301

'What?' Anguish instantly turned to relief, then anger. Alex took a deep breath, unable to express her feelings. 'You better check your facts, DS Oliver. Kat has no children.'

Now Frankie was floundering. Without Stone in support, she had to think on her feet. The only reason she could imagine keeping a secret as big as that had just put an arm around his wife. Suddenly, it all made sense: Timothy Parker's anxiety; large amounts of cash disappearing from his business account; the so-called bad blood between them. Kat's attempt to blacken his name was the only thing that didn't fit. If she was convicted for Justine's murder, she could kiss goodbye to child support. And now she too was dead.

Frankie would debate this when Stone got his shit together. *She couldn't think about that now.* She had a job to do. All that mattered was conveying the awful news as sensitively as she could, offering support to a woman who currently looked like she was losing her mind.

'Alex, we wouldn't be here discussing this if there was any doubt,' Frankie said gently. 'I spoke to the childminder myself. She's known Kat since before the child was born—'

'I don't give a shit who you spoke to. You've got this wrong! As you know only too well, I recently spent a week with my sister. She said nothing about a child. Why would she keep a thing like that from me?'

'That's a question I'm unable to answer. If you'd prefer to speak to the Senior Investigating Officer, I can give you her contact number. All I can say is, the facts have been checked and rechecked. The child's birth certificate was found in Kat's apartment. I really don't know what else to say.'

Alex palmed her brow. 'How old is this child?'

'Three.'

'No, I don't believe it. Kat and I have had our problems, but she would have told me if she was a mother.'

Frankie knew of only one way to ram the message home. It would hurt Alex deeply.

It had to be done.

'Her name is Ali.'

Alex wept openly. Tim Parker did absolutely nothing to help her. With her eyes on Alex, Frankie was unable to gauge his reaction. She hoped, for both their sakes, that Stone was getting some of this.

57

Having taken the seven fifty-five Virgin East Coast train out of Newcastle, Stone and Oliver arrived at King's Cross shortly before eleven. He led the way along the platform, an overnight bag slung over his shoulder, Frankie following close behind. Once through the barrier, he turned right, heading for the taxi rank. It was a lovely day outside. After sitting all morning, and with a couple of hours to spare before meeting the Metropolitan Police SIO at one o'clock, Frankie would rather have walked than taken a cab, but David was on a mission with no stop button.

The news had shaken them both. They had spent the last three hours in complete silence, scanning electronic documents on laptops, familiarising themselves with a murder investigation instigated by a Detective Superintendent whose incident room was almost three hundred miles from their Northumberland base. At no point had Frankie felt able to bone him about stalling the night before. When they left the Parkers to their grief last night, he'd made it abundantly clear that the subject wasn't open for discussion.

'Burlington Arms,' he told the cabbie.

Frankie looked at him. 'Have we got time?'

'We'll make time.'

'We shouldn't drink—'

'Then don't. I need one.'

'Your funeral.'

He looked away.

He wasn't the only one who needed a drink but Frankie kept that to herself. She stared blankly out of the window, a world alien to her. Last time she was in London, she was in and out in a couple of hours. It had taken forty minutes to travel half a mile. Though traffic was light this morning, the closer they got to their destination, the busier it got.

Deciding to walk the rest of the way, they abandoned their cab on Regent Street, an area teeming with visitors, even on a Sunday morning. The West End Central nick wasn't far away, a five-storey stone structure situated in the heart of Mayfair, one of the Metropolitan Police's busiest stations, Stone's former workplace. On the junction of Savile Row and Boyle Street, Frankie glanced up at the building, the Met flag flying on top. An old-fashioned blue lamp caught her eye, beneath it state-of-the-art CCTV, the old and the new, side by side – like her and granddad, Frank.

Thinking about him made her smile.

The pub was at the rear of the station. Whoever had named it the West End's best-kept secret wasn't wrong. It was much less busy than she expected, a traditional London pub on a quiet street, occupying the ground floor of a yellow-brick building, its window boxes stuffed with greenery above a red awning, THE BURLINGTON ARMS picked out in gold lettering.

On the corner of Coach and Horses Yard, empty beer barrels waited on the pavement for replacement and collection. At Stone's request, Frankie took a seat outside, facing the rear of the nick, police vehicles with Met insignia lining the street in front of her. She savoured a moment alone. Time to chill before facing what was undoubtedly the single most important moment of her career. Liaison with the Met was a big deal for any detective, except Frankie had the distinct impression that it wasn't *her* nerves Stone was trying to quell, the beer in his hand testament to his reluctance to cross the road and go inside.

'Now there's a sight for sore eyes.' A local accent.

Frankie looked up to find a detective standing over her.

It took one to know one.

For a moment, she assumed that Stone had arranged to

meet an ex-colleague for the low-down on the case they had travelled to assist, a misjudgement on her part, as it turned out. Stone got up and shook hands but Frankie wasn't feeling the love between the two men, and so it proved . . .

'How's it going, Dave?' the Met officer said.

'Good. It's great to be back.'

'Yeah, right. I heard—'

'I said I'm good. Let's leave it there, eh?'

The local detective put his hands up as if Stone was holding a gun.

David drained his pint, wiping froth from his upper lip with his hand. 'I'd love to chat but I'm running late. Frankie, we need to go.'

The Met officer gave her the once-over. 'Nice meeting you, Frankie.'

'Detective Sergeant . . . Oliver.'

'Come to help us out, have you?'

'Don't we always?'

The man flicked his head in Stone's direction. 'He was a good DCI . . . once.' It was a spiteful dig at David's reduction in rank. 'I'll see you around, Frankie.'

'Not if I see you first.'

His grin was superficial.

Stone practically frogmarched Frankie over the road, making no comment on what had transpired outside the pub or the nature of the unsettling exchange. They were given visitor passes and shown to an office on the third floor. The name on the door said: DETECTIVE SUPERINTENDENT SINEAD FRIEL.

Stone knocked and waited.

'Come!' The woman they had come to see was around forty years of age. Sitting behind a large desk, she looked up as they entered the room, a pair of green smiley eyes seizing on Stone. 'David, welcome back!' She didn't get up to greet him.

'Guv, this is DS Frances Oliver,' he said.

'Frances?' Frankie made a face. 'That's my Sunday name, ma'am. Frankie is fine. I'm very pleased to meet you.'

'Nice to meet a kindred spirit.' Friel's was a firm handshake. 'Let's dispense with the formality then, Frankie. Two expats are now three, so we are. In my case Dublin, should you need to brush up on Irish accents. We stick together – right, David?' Stone nodded a reply. 'He probably told you that we landed in London in the same intake.'

'He did.' Frankie lied out of politeness.

'Oh yes, 2001 was a good year.' Sinead smiled warmly, a brief glance at her office door. 'We formed a secret partnership at training school so we could bitch about the locals. We've since learned that they're a good bunch, on the whole.'

Fifteen years was a lifetime in policing.

This was more than mutual respect.

They were close.

Very close.

Some people you are drawn to instantly. Sinead Friel was one of them. It didn't take long for Frankie to realise what a popular guy David was down south and what he'd left behind when he returned to his Northumberland roots. Almost every detective in the Murder Investigation Team came to shake his hand, offer a kind word, a friendly pat on the back, each one genuinely pleased to see him . . . bar one. The female DS hung back, her reticence obvious from across the room. Frankie couldn't make her mind up whether there was bad blood there or they were close and trying to hide it. An unspoken message passed from the Met detective to Stone: *Not now. Later? Maybe.* Yup, there was unfinished business in the capital. Something that might cause a problem for him. Whatever it was, as his new sidekick, it was Frankie's job to ensure that it didn't.

58

The SIO called for order: those that were standing, sat down; phone calls were ended; conversations abandoned; other work cast aside by the Murder Investigation Team. Detective Superintendent Sinead Friel waited patiently. Only when she had the full attention of her team did she formally welcome Stone back into the fold and introduce Frankie.

'There's a lot to get through,' she said. 'As you all know, Kathryn Tailford Irwin – known as Kat to her friends – was found murdered in her flat the day before yesterday in the early afternoon. Post-mortem results are in. Time of death around noon, give or take. The IP was found by the caretaker at Montagu Square who was checking the building after the fire alarm went off. A false alarm, as it turned out. According to the pathologist, there were no injuries associated with sexual assault, although there was semen present, so maybe forensics will be able to assist us in that respect. One can hope. DI Stone is here at my request. His number is one that Kyra recognised instantly. It was stored on Kat's mobile device and appeared on her call list on Wednesday, June twenty-ninth, a conversation lasting just twenty seconds. A few minutes later, DI Stone called her, a call lasting four minutes and twenty-five seconds.'

'So why is he not in cells, guv?' The facetious comment had come from the arsehole they had encountered in the street.

Stone took it on the chin.

Frankie didn't. 'Because at eleven o'clock on Friday, July the first we were briefing our SIO at Northumbria Northern Command HQ. We were doing police work. You should try it sometime. Virgin trains are good, but they ain't that good. And, as far as I know, my guv'nor doesn't own a private

308

jet to get him to the capital in time to murder Kat Irwin.'

'I see you've met DC Connor,' Sinead Friel said.

Everyone laughed.

The SIO moved on. 'David, you are always welcome here. The floor is yours.'

Frankie was giving the arsehole the thousand-yard stare. There was a Connor in every office. While Stone had given up a rank to move north, it was his choice to do so. He hadn't been demoted for neglect of duty or discreditable conduct and she'd defend him come what may. Addressing his former team might be difficult for him but he was up to it.

He took a moment to gather his thoughts, ignoring Connor's attempt to belittle him, treating the untimely interruption as if it hadn't taken place. 'On June seventeenth, DS Oliver and I began investigating the disappearance of Kat Irwin's nephew, Daniel Scott. Kat and the child's mother, Alex Parker, are sisters. They were in Majorca at the time, leaving the lad in the care of his stepfather, Timothy Parker, a well-connected entrepreneur who lives on our patch.'

A hand went up.

It belonged to the female DS who hadn't come to greet Stone earlier. Nicknamed 'the reluctant detective' by Frankie for giving Stone a wide berth when they first entered the in-cident room, she stood up, the better to see and be seen. She was around the same age as Stone, approximately mid-thirties, average height, dark sultry eyes, hair worn in a messy side braid that appeared a simple look to achieve, only Frankie happened to know that it wasn't.

Stone was smiling at her. 'Kyra? You wanted to say something?'

'Just that Parker's home and mobile numbers are listed in the victim's contacts.' Kyra held up a blown-up image of a man she hadn't been able to identify. 'Forensics found this photograph while sweeping her apartment. I was hoping you or DS Oliver might be able to help.'

'That is Timothy Parker,' Frankie said.

'How odd,' the SIO said. 'Who keeps a photograph of their brother-in-law?'

'I think I know the answer,' Kyra said. 'There are ranting, vicious texts between Parker and Kat on her phone. She was putting the bite on him to increase child support and cared less that indirectly it was being paid for by her sister. Kat saw it as her due. Reading between the lines, she was left out of her parents' will after falling out with them. Alex got the lot.'

This news was gold to Stone, the kind of information that never came to light until wills were read and lawyers got involved. Every family had secrets. He made a mental note to look up the circumstances surrounding the death of the parents of these two sisters.

'Parker said he couldn't pay,' Kyra added. 'It didn't go down well. I gather the family home is worth millions.'

It was all beginning to make perfect sense to Stone. He and Frankie had been wondering why Kat was so poisonous on the phone. Maybe she wanted Parker out of her sister's life and hers. Maybe she thought that, with him out of the way, it would let her back in. Maybe she resented the fact that he'd spent much of what she considered her own inheritance.

Apologising for the interruption, Kyra sat down.

Stone thanked her for her input. 'Kyra's information is very helpful to us. For now, if I may, I'd like to return to Daniel. The investigation into his disappearance was short-lived. It had hardly got going when he was returned home, safe and well, having been for a sleepover at a friend's house. We put it down to a genuine mix-up. Lack of communication between Parker and the family's French au pair, Justine Segal. The missing person's case was wound up, written off as no further action.' He paused. 'However, and this is where it gets interesting, a week later, on June twenty-second, Justine was found dead in an isolated spot in Northumberland, having been attacked and then dragged alive into the middle of a country road, where she subsequently met her death having been run over by a motor vehicle approaching the blind summit of a humpback bridge.'

Stone had the team in the palm of his hand.

'Let me be clear,' he said. 'What happened to Justine was entirely deliberate. She didn't collapse and crawl into the middle of the road. The Home Office pathologist has confirmed that she would not have been able to get there under her own steam due to a severe head injury. She'd been struck with an adjustable wrench and placed in mortal danger by some sick fuck who wanted her dead. We concluded that the offender was attempting to make it look like an accident, but her head injury was inconsistent with being run over. Our underwater search team recovered what we believe to be the weapon from a nearby lake yesterday.'

Stone waited for detectives to catch up.

Frankie's attention strayed to the murder wall where the IP's name was written above a series of crime scene photographs of her lying dead on her living room floor, blood pooling around her head, eyes open as if affronted by the barefaced cheek of her assailant.

If only the dead could speak.

David's soft Geordie lilt brought her back into the room.

'Last Wednesday, Kat Irwin called me out of the blue, that twenty-second call the guv'nor mentioned. I checked she was who she said she was and called her back. She told me that she and Parker didn't get along. From what Kyra has said, that much was true. Kat told me that a third party had told her that he was a serial philanderer, after her sister's money and probably screwing Justine before her death. She put forward no proof and yet she begged me to offer Alex Parker and her nephew police protection.'

Stone glanced at Frankie, her cue to say a few words.

She hadn't expected it and was grateful for the chance to contribute. 'The content of Kat's call may only be hearsay but it rang true, given what we knew of Justine. She had a colourful sex life, multiple male suitors, for want of a better phrase, a diary crammed with the names of various men all requiring a TIE action.' Her audience were all too familiar with the acronym for Trace, Interview and Eliminate. 'We've narrowed the list down to three men we're interested in, the most likely suspect being Kat Irwin's brother-in-law, Timothy Parker.'

Frankie handed back to Stone.

'Despite his out and out denial of an intimate relationship with Justine, Parker's DNA was all over her bedroom and Justine's DNA was in his marital bed. Thanks to Kyra, we now know that our two victims had similar lifestyles, in as much as they were happy to sleep with married men, the same one in this case. Kat's hearsay allegations didn't really hit the mark. Frankie and I did wonder if it was an invention. Sounds very much like a woman scorned, cover story for her own affair with him. Guv, you've put Kat's death at around midday on Friday last. We happen to know that Parker was in London then. He caught a nine a.m. flight to Heathrow, arriving at ten twenty. He flew home at six fifteen p.m. Frankie and I lifted him when it landed at Newcastle International at seven thirty. The slippery so-and-so can't wriggle out of that one.'

There was little doubt that the three incidents were somehow linked. Sinead Friel didn't waste time. Given Stone's insight and his recent involvement with the family, she thought it entirely appropriate that he should take the lead. In no way was she passing the buck. She'd render him every assistance. Intelligence would be shared north and south. Frankie glanced at Stone. In Sharpe's absence on holiday, he was now running the show.

59

The crime scene was on the lower ground floor of a residential block, halfway between Hyde Park and Regent's Park, a twenty-five-minute walk from West End Central, less than ten by car. As the briefing between Northumbria and Met detectives had covered only the main points of the investigation into the death of Kat Irwin, the SIO made sure that Stone and Oliver were driven there by Kyra Thakur. She was the DS assigned to all enquiries and actions relating to family and known associates of the victim. It was quite a responsibility. Statistically speaking, a high percentage of murderers turned out to be one or the other.

Kyra got over her awkwardness the minute they left the incident room and made their way to the car park. The Met DS was a friendly sort, extremely fond of David. It was clear from their chat that they had a good relationship and enjoyed each other's company. He climbed in the front of her car, Frankie in the back. She felt like a spare part, unable to contribute to a conversation about their mutual acquaintances and all that had gone on since he'd left the area, so she said nothing. She couldn't help wondering if their relationship had gone beyond the professional.

Kat Irwin had wanted for nothing. Her apartment was situated in Marylebone, a prestigious address in one of the most sought-after areas of London. It had a shared garden and the additional perk of access to the beautifully manicured Montagu Square. The building itself was impressive, one that a lot of people would love to live in. Not Frankie. She was already longing for her seaport town in Northumberland, the big skies – the peace and quiet of an empty beach.

No amount of money could buy that.

Stone stood in the doorway, fixing the crime scene in his mind in the same way that an artist might. Spatial awareness was key, the ability to view objects in relation to one another and himself in terms of space and distance – for example the positioning of windows, doors and items of furniture – the capacity to see them three-dimensionally and draw conclusions based on what he saw. In due course, when it came to interviewing a suspect, he'd need to know, with accuracy, what was where, how long it might take to cross a room, what the lighting was like and so on. Crime scene stills were one thing. Witnessing a scene for yourself was entirely different. No SIO would could afford to skimp on that.

The interior of the apartment was as classy as it appeared from the outside, airy and light, a much larger space than Stone had expected from the stills Met Police had supplied, the reason it was imperative to view it personally. The light wood flooring was stained with Kat Irwin's blood. She'd ended her days between a cream leather sofa and a marble coffee table, both of which bore the signs of blood spatter. One blow to the head with a blunt instrument – a hammer of some sort – was all it took to end her relatively short life.

The detectives moved into the apartment.

'There was no sign of a break-in or a fight,' Kyra said. 'We're fairly certain she knew her attacker well enough to let them in here without a fuss. The caretaker said the door was open when he arrived. He looked in, saw her lying here and called us in immediately.'

'What time was that?' Stone was asking.

'Shortly after one.'

Frankie turned to look at Kyra. 'Your guv'nor said it was a false alarm.'

The Met detective nodded. 'Someone had set it off maliciously.'

'Unless it was a fault,' Frankie suggested.

'No, it was deliberate. The glass was smashed.'

Frankie met her gaze. She had something on her mind.

'You have a theory?' Kyra asked.

'If Timothy Parker is the father of Kat's child – and I think we can safely assume that he is – maybe he killed her and set the alarm off to ensure that Ali would be found. Which suggests he cares for her. We might use that to our advantage. Is there any suggestion that anyone else was paying Kat child support?'

Kyra was shaking her head.

'Where was the kid found?' Stone asked.

'Through there.'

Kyra was pointing to a door leading off the living room. The three detectives moved through it into a spacious nursery. Like her mother, three-year-old Ali Irwin had everything money could buy. The room was beautifully done out with hand-painted Disney characters across one wall, a tiny table and chair, dozens of well-worn books and a bed stuffed with every soft toy imaginable.

'She was sitting on the floor here, crying,' Kyra said.

Children were often a vital source of information. It was important not to frighten them, to take it slow and build rapport in the hope that they would put their trust in you. Frankie assumed this had all been done in the company of the registered childminder employed by her mother, a familiar face, the person with whom she was living temporarily with the support of social services.

'Did Ali see what happened?' Stone asked.

'It's too early to tell,' Kyra said. 'We don't want to push her. She may be blocking it out. There was a big noise. That's all we could get out of her before we put a stop to the interview. Her bed was as it is now, rumpled, as if she'd been taking a nap. We reckon she may have been asleep and either woke up naturally or suddenly when the fire alarm was triggered.'

'Let's hope it was the latter,' Frankie said.

Kyra was nodding. 'She'll be interviewed again tomorrow. If she's up to it, I'll ask if she saw her mummy on the floor—'

Frankie cut her off. 'What we want to know is: did she see Daddy?'

Stone was delighted to see his two favourite coppers sharing the load. As people, they were very different. As detectives, Kyra and Frankie were similar, driven to investigate crimes without fear or favour, smart and intuitive, vociferous occasionally, with big hearts. Since he'd met Sinead Friel at training school, he'd been fortunate to have been paired with clever women, less egotistical than their male counterparts, often more hardworking if he were being perfectly honest.

He went for his pocket as his mobile rang.

'What's up, Mitch?'

'I have news.'

'Hang on then. I'm at the crime scene with Frankie and an ex-colleague. They may as well hear it too. While you're on, let Dick Abbott know that the incidents are linked. We're now in the driving seat. DS Kyra Thakur is our liaison officer down here. She needs to be aware of what's going on up north. She's up to speed, so no need to repeat what she knows already. You're on speaker.'

'Kyra, hi. Welcome to my world,' Mitch said.

Kyra smiled. 'Polite, isn't he?'

'His appraisal is due.' Frankie was teasing him. 'Quit stalling, Mitch. Give us what you've got.'

'Mason is about to go on leave, so he asked to view the wrench we recovered yesterday before it went off for analysis. Kyra, he's our Home Office pathologist in case you didn't know, and he's as sure as he can be that it's the murder weapon. The jaws are open to the exact same aperture as the injuries he measured on Justine's skull. I've put in an urgent request to the laboratory for forensic examination. They should get to it first thing tomorrow morning.'

'Good,' Stone said. 'Anything else?'

'Yeah, I got in touch with airport administration. Parker's plane ticket was bought on his company credit card, one of two purchased independently . . .' Mitchell paused. 'It seems Curtis was also in London on Friday.'

'*James* Curtis?' Kyra asked.

Stone looked at her. 'How d'you know about him? He's Timothy Parker's business partner.'

'He's a damned sight more than that,' Kyra said. 'He's Kat Irwin's ex-husband.'

60

Kyra dropped them at Stone's place in Pimlico. It felt strange, letting himself in. David had not been back since he'd left London. He'd bought the flat for three hundred and fifty grand in 2001 with a down-payment of half the asking price – money left in trust in his parents' will until he reached the age of majority. His inheritance made owning a London home affordable, something not a lot of coppers his age could hope for.

Losing his parents was a high price to pay.

'It's a bit dusty,' he said.

'David, it's lovely . . . The furniture is divine.' It was a far cry from his Northumberland home. Frankie's eyes were all over what was essentially a modern kitchen at one end of the room, a retro lounge at the other. She scanned art deco prints, ran a finger over the blue and cream Dansette record player his nan had bought him as a moving-in present, then got down on her hands and knees, poring over his vinyl collection. She threw him a big smile. 'I had no idea you were a collector.'

'Just a bit of fun. Besides, there's a lot you don't know about me.'

'Ain't that the truth.' The smile vanished.

David knew what she meant and what was coming now that they were alone with no one party to their conversation. He'd ignored her for most of their journey south, burying his head in his work, knowing he'd have to face her at some point. She'd forgiven his reaction to Alex Parker once. She wouldn't do it twice. The subject needed airing. He was painfully aware of that.

She stood up. 'David, are you OK?'

It was an opener, an invitation for him to share his most guarded secret. Whatever trauma had befallen him in London, he'd faced worse in the north since: two harrowing and deeply disturbing reactions to Alex Parker; the shock of losing Luke in a fatal car crash; the unwanted attention of his nephew, Ben, who he blamed for his brother's death, however indirectly it had come about. It was time he took centre-stage, to prove his worth to his ex-colleagues and his former SIO. David took a deep breath, heart in mouth. It was time to level with her. As his professional partner, Frankie deserved an explanation. If she didn't get one, she might think he didn't trust her, and that wasn't the case. On the contrary, he trusted no one more. Never had. Not even Kyra.

An intense moment followed.

They were two coppers, standing eye to eye in the centre of a dusty throwback to the sixties, his home for fifteen years, the expectation of taking their relationship as colleagues and friends a step further only seconds away. Unable to hold her gaze, David felt a mixture of relief and frustration as his get-out-of-jail card arrived: his mobile phone vibrating in his pocket. The intrusion couldn't have come at a worse moment.

Pulling out the device, he checked the screen.

'Don't answer that!' It was a plea almost from Frankie. 'There will never be a better time, a better place. David, we need to talk and we need to do it now. Whatever is bothering you happened in this city. Let's get it over with and leave it behind when we go.'

Such good advice was hard to come by.

He ignored the call, but his nephew persisted, redialling again and again, until it was obvious that he wouldn't stop. 'I'm sorry, Frankie. It's Ben. . . I'll have to take it.'

'Thought you didn't care about him.'

Ignoring her, David pressed to receive the call. 'I'm in London, Ben. This is not a good time . . . No, that's not going to happen . . . I told you before, you're on your own.' He hung up, aware that he'd already lost Frank.

'Nice.' She didn't even try to hide her outrage. 'Give the kid a break, why don't you? He's the only family you have.'

'I'm better off without one.'

'You don't mean that—'

'I do. And since when did my family become your business?'

The doorbell rang.

Frankie swore under her breath. David gave her the cold shoulder and went to answer it. Kyra knew instantly that she had walked in on something deeply personal. The stand-off between the Northumbria officers was dispelled when Stone grabbed his jacket, telling them he'd go out and get them something to eat.

'I'm not hungry,' Frankie blurted out.

'I am,' he said. 'Kyra?'

The Met detective smiled. 'You know me. Always a pasty on the go.'

Frankie turned away. She stared through the window at nothing that particularly interested her. The world it seemed was moving on without David Stone. She winced as the front door slammed shut behind her. Seconds later, he emerged on the pavement in the street below, hands in pockets. He seemed to take a breath before moving off and didn't look up.

'Well,' Kyra said. 'That was awkward.'

Frankie rounded on her. 'Will you tell me what the fuck is wrong with him?'

'He's in a strop. I would have thought that was obvious—'

'That's not what I meant.' Frankie sat down, dropping her head in her hands. She'd had as much as she could take of the 'Northern Rock' and the feeling was probably mutual. She had to admit that this worried her slightly. Would he be tempted to move south again?

He still owned a home here.

Seeing how upset Frankie was, Kyra sat down opposite. 'Listen,' she said. 'I want us to be mates but I can't break a confidence if he's not ready to share.'

Frankie looked up. 'You mean you won't.'

'That's hardly fair, Frankie. If the shoe was on the other foot—'

'Yeah, you're right. I'm angry with him, not you. It was unfair to ask, I'm sorry.'

'Don't give it another thought. You care about him. I care about him. We all do, except Connor, and he doesn't count. My advice is, don't push David too hard, too early. He'll get there in his own time.'

'He's had time.'

'Frankie, I don't know if you're aware but David and I keep in touch. He just buried his brother. Can't you cut him some slack?'

'Oh, believe me, I have.'

Kyra took a moment, sensitive to Frankie's feelings. She chose her words carefully. 'Is this affecting his ability to do his job? Because if it is—'

'No!' The lie came easily. 'He's a brilliant boss. I love working with him.'

'There you go then.' Kyra smiled. 'Would it make you feel any better if I told you that he's done nothing but talk about you since he went home to the frozen north. If it's any consolation, he thinks the world of you.'

'He's got a funny way of showing it.'

'What did you expect, transparency? He's a bloke. They think they can handle things even when they can't.'

Frankie laughed.

By the time David returned, the atmosphere he'd left on the way out had vanished. The female detectives were down to business, getting on with their work as if nothing untoward had taken place. Hours later, Kyra got up to leave, offering Frankie a lift to a hotel of her choosing. David told her that was unnecessary and suggested she could stay at his place. Frankie declined. He wasn't talking. Well, two could play at that game. Besides, she had a mind to make a call, the purpose of which he wasn't going to like.

61

Monday, the fourth of July really felt like Independence Day in the Northumbria incident room. Morale was up. The forensics lab had completed their analysis of the wrench and found microscopic traces of green fabric in the worm screw which matched to the tool board in Dixon's shed. Stone and Oliver had caught an early train and were thrilled to hear the news, their opposing views on how to handle Ben consigned to the backburner . . .

For now.

Frankie rang the Marine Unit underwater search team to let them know, then Mitchell updated them in Stone's office. Neither Curtis nor Parker denied being in London when Kat Irwin met her death, though both claimed they hadn't seen her. Kyra was checking their alibis in London and Northumbria detectives were left kicking their heels, waiting on results.

The hiatus was frustrating.

Mindful of Kyra's well-meaning advice not to lean on David too heavily, Frankie made up her mind not to broach his difficulties head on. Alex Parker was the link between murders at either end of the country. If he froze again, this wealthy woman might notice his paralysis – if she hadn't already done so. An indirect approach was called for.

'While we're marking time,' she said, 'Alex needs to be seen. I could go on my own if you like. I'm not being unkind, David. I can see it's difficult for you to be around her for reasons I don't really understand, so I want you to know that I can take that on if you don't think you can hack it.'

He looked unsure, not angry.

'As SIO you now have other responsibilities,' she added. 'It won't look odd if I turf up there on my own.'

'And your reason for seeing her?'

'She's the common denominator in all of this: mother to Daniel; employer to Justine; sister to Kat.'

He didn't argue.

Alex was at home, grieving for her sister, saying she was worried for her own safety and that of her son. It was a lovely, sunny morning. She led Frankie out on to the rear patio and seemed pleased to have someone to talk to . . . Initially, at any rate. Tea was offered and politely refused. The marquee was gone, everything back to normal, the garden awash with colour: hydrangeas, rock roses and hibiscus all in full bloom. In due course, Frankie steered the conversation to Tim. He was not around, a bonus she'd hoped for but hadn't expected; this was her chance to talk to his wife off the record. It threw her slightly. She needed to think on her feet.

'Is that why you're here?' Alex said. 'To quiz me about my husband? You don't like him much, do you, DS Oliver?'

'I neither like or dislike,' Frankie lied. 'This is not a personality contest.'

'I thought you must have an ulterior motive for coming here, above checking on my welfare. Why don't I make it easy for you? Stop wasting your time and ask your questions. However hard they are, I won't break, I promise you.'

'OK, but I must warn you that what I have to say may not be what you expect or want to hear. I'm here because Detective Inspector Stone didn't want to drag you into the station at such a difficult time.'

'Why would he need to?' Alex was instantly on her guard.

'We're talking to everyone who might have information to give us.'

Frankie had to be careful. She was there to get information, not give it. So far, she'd failed to mention the evidence they had of Tim Parker's infidelity and it was obvious that he hadn't told Alex of the DNA and fingerprints that proved he'd been in the au pair's bed, or she in his. Frankie didn't intend mentioning the paternity of Kat Irwin's child either, even though she now had conclusive proof that Parker was the father, having rushed to compare his DNA with Ali's.

Frankie needed an in. 'I'm not wanting to add to your distress—'

'Then please don't . . .' Alex wasn't being spiteful. 'Usually I'm bombproof,' she said. 'But even I have a limit. One more revelation will send me over the edge.' She lit a cigarette and gave Frankie a sympathetic smile, as if she'd realised the enormity of the detective's job. It was extremely difficult to talk to a woman whose husband was strongly suspected of murdering two women he'd had affairs with. Then there was the query over Alex Parker's motive for wanting to get rid of Justine and her sister. Did she know about the affairs? The conversation between Stone and Kat Irwin had been playing on Frankie's mind.

It needed further exploration.

'Questions have arisen over a telephone conversation Kat had with DI Stone on Wednesday, June twenty-ninth.'

'What conversation?' Alex turned to face the detective sergeant. 'She never mentioned it to me. Then again, there were other, more important things she failed to disclose.' Her voice was laced with contempt. 'Why did she call him?'

'To ask for help.'

'Oh please, give me the courtesy of a straight answer.'

'She told my DI that you suspected Tim of having an affair. Is that true?'

Alex sidestepped the question deftly. 'We've not been in a good place since losing the baby.'

'With respect, that's not what she meant. Alex, you've asked me to level with you and I expect the same in return. Kat specifically said that you had doubts about him while you were pregnant, not since, and that you told her about it when you were on holiday together in Majorca. She said you'd accused

Tim of putting you under so much stress, it caused you to lose your child. That's quite an allegation.'

'I was drunk. When you've lost a baby, you'll blame anyone but yourself.'

A parallel scenario jumped into Frankie's head. Stone was blaming Ben for Luke's death, unfairly in her opinion. Yes, Luke was on his way to see the lad in hospital. Yes, Ben had taken drugs. But he was not driving the lorry that killed his father. The teenager was feeling guilty enough without his uncle adding to it.

Frankie needed more from Alex Parker. 'So, it's not true?'

Alex avoided answering. 'Do you have children, DS Oliver?'

'No, I don't.'

'Well, joyful though it is, being pregnant does things to your head.' She swept a rogue hair from her face. 'My hormones were all over the place. I wasn't thinking straight. Some women feel wonderful. Beautiful even. Some feel ghastly, fat and unattractive. It wouldn't take a brain surgeon to work out which one I was. I was in a bad place and should never have confided in Kat. It was uncalled for and unfair on Tim. The truth is, I think that my negativity may have damaged the foetus. It was entirely my fault, not his.'

Frankie was tempted to tell her that it wasn't, that these tragedies happen all too often and that she shouldn't blame herself in any way. She let it go. She had to stay on track if she was to get anything from Alex before her husband returned.

'Kat believed Tim was having an affair with Justine, didn't she?'

Alex snapped her head around. 'It was rubbish and I told her so.'

'Are you still of that opinion?' Frankie's eyes drifted over Alex's shoulder to the stable block and the garage beyond, next to which the au pair's car sat on the baking gravel, redundant and unloved. She imagined Justine bombing along the winding country lanes, having fun, so full of life.

Such a waste.

'To be honest, I don't know,' Alex said. 'What's more, I don't care. You know why? I love my husband and, not to sound too melodramatic, I owe him my life. He rescued me from a fate worse than death and made sure that Rob understood the consequences of any approach afterwards. And if you're suggesting what I think you are, I know, deep down, that Tim is incapable of hurting anyone.'

'Even you?'

'Especially me. If he went elsewhere for sex, it was entirely my fault. You could say I pushed him into it.'

Frankie tried a little harder. 'Kat seemed to think he was capable of violence.'

'Doesn't surprise me – the comment, I mean.' Alex was irked now and it showed. 'They didn't get along and fought like cat and dog.'

'Did you never question why?'

'You choose your friends, not your in-laws. Tim thought she was needy. He didn't like her, as simple as that, a feeling that was reciprocated, if the phone call you mentioned is anything to go by.'

'There was more to it than that, wasn't there? Kat described Tim as a serial philanderer.'

'Well, she's a liar! And who could believe a thing she said? She didn't even tell me about her daughter for three years. Three *fucking* years. I've thought about nothing else since you told me of her existence.'

'Did Kat warn you not to marry Tim?'

'Is that what she told you?'

Frankie nodded. 'No different from Rob Scott,' she said.

'She was jealous of me.' Alex sighed. 'It's a long story, DS Oliver, one that I've told few people. Kat went off the rails in her early twenties. So much so, my parents cut her out of their will. She didn't even turn up at their funeral. I got everything. She resented me for it. We lost touch for many years. Eventually, I stopped trying to make contact.'

'That must've been difficult.'

'It was. As kids, we were close. She was always headstrong – a little selfish, if I'm honest. About two years ago, she turned up out of the blue. No explanation. I did wonder why she'd had a change of heart. At the time, I didn't question it. I was happy to have her back. Lately, things had been great between us. It all makes sense now. I'd like to think that, as a mother herself, she saw the value of family. I guess I'll never know now, will I?' Alex paused, eyes on Frankie. 'What else did she say?'

Frankie was so close to Rae, she found it hard to imagine not being able to speak to her, if not daily, then a couple of times a week, not to celebrate in her success or take part in her life with Andrea. Neither could she understand what it must have felt like for the two sisters to lose touch for such a lengthy period. She didn't want to hurt Alex any more than she had already but she was there to do a job and there was still a lot to get through.

'Was there more to the phone call?' Alex said. 'Please, I need to know.'

'She told DI Stone that Tim resented Daniel.'

'Then all I can say is that I didn't know my sister at all. Tim loves Daniel.'

'Then why say it?'

'I have no idea.' Her ambiguity was obvious.

'Alex. I get the impression that there's something you're not telling me. Two people close to you have died. If there's something you know, no matter how small, you must share it before anyone else comes to harm.'

Alex hesitated. 'It's nothing.'

'Let me be the judge of that. You can't go on living in fear. Why do you think your sister didn't tell you about her child?' Frankie waited. 'Alex?'

'Your guess is as good as mine.'

328

'You're a clever woman. I'm sure you have your theories.'

'I had no idea I was so transparent.' Alex looked out into the middle distance. Two rabbits were chasing one another across the lawn. In many ways, she had an idyllic lifestyle, but it was obvious that she also had doubts about her husband she wasn't yet prepared to divulge.

Frankie changed tack. 'Has Tim got a problem with drugs?'

'He has it under control.'

'I think you're wrong. Alex, these are mind-altering substances that have serious side effects. Taken with other medication and alcohol they're dangerous. Even I've noticed a change in his behaviour in the short time I've known him.' Frankie took a moment. 'When I asked you if you were holding out on us, what did you mean when you said, "it's nothing"?'

'He's in financial difficulty.'

'Yes, I know. Curtis told me . . . there's something else though, isn't there?'

Alex folded her arms, on the brink of disclosure. 'I woke up the other morning to find Tim gone. He was making a call outside our bedroom door. It was shut so I couldn't hear what was being said, only that he was threatening someone. James, I think.'

'Curtis?'

She nodded. 'James had called the night before, drunk as a skunk, ranting on about dissolving the company. He wanted to throw in the towel and be done with it. Tim was furious. He believes there's another way and, for what it's worth, I agree with him. They had a massive row. Tim told him to do nothing until he returned from London. He tossed and turned for hours. I guess it was playing on his mind.'

'Can you remember when this was, the phone call?'

'It was Thursday, just before six a.m. I had an early meeting in town and wanted to beat the traffic in.'

'Wasn't Daniel at school?'

'Tim said he'd drop him off.'

'Not a good idea if he's using.' Frankie never hesitated if a child was at risk.

The patio door opened before Alex had a chance to respond.

62

Frankie couldn't wait to brief Stone. She took the stairs two at a time, keen to get into the incident room and tell all. The Murder Investigation Team were taking a break as she burst through the door, a little out of breath, a lull in proceedings as detectives ate lunch, stretched their legs, nipped out for a smoke. Abbott and Mitchell were deep in conversation over Germany's penalty misses at the weekend, the fact that they had nevertheless managed to reach the Euro semi-finals after a tournament jinx lasting fifty-four years.

An updated murder wall instantly took Frankie's attention. Kat Irwin's picture had been added, along with crime scene photographs. A broken line had been carefully drawn, linking the victim to Alex Parker (sister), Tim Parker (lover) and James Curtis (ex-husband); three names that were similarly associated to Justine Segal (employer/lover/lover) respectively. A probable, if not glaringly obvious indication that these two offences were in some way connected.

Frankie's eyes homed in on another broken line that banded together Timothy Parker and James Curtis. Underneath, Mitchell had written *Business partners/In London, Friday, 1 July* – the date of Kat Irwin's death. Neither had a reliable alibi . . . yet. To the right of Justine's picture, a red question mark hung over builder and handyman, Gary Hamilton. He remained on the list of suspects, similarly unable to provide police with an acceptable explanation of where he'd been the day the au pair met her death, though he claimed to have been working in Gretna with his brother. New to Frankie, perhaps the most exciting of all, yet another link, this one unbroken and written in red – stretched between Parker, Curtis, Hamilton, Kat and Justine. Beneath it, Mitch had scribbled the words: *e-voke dating agency*.

'Yes!' Frankie whispered under her breath. 'Now we're getting somewhere.'

'Impressed?' The voice had come from over her shoulder.

Frankie turned to find Stone standing behind her. He seemed pleased to see her, despite the spat over Ben's welfare while they were in London and on the journey home.

'There are more lines linking that lot than on my nan's bingo card.' He pointed at the murder wall. 'It seems e-voke is a well-established, thrill-seeking, no-holds-barred dating agency with a wealthy international clientele – probably what seduced Justine to use it.'

'That's interesting. Remember Parker's suggestion that Alex may have been sleeping with the au pair? I wonder—'

'She's not a member of e-voke. We checked.'

'Right. I was thinking that, if the Parkers were that way inclined, Justine might have been a kind of live-in sexual unicorn.'

'A what?' Stone looked baffled.

'You know, single female, up for anything. A bit of action, excitement, danger even. Mind you, Alex wouldn't necessarily need to be on the site herself to enjoy the fringe benefits. Let's face it, she has more sense than to have exposed herself (no pun intended) or to open herself up to ridicule among the county set.'

'Tell me.' Stone could see that there was more.

'For all we know, Tim may have selected Justine while trawling e-voke. We only have his word that he found her as he said he did, via the employment agency. I never gave any credence to what he said about Alex and Justine sleeping together, until now. If the au pair doubled as a unicorn, it would explain her DNA in their bed and why Alex didn't care that Tim had been unfaithful.'

Stone's eyebrows moved closer. 'She told you that?'

'An unreserved admission. Ever thought that you might be missing out, boss?'

David almost blushed.

Frankie stopped teasing him. 'Any news from Kyra on Curtis's alibi?'

'The man he was meeting in the capital spent the weekend in the Cotswolds with friends. Kyra is on her way there now. Take a seat and tell me how you got on with Alex Parker.' They both sat down. 'I assume you shared the content of Kat's call with her?'

'In its entirety.' Covering all the bases, Frankie had achieved more than she had ever thought possible in an off-the-cuff interview. 'Alex was quick to defend Parker, reiterating the fact that he was with her in the house before she left to pick up Daniel on the day Justine died, though it hadn't passed her by that he was in London on Friday when Kat was murdered. She stonewalled the idea that he might be responsible for either death. Said she was married to the man; if anyone would know whether he was capable of extreme violence, she would.'

'Maybe she's right. With Curtis in London, we could be looking at the wrong suspect—'

'Or maybe not. Tim came home while I was there. It took them all of twenty seconds to launch into a ferocious slanging match. Alex is no slouch either. She challenged him on everything we discussed. I let it run in the hope that words spoken in the heat of the moment might benefit us.'

'And did they?'

'Absolutely. We could do with her on our interview team.' Frankie grinned. 'I don't know where Parker had been, but he looked like he'd slept in his clothes. He was wasted.'

'Did he give you any trouble?'

'Nah, he was in no condition to fight his way out of a paper bag, let alone take on two of us. After a few rounds with Alex, he came to his senses. There was no point denying the affair with his sister-in-law. Just as we'd caught him out with Justine, Met Police were bound to find his DNA in Kat's flat – though he claimed not to have seen her recently. He was adamant that their relationship was over a long time ago and denied killing her. Quote: "Why would I? She's the mother of my only child," unquote.'

'I bet that went down well with Alex. I'm surprised you weren't forced to call for back-up.'

'Naturally, his wife was wounded by what he'd told her. It was awkward being there. She swore she'd never forgive him but then, get this, offered to take Ali in now her mother is dead. She must be desperate for another child.'

'Enough to kill for one?'

'Now there's a theory. I nearly fell on the floor when she said it. I don't think I've ever heard anything so selfless.'

'Ali *is* named after her.'

'Even so. Her sister lied to her for three years and her marriage is on the rocks. Her altruism is misguided in my opinion, David. I know he's come clean, but he'll shit on her all over again. I think Kat was right: there's little between him and Rob Scott. They're takers with not an ounce of decency between them.'

'Anything else?'

'Isn't that enough?' She narrowed her eyes. 'While I was there, it got me thinking. Kat planted the seed that Tim might have been having an affair with Justine while the two women were in Majorca, right? That gave Alex motive for murder number one, but she told me that if it did happen it was all her fault. She pushed him away. It occurred to me that she was giving herself an out there. I leaned on her a bit, asked her why she thought Kat hadn't told her about Ali. She knew what I was getting at but wouldn't be drawn. As I said before, she can hold her own in an argument. She's a clever woman. Far too clever to put herself in the frame for murder number two.'

'That's pure conjecture, Frank.'

'I know . . . just making you aware. Oh, and one other thing: during our conversation, Alex also told me she woke early the other morning to hear Tim threatening someone on the phone. She seemed to think it was Curtis but it got me wondering: what if it wasn't? I'll phone Kyra . . .' Frankie took her phone from her pocket. 'If it was *Kat* he was threatening, then we need to look again at Tim Parker.'

'Whoa! Slow down.'

'I reckon he was still seeing her, David. Maybe they had a row. It got nasty. He walloped her and—'

'I'm sorry to piss on your chips, Frank. The semen found in Kat Irwin's body didn't belong to him.'

'Boss?' Mitchell was holding the internal phone, his free hand covering the speaker. 'Met Police say there's no sign of Timothy Parker yet. James Curtis wasn't so lucky. CCTV captured him a few blocks away from Kat Irwin's flat, around an hour before the estimated time of her death.'

Frankie's eyes were like saucers.

Stone was staring at her. 'What?'

'Curtis knew that Parker was going to be in London. Alex told me.'

The pendulum had swung again.

63

The interview with Curtis was a waste of time. It began at three o'clock in the presence of his solicitor. He didn't deny membership of e-voke or that he'd rekindled his relationship 'for old time's sake' with Kat Irwin through the dating site. It's how they met; how Parker had found Justine; how they had both engaged with countless other women.

Curtis was open and supremely confident. Kat's flat was in an area he knew well, though he didn't visit on Friday the first. Yes, he was in the general vicinity, a business meeting with a man offering him a job, a new start in the south. Curtis was happy to give DNA samples on the spot, in fact he insisted upon it. In Stone's opinion, this was a man who wanted a different life, a new challenge professionally, but was he also a man with something to hide, an arrogant shit who was forensically aware and thought he could get away with murder? They processed and bailed him to await the outcome of further enquiries.

Frankie walked away from the interview room feeling the case slipping through her fingers. Curtis was a clever bastard. The interview hadn't gone the way she'd anticipated. He was openly admitting he was close to the London crime scene when she'd expected an outright denial. Grabbing her car keys from her desk, she left the building without telling anyone where she was going. Stone was in a strop, updating his policy document, re-evaluating where he should go next. There were clues on Curtis's phone, restaurant reservations, weekends away when he was on false business trips, none of that important now that he'd coughed to an affair with Kat Irwin, his ex-wife. Evidence was only useful to prove or disprove a lie and he'd come clean, pulling the rug from under them.

Frankie didn't disturb David. Something was niggling deep inside her brain as she left the station . . .

It took a while to surface . . .

Justine's car.

The vehicle wasn't anywhere near the crime scene when she died and had been left in situ to be processed by crime scene investigators. Frankie had overseen them at work and something wasn't quite right when she'd seen the car again while talking to Alex earlier in the day.

Traffic was light and Frankie was back in Scots Gap in twenty minutes. The ornate gated entrance to the Parkers' property was closed to traffic. She parked on the road outside and entered through an unlocked pedestrian gate. There was no answer at the door, so she walked round the side of the house to the driveway where Justine's vehicle was parked. Lifting her hand to shade her eyes, Frankie peered in through the window. The keys were dangling from the ignition. She tried the door. It opened. She leaned in, then pulled out her phone and called the incident room at Northern Command HQ.

'DC Mitchell.'

'Mitch, it's Frank.'

'Can you hold, Sarge? The boss is looking for you—'

'Tell him I'm busy.'

'He said it was urgent.'

'Yeah, well it'll have to wait. I need a favour. Take a look at the exhibits log and see if the mileage was taken when Justine's car was examined. Quick as you can.' Frankie heard typing at the other end as Mitchell's fingers hit the keyboard, the hum of conversations in the background, phones ringing off the hook – the story of her life for as long as she could remember.

'It wasn't,' Mitch said when he came on the line.

'OK, get the photographs up on screen.'

'Hang on.' More tapping sounds.

Frankie heard feet on gravel.

Everything went black.

64

'Sarge, I have the photographs up on screen. Is it only the mileage you're after?' No response. 'Sarge?' Mitchell strained to listen to what was going on at the other end. It sounded the same as when his brother bum-dialled him by mistake, his phone in his back pocket. The line was open but no one was listening, the phone transmitting random noises. Maybe Frankie was having second thoughts and had climbed into her car to return to base without ending the call properly. Stone's interest in her whereabouts must've changed her mind.

Talk of the Devil.

'Something wrong?' Stone said.

Mitch shrugged. 'It's Frankie.'

'Well, that explains the nonplussed look on your face. What's she done now?'

'Dunno. She was there a minute ago. Maybe she lost the signal.'

'She's driving?'

'I don't think so.'

'Did you tell her I was looking for her?'

'Yes, boss.'

'And?'

'She said it would have to wait. Her words, not mine. She was busy—'

'With what?' Stone took Mitch's mobile from him.

*

Frankie heard David's voice calling her name. It sounded strange and faraway, as if he was speaking through a soggy sponge. Then she remembered the sound of someone approaching from behind. She couldn't see but she could hear and feel an arm holding her up. She tried to break free but the pain in her head was so severe, she couldn't lift her arms to fend off her attacker. The front seat of the two-door vehicle shot forward and she was bundled into the rear of the car, head first, her phone still in her hand. With enormous effort, she tightened her grip on it as she was manhandled into the space. Semi-conscious, she heard the engine start up and the car began to move.

Stone's heart was in his mouth as he turned to face Mitchell. 'She's not answering. I heard a scuffle, a car door slamming, an engine running. Where the hell is she?'

'She never said.'

'Well, think, man!' Stone's eyes were drawn to images of Justine's Renault on DC Mitchell's computer. 'What are you doing with those?'

'She asked about the mileage on the vehicle. We haven't got it logged, so she told me to check the photographs. I did that. She wasn't there when I went back to her. Boss? Should I be—'

Stone held up a hand cutting him off, lifting the phone to his ear. 'Frankie? Frankie, say something if you're there.' He heard road noise and swung round to face Mitchell. 'She's on the move. Justine's car is at the Parkers' home. Hang on to this and keep talking to her.' He handed Mitch the phone. 'Tell her we're on our way . . . Well? Say something, for fuck's sake!'

Mitchell was too shaken to formulate speech.

The DI's eyes found Abbott's.

'Dick, get over here!' David repeated his instructions. Like the professional he was, Abbott took the phone from Mitchell and began to talk to Frankie, his tone calm and reassuring, like it was no big deal. The last thing he wanted was to panic her.

Stone took out his own phone and called her number to make sure that it was her mobile she was using. The engaged tone hit his ear. He grabbed Mitch's phone from Abbott.

'Frankie?' He swore under his breath, Abbott's eyes bearing down on him. Mitchell's face was ghostly white. The DI updated them. 'The line is definitely open but I don't think she's in her own car. She's got a Bluetooth device. She'd hear us. And, if she can hear us and can't answer, she's in trouble.'

Major incident rooms were never silent. This one was. The whole of the Murder Investigation Team had downed tools, detectives' concerned eyes trained on Stone. They were watching and listening to the drama unfold in real time. No matter the age of officer, they all knew a detective called Frank Oliver. If this third-generation model was in danger, there was nothing they wouldn't do to get her out of it.

Painfully aware of his responsibility for her safety, Stone got on to the control room. 'I want all units near Scots Gap to keep observations for DS Oliver's private vehicle and a dark green Renault Clio, registration number . . .' He checked Mitchell's screen. 'N-November . . . 8 . . . 7 . . . 6 . . . P-Papa . . . C-Charlie . . . N-November. We believe Mike 2151 may require urgent assistance. Any sightings of either vehicle to be reported to the incident room and stop and check.' Stone gave the coordinates of the Parkers' mansion and grabbed a radio off the desk. 'I want India 99 in the air and at that location, NOW!' If anyone could find her quickly the police helicopter could. 'I want a fix on her mobile. Call the Parkers' landline. Let me know who picks up. If that's a negative, call their mobiles. I want to know where they both are and if they've seen her.' He was already running to his car. He reversed at speed, then tore out of the station, burning rubber. 'Frankie, if you're hearing this, I'm on my way.'

65

It seemed like a very long journey . . . but how would Frankie know? Everything had slowed down. Her ability to make decisions or even stay conscious was seriously impaired. The car turned off the road, bumped across uneven ground and stopped. Frankie's head was splitting. She felt drowsy, unable to see. Her eyelids felt like they were sewn together. The driver got out. The seat shot forward again. Frankie anticipated being yanked from the rear of the vehicle by her feet and dumped on the roadside, but it wasn't happening. An impasse. Had the driver abandoned her?

Andrea's voice came over the radio: 'Mike 7003 to Mike 7125. Motor patrols deployed north on the A696 and B6343 and south on the B6309. I'm also travelling north on the 696 at Shinningpool Bank.' There was a slight tremor in her voice. When she heard the call go out with Frankie's collar number – Mike 2151 – it would have hit her like a brick.

Stone couldn't imagine what was going through her mind. He hadn't wasted time warning her before going live to all units, asking them to keep observations for the two vehicles. He couldn't afford emotions to get in the way and neither could Andrea, who would be in no doubt that this was about as serious as it got.

David was ten minutes away, making excellent progress, about to turn on to the unclassified road towards Bolam Lake. With his foot to the floor, his advanced driving skills were being fully utilised, his blues and twos easing the way. There was no silent but deadly approach when an officer was down – instinctively, he knew that Frankie was. He wasn't interested in catching anyone, just saving her life. Sirens frightened offenders. If they heard him coming, they might leave her be.

He tried again. 'Frank. I need your help. Come on! You can do this. Give me a clue, anything.'

'Justine's car.' Frankie was breathless, her voice hardly audible.

But she was alive.

'Good girl.' Relief flooded through every part of him. 'Frankie, hold on. I'm coming to get you. All units, target vehicle is the Clio. Dark green in colour. N-November . . . 8 . . . 7 . . . 6 . . . P-Papa . . . C-Charlie . . . N-November . . .'

Liquid splashed across Frankie's body, soaking her jeans, splashing across her upper torso. A dribble ran down the side of her face, seeping into her mouth. There was no mistaking the taste or smell of the vapours filling the rear compartment of the car. Terror ripped through her as she realised what was happening . . .

Petrol.

Oh God!

She prayed that David wasn't far away. The fumes made her even more woozy and nauseous. Mortified by her predicament and powerless to extricate herself from danger, she hid the phone beneath her body so it wouldn't be seen by her attacker. It was her lifeline, her only means of summoning assistance. Her father and grandfather were suddenly in her head.

C'mon, think!

She begged for her life.

Whoever was outside the car wasn't listening. The splashing stopped, the petrol can thrown to the ground. The sound of the cavalry in the distance gave her hope. There was nothing like the scream of sirens when an officer was in trouble. It spurred Frankie on, gave her inner strength that somehow – if she was lucky – she might survive. A sob left her throat. Her life flashed before her eyes. She heard a match strike.

David was almost at the Belsay junction, five minutes away. There was time . . . He flew around the corner, accelerating out of it. Dense hedgerows flashed by on either side. He kept talking to Frankie, telling her he was closing on her location, urging her to hang fire.

'David, hurry!'

'Almost there . . . I'm invoking Rule 6, Frank.' He quoted the Frank Oliver Handbook: '"Low morale is strictly forbidden," you hear me? We've got your back. You let us do the worrying. Andrea's on her way too. ETA two minutes.' There was a whoosh and the phone went dead.

66

'Mike 7003 to Control. I see smoke.' Andrea was only half a mile from the humpback bridge. In the woods beyond were the telltale signs of a burning vehicle. She'd seen enough to know what one looked like from a distance. 'All units, the vehicle is in the clearing. I repeat, the vehicle is in the clearing. Tango 283, leave your position and travel south towards the woods. Tango 269, take a stationary position on the A696 Belsay junction with the B6524.' She made a judgement call. 'Offenders are likely to avoid minor roads and make their way south.'

'Control Room to Mike 7003 and Mike 7125. Fire and ambulance have been deployed to your location. India 99, what's your ETA?'

'Nine-nine: ETA three minutes.'

Stone was apoplectic. That whoosh was unmistakable, the most terrifying sound he'd ever heard, even worse than gunfire at close range. He hoped to God Frankie hadn't heard him scream. The thought of losing her was too much to bear. She was a big noise. Throughout the Northumbria force, work would have ceased once the rumour mill began. Just as everyone would be rooting for her, they sure as hell would blame him if she came to harm. He'd taken it once. He wouldn't survive it twice.

Flames leapt high into the air. The Clio was well alight by the time Andrea reached the vehicle. One of the front windows was gone but there was no sign of Frankie in the front seat. If she was anywhere in the rear or the boot she'd had it. Andrea jumped out of her Traffic car. Lifting the tailgate, she grabbed her fire extinguisher and ran towards the burning vehicle, directing the spray into the interior, working her way around the car.

She needed help.

Where the hell was her crew?

The heat was intense. It was impossible to get close. Smoke billowed from the interior. She was choking as it entered her lungs, her hands burning through leather gloves. She didn't want to open the driver's door to increase the draught to the vehicle, so she concentrated her efforts on directing the extinguisher in through the window.

Her radio went: 'Mike 7125 to Mike 7003: Do you have an update?'

She did, but not the kind Stone was after. When he came upon the scene he'd be as devastated as she was. Frankie had hinted that he was still getting over a trauma of some kind in London. Then he'd lost Luke. She didn't want to be the one to tell him that Frankie might have perished in a fire. He'd see for himself just as soon as he got there.

A sob left Andrea's throat as she continued to work her way round the car. They both loved Frankie so much. Anyone who knew her felt the same. Ignoring his request, she worked fast. She ran around the other side of the vehicle. The wind was against her, blowing flames in her direction, forcing her to back off. Thick smoke stung her eyes. She squirted the extinguisher until it ran out. Like pissing on a forest fire, it had little effect.

What would she tell Rae?

More bodies arrived, including Stone. Outwardly he was calm. Internally, she knew he was broken. The new personnel worked together, used their own equipment to extinguish the flames. They were all aware of the dangers of the job. Coppers' lives turned on a sixpence; one minute they could be having a normal day, the next staring disaster in the face. In

Frankie's case, examining Justine's car, then God knows what, all hell breaking loose as police vehicles set off to find her. There was nothing more they could do but await the arrival of the fire crew.

Andrea was standing beside her Traffic car, speaking into her radio. David was some way off. In a moment of heartbreak and sorrow, their eyes met across the clearing. He walked towards her, put his arms around her and gave her a hug.

She pulled away, her attention on the burning car. 'The passenger door was open, David.'

He looked towards the woods, then at Andrea. 'You think she got out?'

She couldn't answer right off. 'I won't accept that she didn't. All I'm saying is, it's possible. I've seen many burnt-out vehicles. Offenders usually strike a match, hoy it in and leg it. The driver's door was shut. That would suggest to me that whoever drove her here was trying to make it difficult for her to get out in time. There's only one reason why the passenger door would be open—'

'Unless it blew out in the explosion.' Stone wiped the sweat from his face, leaving a smutty mark under his right eye. 'Andrea, I spoke to Frankie. She was incapacitated, slurring her words, fading in and out of consciousness. Whether she'd been drugged or injured, I couldn't say. I'm not sure she'd have the wherewithal or energy to get herself out of a two-door vehicle, never mind run clear of a burning car.'

'Do not underestimate her!'

'I'm not. All I'm saying is she may not have known the car was on fire.'

'No! She got out until I say she didn't.' Andrea's voice broke as her emotions got the better of her. She knew he was trying to make it easier for her and she'd thrown it right back in his face. Stone may not be able to see a way that Frankie could survive but he didn't know her like she did.

He'd gone quiet.

'It's not only the door.' Andrea rammed home the message that there was hope. 'Both front seats are folded forward. If Frankie was in the rear, she'd have found a way to yank the lever and open the door. If you'd met her old man, you'd know that she's a chip off the old block. He's like a freight train. If anything gets in his way, he mows it down. She's an Oliver and proud of it. She'd fight tooth and nail to get out of there. Stop dragging your feet. What are you waiting for?'

Another glance towards the woods.

Stone nodded. 'Get your crew on it.'

As Andrea issued the order, David took a deep breath. If there was any chance that Frankie was alive he'd use every tool at his disposal to look for her, including the dog section. He lifted his radio and pushed the transmit button. 'Mike 7125 to Control: I'd like a Delta vehicle ASAP. Ditto, a search team for the woods. India 99, there's a possibility that the officer may have escaped the vehicle.'

'Copy that.'

'Search the near area first. She's can't have got far.'

'Nine nine: Affirmative.'

An RRV arrived on scene with a paramedic inside. Such Rapid Response Vehicles were used to get medical assistance to a casualty when an ambulance might take longer. There was no casualty to treat yet and Stone asked him to stand by for further instructions.

A fire tender arrived on scene.

Stone felt the blood drain from his face as men and women piled out wearing high-viz jackets. They needed no instruction. They knew exactly what to do. The DI looked up at the force helicopter circling overhead. It hovered over the location, then banked right, the pilot assessing the situation from the air. Using daylight imaging, he'd be looking for a heat source in the surrounding woods, downloading footage from his camera on to digital flash cards, transmitting encrypted images on to monitors within the police command centre.

He went around again.

A few minutes later, David's radio came to life.

'Nine nine: I have a stationary heat source NE of your location, down a slight ravine, thirty metres.' Stone and Andrea legged it in the general direction, guided by their colleague in the air. 'Officers on the ground, turn one degree left . . . Straight ahead . . . Keep going . . . Nearly there . . . Stop, stop . . . It should be right in front of you now.'

67

The journey to the A & E department of Northumbria's specialist emergency care hospital had taken longer than Stone could ever have imagined. Andrea led the convoy, paving the way for the ambulance with her own blues and twos, Stone following close behind, the three vehicles weaving in and out of traffic, compelling others to give way. He'd tried not to visualise what was going on inside the emergency vehicle. He hadn't wanted to know.

Frankie was unconscious when found, face down on the ground in an awkward position. Her blood-soaked hair was the first thing Stone and Andrea noticed as they were guided by the eye in the sky. At first, they thought she was dead. David had rushed to feel for a pulse, screaming into his radio to summon the paramedic.

Frankie had lost a lot of blood and was in bad shape, cuts to both hands and face, clothing soaked with petrol, no serious burns visible. Either she'd collapsed on the edge of the ravine and fallen, rolling down the bank over rough ground, landing in the brambles that caused those injuries, or she'd hurled herself into the valley and managed, somehow, to cover herself up. If Stone had been a betting man, he'd have guessed the latter.

She was quite well hidden.

Justine Segal hadn't been so fortunate. Mason, the Home Office pathologist, was clear on that score. He'd told the Murder Investigation Team that she'd have been incapacitated, unable to move, much less crawl into the middle of the road unaided. The fact that Frankie had escaped a burning vehicle was an indication that she was less severely injured.

Stone willed it to be so.

He'd abandoned his car outside A & E and looked on as she was lifted from the ambulance on a stretcher by a man and a woman dressed in green. There were obvious signs that she'd been worked on in transit: an oxygen mask, wires attached, a pulse monitor, wet clothing cut loose. When paramedics took her inside, Stone caught a strong whiff of petrol. It was the complexity of her injury that bothered him the most. The triage team had been alerted to receive her and were already on standby as paramedics crashed through the door to the treatment room, passing on vital information before handing over her care. Stone hadn't seen her since.

What seemed like hours later, the neurologist appeared, a man of around fifty with a square face, white hair and half-rim pewter metal-framed specs. His expression gave nothing away as he introduced himself to the police officers.

'I've sent her for a brain scan,' he said. 'A precaution.'

Stone nodded, irritated by the lack of information. 'Precaution' was a euphemism for something far more serious in his experience, a one-size-fits-all phrase used by members of the medical profession when they had nothing positive to say. The consultant would be checking for signs of acute subdural haematoma or skull fracture, serious conditions that could kill Frankie if left untreated. At best, they would find no such deadly condition and she'd recover without the need for surgery, at worst there could be permanent brain damage.

The next few hours were critical.

David had many questions – why she hadn't woken up top of his list. He didn't delay the doctor. He wanted him to get on with the job of treating Frankie. The DI told himself not to panic. This state-of-the-art hospital had emergency care specialists on duty twenty-four hours a day. She'd be monitored round the clock.

The relationship between police and medical services had always been positive. Officers were often called in to lend a hand if a patient, their associates or family got abusive or violent. It happened more often than people might think. Stress did things to people. There would be no preferential treatment. Even so, Stone and Andrea had been ushered into an empty staff room to await news, a courtesy afforded to them to ensure that they weren't bothered by the public at such a difficult time. Everyone liked to chat to a copper in uniform, kids particularly, and while that was an everyday occurrence for Andrea, a fact of life for every Traffic cop, today it was the last thing she needed. An officer was down. A family member. Today, she craved the space to worry like everyone else and so did David.

A nurse arrived with coffee – much needed. The DI thanked her and she left them. Andrea was beside herself. She seemed not to notice that anyone had entered or left the room. Out in the Northumberland woods, her police training had taken over. She'd done what she had to do, tackling the torched car without fear for her own mortality. Here in the hospital, where Frankie's life hung in the balance, the gravity of the situation was beginning to dawn.

Sensing his gaze, Andrea looked up, face blackened with smoke, high-viz jacket melted in places, her uniform trousers filthy. She took out her phone, called Control and then Frankie's dad, explaining what had happened, telling him that a vehicle was on its way to transport him to the hospital. She was in tears when she ended the call.

'She's in the best of hands,' David said.

A solemn nod was all he got in return.

'She's tough, like her dad, like you.' He was trying to lift her. It hadn't worked. Right now, they were in a place no member of the police family ever wanted to be. Andrea didn't feel tough or brave and neither did he. They both felt vulnerable and scared. He pointed to a chair. 'She'll be a while. Why don't you take the weight off? I have a few calls to make.'

He had to do something . . .

Andrea sat down to wait, elbows on knees, head in hands.

David took his phone out and dialled Mitchell's number. The phone rang out in his back pocket. He swore under his breath. Stupid mistake. Telling himself to focus, he dialled again.

'DS Abbott.'

'Dick, it's me.'

'How is she?' There was urgency in the detective sergeant's voice.

Stone cleared his throat. He wouldn't lie. He'd called Dick on the way to the hospital to say that she was alive and on route to Cramlington where the major trauma unit was situated. The Murder Investigation Team would have been willing her on. Cut one police officer and the whole force bled.

'She hasn't regained consciousness,' Stone said. 'She's undergoing tests. I've not seen her yet. I'm awaiting the all-clear from the consultant. I don't know what good it will do. Maybe if I regurgitate her daft rulebook, she'll wake the fuck up.' He paused for long enough for Dick to process the information to pass on to the team. 'Did you call Parker?'

'Yeah, no answer on the landline.'

'And his mobile?'

'Ditto. He was asleep in the garden, his missus in the swimming pool when I paid them a visit. They were oblivious to any police activity.'

'That's bollocks. The whole force is out there, including India 99.'

'I was up there sharpish, boss. Their phones were in the house, switched on, I checked. No recent calls.'

'They both saw Frankie earlier in the day,' Stone said. 'They were unaware that she'd returned?'

'So they say,' Abbott paused. 'Mind you, if she was sniffing around Justine's car, maybe she wanted a silent entry.'

'Maybe . . . I wish she'd told me. She should never have gone out there single-crewed.'

'That's not her style, guv. I asked for urgent triangulation from EE. They did it straight away. If Parker moved from the house, he left his device behind.'

'Maybe he took Alex's phone.'

'No, both phones were stationary. There's no CCTV up there so it looks like we're screwed. I sent Mitch out to interview Curtis and shake him up a bit. The guy may have a certain gravitas but I never liked the smarmy bastard. Interestingly, he was home alone, just out of the shower. I'm now waiting on *his* service provider.'

'OK, I'll call in later.'

'Boss?'

'Yeah?'

'Give Frankie our best when she wakes up. Tell her to get her arse back to work. I'm sick of picking up the slack.'

'I will.' Stone hung up.

Dick was a pro, trying his best to stay upbeat. The jury was out on Frankie's condition, David's mind full of words he didn't want to acknowledge: craniotomy, infection, complications. He tried to shake them off but they kept coming, tormenting him. He'd been told that it was possible for a head injury to be a slow burn, blood compressing brain tissue, raising intracranial pressure, fatal in 50 per cent of cases. A large proportion of victims never survived the journey to hospital.

Frankie had . . .

So far so good.

'David? Are you OK?'

He looked at Andrea, almost without seeing her, suddenly conscious of his own vulnerability. For a moment, he'd forgotten she was in the room. He was too slow to cover his distress. She was on her feet, staring at him, waiting for a response. He was frozen in a time warp, unable to shake himself free. Andrea moved towards him. She reached out a hand and then withdrew it as if touching him might make him crumple.

'You've been here before, haven't you?' she said.

He blew out a breath. 'Not exactly . . .'

She apologised. 'I shouldn't have asked.'

'It's fine.' It wasn't. Stone was felled by the sadness all over again. He was in *that* room staring into the face of hell. He thought he was on top of it; and he was, until he'd set eyes on Alex Parker. The likeness was striking. Every time he looked at her, the sadness hit him like a giant wave, rendering him ineffectual. Frankie had propped him up, covered his back – that was the kind of person she was – and he'd given her no explanation. He felt unworthy.

'A colleague?' Andrea had to know.

He nodded his answer.

'And if Frankie doesn't make it, you'll feel guilty for the rest of your life, is that it? We're police, David. Sometimes we get hurt. It comes with the territory. Frankie understands that. What happened to her is not your fault.'

He couldn't speak.

'My God! What the fuck happened in London?'

'My colleague. Partner. She died.'

'Jesus!' Andrea was gutted. 'I'm so sorry.'

David didn't want to talk about it. He walked to the window and looked out, the past slowly subsiding, his thoughts returning to the present. He had a double murder and an attempted murder to solve. He was hoping that Frankie might have seen her attacker and have vital information to give. She was at risk if the offender found out she was alive. He'd deployed two officers to stay with her round the clock. These guys didn't need to work out. They were big buggers. Wherever Frankie went, they went too. Her clothing had been removed and retained for forensic examination. He had no doubt that, if the opportunity arose, she'd have tried to get DNA from the person who'd tried to kill her.

'DI Stone?'

A knife pierced David's back. For a split second, he didn't

want to turn around, didn't want to hear news from the consultant that might affect the rest of Frankie's life or lessen her chances of survival. As her direct supervision, he had to accept the outcome of those tests at some point and face her family. He turned to the voice and waited . . .

'She's conscious and asking to see you.'

68

Despite a family link to Frankie, Andrea insisted that Stone go in first; Frankie had asked for him and the Traffic officer was keen to give them the opportunity to share vital information about the attempted murder of a police officer. More than anything, she wanted the bastard who'd done this caught.

Stone took a deep breath and opened the door.

Frankie's eyes were shut. Now she'd been cleaned up, the wounds to her hands and face were angrier than they'd appeared in the darkness of the woods. He could still see that burning vehicle. He could taste and smell petrol fumes – and not only in his imagination – the odour was in the room, probably from her hair, a large patch of which had been shaved off where staples had been applied to a head wound.

He pulled up a chair and sat down.

Frankie opened her eyes. It took a while for her to focus, a second longer for her to realise she was not alone. She was extremely pale, a bluish tinge, her eyes red, irritation caused by smoke. The consultant had warned him that she had a severe headache, both from her injury and from carbon monoxide poisoning, the effects of which should be gone in a day or two. She'd been given medication that would make her drowsy.

'Hey!' he said. 'Welcome back.'

She didn't speak.

Unusual.

Her eyes travelled blankly round the room and came to rest on his blood-soaked shirt, a moment of frightening clarity. She knew then that she'd been lucky to survive. She looked tiny in the bed. Like a kid, disoriented, afraid and wanting to

357

go home at the earliest opportunity. Stone was about to ask how she was feeling when the door behind him opened.

He glanced over his shoulder, expecting to see a member of the medical team coming to check on her. Instead, he found an anxious male he'd never seen before, a combination of fury and fear in his eyes. David was immediately on alert.

'Who the hell are you?' he said.

'I could ask you the same question, son.'

Stone was on his feet. He had a strong suspicion that this could be Frank Oliver II whose eyes had homed in on the state of his daughter, a fact that he confirmed as he stuck out a hand.

It was a firm handshake.

'Pleased to meet you, sir. I only wish it had been in different circumstances.'

'Likewise.'

An unsaid thank you passed from Frankie's father to Stone, as if he was singlehandedly responsible for rescuing Frankie from the jaws of death. On closer inspection, there was no disputing the man's identity – it was like seeing double. Before David had a chance to introduce himself properly and tell him that it was Andrea he should be thanking, the door opened again and the Traffic officer pushed past the two of them, followed by four others: one elderly male, three females – Frankie's grandfather, grandmother, mum, and sister, Rae. Behind them, a redundant sign on the wall read: STRICTLY TWO VISITORS PER PATIENT.

Stone was overwhelmed. He'd never received so many hugs and thanks from perfect strangers or seen so many rule-breakers huddled around one hospital bed. There was not a dry eye in the room. Tears of joy lifted his spirits and left him wondering if this was what a real family was like. Apart from his beloved nan and brother, he'd not had one since he was six years old – how would he know?

Frankie had eyes only for Stone.

She blushed, sending a silent message: *Get me the hell out of here.*

He shot her a smiley wink and withdrew. This was a private gathering and he had no place being there. He'd step out to allow her nearest and dearest some time to catch up with her, with the intention of hanging around outside. There were questions he needed to put to her. If he was to catch the bastard who'd left her to die in that car, they couldn't wait.

If he didn't ask, her father sure as hell would.

David's phone rang as he reached for the door handle, the last in what seemed like a never-ending stream of calls he'd fielded in the past two hours from the Chief Constable, the force medical officer and members of the Murder Investigation Team, all wanting the low-down on her condition; even Windy offered to supply anything she needed.

As he slipped from the room, closing the door quietly behind him, David answered his mobile without checking to see who it was.

'DI Stone.'

'David, it's Ben.'

Stone hesitated, his eyes on a busy hospital corridor, overstretched NHS staff going about their business, paying him no heed, every one of them involved with crisis intervention, delivering care in a range of cases from minor mishaps to people at death's door. Some emergency admissions would never leave. He blew out a breath. Fortunately, Frankie wasn't one of them.

'David? Are you there?'

'Not now, son. I really am busy.'

'Yes, now! Don't hang up. Frankie said she'd be home around eight. She didn't show. I called her mobile. She's not answering. Should I be concerned?'

'Home?' Confusion reigned.

'She's letting me kip in her spare room until I get my shit together,' Ben said. 'And before you start mouthing off at me,

I didn't ask, she offered. Don't be angry with her, please. She made me promise not to tell you, but I'm worried about her.'

Stone glanced back through the door. The figure in the bed met his gaze momentarily, each member of her family leaning over her in turn, kind words and kisses all round, her grand-dad, Frank Oliver I holding her hand. Stone swallowed the despair he'd experienced since Mitchell lost her on the phone. Frankie was going to be fine. 'I'm not angry with you, Ben.'

'Has something happened?'

'Yes, but she's OK. I'll swing by her place later.'

'I can stay?'

'You can stay.'

69

Stone let himself into the incident room at dawn on Tuesday morning. DS Dick Abbott had beaten him in. The rest of the team drifted into the office in dribs and drabs, hungry for news of Frankie and keen to start work. They were all in by seven thirty and Stone scheduled a briefing for eight o'clock, requiring every member of the Murder Investigation Team to be there. No excuses. They had been working flat out for days and, despite yesterday's drama in the woods near Scots Gap, there were no signs of fatigue. The case had suddenly turned personal. No rest days were allowed until detectives found their target.

Who exactly was their target?

As SIO, David was feeling under pressure to get a result. With Frankie gone, this would be doubly difficult. There was no point stressing over it. The rest of his team were primed and ready to work round the clock to apprehend the bastard responsible for the attempt on her life. Taking out one of their own in the lawful course of her duty was as serious as it could get for them. He was about to call for order when Windy entered the incident room unexpectedly.

The DI stood up. 'Can I help you, sir?'

'Not this morning.' The Superintendent's expression was smug. 'I thought you'd like to know that while you and DS Oliver have been on holiday, working for the murder squad elite, the general CID have collared a team of organised criminals responsible for aggravated burglaries across three counties. Your replacement got a commendation from the Chief.'

Stone had to work hard to keep his face straight.

What Windy meant was the home of one of the Chief

Constable's mates got screwed and he could now dine out on the exceptional job he'd done in ridding the border region of such vermin. David was about to congratulate the self-righteous prick and remind him that Frankie was languishing in hospital for her trouble when his mobile stopped him: *Kyra Thakur.*

'Sir. It's Met Police, I need to take this.'

Windy made a quick retreat, taking his ego with him. Stone watched him go. Kyra had done him a massive favour. If he'd had the chance to respond to Windy's showboating, he'd never have kept it civil.

He pressed to receive the call. 'Morning, Kyra.'

'Mitch told me what happened. How's Frankie?'

'Concussed, but doing well.'

'I've been calling her.'

'Her mobile perished in the fire.'

'Is everything else OK?' Nothing got past Kyra.

'Barring disrespectful conduct, yes.'

'Doesn't sound like you.'

'It wasn't . . . this one had a crown on his shoulder.'

'And we thought Connor was a dickhead!'

'Every office has one.'

She giggled.

'Actually, Kyra, can you call me on Facetime? We're about to start a briefing. It would be good to get your input.' Kyra hung up and redialled. Once the call had reconnected, Stone used AirPlay to wirelessly mirror the display on to an Apple TV so she'd be seen by every detective in the incident room and not just those at the front.

David glanced at the screen. 'All set?'

Kyra nodded.

'Everybody, this Kyra Thakur, the best DS south of Gateshead. She's an ex-colleague of mine, so play nice.'

Kyra smiled.

'How was your trip to the Cotswolds?' Stone asked.

'Enlightening,' Kyra said. 'That job offer Curtis gave as his alibi was genuine. There was a meeting lasting over three hours. The position he applied for is a big deal, requiring him to conduct a presentation in front of a board of directors. Each one verified his attendance independently and CCTV corroborates what he told you.'

'Does that rule him out for the time of Kat's death?'

'On its own, no. The meeting didn't start until two fifteen, enough time for him to commit murder at noon and still get there. Fortunately for him, we've placed him on a train en route to Burford where the meeting took place. It's your call, but I'd say that eliminates him from the enquiry this end, unless the pathologist has his timings wrong.'

'Which leaves Parker,' Mitch mumbled under his breath.

'Or Hamilton or Alex,' Dick Abbott warned him. 'Or any member of the e-voke dating agency. Detecting is a bit like riding a motorcycle, Mitch. Keep looking at the kerb and you're bound to hit it.' Dick's was the voice of reason. As far as Stone was concerned, he was preaching to the converted. Potentially, there were thousands of possible perpetrators out there, though perhaps not all had associations with both victims. There was more work to do.

70

Frankie had still been groggy when David questioned her the previous evening to ascertain whether she could ID her attacker. She couldn't. Over and above that, he'd refused to discuss work or the ongoing investigation, frustrating the hell out of her. What did he expect her to do, lie in bed and mope?

Frankie wasn't having that.

He'd sat there for ages, holding her hand, figuratively speaking. When he refused to leave, she feigned sleep, a plan forming in her mind. He was hardly out the door when she pressed her call button, asking one of the nurses to call Ben. Frankie had helped him . . .

The least he could do was reciprocate.

Ben knocked gently on the door and pushed it open. Frankie beckoned him in. He looked shaken to see the extent of her injuries. Cleaned up, he was a handsome lad, around six two with a good physique, considering his recent lifestyle. He'd made a huge effort to look presentable. She wondered if it was all for her benefit or because there was a chance he might bump into David. Either way, he was heading in the right direction.

The lad winced when he saw the staples on her scalp. 'Do they hurt?'

'They pinch a bit, but it's not as bad as it looks. Did you bring my iPad?'

Nodding, he took the device from his man bag and handed it over. Frankie was desperate to discover what was happening at base. She had as much chance of finding out from her boss as winning the lottery. Stone had forbidden the Murder Investigation Team to worry her with work. Her granddad would call him a prat, although maybe not today. After yesterday's theatricals, he'd more likely hang a medal round David's neck and invite him for supper: she hoped he liked pie and peas.

Frankie tapped her iPad, eyes on Ben. 'This is strictly between us, OK? No blabbing to Uncle Dave. He'll kill me if he finds out I'm within a hundred miles of his case while I'm in here. He can be a pain in the butt sometimes.'

'You don't say.'

'So can you!' It was her way of telling him to back off. She could criticise Stone. He could not. Her boss had earned her loyalty and he'd get it. She changed the subject. 'You're looking after my place?'

Ben was nodding.

'No parties while I'm gone, you hear me?'

'One wrong move and you're out, you said.'

'Nice of you to remember.'

He searched her face for a moment, a question on his lips. It took him a while to get it out. 'Why are you doing this for me, Frank? It's not as if we're family or even friends. My old man said the police trust no one – it's in their DNA – and yet you took me in when you know nothing about me—'

'I know enough.' Frankie couldn't tell him what was behind her benevolence. She had her reasons, of course. None she was willing to share. Where kids were concerned, a united front was what was required. Anything less and they tended to fall through the cracks, sometimes for good. She was determined that wouldn't happen to Ben. 'Besides, I'm not doing it for you, I'm doing it for him. And, for the record, your dad was right, but only where prigs are concerned. Trust is essential between friends. Did you talk to your tutor?'

The lad looked sheepish. Clearly, he hadn't.

She was bitterly disappointed. 'We had a deal, mister. Three conditions, remember: you stay clean; you study and you don't give David a hard time. No matter how he comes across, he loves you.'

'Yeah, well he has a funny way of showing it.'

'Communication is a two-way street, Ben. You get back what you put in.' She gave him a pointed look, then a forgiving smile. 'There endeth the lesson.'

'I made an appointment,' he said.

'Good. Make sure you keep it. If you show willing, so will David. He's not an ogre.' She pulled a funny face. 'Not all the time anyway.' She wanted to tell him why it was so important to get his life in order, stick in at university and find his feet, but she had no words that wouldn't leave her blubbing like a toddler who'd lost her teddy.

Frankie was bored, feeling perfectly well rested after a good night's sleep: redundant, surplus to requirements, left out of the loop. She had to do *something* to push the enquiry along. With Ben gone, she got out of bed. Discarding her hospital gown, she dressed in the clothes her mother had brought in: skinny jeans, a pale grey shirt, a pair of black-and-white snake print pumps. Making herself comfortable in the chair beside her bed, she woke up her iPad and Facetimed Kyra, hoping Stone's directive hadn't travelled south.

'Hello!' Kyra looked pleased to speak to her, a busy office going about its business behind her, the sun streaming in through the window on to her shiny black hair. 'It's great to see you. I just got off a conference call with your office. How are you?'

'I'll be a damned sight better when I get out of here.'

'How long are they keeping you in?'

'I'm waiting for someone to tell me to bugger off home. I'm perfectly fine, so I thought I'd make myself useful in the meantime.'

'I'm intrigued. You have something in mind?'

'A hunch, nothing more.'

'I like!' Kyra smiled. 'Anything you can share?'

'Not yet, but I hope you can. I'd like to look through the

photographs found on Kat Irwin's phone. Can you whizz them across to my personal email?' Ignoring Kyra's suspicious expression, she reeled off the address: 'foliver999@gmail. com.'

Kyra agreed to AirDrop them.

Seconds later, they arrived.

71

Kyra had checked to see how many e-voke members were linked to both victims and come up with only two, the same two that Stone had been chasing all along. Of that pairing, Curtis had been ruled out. Stone looked out of the window, contemplating. Only two people had direct access to Justine's car: both had the surname Parker. Every detective in the Murder Investigation Team agreed that Justine and Kat were killed by the same person. The two women were linked by the e-voke website and had suffered a blunt force trauma to the head, though in Justine's case the killer had incapacitated her and then deliberately moved her into the road to finish the job, an act of unspeakable cruelty. The problem for David was that the Parkers alibied each other for the time of Justine's death.

Although he'd set his team to gather evidence on Alex, on the balance of probability he had to concede that Tim was the most likely suspect, for several reasons: his relationship with both victims; his current financial difficulties; his wish to keep his affairs from his wife and, the most damning of all, his proximity to both crime scenes. It was time to bring him in to Northern Command HQ. This time, Parker insisted on legal representation, a top London criminal lawyer who'd fly north on the first available British Airways flight from Heathrow. In the meantime, the DI had nothing to do except await his arrival while the entrepreneur languished in a cell.

Saul Meyr meant business. He was a small man with a hell of a presence, self-assured and with a gaze that would strike fear into any adversary. His first grievance was that his client was being held on suspicion of murder with insufficient evidence.

It fell on deaf ears. Money and status meant nothing when a suspect was under arrest and charges were seriously being considered. Alex too had complained vehemently, arguing that her husband would offer himself for interview and not flee the area to avoid being questioned. Stone was having none of it. A dangerous offender had killed two women and almost made it three. Timothy Parker was going nowhere until he said so.

Despite Meyr's advice to say very little under interrogation, cracks began to appear in Parker's story halfway through the interview. After spending hours in a police cell, awaiting Meyr's arrival, the entrepreneur was sweating profusely, showing signs of withdrawal from the drugs he'd been taking. A suspect with something to hide – who also needed a fix – was good news for the DI. Driven by a strong suspicion that the man across the interview table was responsible for Frankie's emergency admission to hospital, David went in for the kill . . .

'We never asked your wife if she was the one having an affair with Justine as you suggested in your previous interview because, quite frankly, we don't believe you. Neither have we told her that money leaving your account was being sent to Kat Irwin, or that your business partner was under the impression that the funds were being used to reduce the level of debt to your company, money Alex had loaned you when the business was formed. However, I'm pleased to hear from DS Oliver that you finally had the guts to come clean about your affair with your sister-in-law. Isn't it time you fronted up about the rest?'

'My client has nothing else to say,' Meyr said.

'All the same, I'd like to hear that from him.'

Parker glanced at his brief.

Meyr shook his head.

The prisoner looked at the floor. Thinking time. When he raised his head, his eyes flitted between Stone and Abbott in jerky movements. What would he come up with this time? Stone wondered. Faced with the prospect of a night in the cells, Parker had shrunk in stature since being brought up for questioning. Within the walls of the interview room, he was just another punter who, from the DI's point of view, was in deep shit.

'You were in Kat Irwin's flat on Friday the first of July, weren't you?'

Again, Parker glanced at his brief.

Meyr leaned in and whispered quietly in his ear.

'No, Saul, I have to end this.'

More whispering.

More soul-searching.

Despite the fortune his counsel was costing, Parker was under tremendous pressure to clear himself. No amount of advocacy costing anything between a thousand and five thousand pounds an hour was touching him. He was teetering on the brink of an admission and Stone wondered why he'd asked Meyr to make the trip from the capital if he had no intention of taking his advice. Unless Alex was behind it. She was the one with all the cash.

Parker was practically squirming in his seat. 'I was there in Kat's flat, but I swear she was dead when I arrived.'

Meyr intervened. 'Tim, I strongly advise against saying any more.'

'I have to, Saul. They'll find my DNA and jump to the wrong conclusion.' Parker switched his focus to the detectives. 'You know I lied about Justine. I'm not lying now.'

In his head, Stone was at the crime scene with that three-dimensional image of the apartment, the positioning of the bloodstains on light wood flooring reminding himself that there had been no break-in.

'How did you get in?' he asked.

'I have a key.'

'Describe the scene for me.'

'Excuse me?'

'You said Kat was dead when you arrived. Tell me exactly what you saw.'

'She was lying face down on the living room floor.' Parker shut his eyes, trying to remember. Or perhaps making out that he was. 'There was a lot of blood. I thought she'd fallen. She has this coffee table with a marble top. Italian. I never liked it. I was always worried that Ali would hurt herself on it. Kat was more relaxed about it.'

'You thought she'd struck her head?'

Parker nodded. 'There were no signs of a struggle. If she'd been attacked, believe me she'd have fought like a street kid.'

'Unless she was familiar with the person and turned her back on them.'

There was panic in Parker's eyes. This looked bad for him and he knew it. Stone had to hand it to him: so far, his account was spot on. At the crime scene, Frankie had theorised that Parker might have set the alarm off to ensure that Ali was found. The child was traumatised, unable to say anything to the specially trained officers interviewing her.

'Did you check if Kat was dead?' Stone asked.

Parker shook his head. 'It was obvious.'

'How would you know if you didn't check?'

'I wasn't touching her, was I?'

The tension was building in the room.

Stone remembered the way the light shone through the windows on two sides of Kat's living room highlighting blood spatter on a pristine leather sofa. 'Why not?' he said. 'Accidents happen. If she was still breathing, you might have saved her life.'

'She wasn't.'

'You didn't care if she was dead or alive, did you? In fact, her death put an end to your leaking bank account and the chance that she might one day turn on you and confess all to Alex.'

'My client told you it was obvious Ms Irwin was dead, DI Stone.' Meyr didn't lift his head, much less the expensive pen from his notepad. 'Can we move on?'

That ten-second sentence cost Parker a tidy sum. Meyr got paid for what he did in court, not during interview. He was a charismatic man, able to swing the most sceptical jury. According to Kyra, no litigation lawyer could touch him.

'Where was Ali at this point?' Stone asked.

'In her room. Well, in the doorway. Jesus! I was in chunks when I saw her standing there. I will never forget the look on her face.' Parker was losing it. 'She'll remember what she saw for the rest of her life. I can only hope she didn't think I had anything to do with it.'

'Did you speak to her?'

'No. I just took off.'

Stone glared at him. 'She's three years old and you left her there with her mother lying dead on the floor?'

'I left the door open and started a fire alarm on my way out. There's a caretaker in the building. I knew he'd check it out and find her—'

'With respect, you knew nothing of the kind.' Stone paused, waiting for Dick to stop making notes. 'What if the caretaker had stepped out for half an hour? What if Ali had wandered out of the apartment alone?' Justine's burning car was in Stone's head. 'What if there had been a real fire?'

Even Meyr looked dumbfounded by his client's stupidity.

'I wasn't thinking straight.' Parker began to wobble. 'There's a coffee shop over the road. I waited there to make sure that she didn't walk out of the building. Why d'you think I was terrified when you lifted me from the plane?' It was the most genuine thing he'd said since he sat down.

'Why did you run?' Stone asked.

'Why do you think?'

'I could think of one good reason.'

'No! I lied to you about Justine and was found out. I was scared that you'd think I was responsible for Kat's death. You obviously do. I'm linked to both women. It was over with her, I swear. If she hadn't—'

'Hadn't what?'

'If she hadn't got herself pregnant we'd have ended our fling and that would have been that and I wouldn't be sitting here professing my innocence. I ran because I've been set up, Detective Inspector. You must see that. First with Daniel's disappearance and now these two murders. I swear I had nothing to do with any of this. I may be weak, contemptible even, but that's all I am.'

'Why did you go and see Kat if your affair was over?' Stone was expecting him to say for access to his child, but he didn't . . .

'While she was on holiday, Kat called me. She'd decided to come clean about Ali.'

'To Alex?'

'Yes. Prior to that, Kat and I had an arrangement. She'd leave me out of it providing the money kept coming.'

'So what changed?'

'She'd been getting closer and closer to Alex in the last couple of years and had come up with a plan to tell her that she'd adopted a three-year-old. That was the only conceivable way she could deal with the problem that we'd created. She'd even considered coming north now her divorce was finalised so I could see my child more often, albeit as Uncle Tim. I love my daughter – and Kat too, even though we're no longer together.'

'Even though she was milking you?'

'Financing a child's upbringing isn't the same as looking after one. Kat was doing all the hard graft and making a real fist of it. Ali offered her stability. Kat's never had that. Without her, I'd be childless. Being a father means everything to me.'

'And Alex couldn't make that happen—'

'We'll try again . . . If she'll let me.'

Meyr's head popped up. 'Relevance, DI Stone.' He was making a point, not asking a question.

Stone ignored him as if he wasn't there. 'Kat Irwin was putting a strain on finances that were already stretched, Mr Parker. The way Curtis tells it, you two are heading for financial ruin. That alone gives you motive. If Kat was about to blow the whistle, you just gave yourself another.'

'I was happy to pay her. A year ago, I was making a mint. It was easy to cover the cost. Then things went pear-shaped and I couldn't hide it any more. Curtis found out. He threatened to tell Alex.'

'And did he?'

'Not that I'm aware of.'

Stone wasn't so sure. He had his doubts about her involvement. 'You said you'd been set up. By whom?'

'I don't know. Curtis has been acting weird since he realised where the money was going. His divorce from Kat was acrimonious. She left him, not the other way around . . . I don't think he ever got over it. He'll tell you different, but it's bollocks.'

The more Stone delved into Parker's background, the more he found. Most of the evidence against him was circumstantial. The case was building but it needed to be watertight. At his own admission, he was at the scene. He had means, opportunity and motive, but Stone remained unconvinced. With little progress made, he ended the interview to consult with Frankie, if she was up to it, and lodged Parker in a cell.

72

Parker wasn't the only one ignoring sensible advice. When Stone reached the incident room, Frankie was at her desk as if nothing untoward had happened the day before. She was concentrating hard on her computer screen – images of some sort – and didn't see him walk in. Anticipating a row, Dick raised an eyebrow as David crossed the room, a slight shake of the head.

'I did try and talk her out of it,' he said quietly. 'I can't repeat what she said to me.'

Stone rolled his eyes. 'How did she get here?'

'On her broomstick, probably . . .' Dick grinned. 'She discharged herself, told officers on guard duty to stand down and asked for a lift.'

'They didn't argue?'

'Would you?'

David approaching Frankie from behind. The skin around the staples on the back of her head looked red and inflamed. The rest of her hair reminded him of his nan's old cat whose fur had become matted due to old age. He'd sat for hours detangling it. Unlike the feline, Frankie didn't care about her dishevelled appearance. Work was obviously more important. She still reeked of petrol.

He leaned over. 'Would you like to step into my office, DS Oliver?'

'In a second.' She didn't look up. 'Let me finish this first.'

'Shall I call Windy?'

'Boss, I—'

'Now, Frankie!'

*

375

Irritated by the interruption, Frankie sat down in the chair to explain her presence. 'I appreciate your concern, I do, but the consultant was happy to discharge me on the proviso that I had someone at home to keep an eye on me.'

'According to Abbott, you discharged yourself.'

She grimaced. 'Technically—'

'Either you did or you didn't.'

'Gimme a break -- you're not my dad!'

'And I suppose you failed to mention that the "someone at home" was a teenager with the nous of a three-year-old.'

'Don't be mean. Ben's trying really hard.'

'He's trying . . . and so are you.' David admonished her with his eyes. 'When were you going to tell me that you'd offered him a bed?'

'When you stopped being a pain in the arse.' Frankie was unconcerned that he'd found out about her temporary house guest. 'I'd have got around to it . . . eventually.' She was experienced enough to pick the battles she could win.

Timing was key.

Stone shook his head in a gesture of frustration. 'As it happens, I drove over to your place to catch up with Ben last night. It's the first time I'd seen him look decent in ages. Well, I say decent, he came the door wearing a baby blue undersized dressing gown I presume was yours, his hairy arse on show.'

Frankie laughed.

Stone didn't need to mention that the moment had provided not only relief from a very bad workday, but respite from the infighting that had dogged the relationship with his nephew since Luke died. Last night at the hospital, he'd witnessed a demonstration that family were good and kind. In times of trouble, they pulled together, not in opposite directions. Frankie wasn't stupid enough to think that no other type of family existed on the planet. In her police career, she'd seen many split up with devastating consequences, often involving violence, even death. She'd seen good in Ben where he had not. It was a lesson he might benefit from. Maybe if he gave a little, Ben would too.

Frankie was in full work mode, keen to share new information. The first thing she'd said to him last night, other than 'my head hurts', was work-related. She'd asked whether Mitch had found images on the database showing the milometer in Justine's car. He had, but Stone had steered her away from the subject, refusing to discuss it. It wasn't lost on him that these were the very same photographs she'd been looking at in the incident room a moment ago.

'What is it about Justine's mileage that's so fascinating?' he asked. 'I checked the computer this morning. There's one photograph showing 98,252 miles on the clock, so what?'

Frankie sat up, suddenly animated. 'When I went to see Alex yesterday, I noticed her car on the driveway. It had been moved, David. There were deep ruts on the gravel where she'd come and gone. The vehicle was parked in a different position, I was convinced of it.'

'So you nipped up to Scots Gap to investigate without telling me.'

'OK – I'm sorry. That doesn't negate the fact that the reading I saw was 98,888. I made a photographic record. It's on my phone.'

'I'm sorry to rain on your parade, Frankie. Forensics found your phone – or what was left of it, in Justine's torched car.'

'Really? I thought you'd find it in the woods. I was sure it was in my hand. Could the phone they found be someone else's?'

'The evidence is gone, Frank. Fried beyond belief.'

'But my brain isn't.'

She seemed sure of her facts but Stone had more to say on the subject. 'Without proof to back it up, any self-respecting barrister will pick holes the size of Texas if we put that evidence forward in court. You know as well as I do, they'll question you mercilessly under oath, twisting your words, making out that you're unfit to give a credible statement after being found unconscious. You sustained a nasty bang on the head.'

'I know what I saw, David. And if my maths are correct I'd say that the discrepancy is a return trip to London, wouldn't you? Which means that neither Curtis or Parker is the culprit. They both flew to London on the day Kat died. That's indisputable. But someone else drove.'

73

There was silence in the incident room as Frankie recounted her tale to the Murder Investigation Team. Despite her injuries, she was close to wrapping up their case. 'If Justine's car was used to travel down to London to kill Kat Irwin, only one person could have used it.' Not one detective disagreed. She was pointing the finger directly at Alex Parker and was holding cards she hadn't yet shown. 'The keys were in the car when I arrived there yesterday and yet they were handed over and signed for by Tim Parker following forensic examination of the vehicle. I have a statement from the officer concerned to that effect. He'll swear under oath that the car was left locked and secured on the Parkers' driveway.'

'Makes you wonder how her parents died,' Mitch said.

'Alex wasn't responsible,' Stone replied. 'They were in St Lucia, a boating accident. The British Consulate contacted us. We delivered the death message and she flew out there to repatriate their bodies.'

'Well, she can't have killed Kat,' Mitch said. 'She was at work all day Friday. Put it this way, she went in the front door at seven thirty a.m. and left at six thirty p.m.'

'That's time enough,' Frankie said. 'If she got her foot down.'

'She's right,' Stone said. 'Mitch, check if there's a rear entrance to her business premises.'

'I already did that when Justine died,' he said. 'There's an alarmed fire exit at the rear of the office not covered by CCTV. She could've sneaked in and out unseen.'

'Check it out,' the DI said.

'What she couldn't do is make her son disappear,' Dick said. 'That's where all this started.'

'Unless she was the one who hacked Tim Parker's phone,'

Frankie added. 'An action I initiated but then cancelled when the boy was returned.' She glanced at Stone. 'Blame Windy.'

David was nodding. 'Parker did say he was set up.'

'If that's true,' Frankie said, 'his wife's the one doing it.'

'Revisit the service provider, Dick. We haven't one shred of evidence against her otherwise.'

Frankie couldn't agree more. 'Then we'll have to find it. The more I think about it, the more pieces of the jigsaw fall into place. Alex jogs. She could've been the jogger Marjorie Smith saw running past her cottage – or the cyclist for that matter. Justine and Alex are about the same stamp. Alex could've done the deed, then disposed of Dixon's bike in the lake.'

Dick was shaking his head. 'Not before our guys got their act together. The area was flooded with police vehicles within minutes of Justine's death. Alex would've been seen.'

'Dick has a point,' Stone said. 'And didn't she pick Daniel up from school that day?'

Frankie wasn't put off. 'So she rides home through the woods, hides the incriminating evidence in the back of the car and gets rid on the way to pick up Daniel. It's a small window of opportunity, but doable.' Her eyes found Stone. 'We've been played, boss.'

'We need more than the testimony of an old lady. Something concrete to tie Alex to the crime scene. It's one thing knowing she did it, another matter finding proof.'

Frankie's eyes lit up. 'And I know exactly where to find it.' She paused, several pairs of eyes staring at her. 'All of Alex Parker's problems began while she was away on holiday in Majorca. This morning, I asked Kyra to AirDrop me the photographs from Kat's mobile phone – several thousand of them. I studied them for hours and found something I hope will convince you.'

'Like what?' David was intrigued.

'The villa Kat booked for their holiday last month wasn't

new to her. She'd been to the very same villa four years ago – four months before Ali Irwin was born.'

'You have confirmation of that?'

'Kyra is on it. The evidence is there for the taking, boss. We can be there and back in twelve hours.'

The DI considered this for a moment. 'OK, we'll give it a go. Nothing ventured, as they say. The rest of you: no tipping her off. If Alex is our target and is trying to frame her husband, with him in custody she'll think she's achieved her objective. She doesn't know we're on to her and I'd like to keep it that way.' He focused on Frankie. 'Good job, Frank! Shame you're not fit to travel. I'll take Dick with me.'

'Over my dead body.'

Everyone laughed.

Concerned for Frankie's welfare, Stone insisted on consulting the force medical officer before allowing her to take the flight to Palma. Post-concussion, she was advised that she could travel so long as she stayed hydrated. Long haul might have been a different story. Having been instrumental in the search for the truth, no one deserved to close the case more than she did. Digital images backed up on Kat Irwin's iCloud account had provided a link between the present and the past. Whatever it was, Frankie was convinced that the trip had sparked a devastating chain of events, destroying a family who, on the face of it, led a perfect life.

Before boarding at Newcastle International, Frankie and David put their heads together. Clues on Timothy Parker's phone provided further insight into his double life with Kat Irwin and, later with his daughter, stolen periods when he was on business trips the team hadn't been able to corroborate. Golfing with other entrepreneurs was the only way to do business in his world, a fact of life for Alex who never questioned a prolonged absence.

Using this information, Frankie had done the maths. Ali Irwin was three years and eight months old, born 8 November 2012, a fact confirmed by her birth certificate. Guessing that her mother might have booked through the same travel agency for both trips, Frankie contacted Kyra, who had the details to hand, documents retrieved from the IP's flat, then emailed the company using her work address, explaining that hers was an urgent enquiry.

Minutes later, a reply pinged into Frankie's inbox via the incident room. Taking a deep breath, she opened it and found the confirmation that Kat had booked the villa twice before, the first time in May 2011 and again in July 2012. It was a starting point, nothing more.

Frankie took the opportunity for some shut-eye during the flight, emerging from sleep none the worse for her trip. The villa was a forty-minute taxi ride from the airport. The family staying there were very gracious, allowing the Northumbria detectives to look around and, for that, they were grateful. With a four-hour window before turning around and heading back to the UK, Stone and Oliver had to move fast.

The villa was sublime with a view of mountains they had no time to explore. The house was timeless, an old building, in traditional Majorcan style, surrounded by olive groves, a herd of goats grazing in the field beyond, bells tinkling as they moved to pastures new. Stone looked on as a little boy was taught to swim by his dad. It woke a memory of Luke and four-year-old Ben, one of the few holidays the DI had shared as the lad grew up. It was hard to imagine a more intoxicating scene.

Frankie too was taken by the scenery. She imagined Alex and Kat here, relaxing on sun loungers, reading books, a glass or two of wine, wonderful food and long conversations. Trying to second-guess what had gone on during their vacation was proving more difficult. Frankie wasn't yet sure what they were looking for: a carving on a tree, perhaps. There must be something, a sign that had triggered such destructive behaviour from Alex Parker.

As Frankie reread the email from the tour operator, the penny finally dropped. It took no time to locate what she was after, documentary evidence of the villa's history spanning five years: a visitors' book. Frantically, she checked the May dates. No joy. She flicked forward to July 2012 and found what she was after – a short and happy account.

74

As a victim in the ongoing investigation, Frankie could play no part in the interview of Alex Parker and was forced to observe from the viewing room at Northern Command HQ as Stone cautioned her and began his questioning. The evidence against the suspect was watertight. Once they had identified who the perpetrator was, the rest fell neatly into place. The DI's interview method was sound. Alex couldn't fail to notice his confidence going in. She had a fight on her hands and was probably banking on his evidence being circumstantial. The visitors' book retrieved from Majorca gave her motive, but nothing Stone had said so far physically tied her to a crime scene.

As Senior Investigating Officer, Stone had no choice but to conduct the interview, even though it was difficult for him to be in the same room as Alex. Without Frankie by his side, he felt like he'd lost his right arm. He had to admit, it left him slightly vulnerable. Dick was an exceptional DS – procedurally no one could touch him – but he wasn't a patch on Frank. She looked at things from an oblique angle. Her instinct was spot on. Throughout this case, she'd shielded David from Alex. Now that layer of protection was gone.

He forced himself to meet her gaze. 'On Wednesday, June twenty-ninth, I received a telephone call from your sister, Kathryn Tailford Irwin. She told me that while on holiday with you in Majorca, you claimed that your husband was being unfaithful. Is that true?'

'I've been over this with Detective Sergeant Oliver and I don't intend repeating myself.'

'OK, let's stick with DS Oliver for a second. You told her

that you had pushed your husband away during your pregnancy. Is that correct?' His question spoke to motive. The suspect had been dropping her husband in the shit. It was time to bring this to the fore.

'I fail to see how my marital relationship is relevant to your enquiries.'

'Are you refusing to answer?'

'No. I did push him away. He didn't complain. Why would he, when he was getting it elsewhere?'

'You blamed him for the death of your child, didn't you?'

'No comment.'

Frankie looked on as David presented a printout from Tim's service provider, proof that someone had set up his Twitter account on another device. Whoever owned it had sent a series of direct messages in his name. Maybe that's all Alex planned to do at first – to punish him for the death of her second child – and the rest came later.

'I'm not the first wife to spy on a husband,' she said. 'I doubt I'll be the last.'

'Nice sidestep.' Frankie glanced at Mitch in the darkened viewing room. As his direct supervision, the young detective was her responsibility. She'd been taught by the best and passed on her father's wisdom to the young detective at every opportunity. 'She's avoiding the implication that she used his account to arrange Daniel's disappearance. I doubt she'll admit anything unless we can prove it.'

Stone was talking. 'And what did you find out by doing this?'

'I waited,' Alex said. 'For weeks.' The DI kept quiet, inviting her to continue and she obliged. 'If you must know, I found nothing untoward. Not surprising. Tim is far too clever for that. He has several phones. He'd hardly use a device I could lay my hands on to carry out his sordid affairs, would he?'

'And you went away with Kat to confide in her.'

'The opportunity was there. I took it. What business is it of yours?'

'DS Oliver said you felt desperately guilty afterwards. Can I ask why?'

'Disrespecting him was unforgivable. As I told you once before, he rescued me from an abusive relationship with Daniel's father, Rob Scott. I was drunk. I should never have said anything. Kat was unreliable, the wrong person to share a secret with. She broke my confidence when she contacted you.'

Frankie turned the evidence over in her mind. Just how Kat Irwin had found out that Parker had been sleeping with Justine was unclear. The e-voke dating agency was her best guess – maybe she'd never know for sure – but evidence had come to light that Kat did know and had immediately ended her long-term affair with Timothy Parker, only to regret her decision later. Met detective, Kyra Thakur, had documented the whole thing.

In the interview room next door, Stone pushed on. 'When you shared your suspicions with Kat, she shifted the blame, didn't she?'

Alex shrugged. 'I don't recall.'

'I think you do.'

'She does,' Frankie whispered under her breath.

Mitch was nodding.

Stone again. 'I have a theory about that—'

'I'm not remotely interested in your theories,' Alex said. 'Perhaps you could get to the point and tell me why I'm here.'

If Frankie had to describe Alex's expression it would be contemptuous. She was a clever woman who ran a multi-national public relations company, so successful that she could afford to bankroll her husband without feeling the pinch. An interview with Stone wasn't touching her.

'She's trying to undermine him,' Mitch said.

'It's not working.' Frankie glanced at him. 'The boss is too experienced for that.'

Stone paused, placed his elbows on the table, linking his hands, his eyes firmly on the accused. 'It is my contention that Kat offered Justine up as a scapegoat to deflect attention from herself without realising that she was effectively signing your au pair's death warrant. Isn't that the way it was?'

'I'm sorry, I'm not following.'

'I doubt that. Let me enlighten you. What you may not know is that there was a time when Tim and Kat were very much in love. We found a series of text messages on a device he offered us following your arrest. Although she'd broken it off with him, she subsequently wanted him back in her life and Ali's. Not a real family, but close enough. I gather the feeling was mutual, but then it all went pear-shaped – for her and for you.'

Frankie was getting excited in the viewing room. David was on a roll, taking the wind from beneath the wings of his prisoner, winding her up to the point that she might say something she'd regret.

'Wait for it,' Frankie said. 'This is about to get interesting.'

'He's good,' Mitch said.

'You're underestimating him. He's wasted as a DI. Listen and learn.'

Frankie gave David her full attention as he continued to question Alex. 'Following your arrest and detention and the immediate release of your husband, my team were quick to act. Aided by crime scene investigators, they have done an excellent job. A search of your home and your car was very productive.'

Frankie nudged her protégé. 'You're on, Mitch. Go!'

He got up and left the room.

Frankie kept her eye on the door to the interview room.

'Come!' Stone responded to a knock at the door. 'For the tape, DC Mitchell has entered the room.'

The young DC handed over two evidence bags. It had all been pre-planned, beautifully choreographed by Stone. He was a born SIO. Alex Parker didn't know what was coming. Frankie did and watched her carefully.

Not a flinch.

Mitch arrived at Frankie's side, proud to have played a part in his first murder interview, albeit in a small way. In the interview room, Stone pushed one of the evidence bags across the table. 'For the benefit of the tape, I'm showing the suspect exhibit LH1, a Lycra jogging suit similar to the one Justine Segal was wearing on the day she was killed.' He fixed on Alex. 'I can prove conclusively that this garment belongs to you.' When she said nothing, a second evidence bag was produced. 'I'm now showing exhibit LH2, a baseball cap. Mrs Parker—'

'Ms.'

'Ha!' Frankie said. 'There she goes again.'

Stone wasn't put off. 'I can prove that this is also yours. I have photographic evidence to that effect.'

A shrug from Alex. 'So? I wear a hat and I jog. Most people do.'

Stone began to relax, knowing that he had in his possession the most damning piece of evidence of all. 'I apologise, I should have made myself clear. This is no ordinary baseball cap, Ms Parker. It has been forensically examined.' He opened the file in front of him. 'Traces of green fibre were found on the peak of your cap and in the boot of your car, linking it and you to the burglary of a shed and, more importantly, to a weapon used in the assault on Justine Segal. A weapon we later retrieved from Bolam Lake, along with a bicycle used to transport you home within minutes of your crime.'

'Yes!' Frankie punched the air.

She couldn't have been prouder had she been sitting by his side. In Sharpe's absence, Stone was about to nail a suspect, clearing up murders at both ends of the country, which would please the SIO no end when he returned from holiday, not to mention David's former Metropolitan Police guvnor, Detective Superintendent Sinead Friel. Windy might even crack a smile . . .

Or maybe not.

Stone ploughed on, taking his case to Alex, in possession of facts that would ultimately convict her. 'By your own admission, you have never visited the row of cottages marked on this map . . .' He held up the map. 'Let alone East Cottage, rented by Mr and Mrs Dixon. For the record, I'm showing Ms Parker exhibit RM1.'

'That's me!' Mitch grinned.

'How old are you?' Frankie was smiling and shaking her head at the same time.

Next door, Stone was indicating the point on the map where the burglary had taken place. 'Both tenants have confirmed independently that you have not visited them at any stage, and yet the fibres lifted from your hat match, in every respect, the green felt-like shadow board in their shed. Do you have anything more to say?'

Alex shook her head. 'Do you?'

'Yes, as it happens. The fibres I mentioned are very old. They're also very unusual; forensic experts were unable to trace anything similar, neither is there anything of the kind in the comparison tables on our database.'

'You've lost me, Detective Inspector. Maybe my husband can help you with that.'

'C'mon, Alex, I know exactly when you made the decision that would affect the lives of so many, including my DS.'

For much of the interview, Alex Parker had shown no emotion whatsoever. She'd sat impassively, careful not to incriminate herself while the SIO pulled it all together, each piece of evidence furthering his goal. She was done for now. To give Alex her due, she didn't try to resist when he pushed the Casa Pegueña visitors' book across the table to shake her confidence further. 'I'm now showing the suspect Exhibit FO1: a visitors' book.'

'FO is Frankie Oliver, I presume.'

'That is correct, the same DS you assaulted on your driveway when she was examining the milometer on Justine's car, the same police officer you attempted to murder in woods near your home. Did I mention that we have CCTV of your return trip to London in Justine's Clio? You do like that hat!'

Alex dropped her eyes to the visitors' book. It was open at the correct page, inside an evidence bag. She could see text through a viewing window . . . and it shook her to the core.

Another superb week in Casa Pegueña . . . perfect escape . . . thunderstorms and torrential rain didn't spoil our trip this time. We call it our secret hideaway, just right for two – and a five-month-old bump! Kat and I will be back. Tim.

When Alex looked up, there was no defeated expression on her face. The trigger moment for the killings would be etched on her memory for ever more. Sitting poolside in Majorca with the visitors' book on her knee, she'd read an entry about ants, shuddered and turned the page. The next scribbled note – the one she'd looked at a moment ago – had come as a body blow. Recognising the artistic handwriting produced a panic attack. She'd checked the calendar on her phone while Kat slept soundly on her sunbed, the words poking fun at her. It answered so many questions, not least of which was Kat's familiarity with Casa Pegueña. She had always been an impulsive airhead.

Alex had nothing to say to Stone.

It must've been a heart-stopping, gut-wrenching betrayal,' he said. 'And Kat paid the price, didn't she? Booking a villa that she and Tim had used before was the mistake that ultimately led to her death. She mustn't have known that he'd written in that book or she would never have taken you there.'

The suspect's eyes were like ice.

'You made Daniel disappear to punish your husband, didn't you? It was quite a risk, suggesting that someone had hacked Tim's Twitter account. Pretending that you were supporting him threw us for a while, but then you knew that Daniel was coming home the next day, didn't you? You had us fooled.' Stone sat back in his chair, taking a moment or two before continuing. 'I can understand how angry you were with Kat but did you really have to kill her? You had everything to live for: a wonderful house, a successful business, a great kid. What were you thinking? Divorce wouldn't have cost you your liberty or your son. And why Justine? Did you have one shred of evidence that she was seeing Tim on the sly, beyond Kat's say-so?' He could've added that it was there to find if she'd taken the trouble to look, but it would have been cruel to taunt her with it.

Alex had no such compassion. 'Haven't you ever wanted to kill, Detective?'

'No, I haven't.'

'You're a liar! I saw it in your eyes the first time we met.'

In the observation room, Frankie watched David carefully. He was staring at Alex but not seeing her. Having witnessed the effect the woman had on him throughout the case, Frankie felt physically sick. She knew what was coming and was in no position to take over. She wanted to stop the interview. More than that, she wanted to get in there and turn off the tape. Instead, she turned her head. Mitchell's eyes were like saucers, focused on the DI, wondering what was going on across the interview table next door.

Stone hadn't uttered a word.

Feeling the heat of Frankie's gaze, Mitch glanced at her. 'What's he doing?'

'He's thinking . . .' Frankie flicked her eyes to the door. 'Go and see if there's any update in the incident room.'

'Sarge?' His expression was a mixture of incredulity and disappointment. 'It's about to get interesting.'

'Out!' she barked.

Alex smiled at Stone. 'What's the saying, DI Stone . . . takes one to know one?'

Stone felt his stomach heave. Not long ago, he'd stood in the witness box at the Old Bailey giving evidence in a murder trial. In the dock was the scumbag who killed his professional partner. At the time, he'd wanting to leap over the railings and squeeze the last breath from his lungs, until his eyes rolled back in his head and he fell to the floor. The murdering bastard had shown no mercy at the time of the killing, no remorse in interview afterwards, much less in court. Legal process had left David numb. A life sentence didn't mean life. The man would be out of prison before he turned fifty.

Alex Parker was right.

Stone ached for retribution – except taking a life would never bring his partner back.

'You're in denial, Mr Stone. Don't fight it, do it! We both know you have it in you. What did the arsehole do, take someone from you, someone you loved, perhaps? I think we understand each other, don't you?' She was laughing at him and yet the eyes he'd spent the case avoiding were cold.

Her next sentence felled him completely. 'I remind you of her, don't I?'

Frankie's eyes were on Stone as he took a breather. If she was reading him right, he was finally beginning to see Alex Parker for the evil bitch she was, not her doppelgänger. Alex was defiant, no longer a beautiful-looking woman but an ugly, calculating murderer who took pleasure in hurting people who got in her way. By mocking him, she'd shown what she was capable of. She hadn't admitted her guilt – not in so many words – but it didn't matter now; he had all the proof he needed to put her away.

Stone cleared his throat, calling on all his reserves. Years of training had equipped him to deal with offenders like Alex Parker. He wasn't going to be put off, much less allow her to intimidate him or freeze him out. 'You had the means and the opportunity,' he said. 'The only thing we struggled with was motive, until we found *that* in Majorca.' He was pointing at the visitors' book in front of her. 'Was it really justification enough for murder, Alex? Have the courage of your convictions and own up. You'll feel better for it. As I pointed out when I cautioned you, it may harm your defence if you do not mention when questioned something which you later rely on—'

'The balance of my mind was disturbed.'

'A cunning answer, but it'll never hold up in a court of law. No judge in the land will accept a plea of diminished responsibility. You have no mental impairment and there's been too much planning involved. You found out that your marriage was a sham, that you'd been deceived by the people you trusted most, and you acted upon it with devastating consequences.' There was no doubt in Stone's mind about that. In the time it had taken her to read that tiny paragraph of text in the visitors' book on a Mediterranean island a thousand miles away, a killer was born.

The woman was lost.

Beyond redemption.

'Do you have anything more to say?' he asked.

'Tim killed my baby.'

'And you wanted him to suffer.'

393

'I wanted to *destroy* him.' Her smile oozed ill intent.

'The only one you destroyed was yourself. You lost a son. He gained a daughter.'

'Revenge helps. You should try it sometime.'

Stone closed his file. It was Daniel he felt most sorry for. His only blood relative, Rob Scott, was unfit to look after him. Like Ben, the child was essentially an orphan. There wasn't a hope in hell that Alex would allow him to live with Tim.

She'd rather die than let that happen.

Emotionally, she was dead already.

Stone looked her in the eye, seeing her true nature reflected in those icy pools, separating the past from the present, the first time he'd managed that in her company. He took no pleasure in charging her. 'Alexandra Parker, you will be charged with the murders of Justine Segal and Kathryn Tailford Irwin, the attempted murder of Detective Sergeant Frances Oliver and the burglary at East Cottage, Scots Gap.' Even Saul Meyr would have difficulty defending her against such damning evidence.

75

When DCI Gordon Sharpe returned to Northern Command HQ the murder investigation was wrapped up, written up, on its way to the Crown Prosecutor – a done deal. During his leave period, Sharpe had decided to call it a day, put his ticket in at short notice and return to the South of France where he owned a second home. Detective Chief Superintendent Philip Bright – the man in charge of Northumbria CID – accepted his resignation and summoned Stone to headquarters in Newcastle.

As the man of the moment, he was offered and accepted a promotion to his former rank of DCI. The appointment was received with approval by his peers, a party hastily organised to mark the occasion. The police club was full to bursting, detectives from the MIT and general CID shaking David's hand, all of them keen to offer felicitations. A homemade banner hung across one wall . . .

Northern Rocks the Toon!!
Congratulations DCI David Stone!

Frankie stood at the bar looking lost. Her eyes widened as the door opened and her parents trooped in, followed by her grandparents, Andrea, Rae and Ben, all carrying plates of food: sarnies, pies, a vat of curry to feed a hungry crowd of well-wishers. It was their way of showing their appreciation to David on his big day.

Frankie's father winked at her.

She smiled. There was no way he'd miss the opportunity to offer congratulations and celebrate the ending of a case that had almost taken her away from him. As the food was laid out, Andrea approached, a pint in each hand. She narrowed her eyes, taking in Frankie's new hairstyle: short and spiky. There was still a bald patch around the staples in her head. Andrea kissed her, whispering in her ear as she pulled away.

'You look . . . different.'

'Thought I'd join you on the dark side.'

'Hmm . . .'

'I was joking!' Frankie's attention strayed. Her old man was shaking hands with David. She'd never seen her boss this up since the day he walked into her life.

Andrea followed her gaze. 'He's staying then?'

'Yup. Looks that way.'

They moved away from a group of guffawing detectives. One thing Frankie loved about being a member of the police family was the way officers came together at times like this – be it a wedding, promotion or retirement do – each one with a new story to tell. Funerals especially were hilarious. It wasn't all doom and gloom. The 'Job' had its fair share of good times. No other job would do for any of them.

'It's good to see him so happy,' Andrea said. 'I tell you one thing, he was inconsolable when he thought you'd died in that fire. Me?' She waggled her hand from side to side. 'I always thought you'd burn in hell.'

Frankie laughed out loud.

A flash of guilt crossed her sister-in-law's face. It put Frankie on the back foot. There were things Andrea knew that she didn't.

'Has he told you?' Frankie missed nothing.

'Told me what?'

'What had happened to him in London—'

'Frank, this is not the time.'

'Has he?'

'He told me something. Don't ask me to break a confidence. Let him tell you himself and be happy that he's sticking around. You might not be working together, but you can hang out, right?'

'Yeah, you're right.' The fact that he'd confided in Andrea – and not her – made Frankie's heart sink. And while it stung to be the last to find out, she had to concede that it was easier to share secrets with a stranger than a friend. Alex's taunts had filled in some of the gaps, but there was so much more to tell. David would tell her when he was ready. She lifted her glass. 'To the Northern Rock,' she said.

They clinked glasses.

'You done good too,' Andrea said. 'You ready?'

'For what?'

'Your old man's going to make a speech.'

'What? Oh God!'

'He insisted. Your granddad's been working on his all afternoon.' Andrea chuckled. 'Look on the bright side: it means Windy doesn't have to. If I know Frank Senior, he'll have us both up on his soapbox in a matter of minutes.'

'Great.' Frankie ran her eyes over Andrea. 'Look at you, you look gorgeous. I look like a lavvy brush.'

'There's a pair of trainers in my bag if you want to make a run for it.'

'You'd better not.' Rae had overheard. She sidled up to them, slipping an arm around Andrea's waist. 'Granddad will fetch you both if you don't play ball, and you know what that means.'

Frankie looked at her. 'I feel about five years old.'

Andrea wasn't laughing.

Frankie couldn't help but notice the sudden change in mood. 'What's up with you?'

Rae twigged why her partner was so uncomfortable. 'You haven't told her?'

'Told me what?' Frankie said.

Rae took a deep breath. 'Word is, David can take a DS with him when he moves to the MIT. Don't get excited. Windy has given him two options: Dick Abbott is one. I've not met the other. It's someone recently promoted off the back of the armed robbery case.'

'Mike Lemon?'

'Yeah, Dad said he's a prat. Do you know him?'

'I wish I didn't. Put it this way, his name fits his personality – and the colour of his balls.' Despite her jocularity, Frankie's head was down. With Windy in the driving seat, there was no way she was going anywhere, despite her positive input in their murder case.

'Life sucks sometimes,' Rae said.

Across the room, David caught Frankie's eye. She made a huge effort not to show her disgruntlement. He lifted his pint to toast her, his big daft Geordie grin lighting up the room. The smile slid off her face. Her dad was on the move. Whoever was working the music must have been watching. As her father jumped up on a chair and called for order, *The Sweeney* theme tune blasted out, the volume turned up so loud he couldn't be heard above the din.

'Get off!' detectives were shouting. 'The curry's getting cold.'

Heartfelt speeches were amusing and well-received. Stone and Frankie stood together while granddad Frank waxed lyrical about his time on the force . . . his son's time on the force . . . Frankie's time on the force . . . over fifty years of continuous service, finally getting to the point, offering congratulations to David to the applause of those assembled. The old man ended by presenting Stone with a small boxed gift 'to open later'.

'I'm thrilled to accept this promotion,' David said. 'I've been told by the Chief Super that I can take a DS with me. Superintendent Gail has put forward some suggestions. For me, there can only be one choice, a tenacious, hard-working detective who I know will do a good job—'

'That's you off the list, Mike.' Mitch made a meal of looking over his shoulder.

'Lemon isn't here,' Dick said.

A shout went up. 'He's peeling poorly.'

It was an old joke but laughter filled the room.

'And the winner IS!' someone yelled.

David found his choice in the crowded room. 'Frank, you want to say a few words?'

She wanted to weep as everyone cheered: her family, her colleagues and especially Ben, who was now living with his uncle temporarily. Having been warned that she was not on Windy's list, Frankie knew that her appointment had been approved at the highest level – the Head of CID – and his endorsement meant the world to her.

As she drove Stone home, he opened the gift her granddad had given him. Inside the small box, wrapped in tissue paper, was his old police whistle. The gift card had a simple message:

We couldn't have lost another – Frank.

David didn't understand the message – the drink didn't help – but, deep down, he knew then that something catastrophic had happened to the Oliver family. With Ben in the car, he didn't say anything, just closed the card and slipped it in his pocket.

Frankie glanced at the gift on his knee, breaking into a big smile.

'I can't accept it,' he said. 'It's too much.'

'No, it's not!'

'Yes, it is.'

'You deserve it—'

'It should be yours, Frankie.'

'What would I want that old thing for?' She winked at him. 'Rule 9: Keep me sweet.'

'Done.'

David knew it was her grandfather's most prized possession,

given to him when he joined Northumbria Police in 1966. It was her legacy. One day, when the time was right, he'd find a way to give it back. As they drove on, he fell into a deep and peaceful sleep. The force's newly promoted SIO was about to begin a new chapter in his life. With Frankie along for the ride, he couldn't wait.

Acknowledgements

The Lost is the first title in a new series for Orion Books featuring DI David Stone and DS Frankie Oliver. Many people at Orion have collaborated on this novel: my wonderful editor Francesca Pathak, assistant editor Bethan Jones, not forgetting Trapeze editor Sam Eades who kindly read an early draft, and my amazing copy-editor Anne O'Brien without whose insight, experience and wisdom I would also be lost.

A big wave to all at A.M. Heath Literary Agency; especially to my friend, mentor and agent, Oli Munson – as constant as a northern star – available whenever I need him. A special mention here for Dave (Robbo) Robson, an ex-pat Geordie who I've never met, but whose homesick emails from Australia make me laugh and cry. He is the unwitting inspiration behind the character, DI David Stone.

To readers, bloggers, booksellers and librarians who spread the word, I salute you. Most importantly of all, much love goes to my family: my soulmate Mo; Paul and Kate, Chris and Jodie, Max, Frances, Daisy and a very special imminent new arrival – currently a bump – whose name has yet to be decided. Without their patience and sacrifice, I'd never have made it this far.

Keep reading for an extract from the thrilling second novel in the acclaimed Stone and Oliver series by award-winning author, Mari Hannah.

The Insider

After the success of their last investigation, newly promoted DCI David Stone has been moved to the Murder Investigation Team, taking DS Frankie Oliver with him. But there's a catch: the case they are given is the latest in a series of undetected murders. It's a baptism of fire for MIT's newest recruits.

In the incident room, the murder wall makes for grim reading: three women have been killed within the past year and nothing links the crimes: no day of the week, geographical area, similarity between victims and, most importantly, no forensic evidence.

Joanna Cosgrove is the latest victim, her body discovered fully clothed close to a railway line on the south side of the river in the Tyne Valley. The MO is the same as the other three, but the words 'serial killer' are not welcome in Northumbria force.

And the manner in which she was killed is too close to home for Frankie . . .

'Brand new series, same top-notch writing' *Eva Dolan*
'Nobody understands the many faces of cops better than Mari Hannah' *Val McDermid*
'Mari Hannah writes with a sharp eye and a dark heart' *Peter James*

The Insider

1

It was the news they had all been dreading, confirmation of a fourth victim. For DS Frances Oliver, the journey to the crime scene brought about memories of her father driving her around the county when she was a rookie cop just out of training school, pointing out the places he'd been called upon to investigate unspeakable horrors throughout his own police career, giving her the benefit of his advice along the way. Back then, they were words. Just words. Narratives that, if she were being honest, excited her in ways they should not. And then there was the night he stopped talking: an experience etched on their collective memory for ever more – a night too close to home.

Flashlight beams bobbed up and down illuminating sheets of horizontal rain. The detectives stumbled along the Tyne Valley track, heading east on the Northern Rail line linking Carlisle to Newcastle. No light pollution here. Under a dark, forbidding sky, it was difficult terrain, rutted and sodden, so close to the water's edge. The swollen river thundered by, a course of water liable to flooding. Red alerts for the area were a regular occurrence. At midday, Northumberland's monitoring stations had warned of a serious threat to those living nearby. If the Tyne rose quickly, Frankie knew they would be in trouble. Many a walker had slipped into the water here by accident.

Few had survived.

Lightning forked, exposing the beauty of the surrounding landscape. A high voltage electric charge, followed by the rumble of thunder in the distance, an omen of more rain to come. Frankie's guv'nor, Detective Chief Inspector David Stone, was a blurred smudge a hundred metres in front of her, head bowed, shoulders hunched against the relentless downpour.

Mud sucked at Frankie's feet as she fought to keep up, two steps forward, one back, as she tried to get a purchase on the slippery surface. Her right foot stuck fast, the momentum of her stride propelling her forward, minus a wellington boot. She fell, head first, hands and knees skidding as she tried to stay upright. Dragging herself up, she swore under her breath as brown sludge stuck to her clothing, weighing her down.

Unaware of her plight, David was making headway, sweeping his torch left and then right in a wide arc close to Eels Wood. He had one agenda and Frankie wasn't it. With a feeling of dread eating its way in to her gut, she peered into the undergrowth blocking her passage. Where was a stick when you needed one? As she parted the brambles, there was an ear-splitting crack, a terrifying sound. A tree fell, crashing to earth with an excruciating thump loud enough to wake the dead, unearthed by a raging torrent of water filtering off higher ground, its roots unable to sustain the weight of a century of growth, landing metres in front of her.

Frankie blew out a breath.

Only once had she come closer to violent death. Hoping her luck would hold, she vaulted the tree and ploughed on. From an investigative standpoint, the situation was grim. Had there been any footprints adjacent to the line, they were long gone. As crime scenes go, they would be fighting a losing battle to preserve evidence, assuming they ever found the woman spotted by an eyewitness, a passenger on an eastbound train. Where the fuck was she?

Frankie expected to see the dragon ahead, a wide-eye LED searchlight used by emergency services, an intense beam of white light guiding her. As far as the eye could see none was visible. Worrying. Exasperating. She couldn't be arsed with this. Pulling her radio from her pocket, she pressed the transmit button hoping her link to Control wouldn't be affected by the appalling weather. It would be a heavy night in the control room, for sure.

'Oliver to Control. We're in position. Can you repeat the coordinates? We're seeing bugger all out here.'

Silence.

'Damn it! DS Oliver to Control. Are you receiving? Over . . .'

Her radio crackled to life: 'Control: go ahead.'

Wiping rain from her nose with the back of her hand, Frankie repeated her request, yanking at the drawstring on the hood of her raincoat to stop water getting in. A useless exercise. 'Have a word with first responders, will you? If they're guarding a crime scene, they should know where the bloody hell they are. We need help here.'

'Understood. I'll get back to you.'

Ending the transmission with one eye on Stone, the other on the rising river level, Frankie stopped walking. There was no point continuing without an update. By now it was glaringly obvious they were in the wrong place.

'Guv, hold on!' Her voice was lost on the wind.

David was still on the move, keen to reach the scene and do his job. What happened next shook her to the core. An icy shiver ran down her spine. Her scalp tightened, every hair on her head standing to attention, a physiological reaction to danger. With the roar of the wind, she couldn't hear but she could feel. She looked behind her. Nothing. There it was again, a definite vibration through her unbooted foot. She swung round. Up ahead Stone was oblivious, his worst nightmare was on its way.

She screamed at him to get off the track.

He kept going. A man on a mission with no clue of what was going down. Kicking off her remaining boot, Frankie sprinted barefoot, precariously close to the water's edge, dislodged gravel cutting her feet as she ran – or tried to – a sudden release of hormones providing a vital burst of energy.

'Guv, stop!'

He was too far in front to hear her cries.

As the south side of the river burst its bank, she clung to a tree for safety, self-preservation her priority now. Unable to go on or go back, she had to do something. If she didn't get out of there soon, she'd be swept away in the raging torrent and washed downstream.

If David didn't . . . she didn't want to think about that.

The vibration through the soles of her feet increased. Frankie panicked. Realising she'd never get to him in time, she used her torch – three short bursts; three longer ones; three short – a last ditch attempt to save her SIO from certain death. International Morse code was the distress call every police officer was sensitive to and, finally, she had his attention. As if in slow motion, he turned to face her, lifting his hand to shade his eyes as she shone the torch directly at him. In the distance, over his shoulder, Frankie spotted a pinprick of light.

Oh fuck!

It disappeared as her guv'nor blinded her with his own flashlight, peering through the darkness, with his back to imminent danger. Seeing the depth of water all around her, he'd be more worried about her predicament than his own. Frantically, she waved him off the track, a sob leaving her throat as he walked towards her. He thought she was calling for help.

'No!' she screamed.

A horn blasted behind him. Simultaneously, the light left Frankie's face and the freight train was upon her. It whooshed by, feet away, rattling down the track. Frantic, she shone her torch along the railway line. No movement. She dry-heaved. Thirty seconds later, David rose to his feet. He'd thrown himself clear with seconds to spare. Frankie sunk to her knees, almost waist deep in water. Jesus! That was a close call.

Don't miss out on the next gripping novel by Mari Hannah.

Coming November 2018.